drought

drought

PAM BACHORZ

EGMONT
USA
NEW YORK

EGMONT
We bring stories to life

First published by Egmont USA, 2011
443 Park Avenue South, Suite 806
New York, NY 10016

1 3 5 7 9 8 6 4 2

www.egmontusa.com
www.pambachorz.com

Library of Congress Cataloging-in-Publication Data
Bachorz, Pam
Drought / Pam Bachorz.
p. cm.
Summary: Ruby's blood holds the secret to the Water that keeps her and
her fellow Congregants alive and enriches Darwin West, who has enslaved them
for two centuries, but when her romance with an Overseer, Ford, brings her freedom
in the modern world, she faces a terrible choice.
ISBN 978-1-60684-016-0 (hardcover) — ISBN 978-1-60684-185-3 (electronic book)
[1. Science fiction. 2. Slavery—Fiction. 3. Water—Fiction. 4. Freedom—Fiction.
5. Mothers and daughters—Fiction. 6. Immortality—Fiction. 7. Droughts—Fiction.]
I. Title.
PZ7.B132176Dro 2011
[Fic]
2010039313

Printed in the United States of America

CPSIA tracking label information:
Random House Production • 1745 Broadway • New York, NY 10019

Dedicated to my parents, Paul and Judy,
who read to me every single night.

drought

Chapter 1

I wish it would rain.

On rainy days, we don't have to work in the woods, gathering water until our backs ache and our fingers tremble around our spoons. The Overseers would still find a reason to prod us — maybe the kitchen needs to be scrubbed, or their dock wants fixing. But there would be no quotas, and no woods.

If it rained, there would be water, dripping from every leaf and stem. Our cups would be full to the brim, work finished early, even. Darwin West would be so happy he'd give us dinner.

But it hasn't rained all summer, or most of the spring. For all of these two hundred years, none of us has seen a drought like this. We suffer more every day, each day worse than the last, all of them endured in the dry woods.

I am very tired of the woods. I have been collecting water from them for exactly two hundred years — we all have, slaves to Darwin West and his Overseers.

"We'll be lucky to find five drops today, Ruby," Mother grumbles.

There was no breakfast this morning, not even a mouthful of oatmeal. Darwin said we hadn't worked hard enough for it the day before. Mother will be grumbling all day.

"Otto will provide." My answer is an automatic one, the same answer she gives me when I worry. But she is right. It is already hot, though it's barely past sunrise. Road dust swirls around our skirts with every step. I wonder if there's even five drops of water waiting in all the woods.

Nothing in our lives has been easy this summer.

"Half our strong ones gone," Mother says.

"Not gone. They're just . . . digging," I remind her. "Like Darwin told them to."

"What good are all those holes? Now we're not all harvesting," she says.

I can't answer her. None of us know why some of the Congregants have been digging for nearly two weeks. The holes dot the edges of the woods where we harvest and line the road that connects our cabins and the cisterns. They don't do anything but catch a foot, twist an ankle.

Nobody asks why—asking why means a licking. Darwin gives our men dull shovels each morning and assigns the meanest Overseers to watch them. They dig until they are told to stop.

"Maybe he seeks water," I say.

"A hundred shallow wells? No," she answers.

Soon we reach the clearing where the cisterns sit: five long tanks, raised on rusted metal legs, with spigots near the bottom of each. Our harvests always start and end here. It is on the edge of miles and miles of woods; they all belong to Darwin West—he owns every rock, stick, and person on the entire mountain.

Mother says there are cities farther south in New York. "They must be grown enormous by now," she's told me. "My father said they were beyond imagination, even when I was small."

But I have never seen cities. My entire life has been trees, and leaves, and the tiny lake that our cabins cluster around. It is so tiny that it does not even have a name. It's just the Lake.

I've dreamed of cities—hazy half-imagined worlds that likely don't resemble any true place. When I was small, I built them: streets and buildings made of twigs and mud, jammed with tiny pinecone people. They always had enough to eat, I liked to imagine. Nobody ever beat them.

We join the long line of Congregants waiting to get their pewter cups and spoons.

"On days like today, I dream of chopping this off," Mother says. She twists her thick hair up on top of her head and easily secures it with a single pin. The knot of hair looks heavy enough to tip over her short, slight frame. But Mother is far too strong for that. She is made of boldness and sinew.

"Will you do mine?" I ask. Our hair is the same color—like oak leaves in November—but mine curls in a thousand different directions. It squirms away every time I try to capture it.

"Two hundred years and you still can't tie up your hair," Mother says, but she sounds a little pleased. She does not have to reach up to do my hair; we are the same kind of small, though I am soft where she is hard. I feel a few gentle tugs, a light scrape against my scalp, and then the relief of air on the back of my neck. The sun won't barely touch it; our skin is browner than burned bread from all the days in the woods.

Birds sing from the trees and swoop over our heads, darting from one tree to another. Their song and screeches follow us all day, the only witnesses to our secret existence.

The line is moving now. Once each Congregant gets a cup and a spoon, they stand to the side, waiting for Darwin to decide on the day's quota.

The water can be gathered only from living leaves—scraped from ferns, or the bottom of flower petals—and it can touch only pewter. As for the people who can do that work? Only those blessed by Otto.

Or at least that's what Darwin—and most of the Congregation—thinks. Mother and the Congregation's Elders know different. They protect my secret.

All know that I am Otto's daughter, and that makes me holy. But only the Elders and Mother know all of it. They know I bring my own gift to the Congregation, a gift that must stay hidden.

Darwin is eating something that smells sweet and full of luscious fat. I can almost taste it, even though I stand twenty people away. Congregants can live a long time without food—once, they starved us for two weeks—but I think that only makes me love it more.

Long ago, before Otto, Mother fancied Darwin, and he fancied her. What drew her affection? Was it his height and muscles? Or perhaps the ice-blue eyes that are shaded, always, by a battered leather hat with a broad brim? None would be enough to turn my head. Perhaps whatever she loved left this brute long ago.

Still, his love for her, however twisted, hasn't left him.

Four other Overseers stand around the clearing, their long guns ready, eyes always watching. If one of us tries to escape, they will shoot—and if those bullets miss us, more Overseers wait in the woods.

One last Overseer hands out cups. He is new and younger than the rest of them. Darwin has hired more Overseers this summer, as he works us harder and longer and deals out more beatings. I eye the coppery bristle on the new one's head, so easy and cool. Perhaps Mother is right, and we should crop our hair—though it would be difficult without knives or scissors. Those are forbidden.

The new Overseer holds out the cup, but I fumble, and it falls to the ground. I bend, quickly, to pick it up—but he is there first.

"Sorry about that," he says, looking right at me. I look away fast, but not before I see his lips twitch with the smallest of smiles.

Overseers don't apologize. Overseers don't smile. Perhaps they haven't told him that yet.

We straighten up at the same time, our heads nearly colliding. His fingers brush mine when I take the cup. A burning dances down my fingers, my hand, my arm . . . like the curling designs inked on his skin have crept down his arms to bite me. But it doesn't feel like pain.

I shake my hand to get the feeling out of it. The drought has twisted my mind—all of our minds.

I go to find one of our elders, Ellie. She is standing at the edge of the clearing, in the shade. Ellie is stooped, and her face is drained of color. Her hair is only half braided, the rest of the yellow-white strands straggling down her back. Even her blue eyes seem cloudy, faded.

I stand next to her and squeeze her pinky finger with mine. It's our old way of saying hello. Ellie is the closest thing to family that Mother and I have.

"How are you feeling?" I ask.

"I am better today," she answers.

She lifts her lips in a shaky smile: a lie that she is fine. Her body shows me something different. I fear she is withering. The Water doesn't make us last forever. Already nearly a dozen Congregants have withered—their bodies giving up, piece by piece, until they finally die.

"Only a few months until the Visitor comes," she says.

"The cisterns *will* be full," I say. "We'll find a way."

The Visitor comes just once a year, when the leaves start to turn. He dresses all in white, driving an enormous beast of a truck. He takes away all the Water we've suffered to harvest.

And Darwin will do anything to make sure we've filled the cisterns in time.

"Boone knocked on the last cistern before you got here," Ellie says. "He says it's not nearly as full as it should be."

Boone is another Elder, once a blacksmith, still one of our strongest men.

He's right about the cistern. I check it too, at night, when I make my secret visits.

"Your quota today . . . ," Darwin announces in a loud voice. He takes another bite of his food, and every Congregant's eyes trace the path of his sandwich to his lips. We wait while he chews.

"Otto save us," another Congregant mutters next to us.

Yesterday's quota was a half cup and I barely met it. The plants are guarding their water in the drought, sucking it deep into their stems and pulp.

Darwin finally finishes chewing. His lips are shiny with grease. "Today will be one full cup."

Ellie lets out a soft gasp. My eyes stray to the new Overseer. He is frowning at the ground. I wonder what he must think of Darwin . . . and of our following his whims.

"That's too much." Mother steps to the front of the group so that she's only a foot away from Darwin. The Overseer next to him levels his gun at her, but she does not seem to notice.

Mother is our Reverend. She leads us in worship while we wait for Otto to return. Otto, our savior, gave us his blood so that we could live longer. He passed that blood to my veins too, for he is my father.

But almost nobody knows about his blood.

"I could make it two cups," Darwin muses.

"There's a drought, and we swelter already." Mother holds out her long skirts.

The Congregants wear simple, modest clothes, as if it is still 1812, the year Darwin West imprisoned us. Ellie says ladies used to change bits of their fashions all the time, and likely they still do. I wonder how different we look from modern women now.

Mother says our boots are as modern as any, though—thick, tall, yellow, made to keep us standing for long hours in the woods. The Overseers give us those, one pair every fall, before the first snow.

"Make it a half cup, like yesterday," Mother orders. I marvel at her boldness, even though I have seen it for so long. She is never afraid of Darwin West.

"One cup, full to the brim. Now go." Darwin pulls a heavy chain out of his pocket and coils it in his palm. "Unless you want whippings instead of supper."

Supper will likely be oatmeal tanged by mold, or maybe some greenish bread and cheese. But we will work all day in hopes for it. If Mother speaks again, he might decide we won't get dinner, no matter how much water we find.

"Mother," I say.

She lifts her chin for a moment . . . and drops it. Then she turns away from Darwin.

"You heard him." The Overseer near Ellie and me pokes my back with his gun. I straighten my shoulders and follow Ellie into the trees, close enough to catch her if she stumbles.

"You hole diggers, come get shovels!" Darwin shouts.

Mother comes behind us, and for a moment, I think we will get to walk into the woods together. But Darwin stops her. "You go somewhere else, Mother Toad."

He doesn't like family members working together. I make a small signal with my hand, waving her away. Go. Ellie will be fine. I will take care of her.

Mother pauses, still staring at Ellie, then finally takes slow, heavy steps away. She pushes aside branches as she goes. They swish together as soon as she passes, and soon I can't see her faded red dress.

Darwin stays close to us. I wait to make sure Ellie can kneel,

then I crouch by a clump of goldenrod and pull out my spoon. There is no water on the plant, but Darwin is watching, so I run my spoon along every stem, holding my cup underneath. Nothing drips into it. I move to the next plant, a berry bush. The animals have left a few morsels buried in the thickest thorns. My mouth pricks.

I pull my eyes away fast, not wanting Darwin to notice the berries. As soon as he's gone, I'll return to them. Half will be for me. Half will be for Ellie.

Ellie is on her knees, ten paces from me. Her arm shakes as she runs her spoon along some ferns. Water spills off the tip of the leaves, but it doesn't look like it all lands in her cup.

Darwin is watching her, his fingers opening and closing around his dread chain. Ellie nearly drops her cup and he takes a step closer.

No. I will not let him hurt her.

I stand and bring my foot down on the ground, hard. Sticks break under my boot.

It works. He is watching me now.

Pretending not to feel his eyes on me, I take a berry and toss it into my mouth. The sweetness explodes and I can't help savoring it, even as I know pain is coming.

The chain whips against my stomach. The blow knocks me to my knees, but I clamp my lips shut, crushing the berry against the roof of my mouth. I will at least win this taste.

"No stealing food," he roars.

If I were Mother, I would answer him with strong words. I would say it's not his food — it belongs to the forest. But I just stare

at his feet. The chain dangles over the toe of his boot, swaying a little as if it is a living thing.

Darwin breathes in deeply, like he's trying to take all the air before I steal that too.

"Do it again and I'll beat you until you bleed," he says.

I pick up my spoon and my cup and start working. Water *plink-plops* into my cup.

I'm not afraid, at least for now. He wouldn't hurt me badly in the middle of the day. There is still work to be done.

Darwin saves the real beatings for sunset, after we've put the water in the cisterns. Sometimes he hurts us, and sometimes he doesn't—the worst part is never knowing what will happen. Darwin might shrug if we don't give him what he wants. Or he might lift the chain.

When he does hurt us, we have all night to heal. That's enough time to get us ready for the next day's harvest, unless he breaks bones. Those take two or three days to knit back together, if we've had Communion each week.

There's enough water in my cup now that I can imagine it's a mite heavier. I can feel Darwin's eyes on my neck. I draw in deep breaths as I work, trying to ease away the feeling of his stare.

Darwin leans over me and peers into my cup. "Should have made you Toads collect two cups," he says. I brace for a slap, but he reaches past me into the bush and plucks every last berry. He crams them into his mouth. "Harvest well, Toad."

That is what they call us—toads. I guess that's because we can survive their beatings and starvings, like the toads that sleep in the mud all winter here. Or maybe we are that ugly to them.

He shuffles away, down the hill. I imagine he'll sit in the shade with his favorite Overseers, playing cards and eating the lunch we never get.

As soon as he's gone, Ellie stops working. She sits on the leaves, the cup in both her hands. I check to make sure we're alone, then hurry over to her.

The bottom of her cup is barely wet.

"Hard for an old woman to keep up," she says.

"You don't have to apologize." I hold my cup over hers and pour. Everything I've collected is hers now.

Ellie puts her hand out to stop me, but she's too late. There wasn't much to pour. "I won't have you beat," she whispers.

"There's enough water out here for both of us," I tell her, even though I'm not sure.

She grips my hand, fingers quaking. Her skin feels soft. "Don't you give your life up for anybody, girl. You've barely begun."

A soft laugh escapes me; we both look down the hill. But there's no sign of an Overseer. "I've already lived enough life for four girls, every day the same," I whisper. And there's no change in sight.

The Water slows our aging—or growth, for me. It's taken this long to grow from a baby to this.

"You're a woman now," Ellie says. "We all see it."

She sounds so proud—but of what? "And what new wonder does womanhood bring me?" I ask.

"The Elders . . . we want to talk to you about just that," she says.

Curiosity flickers in me, like a leaf trembling in the wind. "What?" I ask. "What do the Elders want?"

Ellie wags one finger gently. "Wait for the next council meeting."

Irritation washes over me—and then I feel terrible, small. What has Ellie earned from me but love, and gratitude?

"Sit and rest a bit," I tell her. "There's enough water for me to find and share."

I help her ease against a tree trunk, but then there's the crackle of sticks underfoot; someone is coming. Ellie grips her cup tight and I spring away from her, my heart pounding. I scramble to a patch of wildflowers and run my spoon under their petals, praying some dew still dangles there.

A shadow hovers over me.

"Your cup is empty," Mother says.

"I gave it to Ellie."

"As will I." Mother takes light steps to Ellie and pours everything she's collected into Ellie's cup.

She fishes a cloth from her pocket and wipes it over Ellie's forehead. The older woman's eyes are fluttering shut.

"You should go," I tell Mother. "I'll take care of Ellie."

"We are all helping Ellie today," she says, nodding her head toward the cup. It's more than half full. There's no way Mother could have collected so much. I am not the only Congregant who risked a gift to Ellie today.

"Who?" I ask.

"Hope. Asa. And others," Mother says.

That is when I see Darwin peering at her through the leaves.

I purse my lips and make an imitation of a robin's call. It's our signal, one we've used for a very long time.

She does not look; that is a waste of time. He has seen us do something we shouldn't have, and it will not be ignored. The only question is what the punishment will be.

"No matter what," Mother whispers, so quiet I can barely hear her, "protect yourself."

Rebellion burns my guts. She doesn't know I took a lashing for Ellie this morning, already. I don't have to sit by anymore and let her take all the pain. I am strong too—stronger than her now that I'm grown, I think.

But I nod, because we have argued about this since I was as tall as her shoulder. She says it's her job to protect me, and my job to sustain the Congregation. But I say it's my turn to help her.

And then Darwin is standing by us, grinning, like he's happy to have caught us doing something wrong. When he looks at the cup, and then Ellie, his head nods.

"Knew you were up to no good. You helped her." He aims a thick finger at me.

We are never supposed to help one another. I start to nod my head yes, but Mother lays a heavy hand on the top of my head: a reminder.

"I did it all." Mother stands up and gives him a smile that dares him.

He takes the bait and deals her a hard slap. Mother's head jerks to the side, but she does not cry out.

I bite the inside of my lip to stop from screaming.

His hand hovers near her head, ready to strike again.

"You Toads don't have to suffer," he says.

"Then release us," Mother snaps.

Darwin's hand sinks back to his side. He drops to his knees and grabs Mother's hand.

She tries to pull her hand back, as if his skin burns hers. But his grip is too tight.

"I'd still have you, Sula Prosser," Darwin says.

A groan escapes me, but neither seems to notice. He has asked her, again and again, and I feel sickening shame for his desperation. I hate it more than his brutality.

Once, before Otto followed my grandfather out of the woods, before we were slaves, Darwin asked my mother the same question. That time she said yes.

But Otto changed everything. Darwin West did not win my mother, after all—but he did win the Water, and all of our lives.

Bile rises in my throat as I imagine the life we'd have under his roof. Cruelty does not change; he would only find new ways to hurt us.

But at least the Congregation would be free.

"I wait for Otto," Mother replies.

It is what she always says.

Darwin hitches up his pants and pulls out his chain.

"There is still work to be done," I murmur. "It's not near sunset."

His hand falls slowly, the weight of the chain pulling it down, maybe. Darwin looks up at the sky. "That savior of yours is never coming."

"You'll see," Mother says quietly.

I press my lips together and say a secret, silent prayer to Otto in my mind.

Please stop him. I pray. *Don't let him hurt her.*

Otto must be listening, for Darwin slides the chain back in his pocket. "You'd better get your lazy Toads working."

"There's no way they'll fill a cup today," Mother snarls.

"Then maybe you'll feel my kiss at sunset . . . if you're lucky." He pats the chain in his pocket. A shiver down my back turns the day as cold as January.

Darwin's eyes turn to me. "You, little Toad. Find some other place, away from Mama Toad."

I can't help looking back at Ellie. He wraps a beefy hand around my arm and yanks me to my feet. "Go now, or there's no mercy for your mother."

There's no use arguing. I find a patch of woods shaded by brown-edged leaves and spend the day doing the same as always. Gathering water . . . and praying there will be enough for Mother to escape a sunset beating.

Chapter 2

When the sun slips below the trees, I creep back to Ellie. She is so still that I race the last few steps to her. A few drops splash from my cup onto my hand, but I do not slow.

"Ellie? Ellie. Ellie!" I call. "Harvest is done for the day."

But she does not stir. Is her chest moving? I cannot tell.

I set down my cup, nestling it by a branch so it doesn't tip. Then I put both hands on her shoulders and shake, gently. Her braids swing against her thin shirtwaist. She is as limp as the doll she fashioned for me, long ago, out of scraps and scavenged buttons.

"Wake!" I tell her, loud enough to make the birds scatter from the tree overhead.

Ellie's eyelids flutter. Cool relief steadies my breath.

It's even darker now. I'll need to get her down the hill to the cisterns quickly. We need both our cups to be counted, if we want dinner tonight.

The cup tucked beside her is full to the brim. How many

visited her today? How many would bring half-empty cups because of what they did for her?

"You are a good girl," Ellie says. She struggles to her feet and reaches for the cup.

"I'll carry both," I say, offering her an elbow to grasp.

Even though the color has fled from her lips and she hunches to one side, Ellie's grip is strong. "We'd best hurry," she says.

When we reach the cisterns, the clearing is crowded with exhausted Congregants and Overseers inspecting the day's harvest. We step to the back of the line, behind the second-to-last cistern. By now we should have four cisterns full, filling the last. But the drought has made that impossible.

The cisterns sit directly across the road from the Common House, where we gather for food—when we get it—and Sunday Services. Trees edge the clearing around the cisterns, always growing a little closer, it seems, wanting the Water for themselves.

Nothing can come out from the cisterns unless Darwin unlocks the spigots at the bottom. All that's open are the valves on top. We can only add, never steal.

My first memory is coming here at night, with Mother.

"Quiet," she warned every night. "He must never find us here." She meant Darwin, of course.

I pulled out handfuls of the lush grass that grows under the cisterns, even in winter, while Mother climbed to the top of a cistern and muttered a fast prayer to Otto. She counted out loud: "One, two, three drops," then hurried down.

She always carried that vial of Otto's blood so carefully, even as we hurried back to our cabin. All the vials are empty now, but she saves them in a wooden box beneath her bed, still careful to keep them whole.

Now it's my blood that drips into the water inside the cisterns. But since this year's drought—since Darwin found a new depth to his cruelty—I've had to come to the cisterns alone while Mother heals. She takes other people's share of the beatings, as much as Darwin will allow.

We are near the front of the line now. The new Overseer is standing by the cistern, his long gun set against his shoulder, only loosely holding it. His sweaty shirt clings to his body, hinting at the muscles underneath.

He shifts his weight from one foot to the other, his eyes flitting from person to person. For only a second we stare at each other. He looks away first.

I draw in a deep breath and crane my neck to see whether the others have filled their cups. Boone stands a few feet ahead of us, hands empty—he spent the day shoveling. He is talking to Hope, once my playmate, now a grown woman and Elder. She holds her cup carefully with both hands. I pray that means it holds enough, after giving to Ellie.

But Jonah Pelling, directly in front of us, has a cup so empty that I see its pewter sides. He tilts it to the side a bit, careless, and looks about him with far too much energy.

Anger flashes over me, hot and merciless. I do not care how dry the woods are. He should have found a way, somehow, like the rest of us. Those Pellings always find a way to rest their feet and make the rest of us pay for it.

I nudge Ellie with my hip and nod my head toward Jonah.

She lets out a small *tsk*, but then lays her hand on my arm. "It's been a hard season," she whispers.

"Not so hard for some," I answer.

"Jonah is a smart boy," Ellie says.

Why does she defend him? "Smart and shiftless," I tell her.

Jonah looks back at me, then, and I feel a flash of guilt. Did he hear me? But then he raises his eyebrows and grins before whipping his head back round to the front.

Once, there were four of us young enough to be considered children. Jonah was eight when he came here, and his brother Zeke was twelve. Hope was the oldest—fifteen—fleeing a forced marriage as much as she was following Otto.

Nobody has borne a child since the Congregation came to the woods—save Mother. Some say Otto doesn't want another child born into slavery. Others think the Water does it. Only Otto knows.

Being the only children meant the Congregation spoiled us some. They helped us steal time to romp in the woods—I, the baby, struggled to follow the other three everywhere. But with time came more duties, and less indulgence. I haven't chased Jonah through the woods for dozens of years.

Now, he lounges and lets others do his work.

One by one, the Congregants in front of us show their cups to an Overseer. They check it, and make a note on their clipboards if someone has not met the quota. Then each person goes to the ladder.

The Overseer who checks my cup does not meet my eyes. He finds lower parts of my body to examine. They never touch us that way—but it does not stop some of them from looking. I turn away too fast, and a drop slips from the cup.

"Do that again and you'll feel the chain," he warns me in a loud voice.

Someone draws in a sharp breath. I look back and see the new Overseer staring at the man who threatened me. He is gripping the gun so hard now that his knuckles are white.

"Go patrol the perimeter, newbie," the man tells him. The new Overseer turns away without looking at me.

I slow my walk on the way to the cistern, trying to hide that my legs are shaking.

"Steady." Mother's voice, behind me. She presses her hand against my back as I climb the ladder.

"Have all met their quota?" I ask her.

"Enough, maybe," she answers. "Now pour, and carefully."

I tip my cup into the open valve at the top of the cistern. Then I see the new Overseer making a slow path around the clearing. He looks up at me and stops walking.

My hand falters and water escapes onto the side of the cistern. But I correct myself quickly and soon the pouring is done. I hope that an Overseer didn't see my sloppiness. There would be punishment, and Mother would bear it on her shoulders.

When I reach the bottom, Mother holds up a wet fingertip. "You are distracted," she says.

Shame burns in me, and I cannot meet her eyes. "It was just a slip."

She raises her eyebrows, then climbs the ladder with her cup.

Nobody can leave until all the water has been poured into the cistern. Then Darwin decides if we get supper—or his fist.

Soon as Mother has climbed off the ladder, Darwin pulls the chain from his pocket. "Five of you Toads failed today," he shouts.

"Five people," Mother breathes.

Yesterday was three. How can she possibly bear it for five?

"Get up here, Toads!" Darwin cries.

The Overseer with a clipboard calls five names; five failed Congregants shuffle forward. All but one is a Pelling, including Jonah, not looking so merry now. They dart their eyes toward Mother, waiting for escape. The last one is Meg Newman. She's a hard worker, and strong, with a body young enough to show barely any gray hair. But even hard workers don't get lucky, sometimes. She stands tall and does not look our way.

The Overseers form a tighter circle around us; we gather closer. The new one is standing behind Darwin. Another guard is telling him something, his voice too low to hear. When the new one nods, his lips pressed tight, the two men take a few steps from each other and turn their guns to point them at us.

Darwin folds his arms over his chest and looks at Mother.

"We want supper," Mother says.

"And I want my Water," he growls. "The truck's coming soon, and what'll happen when the cisterns stand half empty?"

Mother keeps her eyes steady on him. "We'll work harder if we have food."

"You think I'm a brute?" Darwin shakes his head. "You see what happens if we don't have that Water."

I don't know much about the man who comes with the truck

every year, to pick up our Water. But I know it's the only time I see Darwin's hands shake.

Darwin nods to an Overseer, the one with the scar over one eye. He stands behind Meg and pushes her to her knees. Darwin lifts his chain.

"No. Not tonight," Mother says.

"It's your fault. If you loved me, none of these people would suffer," Darwin says.

"I'm not the one who hurts them," she snaps back.

Darwin's thick arm muscles bunch, and he slides the chain over his shoulder, ready to strike.

"Take me instead," Mother says—like she does every night when he's got a taste for hurting.

"Mother, no, please." I grab her hand and try to pull her back. It is selfish of me, I know. She has a secret way of healing from these beatings that nobody else has.

She has my blood to rely on.

"Trade accepted." Darwin smiles and nods.

The Pellings melt into the crowd without even a thank-you. I fix a hard look on them, but if they feel my stare they don't show any sign.

Still Meg will not stand up.

"Don't take it for me," she says behind gritted teeth. "I can bear it."

Most of the time, people step aside for Mother. She kneels beside Meg. "Let me carry this load for my Congregation."

"Why? It's not your fault that he beats us." Meg spits on the ground, dangerously close to Darwin's boot.

drought

I want to step forward. I want to take the lickings, for once. But I've promised Mother, and the Elders, not to put myself in danger. I'm the only one who can heal Mother . . . heal our leader. I'm the only one who can make the Water what it is.

Until Otto comes back, that is.

"So it'll be two of you tonight," Darwin roars.

Meg's husband John—third husband, since after a while even good people tire of each other—pushes to the front.

"Don't do it," he tells her. "Listen to Sula."

She shakes her head.

Then there is no more arguing or waiting. Darwin smashes the chain onto Meg's back, and she lets out a gasp. A small smile plays on Darwin's lips. He looks at Mother again.

"No more," Mother says. "Let me take it."

But Darwin hits Meg again.

"Meg!" John cries in a strangled voice.

Next to me, Ellie starts the prayer. It is a chant, really, the same simple thing over and over. We say it soft and low, but together we make enough noise to reach the top of the trees.

Otto will come.

Otto will come.

Nobody leaves during the beatings. We are a family. So even though we cannot stop the chain's blows, we can bear witness—and pray.

Meg is crying now. Mother reaches out, as if to pat her back, then stops herself. Then she slides her hand on top of Meg's and squeezes.

Otto will come.

Otto will come.

Why do we only watch? Why don't we stop him? Am I the only one tired of waiting for Otto—and of protecting me? Hate burns in me—hate for Darwin and hate for us, standing by while he hurts another Congregant.

I look up and see Jonah staring, fists clenched, eyes narrowed. He was too weak to offer to take the beating—but at least he wishes he could fight too. My anger fades a little.

One more strike, and Meg falls onto her stomach. Darwin lets the chain fall to his side.

The chant fades away.

Meg's dress is not ripped, but blood darkens it from underneath, a fast-spreading stain that shadows her whole back. John reaches for her, and Darwin doesn't stop him. He's looking at Mother.

"Are you sure?" Darwin asks softly, tender for just a moment, like he sometimes is with her. It doesn't stop him from using every bit of muscle when he swings the chain.

"Are *you* sure?" Mother doesn't bow her head.

I start the chant again, and so do all the other Congregants. It's louder this time, and the Overseers shoulder their guns. I look for the new one.

The chain speeds toward Mother's back. There's a horrible thump when it strikes—a sound that makes me cringe, no matter how many times I hear it. But she does not cry out.

"Eight more," Darwin says.

The new Overseer's gun is dangling in his hand now. His mouth hangs open. One of the other Overseers nudges him with the barrel of his gun, and he shakes his head. Then he slowly lifts his gun back into position.

I chant louder.

Otto will come.

And I stare at the new Overseer. His face looks wet; could he be crying? Overseers don't show emotion, unless you count anger, or lust.

Darwin strikes Mother again, and this time a groan escapes her. She presses her hands into the ground, no longer staring up at him.

I creep forward and kneel next to her. "Let me," I say.

"Get back, you useless girl!" she roars, and then the chain strikes again, just an inch from me. Somehow she finds the strength to kick me.

She's only protecting me. She wants me away from the chain, and from Darwin. She knows I'm not useless.

I tell myself these things like my own chant, and the Congregation continues theirs.

Otto will come.

The new Overseer steps into the circle they've formed around us. He's only a few steps from Darwin now.

The chain lands again.

Mother slumps to the forest floor. I want to hold her. I want to shield her. But I know what I am supposed to do—and that she would not forgive me for taking a blow. So I wait until I can help her.

"Four more," Darwin says. He runs his fingers along the chain and wipes the blood on his pants.

"You have to stop." The new Overseer is right next to Darwin. His eyes flick fast from the chain, to Mother, to Darwin . . . and then to me.

Darwin blinks at him, draws a breath, then says nothing.

"Don't they suffer enough?" the new one asks.

The Congregants' chant falters, then dies. Are they all feeling hope flaring in them, like I do—and hating themselves for it? Perhaps this new one is softhearted, but Darwin will squeeze that out of him soon.

"You work for *me*." Darwin says it low, and calm. But his hand grips the chain even harder. "No questions, no complaints, remember?"

"I—I know. But this is . . ." The Overseer swallows. "Nobody should stand for this."

Fear thrills through me as if he is one of ours. Doesn't he know he's asking to be hurt? Doesn't he know that defying Darwin will always, always bring pain?

"How is your mother feeling?" Darwin asks in a silky voice.

Now the bold, foolish Overseer stares at his feet. If he answers, I cannot hear it.

"Seems like she'd have a real hard time without that nice insurance that I pay for," Darwin continues.

The Overseer nods. "I'm grateful."

"Who do you care about? These Toads or your own mother?" Darwin arcs the chain up high, high, higher than any of the other hits, and lands it straight down on Mother's spine. This is the worst I've seen him beat her in a long time.

Her body jerks from the impact. I know it means she's

fainted, gone to a place without pain . . . until I bring her back with Water.

Please, Otto, I pray. *Let her be strong enough for three more of those.*

"Got anything more to say?" Darwin asks.

The Overseer stares at Mother. Slowly, he shakes his head.

I hate him for it. It's not fair, maybe. What's he supposed to do? But his noticing the wrongness of Darwin made me hope, just for a second, that things will change. I wish he hadn't said anything at all.

The Congregation begins to chant again, and the last three hits are hard and fast.

"All done," Darwin sings. He coils the chain and slides it back in his pocket.

I rush to Mother. The ground around her body is wet with blood, and her sleeves have split where I've already mended them countless times. But her chest moves; her body is still fighting him, even though her mind has eased elsewhere. I smooth her hair. Darwin never touches her face, or head.

The new Overseer dares to speak again. "I'll call an ambulance."

Darwin's answer is to grab the new one's shoulders and spin him so he's directly facing Mother. Then he strikes the back of his knees with the chain, so the new one falls to the ground beside Mother. Our eyes meet, and I see that his cheeks are truly stained from tears.

But I look away, and fast. There's no good in feeling for this boy.

"Take a good look," Darwin snarls. "And decide if you're with me or not."

The boy turns his head and vomits into the leaves. He heaves, and heaves, until all that's left are the sobs ripping out of him.

There is no one to console him; Darwin slides away and the Overseers do too. The Congregants, most of them, begin the trudge home.

But not all go—as always, Boone stays, and Hope with her new husband, Gabe. Ellie is here too, of course.

"She'll heal," Ellie says. "We just need to get her home."

Boone lifts her feet; Hope and Gabe lift her upper half while I support her middle. When Ellie makes a move to help, I shake my head. She frowns, but lets her hands drop.

The Overseer is still on the ground, but he is watching us now.

"I'd help if I could," he whispers.

Gabe snorts and hawks a glob of spit on the leaves next to him. It's a foolish thing to do, something he wouldn't dare with any other Overseer.

"Her breath is going funny," Boone says.

"Hurry," I answer, turning my back on the new Overseer.

Chapter 3

By the time we reach the cabin, it's gone entirely dark outside. The only sound is our feet scuffing the road—the frogs stopped croaking a few weeks ago, maybe too thirsty for song.

Something flits past my head. The bats are out for their breakfast.

I'm so hungry. If I could catch bugs, I'd make them my every meal. With Mother hurt so many nights, she hasn't been able to creep out enough for nighttime trapping. Nobody gets food unless the Overseers give it to us.

Mother's body sways heavy between us. The walk is slow and careful. Our feet know the road, but one slip could jar a body that's barely holding on.

"I'll get the lantern." Ellie eases ahead and through the door.

It's not locked—we haven't got locks. Mother's told me about grand houses with so much inside, they have locks, perhaps more than one, on them. I've seen locks only on the fine house that the Overseers share.

Light flares in the crack of the open door. We ease Mother inside.

Like all the others, our cabin is a single small room, thrown up against winter winds the first year that the Congregants fled to these woods—and were followed by Darwin West. It has a small stove, a single rough window that looks onto the Lake, and bare log walls. The cracks between the walls are crammed with years of dried mud.

Our only furniture is two beds, a sheet hanging between them. It was Mother's Christmas gift to me this year. "You're almost a woman now," she said. "And you deserve your own small space."

Ellie smoothes the bloodstained muslin on Mother's bed before we lay her on it.

"Poor child," she sighs, laying a light hand on Mother's cheek.

I have had only a mother for as long as I've lived, no father with us, but it was the opposite for Mother: she just had her father, a trapper who was gone for months at a time. And then she had Ellie, who rented them two rooms in her house.

The shadows hide the worst of Mother's wounds. I pretend that it's been this bad before, that this is a normal night. "Gently," I say, more of a prayer than an order, as we lay her down.

"I'll get the water," Gabe says.

Boone draws in his breath sharply. "What did you tell him?" he asks Hope.

Gabe isn't an Elder. He shouldn't know how Mother heals so well and fast after each beating.

Hope's cheeks are pink, but she meets Boone's stare. "He is my husband now."

"Now, but not for always, maybe," Boone says.

Not many of the Congregation's couples have proven to be for always.

Gabe slides close to Hope and puts his arm around her shoulders. "For always," he says—simply, without anger. I see why Hope chose him, even though it meant his setting aside another.

Jonah doesn't understand it, I'd guess. We all knew he'd set his heart on Hope, years before he was old enough.

He'll be waiting a long time, maybe forever, I think.

"Your secret is safe." Gabe looks at me—not at any of the Elders. But he frowns.

"I know," I tell him. And then I give Hope a small smile. I know why she told him. Hope stopped whispering her daily secrets to me when Gabe's eyes fell on her.

I miss our stolen time in the shade, whispering, giggling.

"We're wasting time while Sula suffers," Boone says.

Gabe pushes out the door. He'll be lucky to get one clear bucket. The Lake is victim to the drought too, dwindled to puddles and wet mud. I don't remember ever seeing it like this. When we go to bathe, or find drinking water, it's nearly impossible to find clear water.

After Gabe's gone, Hope speaks. "Ruby's secret is hard for him to accept."

"You shouldn't have told him—and that's one of the reasons why," Boone says.

"He'll be easier with it, in time," Hope says to me.

At least I understand why he's been so strange and unfriendly lately.

While we wait, I reach under Mother's bed and pull out the sharp-edged stone we keep concealed beneath her mattress. It's jagged, but it does its work well enough.

Boone is looking at the picture of Otto that hangs on the wall. Mother has lined the walls with the few special things she brought from the village: a fur muff her father made for her, a silver mirror from the mother she never knew, and the drawing of Otto that Boone made for her, years ago.

People had time to pack their most treasured possessions when they fled Hoosick Falls. Darwin never bothered to take any of it away. He wanted only us . . . and Water.

"I should have drawn it the night he ran way," he says. "My memory is already fading."

"We thought he was coming back any day," Hope says.

"Why does he let us suffer for so long?" I ask.

Boone does not answer.

Ellie lays her hand on my cheek, just as she did on Mother's. "We suffer because we are Otto's chosen children."

"He chose us to suffer?" I ask, hating how small and petulant my voice sounds.

"He chose us to live!" Hope exclaims.

"In time he'll come," Boone says. I notice, now, how pinched his face is.

"You'll not leave until you're healed tonight," I tell Boone.

He shakes his head. "There's no need."

"And who will fill Ellie's cup tomorrow?" I ask. "Not you, with a lame foot."

"He needn't take the Water," Ellie says. "He needn't do that for me."

"Not every person has to be as stubborn as you," I tell her. "Let me heal him, especially since you won't let me heal *you*." It has been a long, painful argument between us. She will not accept a single extra bit of Water. She will only take what Darwin permits at weekly Communion.

Mother says that most Congregants would not be so selfless. "If they all knew, they'd bleed you dry," she always tells me.

I discovered my blood was special long ago, back when I was barely half the height of Mother . . . long before Otto's blood ran out.

Mother had forced me to come on one of her trapping trips, sneaking into the woods on a drizzly, dark night to steal extra food for the Congregants. I liked the food. I hated the trapping.

We had to be silent in case one of the Overseers cared to check the woods at night. Darwin thought he controlled every morsel that went into our mouths.

There was barely a moon, and the clouds curtained the stars. But Mother was silent in the woods, as if she could see a clear path in front of her. My feet seemed to find every crackly branch and leaf.

"Toe to heel, toe to heel," Mother whispered. Still my feet stumbled. With my every sound her shoulders raised and her fists clenched, but after a while she gave up trying to remind me.

I hoped, after every trip, that my clumsiness would save me from checking the traps with her. But she still insisted that I come along. "You'll learn how to trap," she said, "the same way my father taught me."

So I followed her that night as she glided to the squirrel trap tree. It was deep in the woods, so deep that we didn't even come this way for gathering water. Mother had baited loops of rope hanging off limbs, and at least a dozen squirrels had fallen into her trap. They strangled before they even got to eat the bait.

Mother let out a small, triumphant laugh and clapped her hands together once. Then she set off to the nearest squirrel. Their shadowed small bodies swung from the ropes, moving slightly in the night wind as if they'd just been caught. I hung back, feeling like I'd come across something private, something I shouldn't get near. But Mother didn't even pause. She strode up to the first one and cut it loose. Then she tossed it back over her shoulder.

It was my job to catch them—and hold them, all the way home. That night I was feeling especially reluctant. I let the first one drop in the leaves, then bent to pick it up by the bit of string left around its neck. It smelled like musk and blood.

"Use the tail. We can't afford you dropping even one," Mother whispered.

"They're only a bite or two," I told her.

Mother came to my side so fast, it was as if she flew. "Every bite matters," she said, her voice low and intense. "Never turn aside food."

My stomach growled like it was agreeing with her.

"Hold it tight," Mother ordered.

I'd been alive for decades. I knew I should be able to carry a few dead squirrels, especially if it meant feeding hungry Congregants. So I swallowed and grabbed the tail.

It was cold and bristly, nothing like the way I thought it should feel. Squirrels never stopped twitching their tails; it seemed wrong that this one was so still.

"I'm sorry," I whispered.

"You're too soft," Mother said, patting my cheek three times with her rough palm. She didn't understand that I was apologizing to the squirrel. I didn't try to explain.

Mother returned to the tree. While I stared at her first victim, two more landed by my feet.

Then my squirrel's tail twitched—just a bit.

"Mother! It's still alive!" I called.

She turned back swiftly to look at me. "Did it bite you?"

"No." It was far too weak for that.

"Break its neck," she said.

I shook my head.

"It's the kindest thing to do." Her voice was softer.

When I didn't move, she started back toward me. "Must I do it?" she asked.

"I'll do it!" I cried. I couldn't stand to see her kill this squirrel.

"Best hurry. We've got the fox traps to check, still," she ordered. Then she turned back.

I put my hands around the squirrel's tiny neck; I imagined I could feel the blood pulsing in its veins. "Could you run away?" I whispered. But I knew that the squirrel was far too weak for that.

The rain was falling harder; I felt drops running down my face. I imagined what I could do if this was consecrated Water, with my father's blood, coming from the sky. I could tilt the squirrel's head back, let it fall in his mouth just like our Communion.

I wanted to save the squirrel so badly.

The squirrel's paws hung limp, but its claws felt sharp. I wondered . . . I wondered if I carried its salvation in my veins.

It was something I'd thought about before: if my father's blood was holy, then could my blood be holy too? But the only time I'd asked my mother, she'd slapped me.

"Never speak of that," she'd ordered.

Five more squirrels were sitting in the leaves near me. Mother would finish soon.

I drew the claw across my wrist, but it left only a white scratch. I pressed harder, and blood welled along the line of the scratch.

Then I turned the squirrel on its back, cradled it in my hand, and held my wrist over its mouth. Rain ran over my hand, blending with the blood. At least one, two, three drops fell, I was sure.

"Praise Otto," I whispered, because it seemed like something had to be said.

The tail twitched again, and again, and then the squirrel sprang to life. It flipped in my hand and gave my finger a good, hard bite.

I cried out and dropped the squirrel. My finger hurt, but I was exhilarated. I had saved a life.

"Ruby?" Mother dashed back to me, her eyes searching and quickly landing on the hand I was cradling close to my chest. She grabbed my hand to inspect it.

"It bit me and ran away," I said.

"You're bleeding," she said.

"It bit me hard."

But her fingers ran over my wrist, and her eyes met mine. In the dark I couldn't tell if she was angry, or confused. But then she let out a half groan, half sob and pressed her fingers against the cut on my wrist.

"I didn't want it to die," I said.

She tilted her head back and stared at the sky, then wiped tears—or perhaps just raindrops—away with her free hand.

"Now we know," she said.

Mother never made me go out on trapping trips again. She swore me to secrecy. It was only years later that we told the Elders about my blood—only when they had to know.

Gabe is back with the bucket. It's barely half full, swirled with mud.

"Thank you," I tell him. "Now, please, go home—both of you. Rest for tomorrow's harvest."

"Yes. We should." Gabe cannot seem to stop staring at my arms. He swallows hard.

"Good night," Hope says.

Boone moves for the door too, but I block his way. "Not until I've healed your ankle," I say.

He frowns, but he does not leave.

I hold my arm over the bucket and ready the rock, hovering over my vein. Then I make a quick, hard slash.

Boone sucks his breath in through his teeth. Some of the Elders never have been easy with seeing me cut myself.

"It'll heal in minutes," I remind him.

He nods and stares at the wall over Mother's head, far from the bucket.

My blood drips into the water; I squeeze above the cut to

make it flow faster. That should be more than enough, really. The muddy swirl has become Water.

I grasp the bucket and move it in a slow circle to mix it. Then I dip a metal cup into it and pour it over the worst of Mother's wounds. While I wait for that to sink in, I can heal Boone.

"Drink," I order, giving him a fresh cupful.

Boone takes a tiny sip. I catch Ellie's pursed lips from the corner of my eye. He must feel her disapproval too.

"You'll need more," I tell him.

"That's more than the rest will see for Communion all month." Boone shakes his head and turns to the door. "Give it to Sula. All I need is rest."

"Good night, then. And thank you," I say.

He raises a hand good-bye, and then it is just me, and Mother, and Ellie. She hands me a rag soaked in the Water, and I press it to one of Mother's wounds. And then another, and another.

"Why don't you frown when I heal Mother?" I ask her.

"Otto will need her here, when he returns," she says.

"Won't he need *all* his followers?" I ask.

She holds up her hands to ward away the full cup I am offering her. "If Otto wishes me to live, he'll come in time. And if I'm meant to pass, then that's what I'll do."

"You take Communion," I remind her.

"As Otto taught us—one drop, every week. After that, it was his choice."

"He never denied anyone," I say, even though I never knew my father. All I know are the stories my mother tells me.

"You are as generous as he was." Ellie lifts a rag off

Mother's skin to inspect it. "She is improving."

But her body is still striped with deep cuts, some of them down to the bone. I swallow back revulsion, watching the muddy Water seep into her body.

"We could fight," I burst out.

Ellie sighs and lays another bit of cloth over the cuts that circle Mother's wrist like a bracelet. "We are not fighters."

"Not until now." I tilt some Water over one of the deepest gashes on Mother's torso.

"That's enough. A grown woman has to think more wisely." Ellie pulls my hand away, and a little of the Water splashes on Mother's bed. It soaks into the mattress; a bit of dried blood turns vibrant red.

Then she peels away the cloth that's layered on Mother's skin.

"Put it back. Mother's still bleeding," I say.

"She'll need to have some bumps and lumps, still. Darwin must never suspect what we do for Sula." Ellie's voice is hard now, and she does not put back the cloth.

He likes seeing her scars and scabs, I think. Some mornings, after he's beaten her hard, he smiles when he sees her—smiles like a man proud of his handiwork.

"I hate him," I say.

"All of us hate him." Ellie presses a dry cloth against the closing cuts on Mother's skin.

"Mother didn't, once," I say.

"True. Things were different, then." Ellie straightens up now, walking away from Mother's bed. The floor creaks beneath her dust-streaked boots, even though her step is light.

I slide another wet cloth on Mother's skin when Ellie's back is turned.

"Tell me," I say, because I love any story of the days before Darwin trapped us in the woods, even though I've heard them all hundreds of times. Besides, when Ellie tells tales, her mind travels back. She doesn't notice if I give Mother just a little more healing, take away just a little more pain.

"After your father . . ." Ellie swallows. "Disappeared from us . . ."

That is another one of the old stories I know by heart. Mother crept away to their secret meeting place, but Otto wasn't there. Just a wooden box waited for her, with the four vials of his blood inside.

She went there every day for a month. But he never returned.

"Darwin hoped he might have another chance with Sula." Ellie eases herself onto my bed, feet dangling off the edge, not quite reaching the floor. "He wooed her."

"What did he give her?"

"Oh—anything he thought would please her. His father owned the big store at the end of Main Street."

"That's how she met Darwin," I add.

"Your mother found every little excuse to visit that store and see the beautiful things there. She longed for so much." Ellie folds her arms and gives me a small smile. "Like her daughter does today."

I want freedom, not trinkets. But I don't argue with her, not right now. While she talks, I've been sliding just a little more Water over Mother's cuts. Her skin is knitting together, only faint lines left to remind her of Darwin's cruelties.

"After Otto was gone, Darwin brought her the finest cloth for sewing and cunning little carvings of animals. But it didn't change her heart."

Mother lets out a small groan, and Ellie's eyes swivel to her. She sits up straight to get a better look. The shadows hide how much healing I've done.

"Her breathing is better," I say.

Ellie's body relaxes and she continues.

"When he saw that Sula wouldn't have him back, Darwin turned to the town church in Hoosick Falls. He told them that we worshipped a false idol."

"Otto," I say.

"Yes. The minister told Mother we had to stop meeting, that she couldn't give us Communion anymore."

When Mother saw those vials of blood, she knew what Otto wanted her to do. She secretly mixed a bit into a crock of water, every week, and gave sips to his followers—just as he had done for them, when they needed healing or comfort. They came to call it Communion, just like at church.

Soon she was giving Communion every week.

At first, she refused the minister's demand that Communion stop. Soon crowds came to Ellie's door. They shouted hate, and threats.

"Darwin struck us a bargain." Ellie smoothes her skirts, the action firm and fast, and in the dim I can imagine she is still the youthful, confident woman who helped raise me here in the woods. "Darwin told your Mother he'd get the minister to leave her alone—that he'd make sure she was safe—so long as she'd leave Hoosick Falls before the winter."

"He didn't want to see her face anymore." I run one finger over Mother's cheek, more intimate a gesture than I'd dare if she were awake.

"Sula told Darwin she'd take his bargain, and the minister stopped calling. The crowds died away. But she didn't have anywhere to go. And by then, anyone could see that she had another to care for," Ellie says.

Before Otto left, he promised himself to Mother, and she to him. That was as good as married, Mother says.

"We told her she couldn't leave, not without us," Ellie continues. "After all, she was carrying Otto's child."

That's me. My father left me behind in Mother's belly. I slept there while Darwin wooed her, and the minister threatened, and the Congregants tried to protect her. What would she have done without me, I wonder. Would she have tried to follow Otto? Might she be with him today?

I've always been too afraid to ask her.

"So you all left," I say.

"We did. We packed what we could on wagons, and we headed up the mountain. Asa knew this place from his hunting trips."

Asa is our oldest Elder, after Ellie. I'm glad his daughter grabbed his elbow to stop him from coming tonight. He needs rest.

"But Asa never knew who owned it," I say.

Ellie looks down at her hands, knitted in her lap. I pour just a little more Water down Mother's throat. Even though she sleeps, she swallows it. Then I give her a little more.

"The men put up a few cabins—this one first, so your mother would be comfortable. She was very round by then." Ellie stands and comes behind me. She lifts my hair and starts to braid it. I close my eyes and savor the feel of her tender touch.

"How many were you?" I ask, not wanting the story to end.

"Nearly six dozen came to the woods," Ellie says. "Plus you."

And now ten of them withered, the rest of us still here.

"Not a single one has left. We all wait." Ellie tugs at my hair, lightly, as she makes the braid. It feels good. I tilt my head back a bit and look up at the ceiling. I pretend Mother is only sleeping, not healing once again.

"What was it like in the woods, before Darwin found you?" I ask.

"It was busy. We knew we had to get up shelters, find food sources, before winter." Ellie sighs. "To think winter was our biggest worry."

"But then Darwin came."

"He brought so many cruel men. They all had clubs and chains."

They hadn't escaped him after all. Darwin's family owned the land they had fled to.

"He said we'd either give him some of Otto's miracle Water . . . or he'd kill your mother. He'd kill *you*." Ellie's hands stop their braiding.

"Mother should have told him about the blood."

But she didn't. She made something up, and fast. She said

43

the Water could only be harvested from forest leaves, by Otto's consecrated followers. She lied to Darwin and she lied to the Congregation.

"She was protecting Otto—and you." Ellie rests both her hands on my shoulders for a moment, and squeezes. "If Darwin knew what made the Water special, he'd have taken all the blood . . . and then he would have gone after Otto."

"Now we're all stuck with pewter cups and spoons." Mother was scared. When Darwin asked her how we harvested the Water, it was the only thing she could think of.

"We thought it was a bargain we could live with." Ellie starts braiding again. "We thought Otto would come, and soon."

"This summer has been terrible," I say.

"The worst yet. The drought . . . it's made them all meaner than ever," she says.

Not all. My mind flashes on the new Overseer, his eyes wide with horror as the chain fell. My skin flushes warm. Suddenly it feels wrong to have Ellie touching me.

I pull away, taking my hair into my hand to finish my own braid.

"What do the Elders want to ask me?" I ask.

Ellie draws in breath, but pauses.

"In the woods," I press. "You said there was something you all wanted to ask me."

Ellie frowns, then shrugs. "I forget so much these days."

"Hmm," I answer. I want that to be a lie—not the truth, not something that means she's withering away even faster than I fear.

Ellie lets out a soft gasp. "Sula," she says, leaning close.

When I look closer, I see why she sounds afraid. Mother is healed . . . not a little, but completely.

"She hasn't got a single scar." Ellie accuses.

"I didn't know . . ."

"You knew. But you chose to heal her anyway. Don't you see?" she says. "She'll only be hurt worse, now."

"We'll hide it. We'll . . . She'll cut herself, if she has to," I say. "She can have a fresh wound or two for him to see."

Ellie drops her head, silent for a long time. Finally she draws in a deep breath. "It's time I went home."

"I'll walk you." I stand, but she waves me away.

"I know the road. It's been a long time, hasn't it?" She turns to face me. "Waiting is hard. But it's all we can do, Ruby. It's all we know how to do."

"We could fight." It comes out as a whisper.

"With what tools? And what spirit?" She shakes her head. "All we can do is pray, and wait."

It is an old fight between us, and one I am too tired to have again tonight. So I clasp her in an embrace and offer her our lantern for the walk home.

She refuses it, of course. But she is as dear as any blood relative, so I have to try.

"I only want things to be better," I tell her before she leaves.

"Then pray," she says. "And find a way to wait."

When I go to sleep, Mother's breathing is even. I do not feel guilty that I healed her. I am proud that she has healed, all thanks to my blood.

I have helped, even if nobody wanted it.

Chapter 4

We wake even earlier on Sundays. It's our day to gather and pray to Otto.

But our Services will end before sunrise—Darwin will make sure of that. The daylight belongs to him.

We gather at the only place big enough to hold all of us: the Common House, across from the cisterns. It is where we eat all our meals too. The Common House is a low, simple building made of wood frame covered by grayed boards. The windows look too small for the wide walls. But at least some look over the Lake, bringing a little light to the gloom inside.

Mother and I walk to Services in silence. She was angry when she woke to find her scars were gone.

"You went too far," she told me.

"As did you. Let others take their licks, for once," I told her.

After that we had nothing to say to each other.

Darwin is waiting at the door, lips pressed tight in the shadow of his hat as he watches us approach. Nothing escapes his stare—and as his eyes flit over Mother's body, I hear Ellie's voice echoing in my head.

She'll only be hurt worse, now.

"You look well," he says. No part of him moves except his eyes and his mouth. The rest of him stays leaning against the door of the Common House.

"As well as any day." Mother tries to push past him, but he grabs her arm.

"Too well," he says.

Congregants move past us, quiet, nearly creeping. They don't want Mother hurt, I know it—but they don't want Darwin to notice them either. Now is the time to slip past and find a seat as far from an Overseer, and Darwin's eyes, as possible. They only want Communion and maybe some of Mother's Word.

"I slept well," Mother says. "That is all."

"You slept alone. That is not *well*." Now Darwin moves, his body pushing toward her. Mother does not back away, even when he stands just inches from her.

"The sun is nearly up," she says. "Let me inside."

He's taller than her, towering, a wall of muscle against her narrow bravery. I imagine his fist circling her entire waist, crushing, stealing her breath away. He could nearly do it, if he wanted to. And who would stop him?

"Are you stealing from me?" He asks it in an even, low tone, but there's danger in his eyes.

"Never." Her answer is not scared, or too fast. It is a perfect mix of hesitation and assurance. She keeps her eyes on him.

"I don't know how you would." But he doesn't seem satisfied.

He slides his look to me, even as he grips Mother's wrist in his iron hand. "Little Toad, does your mother lie?"

"No. No, never." My answer is too fast, too eager, no matter how hard I try to be like Mother.

Darwin's eyes narrow, and he turns his stare back to Mother. "Her father was a liar too."

"Let me go," she says.

He steps back to let her pass, but he keeps talking as we walk by. "There's only one way those cuts went away so fast," he says.

We're nearly to the front when he shouts the rest. "You're stealing!"

They all turn to look, Overseers and Congregants alike. But Mother just raises her chin and walks to the front.

I sit in the chair next to Ellie, and we listen to Services, same as any other Sunday. But today my heart pounds, and Mother's words are a stream running over pebbles—too fast for me to catch, only sound, nothing of meaning.

Ellie squeezes my pinky finger with hers, then covers my hand with her own. Her skin feels like paper next to mine, her heart's beat pushing too hard through it. How much longer does she have?

"I should have been more careful," I whisper to her.

"You did it for love," she answers. "Just like Otto."

Services never last too long. Mother starts with a reading from the small Bible in her skirt pocket—Old Testament, always, since it's what she read in the woods with Otto—and then we follow her in a psalm.

Mother stands in front of the windows that face the Lake.

A small altar—a table, really, brought from someone's home in Hoosick Falls when the Congregation fled—is in front of her. A single, small bottle of Water rests on it. That is what they are all waiting for—the Water made from my blood.

Even when I stare straight at Mother, the Overseers hover at the edge of my vision. Darwin stands the closest, one hand in his pocket. His eyes never leave Mother. Then there're always three more men, all in reach, all holding guns.

My tongue stumbles over the psalm while my eyes rove. Where is the new Overseer? Is he here, or waiting in the woods for the harvest to start? Or has Darwin already dismissed him? I can't find him.

"It is too hot for the word today," Mother says, reaching for the bottle of Water. I know why she is really skipping her sermon: she wants no excuse for the Overseers to deny Ellie's turn at Communion.

"Ten minutes," Darwin growls from the corner.

"Come forward," Mother tells the Congregation. The Overseers come close now, making sure that we're lining up in the same order as every week. Once in a while they make small adjustments, pushing one person ahead of another.

Usually I stand near the front of the line. The strongest Congregants, the most valuable ones, are in the front. The weakest are in the back—just in case the Water runs out. Sometimes the Overseers don't give Mother enough.

Ellie walks to the back, and I follow her, away from my place. I take hold of Ellie's arm. She will be last, but I will be certain that she makes it there.

"Not your spot," an Overseer growls at me. His breath smells bitter.

"Go," Ellie whispers.

I tighten my grip on Ellie's arm and shake my head. The Overseer lifts his gun higher in the air. Somehow I find the courage not to flinch.

"Your loss," he mutters, then walks away.

Now I see the new Overseer. He's in the back corner of the room, watching, his face rigid. As soon as I look at his face, he looks at mine. He lifts his other hand—the one not holding a gun—to touch the gold medal at his throat. His face softens a little.

I turn away fast, but my face burns as if he's touched me.

Mother puts a single precious drop of Water on each Congregant's tongue. Her shoulders, draped in white linen, glow in the predawn gloom. Darwin edges closer, until he's nearly pressed against her. Every Congregant faces Mother and Darwin at the same time.

Her low, rich voice says the same thing with each drop.

"In the name of Otto." Drop. Swallow. The Congregant steps away fast enough to satisfy Darwin.

Another Congregant is ready.

"In the name of Otto."

But this one is too slow. Darwin deals him a hard slap.

"Move faster," he barks. "You've got to meet quota by noon."

Mother freezes, only her eyes turning to stare at Darwin.

"Every single Toad gets a shovel when you're done getting your Water," Darwin announces. "We got big plans."

A groan creeps through the Congregation, like fog over the Lake. I wonder what plans Darwin has, other than tormenting us and stealing our Water.

"We'll never—" Mother starts.

"You want to waste your precious Communion time arguing?" Darwin asks.

Mother shakes her head and lifts the dropper high. The line hurries now: drop, swallow, step away. But then another Congregant is too slow. He gets a poke with the barrel of Darwin's gun.

"You keep up this pace, no dinner," Darwin bellows. "You'll live."

Ellie is leaning heavy on my arm; I struggle to make it look like I'm not dragging her down the aisle.

"I should sit down," Ellie whispers.

"Not before you get Communion." I tighten my arm around hers.

"They won't give me any," Ellie says.

All the Overseers care about is having strong bodies to harvest the water. If someone is too sick to work, they don't get Water—or food. It is, they say, a waste.

I hush her, my eyes flicking to the Overseers. They hold their guns against their shoulders like old friends, watching to make sure Mother puts only a single drop on each person's tongue.

"Just be steady and try not to shake," I say. "I will hold you up."

Only three people in front of us now: Boone's aunt, Mary, one of the oldest but without a palsy. She gets her Water. Next comes her brother John. Darwin doesn't pay much attention to him, or to Gen Duncan, when she takes her turn. He's looking at Ellie, sharp eyes like a crow watching from a low-hanging branch.

Then it is our turn. We take one more step forward.

"You first," Ellie says.

I shake my head. I don't need the Water. But she pokes me in the back, suddenly strong. I open my mouth and the Water drops on my tongue. It doesn't taste special—it's just like drinking from the Lake.

Next comes Ellie. Her mouth opens, trembling, and I gently tip her head back. Mother dips the dropper in the bottle.

Darwin grips Mother's arm. "Stop."

Her body goes stiff. She stares at the meaty hand wrapped around her arm.

Then he looks at me. "Let go of her."

Ellie's body is shaking under my hands. I let them slide away, slowly, imagining leaving my strength behind to help her.

"You were sleeping in the woods yesterday," Darwin says.

"It was only for a moment." Her voice is strong. If I close my eyes, it's easy to imagine Ellie as I have known her for my entire life: strong-bodied, confident, never needing help from anyone.

"And the day before?" he asks. "I saw you lying in the shade then too."

Now Ellie is sagging to one side. I nudge her with my shoulder to set her upright. She lets out a low moan, her strong voice leached away.

Darwin turns to Mother. "Is it hard to see your mother dying?"

drought

Of course Ellie is not her mother—her mother, my grand-mother, was taken by fever before my mother could walk. But Darwin knows we love Ellie like our own, and she us.

Mother does not answer. Instead she reaches out to lay her hand on Ellie's shoulder. Darwin slaps it away.

"The old Toad must pass a test," Darwin says.

"A test?" Mother's eyebrows twitch high.

"God tested man, now man tests Toad." Darwin's broad smile tells me he's very pleased with himself.

He's never done this before. Either he lets the old person have the Water, or he doesn't. Then he makes us hurry into the woods for a harvesting.

"No tests." Mother lets out a huff of air. "Services are sacred. Let me finish the Communion first."

"You don't tell me no, Sula Prosser." Darwin takes the butt of his rifle and slams it on the floor, just an inch from Mother's boot.

Her face tightens, but she does not flinch. She keeps her eyes steady on him.

This time his rifle lands square on her toes. Someone in the Congregation lets out a low cry. But not one of us stands or stops him. It's better that way—but it's not easy. I squeeze my fingers together and stare down, away, to stop myself from saying some-thing.

We have been living this way for a very long time. I should be better at accepting this. But it gets harder every day.

"Please let her take the Communion first," Mother mutters.

She does not usually beg. But I know why: the Water will help smooth away the shakes and help Ellie to stand tall. It might be enough to pass any test the Overseer chooses for her.

But without the Water, she doesn't have much of a chance.

"I don't think so." Darwin motions to the back of the room. "Get a broom, boy."

The new Overseer sets his gun in a corner and goes to the closet. He keeps his eyes low, staring at the tops of his boots, as he walks to the front.

Darwin points at me next. "And you'll help."

He arranges the new Overseer and me, one at each end of the broom. Our eyes meet for a second; a flash of heat makes me look away fast.

Darwin lifts the broom until it's as high as my shoulder.

"Now, Toad." Darwin lets out a bark of laughter. "Limbo."

"What is limbo?" Ellie's head is bobbing but she holds it high.

"You dance under it. Like this." Darwin holds both arms out to the side, twisting, sliding under the broom without his face touching the handle.

Darwin knows modern things like limbo. He has a modern house with modern books and the glow box you can see moving pictures on. His truck takes him anywhere he wants to go.

I dare to raise my eyes to the new Overseer again. His lips move; he's saying something to me, without any sound. But I don't understand. He tries again, his eyes flicking to Darwin.

Then he lifts the broom, just a tiny bit higher. My hand holding the broomstick is slick and quivering. The boy grimaces, for a second—from sympathy or hatred of me, I don't know—then puts a second hand on the stick. It steadies . . . and then he raises it again, a small amount. I follow his lead and edge it even higher.

Mother's face is white. "Let me give her the Water."

"I feed and clothe you people. I give you firewood in the winter. You think those things are free? You greedy guts cost me!" Darwin's last words are a guttural shout. He takes in a shallow breath. "Especially when you steal from me. Someone's going to pay."

"Nobody's stealing," Mother says. But Darwin doesn't seem to hear her.

"She's useless if she can't harvest." He gestures to Ellie. "Now go. And mind you tilt your head back. Do it just like you're getting your precious Communion."

I want to make this stop. Why should we be this man's playthings? We are dozens to his one.

But Mother says the Congregation does not fight back.

So I remind myself: we endure. We endure, and we wait for our Savior. Otto will fight our battle.

I remind myself, but deep inside I don't believe it.

Ellie takes one shaky step, then another, to the broom. I hold my breath. The room is silent, save for Darwin's heavy breathing.

She tips her head back. Her white-yellow braids slide down her back. I long to reach out and steady her.

Then Darwin starts singing. "La la la . . ."

Ellie startles at the song. But she closes her eyes and straightens her shoulders. And then a miracle happens. She walks under that broom, head tilted back, chin tucked, without brushing it. She has inches to spare.

She doesn't even falter.

An excited murmur travels across the Congregation. I can't help grinning. When I look at the new Overseer, I see he is smiling too, his lips lifted just enough for me to be sure he's happy. None of the other guards are smiling.

"She has passed," Mother says. She lifts the eyedropper.

I set the broom on the floor, slow, not wanting any clatter to attract Darwin's attention. His face is flushed red—the man is angry, I imagine, at losing his cruel game.

"Fine. She passed." Darwin steps so close to Mother, her skirt touches his boots. I step forward to help Ellie, but she motions me away.

The drop of Water dangles over Ellie's open mouth.

But Darwin's arm snakes out. He knock's Mother hand and the drop of Water goes flying.

"No!" someone shouts from the Congregation.

Never waste the Water. Every single drop is meant to be drunk—or delivered. Darwin is breaking his own rule.

I look for the mark: where did the Water land? Everyone is craning their necks to see. Someone points at a dot on the floor. Darwin treated the Water like it was garbage—something only fit for washing the floor. I suppose he doesn't mind wasting Water, not if he ean spend it with cruelty—he has plenty more in the cisterns.

"Psych," Darwin says.

I don't know what psych means. But I think it's certain that Ellie will not get Communion today. She will probably never get it again. I slide an arm around her shoulders. She does not refuse me this time.

"Another drop for her?" Mother asks through tight lips, though we all know the answer.

"I think not. This one is done for good." Darwin folds his arms and shakes his head, the smile stretching his lips wide as he fixes his eyes on Ellie.

Ellie lets out a shuddering breath. Her time is nearly gone, then. We will have only days to say good-bye.

"But she passed," I burst out.

"Ruby." Mother's single word is an order I know well: Silence, Ruby. Let well enough alone.

A small smile flickers on Darwin's lips, and he stares at me. "You think I'm unfair, don't you, little Toad?"

"I . . . No." I shake my head and stare at his feet. My mouth is dry with fear now, too dry to form any more foolish words.

"It's sunrise," the new Overseer says.

Darwin is squinting at the new Overseer as if he's never seen him before. Then he gestures to Mother without taking his eyes off the new Overseer. "Wrap it up, High Priestess Toad," he barks.

Mother sets the dropper on the altar, careful to make sure it doesn't roll off, and recaps the bottle. Then she gestures with both hands, palms toward the ceiling. "Please rise for our final prayer."

The old oak benches creak as the Congregation pushes to their feet. I speak our special prayer with everyone else, even though I feel doubt. If Otto loved us so much, if he were truly divine, wouldn't he have come back to save us a long time ago?

Otto, our savior
We seek thy deliverance
Take us from our pain
And show us to heaven
Where Water flows freely
And we live in thy presence
Amen.

Darwin stares straight ahead as we recite the prayer. He does not join us, nor do any of the Overseers. I wonder if they pray to anybody, and if they think their god loves what they do to us.

Chapter 5

The days get hotter and the woods yield less and less water. Darwin's hand grows heavier. There are more days when he beats us than not.

I'm more careful healing Mother, now. But even so, it took two buckets of murky lake water to ease her wounds tonight. Now she breathes easier, and everyone has left us. It is time for my nightly trip to the cisterns.

It is a hot, still night—barely better than the day. The air is cooler than the cabin, at least. There could be an Overseer waiting, even though we've never seen one in the woods at night. I walk toe to heel, toe to heel, like Mother taught me. I keep my feet on the dusty road, away from branches, barely making a scuff or crackle on the road to the clearing.

Mother's warnings of Overseers terrified me when I was smaller.

"Always be careful," she reminded me every night. "Always expect them to be there."

To still the fear, back then, I pretended I was nothing more than a mouse rustling through the weeds. If an Overseer happened to be out at night, all he would see is a little brown mouse creeping to its nest. I wasn't a girl. I wasn't even big enough to trap and eat.

Now I pray silently to Otto—and listen like a deer tiptoeing past a wolf.

It's dark out tonight, barely any moon to see by. But my feet know the path well, and I do not stumble once. When I reach the cisterns, I pat my skirt to make sure the sharp stone is still tucked there—yes, an edge threatening to poke through the threadbare fabric. Then I climb the ladder to the top of the cistern we've been filling these last weeks.

A breeze comes from somewhere—sent by Otto, maybe. It catches at my hair and swirls the curls around my face. I pause to push it behind my ears. Why didn't I think to bring a piece of twine or some hairpins with me? Mother would say I'm still a child who needs minding.

I screw open the valve and peer inside, even though I know I won't see anything in the dark—unless it's nearly full to the brim. There's only darkness. I roll back my left sleeve—the arm I haven't already cut for Mother tonight—and hold my arm over the opening. My skin is smooth, even though I've cut it in this place hundreds, maybe thousands of time. My body heals just as fast as the Water heals everyone else.

Mother cried the night when the last drop of my father's blood fell from the last glass vial. She collapsed onto the cistern in a kind of desperate embrace, not worrying for once about how loud she was or who might hear us. The empty vial slipped from her fingers and fell onto the grass without a sound. I picked it up and tucked it into my skirts.

Now the vial sits with the other three, four nestled in the little box beneath Mother's bed. Empty all, Otto's promises used up.

I held my arm up high when she descended the ladder that night. "Let me do it," I said.

We'd never talked about what would happen when his blood was gone. But she didn't argue. Instead, she took my hand in hers, turning it so she could see the tender underside of my arm, my veins a faint blue trace in the moonlight. "There's no other way for us to live," she said. "And live we must, if we wait for Otto."

I have visited the cisterns every night since.

One quick slash of the stone and my blood is flowing free. I let it drip into the cistern—one, two, three . . . ten drops altogether.

Back when Mother added Otto's blood, she counted to three and stopped. But mine's likely not as strong as his since I am half from Mother. Besides, I've got lots more to give.

Mother always whispered a prayer, so I do too. "Deliver us, Otto."

Does he hear me? Does he see me, pouring the blood he gave me into our captor's cisterns?

"Why don't you come?" I say, too loud, and warning fear makes my skin tingle.

Of course there is no answer—he never answers me, not in my mind, not in the wind or the birds singing in the trees. When I talk to Otto, I feel like I am throwing a pebble off a vast mountain. I have thrown enough of those pebbles to have made my own mountain.

I've added enough blood to the cistern now. I press my hand to the cut.

It barely stings tonight, probably because I'm more tired than usual. I peel away my hand to peek at it; it still looks wet, so I press my hand back on the wound. The wind pulls at my hair again, and this time I toss my head to push it away. The movement makes me tip to the side, and I make a quick grab at the cisterns.

My hands echo on the near-empty cistern, like a clap of thunder.

Then an even louder sound—a crack of sticks, only a few feet away, perhaps by the next cistern. This is a sound I've never heard here before.

I freeze, waiting for another sound, any sound, to tell me what's waiting at the bottom of the ladder. Let it be a fox, or a bear. Yes, it's probably an animal, driven by the drought to find water farther from home, closer to people.

Any animal will be kinder to me than an Overseer.

"Who's there?" a man's voice says in the darkness.

Cold fear sweeps over me. I squeeze my eyes shut, like a child, praying he won't see me if I can't see him. If I stay still enough, maybe he won't even think to look above his head. Maybe he'll go away, and I'll be able to slip back to our cabin.

There's rustling below me now, and another stick cracks underfoot. This man, whoever he is, knows less about creeping around the woods than I do.

"Hello?" he asks.

He doesn't sound cruel. He sounds a little afraid, maybe. And he sounds uncertain — nothing like an Overseer. Maybe he's a stranger. Maybe he's someone who could help, even. Might someone slip into our woods at night, someone who doesn't belong?

I could get us help. For a second, hope surges in me. My foot aches to step down the ladder, five quick steps, and beg for this man to save us, to do what Otto hasn't.

But Mother's warnings stop me. Otto will save. Strangers won't help us. They didn't help us when Darwin turned the town against Otto, and Mother. They didn't help when the Congregants had to flee. And they won't help now either.

There's a loud squawk below, one that pushes new dread through my body. I know that sound. This is no stranger.

"You out there, boy?" It's Darwin's voice, on one of the talk boxes that the Overseers wear on their belts. They can speak to each other without even being within eyesight.

How close is he now? Dread makes my limbs feel heavy. Can I even stay standing up here? Or will I fall backward, heavier than a stone, and lie on the ground waiting for discovery?

The man near me speaks. "I'm at the cisterns, like you told me to."

"Any sign of the little thieves?" Darwin asks.

Silence, for a moment. I lean over the cistern and dare to look down. Should I run? Or pray he hasn't seen me?

A pair of eyes meet mine, looking up from below. It's the new Overseer. I am frozen with fear. But a slow, wondering smile settles onto his face.

"It's you," he says.

"Don't tell," I whisper, both a prayer to Otto and a plea to this man who can hurt or save me.

He lifts the talk box to his mouth. "All's quiet," he says. "No sign of anybody."

Relief rushes through me so fast, so hard, that my body trembles. I can barely keep hold of the ladder.

Darwin answers fast on the talk box. "You keep an eye out. Find out how those Toads are stealing from me."

"You got it." The man below me disappears, but I hear him coming closer, and I sense him at the bottom of the ladder. I run one finger over my arm—healed, though streaked in brown—and pull my sleeve over the place where I cut myself. My hand still shakes.

Then I descend, slowly, my mind racing with plans for escape. Halfway down he shocks me—he puts both of his hands on my waist. They feel warm and wide, but gentle.

I let him lift me down and turn me around to face him. When he takes his hands off my waist, it feels strangely cold.

"There you go," he says.

I can't see his eyes, but I see some of the drawings on his right arm, twisting from shoulder to wrist. There's the glint of an animal's eye, and flames reaching over his forearm. I imagine tracing each one with the tip of my finger, lightly, trying to feel where the colors blend.

"I'll never come back," I say. "I'm sorry."

Then I lunge, try to get past him.

"Wait . . . please," he says.

The word stops me. An Overseer never says please, especially to a Congregant. That is a word we use to pray to Otto, or to beg Darwin for mercy.

He could have grabbed me, or whipped his chain at me. But he *asked*.

"Don't go yet. I just . . . I just want to talk for a little bit," he says.

"My mother . . . ," I start, but I can't make any other words come out. My breath is too short.

"Darwin hit her pretty hard today." He folds his arms. Even though it's dark, I can feel his look, steady.

He wants me to say something, I know it. But there's no use complaining to an Overseer. I only stare at the ground.

"It makes me sick. I want to stop him but . . ." He trails off.

I look back up; now he is staring at the ground too. He shakes his head, not raising his chin. "I'm sorry."

"Only Otto can stop him," I whisper.

But I don't know if he hears me, because he turns away and walks to the grass under the cistern we've been standing next to. He sits in the softest, lushest grass beneath the belly of the cistern and pats the ground. "Maybe—maybe you could stay? Just for a minute."

"No, I can't." I wrap my arms around my sides.

"I won't touch you," he says softly. "If that's what you're worried about."

Only a fool wouldn't be worried about that. Mother has warned me about what men want to do to girls. And this man belongs to Darwin West. Every part of me wants to run—except a small, dangerous part, a part that wants to know why he lied to Darwin for me. He's more Congregant than Overseer. Or maybe he's something I've never known before.

Things have been the same here for hundreds of years. He's something different, maybe something safe, even.

I keep my eyes on him and edge a little closer to where he sits. But I stay standing.

He doesn't coax me closer, only watches. "Darwin posted me as the guard for the night. Nobody else is coming."

Be ready to run, I remind my legs. You can leave at any moment.

"I'm Ford," he says. "And you're Ruby. I heard your mother say it, the other day."

He called me Ruby. He knows my name. It's not "*little Toad*" or "*girl*." I'm a person to him.

Slowly, slowly, I settle into the grass. Still I'm far enough away to run, if I need to. But I'm close enough to hear his soft breathing. I brush my fingers over the tops of the soft grass, softer than the bed that I should be sleeping in right now. It's cool, and a little damp.

"Ford," I repeat, liking how the short, strong word sounds. It's not modern; it's something that fits in my old, simple world.

"How old are you?" he asks.

I don't answer him. Maybe he's strangely kind for an Overseer; gentle, even. But I won't give him my secrets.

"You're seventeen, I bet. I'll be nineteen in September," Ford says. "Am I right? Seventeen?"

"Nearly." I push down the hysterical bubble of laughter that wells inside me.

"I've lived in Hoosick Falls my whole life and I've never seen you. You go to school near here?"

All my schooling has been what Mother and the others have taught me in winter nights, or in stolen moments in the shade. I shake my head.

"You're homeschooled, then," he says.

Longing fills me. School is one of the hundreds of things I've dreamed of, but never had.

"Tell me about school," I say.

"My school? It's not too big. Maybe fifty kids in class. You get pretty sick of each other." He lets out a short laugh. "But nobody leaves, not even after they graduate. Including me.

"I'm just like the rest of the guys here," Ford says, his voice heavier now.

His troubles are nothing close to mine. But he helped Ellie at Services, and he didn't tell Darwin I was here. I owe him something small, I think. "You're kinder than the others," I say.

"I'm nothing special." His voice is low and bitter. "All I do is watch."

"But tonight . . . you didn't tell Darwin I was here."

"Yeah. Yeah, I guess I did that," he says.

"Thank you," I tell him, looking over. The shadows make the lines of his face even stronger, outlining the jut of his chin and nose.

"Don't. I don't deserve that," his voice cracks.

"Maybe you're right," I say.

He'll hurt me now, I know it. I brace my legs to spring, to run, to duck. But he doesn't move at all . . . and I don't either.

We're quiet for a while. The backs of my legs feel wet from the damp seeping through my skirts. I swing my legs under me, even though it will make it harder to leave fast.

"You have a hobby?" he asks me.

"What's a hobby?"

"You know. Something you do for fun," he explains.

"There's not much room for fun here," I say.

"There must be something." His voice is soft. Part of me knows I'm never safe with him. But part of me wants to tell him things.

"I like to sing." I think of our songs to Otto, drifting over the tops of trees.

"You don't want to hear me sing." He laughs. "I'm more of a fix-it kind of guy."

"What do you fix?"

"Anything with an engine. Cars, trucks . . . I've been giving my mom's car oil changes since I was twelve."

"Do you fix things here?"

He lets out a sound that's more of a bark than a laugh. "I'm just a guy with the gun, around here."

"And the chain," I say softly.

"I hate it. I hate all of it." He turns so he's facing me, full on.

And I turn too, so we are looking straight at each other, though still far away.

"It used to be there was nothing I couldn't fix," Ford says. "But now . . ."

"But now?" I prompt him.

"My mom's sick, real sick. The kind of sick you can't fix."

I think of the buckets I poured over Mother tonight. What would I do to help her, if I didn't have that? "That . . . That must be hard."

"And this place . . ." Ford makes a loud sniff. Then he swipes his arm over his face, fast.

"Are you crying?" I ask.

"These days I do that a lot." He clears his throat and looks up at the sky.

His entire life is so easy compared to mine. And he is here to keep my world terrible. But I still feel tears welling in my eyes, a response to his pain, even though I should hate him. I reach a hand out. I imagine laying it on top of his hand, cool skin on warm. I drop it fast.

"What happens here . . ." He trails off. "I can't—I can't stop thinking about it."

"It doesn't help to think about it," I say.

"That doesn't make it right. Darwin West makes me sick." His voice is low, rough, like it hurts for the words to come out.

"Why are you here, then? If he makes you ill, why don't you leave?"

"My mom needs medicine, and hospice, and . . . I can't let her suffer," he says.

"Seems like there's better work than this," I mutter.

"Round here, there's not many choices. But you know that— you're working here too," he says.

Should I tell him the truth? Would it change anything?

No. Ford is not Otto. It is not his job to save us. It is his job to imprison us.

"I haven't any choice," I say. But I do not tell him more.

"Is it because you're a cult?" he asks.

"A cult." I taste the word—strange, brand-new. "What's that?"

"No offense. That's what the other guards told me—that's why you wear those old-fashioned clothes and have all the Otto stuff on your church days . . ."

"Is a cult a Congregation?" I ask.

"Sort of." He draws out the words. "But you can't leave them, really. You're stuck."

"Then maybe that's what we are," I say.

"Maybe someday we'll both find something better," Ford says.

"Someday," I say, sending Otto a silent prayer.

"How's that lady doing—the one who's so sick?" Ford asks. "I didn't see her in the woods today, or the day before."

It's been six days since Ellie was denied Communion. For the last two, she's been too weak to be out of bed. I brought her the last of our squirrel jerky this morning.

But she made me eat it while she watched.

"She was in the woods," I lie, trying to keep my voice steady. "She's much better."

"I see. That's . . . good. I thought maybe it was something serious."

"Ellie's real strong. You don't have to worry about her," I say. But I like that he asked. He cares, at least a part of him does.

"You're strong too," he says.

His voice is too familiar, too warm. I push to my feet. "I have to go."

"Wait," Ford says. There's enough command in his voice

to make me brace my body. "Why'd you come here tonight?"

"I only . . . I . . ." I will myself not to touch my arm. "I come to pray. And I bless the Water. My mother taught me how."

He shifts in the grass and I feel his eyes on me. "Maybe you'll come to bless the Water tomorrow."

"My mother—" I shake my head and back away, slow at first and then faster, faster.

"I'll be here," he says.

I might stutter a few more words—I'm not sure. My heart is beating too fast to hear. I turn, run, so panicked that my feet find every rut and hole in the road. But it doesn't slow me down.

Chapter 6

The Elders are meeting tonight, and they want to talk to me—just as Ellie said they would.

Hope found us in the clearing, after we emptied our cups. "We're meeting at Ellie's tonight," she whispered. Her eyes darted about, hunting for guards, I think. Only the Congregants even know the Elders exist.

"I'll come if I can," Mother told her.

"We need Ruby too." Hope gave Mother a strong look, then me. "You'll come?"

I remembered that Ellie said this would happen. Now I'd finally find out what they wanted.

"Of course I will," I told Hope.

She pulled me into a tight hug and whispered something. *Just say yes,* I think it was. But before I could ask, Gabe was there, and then Hope was gone.

The Elders have met with Mother at our cabin every Tuesday night for as long as I can remember. Some of the faces have changed: Asa's wife Mabel and Christian Banks are both withered and gone, with Hope and Asa taking their places. But the meetings are mostly the same. They sort out arguments between families, give our meager extras to those who need them the most, and they always pray to Otto.

Sometimes other Congregants come too, pleading their case or complaining about a neighbor. They all trust the Elders, and Mother, to smooth things over, to protect us, as much as anyone can.

When Hope asked us to come, I wondered whether Mother would be too hurt, too beaten. And when we didn't meet our quota today, I was so afraid for her.

But Darwin only lifted a hand to Mother's cheek and smiled.

"Remember I love you," he said.

Then they gave us hard biscuits and chopped fish that tasted mostly like the metal cans it came in. The Congregants were jolly, as if it were a holiday. I suppose it was. And all of us know it could be very different tomorrow.

The walk to Ellie's is short; her cabin is the closet one to ours. I remember all the times I ran there, my heart burning from Mother's careless or hard words. Ellie knows all my secrets . . . except for this new one about the Overseer, flourishing like a summer weed while she slips away.

We have arrived at Ellie's door. Someone pushed fresh flowers in the knothole near eye level; they are limp, but the tiny yellow petals are pretty.

There's a burst of laughter from inside the cabin, the same

kind of joy we all felt at dinner. But Mother lets out an irritated sigh and pushes inside.

"Have a care," she warns as we enter the cabin. "Do you want the Overseers finding us?"

Hope is sitting on Ellie's bed, holding one of her hands. A smile slides off her face, and she looks away from us. Her thick black hair swings to cover her face like a curtain.

"I'm sorry I was loud," she says.

"We're telling stories about the old days." Boone is tending a small fire in Ellie's stove, poking twigs into the fledgling flame. He pauses to offer us one of his rare smiles, and I see Mother's shoulders relax.

It's hotter than noontime, but Ellie has drawn the blankets tight up to her chin. The evening's slight chill must be soaking into her bones. I pull at my bodice to free it from my sticky skin.

Her bed is plumped with pillows I've never seen in the cabin before. They're made from faded fabric, lumpy with pine needles or dried grasses. It's a luxury for any Congregant to have more than one pillow—or even that.

"Who brought these?" I ask. One has faint yellow stripes on it; another shows brighter spots of blue where buttons used to be.

"Joan made them, but Mary gave her the fabric. She'll wish she had those shirts come wintertime." Ellie frowns and reaches back to touch the pillows.

Come winter, will Ellie even need the pillows? I swallow hard and twist away, pretending to study the careful dried daubs of mud that seal the logs of her cabin.

I helped Ellie add more mud, every fall, keeping the wind

away from her. She followed behind and smoothed each bit until it was perfect. Our walls never looked so nice. Mother didn't have the patience for making them perfect, and I didn't have the steady hand.

Mother sets her stool next to Ellie's pillow and takes a seat. She brushes a light hand over Ellie's forehead. "And how are you tonight?" she asks.

"Better now that I see all of you," Ellie answers in her worn-down voice. "Give me a hug, Ruby."

I draw Ellie's shoulders up for a hug. "Let me give you Water," I whisper.

"Don't you start that," Ellie warns.

I ease back and retreat to the corner farthest from the fire.

"Remember how you used to mix beans in the leftover mashed potatoes, Sula? And feed them to the cat?" Ellie asks Mother.

The corners of her mouth twitch as she stares into the air, as if she sees something the rest of us cannot. "Snowball spit out every single bean, no matter how much I hid them."

I know that story—I know every single one they tell—but I still love to hear them. What was it like, living in a time when you had more food than you could eat? When you could spare food to feed a picky animal?

"That durn cat wasn't fussy about eating Mabel's flowers." The last Elder, Asa, is leaning against the wall, farthest from the group. His face is in shadows, but I can imagine the sour look on his face—it so rarely goes away since Mabel withered a few years back. That was when Hope took her place as an Elder.

"Mabel didn't mind," Hope says.

"She was soft like that. Always falling for the strays, like your mother here, Ruby," he answers. "Otto came out of the woods. Biggest stray of them all. See what trouble that got us into?"

Nobody else could talk to Mother like that, but she only shrugs. We're all accustomed to Asa's vinegar, and the loyalty that lies beneath it too.

"Why so grumpy, old man?" Ellie asks in a light voice. "Was our dinner too rich for you?"

We all laugh at that one, even Mother.

"Truly . . . Darwin West was merciful today," Hope says. "We got biscuits *and* fish. And no beatings."

"Sula must have thrown him a smile," Asa says.

"No. Nobody can predict that monster." Boone gives Mother a quick look. "And Sula doesn't control that man."

Mother draws in a deep breath and squares her shoulders. "Shall we begin?"

The Elders settle into a rough circle, Asa and Boone perching on low stools they must have brought from their cabins. Hope stays on Ellie's bed. Once we two played childish pretend games in Ellie's cabin, especially in the long winter months—right on that bed.

"We can talk about Ed and Posey first," Boone says.

"Or maybe those shiftless Pellings," Asa growls.

But then they look at Hope, who is bouncing a bit on the bed and frowning—and the men laugh.

"Only teasing, Hope," Asa says. "It'll be Ruby first, of course."

"What is this about?" Mother asks, looking at each Elder in turn.

But they are all looking at me.

"Ruby, you were born two hundred years ago," Boone starts.

"The tiniest, prettiest thing," Hope adds.

Ellie nods.

"Now you're nearly as ugly as the rest of us," Asa says.

"A woman, now," Ellie says.

Mother seems as lost as I, still looking from face to face—and then at me. "Ruby?" she asks.

I shrug.

"We've been . . . watching you for a while," Hope says.

"Seeing if you're ready," Asa adds.

"For what?" I burst out. I've tried to be patient, but I can't imagine what they want.

"We want you to be our Leader," Boone says.

"Until your father—until Otto comes," Hope adds quickly.

They all look up at the sky, for just a moment.

The heat presses on me like someone is holding a blanket over my face. I gasp for air. The dim-lit room sparkles and shifts.

"You already have a Leader," I say—too afraid to look at Mother and see what her face must be like.

"We have a Reverend—and that won't change." Boone stands now and puts his hand on Mother's shoulder.

I dare a glance, then. She doesn't look angry. She is only shocked, I think. Our eyes meet, and I know she must see a mirror of her expression on my face.

"Mother is all the Leader you need," I say..

"There's four Elders. We need a fifth," says Asa.

"Then get another Elder." I must sound ungrateful, whining, even. But I have never expected this—never wanted it.

Ellie answers, the words said with careful effort. "You carry Otto's blood. You're the one meant to lead us."

"What does that mean for her then—lead?" Mother asks. She stays on her chair, Boone's hand on her shoulder.

"You'll come to the Elders' meetings. You'll talk to anyone who has a problem, or dispute—and you'll pray with them," Hope says.

"That's what Mother does," I say.

"Not this summer," Mother whispers, and Boone squeezes her shoulder.

"You'll do what Otto did—mostly. Some you already do, with your blood," Asa says.

"I won't have her beat," Mother warns.

"No," Boone agrees. "We'd protect her, like we always have."

"It's a good idea." Mother stands to come close to me. She takes my hand in hers. "You can lead. Darwin never has to know. You can be what the Congregation needs . . . what I haven't been, this summer."

"Because of *him*," Boone says through gritted teeth.

Mother nods.

"So many people want you to do this," Hope says. "They want *you*."

"They do?" I can't imagine who.

"We all see how you've grown," Ellie says.

"And we all know who your father is," Hope adds.

"I'm not my father," I say.

Asa shifts his weight and aims a finger at Ellie, or perhaps Hope. "Told you she'd balk."

That raises my hackles. "I'm not balking. I'm only—"

"Shocked." Hope's smile warms the cold, afraid feeling that's stealing over me.

"Shocked," I agree.

"Come here, Ruby," Ellie says.

Hope slides off Ellie's bed and I climb up, gently. Ellie hooks her pinky finger through mine. I can feel her pulse, fast and light.

"You would be sustaining us, like always," Ellie says. "That's all."

"No, No. If I'm to lead us . . . I want to change things," I tell them.

Ellie pulls her hand away. "*Sustain*," she says, stressing the word.

Mother walks to the bed. "You must accept things as they are. You can't try to *save* this Congregation."

Tears are pinching at my eyelids, trying to push out. I bow my head and will them to go away. "I want to help," I say.

"Not this again," Asa sighs.

"You will help," Ellie says. "As we need you to."

"Can you promise us that?" Hope asks.

"And if I don't?" I say. Rebellion burns in me. "Or if I won't lead?"

They look at one another; they didn't expect that question.

Mother finally answers. "If you don't do as the Elders ask, then . . . Otto will condemn you to hell."

Hope gasps. But no one disagrees.

"To hell?" I stand up and so does she; we are eye to eye, so close that I could breathe in the air she pushes from her lungs. "Do you really think my father would send me to hell for trying to help?"

"Yes. Yes, I do." She does not seem to blink or even breathe, only stares at me.

"Please just promise, Ruby," Hope says. "We only want you to be safe."

"Promise for me," Ellie says.

I should try to make them see what I know—that I can save all of us. But maybe Otto would condemn me. Maybe we are meant only to wait.

So I swallow and say it. "I promise. I'll lead. The way . . . The way you want me to."

"Good girl," Mother says, and she pulls me into a hug. I do not hug her back.

"Congratulations," Boone says.

"Thank you," Ellie says, and the other Elders give their thanks too. But hearing their voices only flames the anger in me.

"I have to be alone . . . for now," I say, and nobody stops me.

Nobody even walks me outside.

Chapter 7

Soon all of the Congregants know I am Leader.

It starts with a strange glance, a quick squeeze of my hand—people telling me they know, without saying.

But then the pleas begin.

Yesterday I was alone, harvesting, when Gen Baker found me.

"Those Smiths stole the last of our dry hay, I know it," she said. "What'll we do for fresh beds this winter?"

"I'm . . . sorry?" I was too startled to say anything else. Besides, the Bakers and Smiths were always feuding.

Gen tapped her spoon against her cup. "You're the Leader. Fix it."

Mercifully, an answer came to me. "Come to the next Elders meeting."

She left me alone after that, though she wasn't entirely satisfied.

Harvesting has become a new torture, for it's a time when the Congregants can find me. More and more come, wanting small things that are large in their lives. We will have a very full Elders meeting next.

Today's harvest is a little better, at least. They took our cups and spoons away today just as the sun reached its peak in the noon sky. We'd met quota, most of us, the morning dew kinder than it had been in a while.

Darwin didn't take the time to punish us for anyone's shortfalls. Instead he told the Overseers to give us shovels.

"You'll all dig," Darwin bellowed. "Four holes each, and then more if it's still light out."

I hate scraping and bending for water, but digging is worse. The ground is baked hard, reluctant to give up its grip on the rocks and roots around it. And the Overseers watch us the whole time. There's no slipping into the shade for a moments' rest, or watching a bird flit overhead.

At least we're paired, two to every hole, so one can dig while the other tosses the dirt.

"I'll pair with Ruby," Mother tells the Overseers. They only grunt and give us our shovels—long sticks with narrow heads on them.

I'm glad to hear her claim me. Maybe fewer people will ask me for things if I have her company.

"There's a spot with shade," I whisper to her, pointing to the area marked with a painted orange X. Most of today's digging areas are right along the road, where only tall weeds grow.

Mother gives the earth a heavy jab with her shovel. "I'll start it for us."

She pulls her hair higher on her head and bends to the task.

Red welts stand out on the back of her neck. Darwin hit here there two, perhaps three nights ago. I've been careful to let those stay angry and sore, so he thinks every part of her is healing as slow as he'd like.

"We can both do it," I tell her. The ground is too hard for her to break alone. It will get easier when we reach the crumbly underlayer.

But it will still be hard work. The holes must be narrow, and deep, so deep that the Overseers can reach down and feel nothing but air beneath their fingertips.

"You sleep like the dead these last few days. Are you staying too long at the cisterns?" Mother asks.

I haven't been back to the cisterns since Ford and I talked. I'm afraid he'll be there—and I'm afraid that I want him to be.

Never have I missed a night, not when we've added any water to the cisterns. Mother says I must give only a little blood at a time, that if I tried to do it every few days, or every week, I could weaken. She doesn't know how much of my blood pours into the buckets at night, trying to make stronger and stronger Water to ease her wounds.

I'll make up the difference soon, giving extra blood to the Water . . . as soon as I figure a way to go to the cisterns without seeing Ford.

"I'm sleeping enough," I tell Mother.

"Perhaps you're still growing." She stops digging for a moment to study my face, and a slight smile softens her hollow cheeks. "In some ways you're still a child."

"I suppose." I duck my head so she can't see the lie in my eyes.

I manage to flip a clod of dirt off the surface of the soil, and then another shovel, this time full of sand. "I wish I knew what he was planning."

"Darwin West will do what he wants, whether or not we know what it'll be," she answers. "You needn't worry."

"Knowing when something is coming helps," I argue.

I've heard other Congregants chattering about the holes. Some think there's going to be a fence—though this makes little sense, since the holes are cut in strange angles throughout the woods. Others think they'll be used for some strange punishment. None can imagine what that would be, though, and none wish to discover it.

One thing is for certain: these holes can only make our lives worse. When has Darwin ever done something to make us live more easily?

"Dig!" an Overseer bellows at us. But he is too lazy or hot to come closer. Perhaps the heat has drained the fight from him too. Even with the shade, the heat seems to slink up from the ground like fog. Humid thick fingers twine up my skirts, over my neck, trying to pull me to the ground.

"Whatever Darwin West has planned, I'll protect you, Ruby." Mother's voice is softer. She reaches out to grasp my elbow for just a second before taking her turn at the soil.

I remember how she used to fill my cup for me, when I was smaller, allowing me to rest in the shade or build fairy houses with sticks. Even this summer I think she would slip by with extra water, if it weren't for Ellie's need.

But things are different now. "I'm Leader. I'm supposed to protect you," I say.

"No. Sustain, Ruby." Mother gives me a sharp eye before stabbing her shovel into the dirt.

We fall into the same rhythm we've used for the last few days he's made us go out digging.

"Suppose we should be glad we're not digging with spoons," Mother sighs. She dumps her dirt just behind her, not giving an extra effort to the task. But even so, she staggers back once her shovel is lightened and nearly falls to the ground.

"Let me dig twice for your once," I urge her in a low voice, making sure not to look over at the Overseer in the deep shade.

Mother shakes her head and grips her shovel hard with both hands. "No, Ruby. Mine is to suffer. Yours is to sustain. That is how Otto would want it."

"What was he like?" I ask my mother, like all the other thousands of times I've asked the same question. But she always gives a new scrap of a story, or reminds me of something that's grown fuzzy in my mind.

"When I met your father, he was half wild, and as thin as a river otter," Mother says. "He followed my father out of the woods."

"He wanted your father's food," I say.

Even as Mother works, a smile softens her face. "Yes. Even though Otto lived off the land, he was a terrible trapper. I don't know if he ever managed to kill something."

"Otto was good at some things," I say.

"Not at first, I didn't see that." Mother laughs. "He was nothing next to my fiancé."

We both stop for a moment and look at the Overseers. Darwin isn't near today, though I know we'll see him at sunset.

"He wasn't always this cruel." Mother bows her head and looks at the hole. "Though I didn't choose him for kindness. He was rich, and he promised me an easy life."

We both let out a short laugh.

"Dig!" The Overseer closest to us bellows, this time taking a few steps toward us.

The hole is deep enough now that I must bend to get my shovel to the bottom and scrape the dirt up the side to the top. I try not to struggle as I do it. I don't want Mother to know how hard this work is for me.

"Otto was kind, wasn't he?" I prompt Mother.

"Yes. He was so . . . easy with being kind. He gave all that he had as if it cost him nothing," Mother says.

"He didn't have much," I say.

"Nothing except his blood." Mother's lips press together, and her eyes dart to my arms.

A crack of sticks, and Jonah Pelling is there. His shirt is wet against him—has he been working, for once?

"The Overseers are on the lookout," I warn him.

He waves his hand. "They sent me to get them water."

Mother crosses her arms around her shovel, leaning on it. "You're their message boy?"

"Whatever is takes to duck the lash." Jonah gives me a wink, not seeming to notice Mother's wince. "So you're Leader now. Fine news, little Ruby."

I bite back the urge to tell him I'm not little anymore. None gets under my skin like Jonah. "Your Overseers are likely thirsty," I say.

"I provide what's needed." He gives me a smile that is too bold, too familiar.

I've had enough of the Pellings. I'm glad to see him saunter away.

"Where'd my father come from?" I ask.

"I've told you, Ruby," Mother sighs. "The woods."

"Who was *his* mother?"

"We'd best speed up, Ruby," she warns. "Else we'll never dig more holes before the sun goes down."

I give the sand and rocks a vigorous scoop. "Tell me about Otto's mother, please?" I try to use the same sweet tone that won me tiny triumphs with her when I was smaller.

She sighs again. "He was only a child when his parents were taken. Then he had to survive on his own."

I've heard the story before, but I'm always certain she's keeping parts of it from me. Surely she knows more about this. "Who took them? Where did they go?" I press.

"He never said more than that." Her voice is sharp.

And then I ask the same thing I have always wanted an answer to, hoping maybe this time she'll say something different. "Were they like Otto . . . and me?"

"I don't know." Her answer is quick. "We'll never know."

"I suppose not," I mutter.

"Just one more foot," Mother says. "Why don't you pick our next digging spot?"

I pretend to look around, but I'm only thinking of how to move our talk to Ellie . . . to the thing that's been burning me like the middle of the hottest flame.

"Maybe we'll have dinner tonight," I say.

"Unlikely."

"We can bring it back to Ellie."

She nods. "We'll find something for her tonight."

I try to slow my breath and think before I say the next thing, but it's so hard. "Did Otto ever deny anyone?"

"He gave Water to all who asked. But nobody knew it was his blood. Nobody except me, and then Ellie . . ." Mother squares her shoulders and pulls a good amount of dirt from the hole.

Nobody else knew the secret of Otto's blood until they'd followed her to the woods. She told the few people she trusted the most. They became the Elders.

"I want to help everyone, just like Otto," I say.

Before I even look at Mother's face, I send Otto a fast prayer: *Help me, Otto. Help me, my father.*

Her eyes are narrowed, and she stares at me like she's trying to burn holes with them. She knows already where my mind is, I think.

"Sometimes we must wait for what we want," she says.

She's been saying that for two hundred years. I'm very tired of hearing it.

"Haven't we waited long enough? Ellie is dying," I burst out.

"Ruby, quiet!" Mother warns.

"How will he do it?" I ask. "How will Otto free us?"

"I don't know," Mother says.

"He'd need a plan. He'd need our help," I tell her.

She doesn't answer. She's looking over my head. And then she starts to shovel faster.

"He's coming over," she whispers.

This time the Overseer comes close to us, so close that I can smell the sweat on his clothes. "You two finish this hole yet?" he growls.

"Nearly," Mother says.

He gives her a dubious look and kneels to put his arm in it. Dark fantasies fill me: how easy it would be to lift the shovel and drop it on his head, or simply kick him hard enough to make him stay down.

The Overseer stands and pulls the chain out of his pocket. He looks at it like he's considering something. I stand steady; Mother slips her hand in mine.

"No more talking, Toads," he says, aiming a wad of spit at the ground by my feet. "Dig. You've got a foot more to go, at least."

But he retreats to his shady spot, which is shifting farther from us as the sun sinks in the sky. He won't hear if we whisper.

"Wouldn't he love us, still, if we freed ourselves?" I whisper.

Mother acts as if she has not heard me. But I'm certain she did.

"If we could escape—Ellie might not die. Not so soon," I say. "She'd have to drink Water, then."

"Let me do it," I tell Mother.

"No." She uses the same voice I heard when I was a child

and wanted to eat dirt, to fill my stomach, or cram my cup with flowers and sticks. It is her warning voice.

"Please," I tell her. "Let me find a way to free us."

"I said no. We won't speak of it again."

Her shovel is jammed into the ground, her arms crossed against the top of it. I realize I've done the same. We are staring at each other like enemies, not mother and daughter.

Chapter 8

I can't wait any longer to go to the cisterns.

The woods are noisy tonight—windy, and crackling with animal sounds. I'm not afraid of the animals, though. My heart is pounding because I know I might see Ford again.

When I get to the cisterns, there is no shadow beneath, no man lurking around the edges. Good. He shouldn't come. And I should be relieved—I'm safe. But mostly I feel a lump in my throat. Part of me—maybe all of me—wanted to see him.

Just before I put my foot on the bottom rung of the cistern's ladder, I see a shadow in the trees, at the other side of the clearing. It's tall and narrow, too still and too dark to be a tree's shadow.

I freeze and look harder. The shadow shifts, slightly, and I know for sure that it's a person. A person, watching me from the woods.

Ford came, after all. But he didn't hide, before. Why does he lurk in the trees? I can't add my blood, now.

My breath is short, and my fingers and arms are tingling. I

could walk over to him. I could confront him. Or . . . I could run.

But instead, I take a step toward the shadow. And then another, and another, until I start to see the edges of it: the person is wearing long pants, and long sleeves.

"Why are you hiding?" I ask in a low voice.

"Why are you here?" A man's voice, answering—but it's not Ford. It's a lighter voice, a laughing voice.

Finally I find the resolution to run. My feet pound toward home, fast faster faster, and my breath comes so hard that I can't hear if the man is chasing me.

But then I feel a hand around my elbow, and I'm spun, hard. "Am I that bad?" he asks.

It's not an Overseer, after all. It's Jonah Pelling. All my fear rushes away and is replaced by a deep, familiar irritation. How like a Pelling to lurk about the woods and scare people. How like a Pelling not to call out a warning, an assurance, anything to stop me from running in terror.

"You scared me." I yank my arm out of his grip. He lets go with a low laugh and a grin.

We stand on the dirt road, facing each other—I panting from my sprint, he barely winded. Jonah jams his hands in his pockets and looks around at the woods.

"Remember how we used to play hunter? We always made you be the rabbit," he says.

"And you never caught me," I retort. I remember: Jonah, Zeke, even Hope sometimes, letting me run ahead for a minute and then chasing me with sticks held high. They found it amusing. But it terrified me.

"Caught you tonight," he says softly, reaching out to touch my hand lightly, then pulling his arm back again.

"You're not supposed to be out here," I tell him.

"Nor are you. But . . . I knew you would be."

I think of how still his shadow was in the woods, how easy it would be to miss it, if you were distracted. Did he see me talking to Ford? Did he hear what we said?

I am suddenly aware of how exposed we are, standing in the middle of the road. Anyone might see us—and if an Overseer's truck drove round the corner, we'd be trapped in its lights.

"Follow me," I tell Jonah.

"Anywhere," he breathes, and a nasty chill washes down my back. I don't like the way he's talking to me. It makes me think of how he used to pursue Hope, in the years before Gabe made his play for her.

I couldn't possibly be his new target . . . could I?

I lead him into the woods, doubling back toward the cisterns. Maybe Ford will be there soon. He'd protect me, if Jonah goes strange.

Jonah leans against a tree and reaches back to smooth his short, ragged ponytail. We all do the best we can with sharp-edged rocks to keep our hair manageable.

"Why did you think you'd find me out in the woods?" I ask him. My heart pounds as I wait for the answer.

"You think you're the only one who creeps around at night?" He shrugs. "I see you sometimes."

I never heard him, never saw him. How close was he? How many times did he stare at me, without any part of my body warning me? It's as if I'd been trailed by a bear and never knew it.

"Why do you go out?" I ask.

"There's good hunting and berries to find too."

"That's . . . That's why I go out," I say.

"To check your mother's traps." He lowers his chin and meets my eyes squarely, no hint of a smile left on his face. "Is that all?"

"That's all," I say, trying to keep my voice steady.

Then he flicks me a smile. "I'll keep your secrets if you keep mine."

I don't know how to answer, and I don't want to tell him anything he doesn't know. So I simply take a step away and bend to inspect a bush, pretending I'm searching for berries.

"You won't find anything on the bushes around here. But there's some fine mushrooms that grow on the shady side of these trees." Jonah turns and pulls something off the trunk he was leaning against. Then he offers it to me.

"Mother says they're not safe." I shake my head.

"Guess trappers like killing more than picking. That's fine, more for me." Jonah tucks the mushroom in a small bag that hangs around his waist.

My mouth waters as I watch the mushroom disappear. "Maybe if you took a bite," I say.

"And see if I fall dead?" Jonah tilts his head and gives me a narrow-eyed look. "You're not too fond of me, are you, Ruby?"

"No—I mean, that's not it. I only wanted to make sure it was safe," I stammer.

Again, the grin flashes over his face. Jonah has always had

quicksilver moods; when we played together, he'd be sunny one moment and stormy the next. We never knew how to predict the changes.

"Just joking," he says. "Here."

He reaches into his waist bag and then holds his palm out to me—six perfect plump berries glint in the darkness.

"Thank you." I take three.

Jonah shakes his head and stretches his arm out farther. "Take them all. I picked them for you."

If he doesn't want food, I won't argue with him. I take the rest, then bite into the first. The juice fills my mouth and I can't help closing my eyes, for a second, in pure pleasure.

When I open them, Jonah is standing closer. And then . . . he drops to one knee.

"I'm not much for talking," he says. "But I'm a good provider. One of the best."

"What are you doing?" I ask. I can think of only one thing he'd be doing, kneeling in front of me, but I can't believe it. We've never courted. We've never even whispered a single romantic thing to each other.

Jonah looks up at me with an intense stare. I take a step back. He continues his speech. "Pellings never want for anything . . . at least, nothing they really need."

"Otto provides," I mutter.

"You could be a Pelling too," Jonah says.

I nearly shout "No!" but collect myself just before the word bursts from my lips. There's no use hurting Jonah. For he seems to be very, very serious.

"I'm not . . . I won't be marrying," I say.

He takes a step forward on his knee and reaches for me, but I slide both my hands behind my back. He keeps his hand in the air, suspended, as if waiting for me. "Why not?" he asks.

I'd never seriously thought of marrying any Congregants. For my whole life, I've watched them marrying and leaving and marrying again. Few bonds last forever, or even a hundred years. Maybe that's why I never thought to marry: I know nearly every Congregant I could marry will eventually sicken of me, or I of him. I know them too well. What mysteries could there be left to discover?

"I don't want to," I answer simply.

"Marrying has its joys. Ask Hope." He swallows and looks down at the ground.

Then I hold out both hands to him. "Please stand, Jonah."

He lets out a sigh and stands without my help. "She never wanted me," he says.

"I know you fancy her. And . . . I see why. Hope is kind."

"And beautiful." Then he smiles again, his dark mood dropping away as fast as it came. His voice is light. "But so are you. You're a woman now, all grown."

I'm conscious of my dress, too tight across the chest—once Mother's, now mine, with no more room to let out the seams. Even without enough food or drink, I'm bigger than she ever was.

"You should marry me, Ruby. That's what you should do. Think of it: the Congregation's Leader, and the Pellings—one family. We'd be the highest family in the Congregation."

"There are no . . . *heights* . . . in the Congregation," I tell him.

He waves his hand as if shooing away a fly. "You know what I mean, Ruby."

"I do, exactly," I say. I'm not going to create some terrible royalty in our Congregation: Otto's daughter marrying the prince scoundrel.

Besides, I don't *want* him. I don't tingle when he nears. I don't want to trace every bit of him with my eyes.

"Think of it: you'd have pillows . . . plenty of firewood . . . and food. I can forage from anywhere," Jonah says. "I've even stolen from the Overseers' trash."

I let out a gasp. "They'll shoot you if they see you."

"Hasn't happened yet." He crosses his arms. "I'll do whatever my family needs. And you could be family."

"Why do you want me?" I ask. "Me, and not Hope."

"I'm no fool. She's only got eyes for Gabe. But you . . . you're unclaimed. Untouched. I wouldn't mind laying eyes on you every night . . . every morning . . ." The edge in his voice makes my skin crawl.

"I'm not wanting to be touched," I warn him.

"It's not just that." Jonah shakes his head. "I think you want what I want—I see you, watching Darwin and the Overseers. I know how mad you get."

"I never say anything."

"Nor do I. But I hate them, just the same. I hate them the way the rest of them don't."

"Otto loves, never hates," I say.

"Yeah, and most Congregants . . . well, they try to be that way.

Me? I'm not wasting any *love* on Darwin West," he says.

"Me either," I whisper.

"I want to fight," Jonah says. "Don't you?"

"Yes." The answer flies out before I can stop it. I clap my hand over my mouth and look around. "I mean, no. It's wrong. We're only supposed to endure."

"Endure, and wait. I'm sick of that. Aren't you?" He takes a step closer and stares at me, and this time I do not back away.

"Yes," I admit.

"We could plan it . . . we could plan a whole battle, Ruby." His voice is high, and excited. I remember how he used to arrange stones in formation, soldiers marching toward one another, making quiet explosion sounds with his mouth.

"It's not a game," I tell him.

"I know. But Ruby—if we were married, we'd be together all the time. We could plan, night and day. I'd get us our own cabin. Nobody would have to hear . . . not until they're ready to hear." His words come out fast, and fevered. I wonder how long he's wanted this, planned for it.

A very small part of me wants to say yes. I want someone to listen to me, someone to agree that Otto wouldn't mind if we fought; maybe he'd even be proud.

But then I look at him: Jonah Pelling, the one whose cup always seems to be half empty; Jonah Pelling, the one who steps aside the fastest when Mother volunteers to take the beatings.

And then, Ford. I can't have him. But he makes me want Jonah even less.

"Say yes," Jonah urges.

"No," I say. "And don't ask again."

"I will. I'm going to ask, and ask . . . and one day, Ruby, you'll say yes. You'll get fed up with *waiting*. You'll get fed up with being a woman and living with your mother."

"Maybe I will get sick of those things. But I won't marry just to leave them," I say.

"You'll get fed up with being alone. I know that too, Ruby," he says.

"I'm sorry about Hope," I tell him.

"Don't be. Just—think about it. Think about what being my wife could mean." Jonah pats his waist bag. "Food. Comfort. And . . . we could fight Darwin West."

I don't tell him no again—and he doesn't stick around to hear it. Instead he simply turns and melts into the woods, heading uphill, away from the cisterns and me.

I wait for temptation to flicker. I wait for second-guesses to flood in. But none of that happens. Saying no to Jonah is the easiest thing, yes—and it's also the entirely right thing.

The cisterns will have to wait till another night. I walk down to the edge of the road and begin my careful walk home. Toe heel, toe heel, I go, not wanting anyone—Overseer or Pelling—to find me tonight.

Chapter 9

Ford heads the early-morning line for cups. His eyes linger just a little too long on me. Then he smiles, only a little. I have to fight the urge to smile back.

When it's Jonah's turn in line, Ford gives him a hard stare. He looks like he'd like to give Jonah ten lashes with his chain.

"A full cup!" Darwin bellows.

He looks at Mother, waiting for her to argue, but she stays silent, just as she was when we woke this morning. We argued yesterday, and there hasn't been much for us to say to each other.

"Any problem with that?" Darwin sneers.

Mother shakes her head.

I think she's afraid he'll drag us to dig more holes. Already he's pulled half the men away to help.

"Then get to work, Toads!" He points into the woods and we all obey.

I cut a path high up the hill. Start up high and work down-hill as the day wears on: that's the way to get the most water, I think. Everyone has their own theories about how to fill their cups.

After a few minutes of searching, I find a patch of coolness, as if this part of the woods has forgotten that it's the height of summer. Water waits for me under clumped, gold-flowered weeds, and I whisper a quiet prayer of thanks to Otto while I spoon it into my cup.

The drops make a quiet *plink-plink* in my cup. Above me a bird trills a song. I work and work, until my cup has water half the height of my pinky. I should make quota today, especially without Ellie's cup to help fill.

Ellie. Thinking of her hurts like Darwin's kicked me in the stomach. She seemed paler when I checked on her this morning, and she barely smiled.

My body feels heavy with grief, the magic of the morning gone. I'll rest, just for a moment. I set my cup carefully on the ground, twisting and pushing it until the dirt holds it tight. Then I sit on the leaves and pull my arms tight around my knees, resting my cheek against my knuckles.

"Ruby." A man's voice, whispering. I jerk my head up and look around.

Then I hear the footsteps, soft ones, careful like Mother approaching one of her traps. I unfold my body and pick up my cup.

Ford steps out of the woods, quietly, carefully. He is getting better, much better, at creeping. Every bird in the woods seems to grow still. For the first time today, I notice the light wind ruffling the leaves far above our heads.

He's wearing the same as all the Overseers: khaki pants with many pockets and a shirt without sleeves. The shirt clings in patches to his chest.

My skin tingles. I imagine a thousand tiny lines of lightning sparking across the space that separates us.

"Hey, Ruby." Ford's voice is gentle.

I scramble to my feet. "I'm working as hard as anyone could."

"Who said you weren't working hard?" he asks.

"You're here and you talked to me and . . ." My voice is shaking.

"You're not in trouble." He wipes one hand up and down his face, pulling his mouth open wide for a moment. What would it feel like, running light fingers over the stubble I see on his chin?

But then his hand slides in his pocket, and every part of my body wants to run.

Ford holds up both hands, empty, and gives me a sad smile. "Do they do anything except beat you?"

"Sometimes they only yell." I don't mean for it to be amusing, but a smile quirks across his face.

"I only wanted to talk again," he says. "I liked that . . . the other night."

"I have to work." I edge away from him and kneel in front of another plant. There's not a spot of water on it, but I run my spoon over the leaves just the same.

He crouches next to me. I edge away. Ford follows, staying low like me.

"That . . . *boy* . . ." Ford says. "I heard what he asked you."

I keep my eyes on the plant. Even if I don't want Jonah, he's still a Congregant. We protect each other.

"You're a million times better than him," Ford says.

"I don't want him," I say. I don't mean to emphasize the last word—*him*—but I think I might have.

"I can help you, too, you know." Ford pulls a small white bottle out of his pocket and holds it out to me. "For Ellie."

"What is it?" I ask.

Ford shakes the bottle. "It's just some Advil. She'll hurt a little less if she takes it."

"Thank you." I take the bottle and tuck it into my pocket. "Does Darwin know you gave this to me?"

Ford picks up a fallen leaf and pulls the green away from the spindly veins in the middle of it. "No."

"He'd hurt you."

"Maybe that's not the worst thing that could happen to me." Ford lifts a hand to his neck and fingers the oval gold necklace hanging from a chain.

"What would you do if he found out?"

There's a noise near us—sticks breaking, someone walking, not trying to be quiet.

"You have to go," I tell him.

Quicker than a bird's wing, he reaches his hand out. I think he's going to take my hand, but then he pulls away.

"I'll come back," he whispers, and then he's on his feet, stomping toward the noise.

"You Toads keeping up with your quota?" he roars. A shiver runs down my spine, hearing him talk like that.

But I can't help tracing the places on my hand where his skin nearly touched mine.

"Are you ill?" It's Boone, standing over me, a frown on his face.

"No. I'm just resting."

"Careful. There's an Overseer walking around here." He looks back over his shoulder. "More alert than the others, that one."

"I didn't see him," I say. I stand and walk away from him, careful to stay slow and steady, searching the leaves for any sign of water. He can't suspect how nervous I'm feeling. Boone has known me for so long. Won't he see the lie on my face?

"Don't rest for a while," he says, an order, but a tender one, like a father would give. "That Overseer might be back."

The thought makes fresh heat rise in me. "I'll be careful," I say.

There, a few drops under the bushes. I kneel and the bottle in my skirt pocket rattles a bit.

Did Boone hear it? I look to see. He's frowning, but I think it's just his cup he's looking at.

"It's a dry day," he says.

Why won't he go? I want more of Ford, even a moment more.

I stand again and hear another rattle, but Boone shows no sign of hearing it. When I come close to him and peer inside his cup, I see there's barely enough to cover the bottom.

I tip what I've got into his cup before he can tell me to stop. "There. Now it's almost a third full," I tell him.

He gives me a small smile. "Thank you, Ruby. But what will you do?"

"I'll work harder," I say.

"When I'm done, I'll come back to help you."

"No." I say it too quickly. "Help Mother."

He nods once and moves away. I walk a little downhill—water runs downhill, after all, and things will only get drier the higher I try. There I find a little more water, and the bottom of my cup is wet again.

It might not be enough, though.

Let Darwin beat me. I'm the Leader. It's time I stepped forward. My wounds will heal fast; I might even forget the pain.

I stop harvesting to check—Boone's gone. And when I peer into the leaves, I see a different face. Ford is back.

He stands over me and holds out one hand. "Talk for a minute more?"

"Only for a little while." I stand up without his help. Then I slowly slide the near-empty cup behind my back.

"I have a present for you too." He pulls a packet of something out of his pocket; the sun flashes off the surface and I have to squint.

"Take it," he says, thrusting it into the space between us.

The packet feels heavier than it should, for the size. It's as long as the span from my wrist to the tip of my pinky, and about as wide as two fingers. The wrapping is bright silver and yellow.

"What . . . What is it?"

"You never saw a protein bar before?" He rolls his eyes. "Come on."

"Haven't you seen what we eat around here?" I ask him.

Shame settles on his face. "Sorry. It's . . . good. It's the best flavor they make."

"Cho-co-late . . . and . . . ba-na-na?" I read. The smell is heaven, even through the wrapper. My stomach growls.

Ford nudges the bar with his finger. He's so close I can smell the half-sweat, half-scrubbed scent of him.

"You're hungry, aren't you?" he asks.

"Thank you, but . . . no." I hold the bar back out to him, trying to control the quavering in my fingers. I want to rip that shiny wrapper off and cram the whole thing into my mouth.

"Why?" He doesn't take it from me.

"Overseers don't give presents. And . . . I don't have anything I can give back." My face burns.

"You took the medicine for Ellie."

"This is different." I drop the food on the forest floor and back away fast.

"Come on, don't be like that." Ford picks up the bar and holds it out. "Overseers give Congregants food."

I shake my head. "You know this isn't the same."

"All right, then." He shrugs and drops the bar on the ground. "Guess I'll get back to work."

His voice isn't warm anymore.

"I'd best work too," I say. I can't help looking down at the food, just sitting there. Would Mother want me to take it, and she'd decide who needed it the most? Should I bring it to the Elders instead? Isn't that what a Leader should do?

But there would be too many questions.

"Take it," I say, my voice rough. "Don't leave it there."

"Fine." Ford shoves the bar in his pocket. But then he reaches into another pocket.

"Maybe you need this, at least?" He's got a clear bottle of water. The paper wrapper makes a crinkly sound as it comes out of his pocket.

"I'm not thirsty."

"I didn't mean for drinking." He looks at my cup.

"It has to come from leaves," I whisper.

He stares at me, steady. "Really, now?"

"You have to go," I tell him. "Someone will come."

Ford holds the water bottle up high.

"It's not consecrated," I say.

"Only a priest can consecrate something." Again Ford reaches for the medal that hangs around his neck.

"Please just go," I tell him.

He uncaps the water bottle and pours it, slow and steady, over the bush that he's standing next to. He makes sure to cover the leaves in the water, until drips fall from every surface.

"Just in case," Ford says.

"I won't use it," I say, but he smiles anyway.

"Come to the cisterns," he whispers.

I stare down at the ground, not watching as he walks away— but I hear his footsteps, lighter, lighter, and then gone.

Then I kneel by the bush and hold my cup under the dripping water. It's a gift I can't give back, and one I can't bear to waste.

Chapter 10

I long to bring Ford's modern gift to Ellie. It's rattled in my pocket all day, reminding me—though I need no help remembering Ellie's need.

Mother needs me first. Darwin lifted the chain against her tonight. I rush the healing, sloshing more Water than I should over her body. There are small puddles on the floor by the edge of her bed.

"Rest well," I tell Mother.

"And you," she whispers back, before her eyes slide shut.

I straighten the covers that lie over her body, just as I remember her doing when I was small.

Before I go, I empty the bucket of bloodied Water outside the door: this is a shortcut I know I shouldn't take. Tomorrow lush plants will spring from the ground where only dry, cracked earth should be. If I were wise, I would take the time to return the Water to the Lake, like usual.

But it's all taking too long. So I set the bucket by the door and run all the way to Ellie's cabin. It is full dark outside, with no moon; clouds cover the stars too.

I sense something is wrong before I understand what I am seeing. There's a large something on the road by Ellie's cabin. My heart leaps, and my first thought is that it's a bear watching me. But then I realize it's bigger than that: an Overseers' truck, parked half on, half off the road. The truck is dark. I can't tell if anyone is inside it—or the cabin.

I creep to the deeper shadow of the trees, a little closer to Ellie's cabin. But I hear nothing: no voices inside the cabin, nothing coming from the truck either. A night bird in the tree above me bursts into song. I wish I could call to Ellie the way this animal is calling to its family.

Why are they here? The Overseers hardly ever come to our cabins—save for Darwin's one terrible visit to our cabin, every year. But I don't want to think of that, not now.

The medicine in my pocket rattles again. Until now, I thought my only problem tonight would be convincing Ellie to take the pills. How would I explain where they came from? I didn't know exactly. I didn't even know if they were truly safe.

When Asa's wife Mabel was alive, she knew how to brew teas to ease pain. She sent Asa into the woods at night to find roots and leaves whenever someone was especially suffering. But now she's gone, and her secrets gone with her.

I have to trust that this medicine is like her tea.

There's a loud squeak, and a light inside the truck comes on. Two Overseers climb out of the truck and start down the small, steep hill to Ellie's cabin. One of them carries a flashlight. The beam bounces from rock to rock, and I shrink deeper into the shelter of the trees.

If only I had come a little sooner. I could be inside with her, helping her. But now I don't know what to do. Should I rush ahead of them? Try to protect her? Or is it better to wait here in case I need to run for help?

For now, I will stay behind the trees. I hold my breath as they get closer to the door, closer to me. The one holding the flashlight looks up just as they reach the door. My breath stops. Something about the man's shape is familiar—something I've studied. I can't be sure, but I think it's Ford.

Did he bring more medicine to Ellie? Do I dare to hope?

I remember only one time that the Overseers came to our cabin. It was long ago, one of the snowiest winters ever. I was young enough to dance outside when it snowed, catching snow-flakes on my tongue.

So much snow had drifted against the side of our cabin that we couldn't see out the window. The morning light was a strange filtered blue, as if we woke at the end of the day instead of the start.

That night there was another storm.

"Wake me every hour to mind the door. This one looks bad," Mother warned me. She'd have to push the door open and shove the snow away from our only entrance . . . and exit, each hour. Otherwise we could have found ourselves buried, come morning.

We're still expected to work in the winter, with beatings doled out to anyone who comes to the Common House late. There's still water to find, by midday. Snow melts off branch tips and we catch the drops in our pewter cups. There are always things to do around the Common House too: cleaning, patching holes in the roof, chasing away the mice that are fatter than us.

When we aren't working during winter, all the Congregants retreat to their cabins. Once the snow is high, nobody visits one another, not even the Elders. Every winter night it's only Mother, and me, and the stories she reluctantly tells me in front of the fire.

But that one night, there was a knock. A knock, just like now.

The Overseer with the flashlight is knocking on Ellie's door. One, two, three polite knocks.

"Quit being so nice." The other one bangs a fist on the door. The sound makes me jump. "Open up, old lady!"

There's no answer. They push open the door. It's dark inside.

When the Overseers came to our cabin that night, we'd already put out the fire and climbed into Mother's bed to huddle for warmth. We'd been conserving our small pile of firewood, not knowing when we'd be able to dig through the piles of snow for more.

When Mother slipped from under the blankets to answer the door, I curled against the sudden cold of being alone in the bed.

"You alive in there?" a rough male voice called.

Mother shrank back from the door and glanced back at me. Then she squared her shoulders and opened the door a crack.

"We're barely alive. It's freezing," she said.

"Yeah, well, Merry Christmas," the voice said.

Christmas had come the week before. We had prayed to Otto and worked. Mother tied a fragrant bough of pine to the foot of my bed.

"What do you want?" Mother asked, voice wary.

"You want this stuff or not?" the man answered. I strained to see him through the crack in the door, but it was too dark.

The Overseers at Ellie's cabin tonight brought nothing but their flashlights—and whatever was in their pockets. They shut the door behind them, so I can't see inside. Flares of light show in the window, then are gone, then flares again. They must be looking all around her cabin with that flashlight.

"*Aw, shit!*" I hear a man shout from inside. It's a favorite curse from the Overseers.

Did she hurt him? Will they hurt her? I slide my feet over the dry leaves to come closer, closer, even though there's nothing to hide behind.

Then I hear the scrape of a chair. Feet thumping on floorboards. But there are no more voices—not the Overseers' and not Ellie's.

A steady glow of light illuminates Ellie's window. Someone must have lit the lantern inside.

When Mother saw what the Overseers brought us that long-ago night, she let out a gasp. "Is that all for us?"

"Unless you'd rather freeze to death."

"Is there—is there enough for everyone?" she asked in a low voice.

"We're making deliveries all night," he answered.

Mother stared out the door for a moment; in the dim I

thought I saw her shake her head as if amazed. Then she called to me.

"Ruby, come help."

I half hopped to the door, the floor like a sheet of ice, even though I was wearing my thickest socks. Mother drew me close and rubbed one hand over my arm as we looked outside the open door.

There, hurrying away from our cabin, I could make out two thick figures wearing coats splotched with green and brown. They were Overseers, wearing their plush coats that reached from neck to ankle.

"What did they want?" I asked.

"They brought us this." Mother pointed at what I hadn't noticed—a big pile of wood sitting on our doorstep.

"We could make it as hot as summer in here," I said. I remember imagining thick flames leaping up, pushing out of our stove, so warm that we would have to edge away from it.

But Mother didn't answer. She didn't pick up the wood either. She was staring at the place where the Overseers had been, a moment ago—now it was only blowing sheets of white snow.

She let out a sob.

"Thank you," she whispered.

The door to Ellie's cabin flies open, and I take a quick step backward, remembering too late that I've crept far from the shelter of the trees. One of the Overseers backs out the door, moving slowly, and then I see he is carrying something: a bundle of sheets, Ellie's sheets. In the dark, they seem to glow.

I don't understand what they're doing. They can't take her bedding. We're allowed that, at least. And she's sick. What will she lie on?

I open my mouth to speak, but then the second Overseer steps out the door. The lantern lights his face and a thrill races over my skin. It's Ford, sharing the burden of the sheets with the other Overseer.

Ford looks up and our eyes lock. I've been discovered. He blinks, so slowly that his eyes are closed for a moment.

Sheets shouldn't be that heavy.

Sheets shouldn't be long, and narrow.

Otto save me. Otto save Ellie. That can't be her.

They are lifting their burden, staggering up the hill.

There is nothing so heavy in Ellie's cabin like this . . . nothing but Ellie.

"Stop!" I scream, and there's no safety or intelligence or planning left in me anymore. My feet fly me to the Overseers.

Mother and I piled all the firewood next to the stove, under Otto's portrait. We stacked it neat and pretty, like it was our finest treasure. And it was: we coaxed weeks of warmth from it. Once it was gone, I had hoped for more firewood. There was still plenty of snow on the ground, though we had started to gather the snowmelt that crept from under the icy bottoms of snow banks.

"They'll not be back with more," Mother had warned me. "We'll need to gather our own."

"But why wouldn't they come back? They did it once," I argued.

"Darwin was afraid we'd all die," she explained. "But it's warm enough now that we'll only suffer."

And suffer we did. Overseers never came with firewood—or anything else—ever again.

I stumble-run up to the Overseers carrying the bundle from Ellie's cabin. When I reach them, Ford bows his head. The other one makes an angry motion with his hand, nearly dropping his end of the bundle.

"Get out of here, Toad," he growls.

"Is that . . . Is she . . ." I swallow hard.

"Get back," the man orders. He tries to start walking again, but Ford stays still.

"The game's on soon." The other Overseer gives Ford an angry look.

But Ford shakes his head. "We can wait for a second."

"Thank you," I whisper, daring to glance at him for a moment. But he isn't looking at me.

I reach one hand out to touch the sheet. I can't make myself move one last inch and actually touch what they're holding. That same night bird bursts into song, and a strange wave of fury overwhelms me. I hate that bird more than Darwin West and all the Overseers.

Tears flow out of my eyes and drop onto the sheet, leaving large dots on the yellowed fabric. "Is that Ellie?" I whisper.

"The, uh, lady that lives here died." When Ford speaks, he keeps all the warmth out of his voice. His eyes go heavy-lidded and dead.

The Overseer shifts their burden and turns his nose higher

up in the air. "And she's getting ripe. You smell that?"

This is what I should feel fury for—are our lives worth so little to them? But I don't feel anything now, even though tears are still flowing down my cheeks, into the corners of my mouth. I find the strength to touch the sheet, to trace my fingers over the length I think is her arm.

"I love you, Ellie," I say.

"Let's go." The other Overseer starts walking, and this time Ford doesn't stop him from moving. They trudge up the hill and I follow, still holding the sheet.

She was alone when she died today. When did it happen? Was it after I brought her breakfast and found her still asleep— but breathing? I checked that, I know I did.

Did she see the sun set today, or was she already gone? When did she give up waiting for us—and for Otto?

"I'm sorry I didn't come sooner," I tell her.

Ford pulls in a deep breath and looks up at the stars.

"Like I said, *rank*." The other man lets out a harsh laugh.

They're near their truck. "Put her down while I open the tail-gate," the other man orders.

Ford gazes at me while his partner yanks open the back of the truck. He gives me a tiny smile that vanishes only a second later.

It gives me strength. "Wait. We'll want to bury her." I look over my shoulder. "Will you just take her to my cabin?"

"We could do that," Ford says, his voice quiet and deep.

"Please. Please, she means everything," I say.

"Forget it." The man wrinkles his nose and bends to lift Ellie.

"You think the boss wants them Toads wasting burying time? Or energy?"

"Right." Ford stares straight ahead. He's a lot gentler easing Ellie into the back of the truck than the other Overseer is.

"You want this job? Keep your ideas to yourself." The man shakes his head and gives Ellie's body one last shove before he slams the back shut.

"Right," Ford says again.

Ellie is lying next to all the dirty shovels we've used to dig our holes, next to the discarded wrappers and cups from the Overseers' favorite food places. It's like she's nothing more than garbage.

They're walking toward the truck doors now.

What did Mother say when the others withered? What did she say over their graves? Shouldn't I say some of it, any of it, now?

But I can't remember.

"Please just tell me where you're taking her," I say. My voice breaks over the words like a stream over rocks.

There's no answer. Two doors slam shut. Ford doesn't look back.

I go to his side of the truck and slam my open palms against the window. He jumps and looks at me. In the darkness I can't see his eyes.

"Where are you taking her?" I scream.

The truck starts with a rumble and a blast of sound from the inside—music, loud music that sometimes we hear the Overseers playing in their cabin at the top of the Lake. My palms vibrate on the window. Still I shout. "Tell me! Please tell me!"

Just in time, I step back before the truck jolts forward. The words from Mabel's funeral come back to me.

"Walk with Otto," I say, just as Mother did when we sprinkled the first bits of earth on Mabel's body.

The truck spits gravel and dirt as it moves away from me, but I stay standing, even as a piece of gravel stings my cheek.

"Otto will carry you home," I say.

They've nearly reached the curve of the road; I see red lights and reach out, as if I could stop them, wrap my fingers around that truck and pull Ellie back to me.

"Otto will never abandon you," I say.

And then the truck is gone. Even the sound is swallowed into the night.

I remember the bottle of Ford's medicine in my pocket. I pull it out and fling it into the space the truck left behind. It makes a rattle and a cracking sound when it hits the road. And then that noise is gone too.

All that's left is the sound of my sobs.

Chapter 11

I stumble home to Mother.

"Wake up," I sob. "Ellie's dead."

I shake her, none too gently, and call her name loudly. But she doesn't stir. She only breathes, and breathes, and heals. Why did Darwin have to beat her tonight? I need her more than ever.

I can't stay here all night, as good as alone, thinking of that white bundle that was once Ellie being carried away. I can't stay here wondering where she is, and what I could have done to keep her living.

I can't keep this secret from the rest of the Congregation. She is theirs too. And they were all her children—nary a skirt or blanket remains in the Congregation that doesn't have some small mend or patch from Ellie.

Until now, it was Ellie I would creep to for comfort—Ellie's cabin I'd go to, at night, when I needed refuge from Mother, or just wanted company as she healed. Ellie always knew when to talk, and when to be quiet. Sometimes I'd come to her cabin and sit, no words in me. She'd braid my hair, or take my boots and brush them clean. We would embrace, and I would return to my own bed, ready for sleep.

But no more. Ellie is gone. There isn't any time left for visiting with her. How could I have had nothing to say, then? I have a million things to say now—and no Ellie to hear them.

Hope used to come to Ellie's cabin too, sometimes. She lived in her own small place, not so far away from ours, but it was lonely, she said. Once she married Gabe, though, I never saw her make a special visit at night.

I'll go to Hope. It is the easiest place to start, to tell the awful truth: Ellie is gone.

The quickest way is along the road, but I'm afraid the truck will come back. Ford might be in it, but tonight he's just another Overseer. He's one of the men who took Ellie away.

Instead I slide along the dried-up Lake shoreline, fitting my feet carefully around the stumps and rocks that usually sit at the very edge of the Lake. Not this summer: now the waters glisten, dark and sullen, about ten paces from my path. It smells like dead fish, and earth.

Even water needs more water to thrive.

Hope left her small cabin when she married Gabe. I pause by it, looking up the hill at the house—small, even for our homes. There are still traces of the gay red paint she coated it in one year, back in a time when Darwin was feeling indulgent.

Ellie loved that red paint. Once she brought a pot of red paintbrush flowers so Hope would have red inside and out. Hope

kept them alive until winter. Then she put them by the stove—
but it was still too cold for a wildflower to survive.

I have to tell someone Ellie's gone. The secret bulges inside
of me, makes it hard to swallow, hard to breathe.

Gabe's cabin is just a few past Hope's old one—though I suppose it's Gabe *and* Hope's cabin, now. There aren't any tall trees
around the back of the cabin, on the side by the Lake; over the
years Gabe has rooted out any sapling that's tried to take hold.

The cabins between Hope's old one and Gabe's are dark, and
so is theirs. For the first time, I worry that I'll be waking them, or
worse, disturbing something private.

But a voice calls out to me before I even walk up the hill to
their cabin.

"Ruby! Come for a visit?" Hope's voice, light and joyful,
comes from behind the cabin.

Instead of answering, I walk up the hill as if in a dream, my
feet far too light and my head far too heavy. I stare at the ground,
hot tears running down my nose and dropping on the earth below.

Hope is standing behind the cabin. Gabe's greatest secret
from Darwin West winds up the wall that she stands near: vines,
full of vegetables—or at least they would be, in a good year.
Before he came here, Gabe was a farmer.

She doesn't look as I approach; instead she's got her back
turned to me, hands lightly traveling over the vines. "I was just
trying to find some peas," she says. "To tempt Ellie into eating."

I want to tell her Ellie is dead. I want to tell her I can't stop
dreaming of an Overseer. I'm afraid of what I'll say, so I stay silent.
I stop a few paces from Hope and wait for her to turn.

"There. Six! Six whole pods. Remember how we had buckets of them last summer . . ." Her voice trails off as she sees my face.

Then, without even knowing, without hearing what I have to tell her, her face crumples into tears too. She's the one who closes the space between us; she's the one who throws her arms around me.

"Ellie's gone, isn't she?" Hope asks, her head pressed close against mine.

I nod; she must feel the movement and understand, for her hug grows even tighter.

"But I picked peas," she sobs. The peas fall from her hand and land on the ground. Even in the dark, their green is so bright they almost seem to glow. Nobody grows things like Gabe.

All I want is to cry, to be held. But I know I've got to tell her all of it—or at least all of it, except Ford.

Gently, I pull away. Ellie keeps her arms around me, loosely; we stand like a couple waiting for their wedding waltz to begin.

"I went to see her," I say, "but there was an Overseer's truck there."

There. I started. I swallow and remind myself: tonight, Ford doesn't exist. I can't say a thing about him.

Slowly, carefully, I tell her how they carried her body out and put it in the truck. I don't tell her how they wrinkled their noses at the smell of her, or how they shoved her beside discarded food wrappers and cups. Losing Ellie hurts bad enough. The rest of it can be my burden.

"Did they take her things too?" Hope asks. "Filthy Overseers."

Ford's not filthy. I know he would never take any of Ellie's few belongings—or let anyone else do it. "Of course they didn't," I say. It's the wrong answer, I know immediately.

"They're *Overseers*. Why wouldn't they?" she asks.

"They were in a hurry," I answer, and it seems to be enough for her.

Hope guides me to a set of low, weathered stumps set beside the wall. We both sit. Her shoulders slump, and they seem to pull the rest of her body down too.

I reach out and take her hand, lacing my fingers between hers.

"We . . . We can't bury her?" Hope asks.

"They wouldn't tell me where they were taking her."

"Ellie was the one who said I should run away with the Congregation," Hope says. Then she looks back over her shoulder, as if making sure nobody else is listening.

"She loved you," I say.

"She protected all the women in Hoosick Falls—meals for the sick ones whose family couldn't work a kettle or stove; shelter for ones whose husbands were too . . . rough." Hope reaches up with a free hand to wipe a tear away. "That's why she said I should come with her. Life with John would have been a short, hard one."

Instead she's got a long, hard one. I give Hope's hand a squeeze with mine, still linked to her. "Are you sorry?" I ask.

"Sorry?" Again Hope looks behind her, but this time her look lingers on the plants that climb the wall behind us—and she smiles a little. "No. I'm glad I came here."

"Too bad Darwin West came too," I say.

Hope surprises me with her high, silvery laugh. "That was the fly in the ointment, wasn't it?" Her face falls back into a frown.

Then she slides her hand away from mine and bends to pick up the peas. She holds them out. "Ellie would want you to have them."

"I'm not hungry," I say, even though the pea pods look so beautiful.

"We're always hungry," Hope says. "We just forget what it feels like, after a while. Eat them."

I think of how Ellie always pushed me to take the extra apples, to eat the bit of food left on her plate. She wouldn't want me to refuse this either, so I pop one pod into my mouth. It's limp and not very juicy, but it's very delicious.

"You eat half," I say.

Hope puts one in her mouth and smiles again, her eyes half shut.

"Will Gabe be angry?" I ask.

"Gabe says what's his is mine. He wouldn't care," Hope says. But she looks down at the ground when she says it. I don't think she would have picked those peas for anybody except Ellie . . . or Gabe. They're family, each other's protector.

Jealousy swirls in me. She can be with somebody, somebody she wants and loves. The only person who's sparked anything in me is an Overseer. How could I choose so badly?

"You're lucky . . . and he's lucky," I say. "Having each other."

Hope bites another pea. "Gabe takes care of me."

I think of Ford offering me the food in the woods, pouring his water over the leaves—and I think of Jonah's promises to provide. But neither boy is the right choice for me.

"Are you lonely?" Hope shifts her legs so our knees meet, and she's looking straight into my face.

"I have Mother—and you, and Asa, and Boone," I answer.

"But you don't have . . . this." A shy smile curves the bit of plumpness in her cheeks, and she tilts her head toward the cabin.

"Maybe I never will," I say.

"But you want it." She lets out a small sigh.

There's so much I want to tell Hope about Ford: about how he cared about Ellie too, and how he tried to help in some small way.

"Jonah asked me to marry him," I confess.

"Oh . . . really?" Hope ducks her head.

"Is it such a surprise?" I ask.

"No, I just didn't know Jonah had set his cap for you," she says. "But I don't talk to him much anymore."

"I said no," I tell her.

Even in the dark, I can tell Hope is still smiling. "I wouldn't expect you to say yes."

"What do you like about Gabe?" I ask.

"He's patient and he sees good things in people," Hope answers. "And he's strong."

I wonder what he loves best about Hope. She's easy to love—easier than me, I think. Hope doesn't have prickles or doubts anywhere in her.

"What do you want—who would you love?" Hope asks.

I hide my face so she can't see the secrets in it. "Somebody brave, but gentle," I say. "Somebody worth taking risks for."

"Sounds dashing," Hope says.

"He is," I say.

"Is?" She giggles, and only then do I understand what I've said. "Who's your secret suitor, Ruby Prosser? Are you stringing along *two* men?"

"There's nobody. Nobody!" I stand up quickly and pretend to study the vines on the wall. "I think I see some more peas. You could pick some for Gabe."

"Shall I guess?" Hope teases.

"There's nobody," I say—firmly enough that she doesn't say anything more, but I don't think she believes me.

"You'll find love, I promise," she says softly.

I can't bear to talk about love anymore—and I can't afford to let my secret slip out again. So I bring up Ellie, even though it's far more painful to talk about. "We'll have to tell people about Ellie tomorrow morning," I say.

"Ellie wouldn't want any fuss," Hope says.

She wouldn't have minded a few prayers over her body, I know. She wouldn't have minded if we all gathered to say good-bye.

But the Overseers took that from us. Hate flares in me, strong enough to burn away any sentimental thoughts of Ford—for now, at least.

"We'll each tell one person and ask them to tell another," I say.

"And to say a prayer to Otto," Hope adds.

I should have thought of that—a Leader thinks of things like that. "She'd like that. So would Otto," I say—then feel foolish, for pretending I know what Otto would really like.

Hope stands and folds me into a hug. Her body feels warm, and softer than Mother's angles and edges. I rest my head on Hope's shoulder for a moment.

"You can always come here to talk to me," she says.

I step out of the hug. "And you to us," I add.

Hope turns to inspect the vines. "You were right. We have a few more peas." Then she reaches deep into the leaves and plucks.

"Save it for Gabe," I say.

"Gabe has plenty." She holds it out. "Take it."

"Thank you." I slip it into my pocket and resolve to save it for Mother, for the morning. I'll be sure she eats it before I tell her about tonight.

I'll give her that tiny happiness before she knows Ellie is gone.

Chapter 12

Mother didn't cry when I told her that Ellie was dead. She only bowed her head and murmured a prayer to Otto. "Rest in peace," she said. "Rest with Otto."

I'd sat up half the night crying and slept in fits the other half.

"Your eyes are swollen," Mother said. "Ellie wouldn't want that."

It was all we said about her.

But when we reach the clearing the next morning, everything feels different. The Congregants whisper to one another, many with bowed heads. A number stop to give Mother and me a nod; some reach out to squeeze our shoulders, or our hands.

It's all the funeral she will get.

My grief makes me heavy, slow. I don't notice that something else is different until Mother takes my hand and squeezes it—not in sympathy, but to wake me from my stupor, I think.

"Where's Darwin?" Mother says quietly.

Darwin West never misses a morning in the clearing. The

drought

Congregants are still whispering, but not about Ellie anymore. They've noticed too.

It seems like the same number of Overseers as ever. They've got their guns and the bulge of chains in their pockets. I see the man who took Ellie away with Ford. But Ford is missing.

Disappointment slides over me.

The sun is nearly up. A few stragglers reach the clearing, eyes big with fear, breathless from running. But the Overseers don't lift a hand to them.

"Otto deliver us," Mother whispers to Asa, who is standing near us. He nods and whispers it to the next person, and the next, until the whispers change to prayerful murmurs.

Just as the sky above the trees lightens, one of the Overseers takes the chain out of his pocket and snaps it against the group. It bites at the dirt like an angry snake.

"That all of you?" he shouts. This man is one of the most brutal ones; last week he drove his rifle butt into Gen's head when she stumbled in the midday heat.

Mother steps forward and even the prayers go silent. "It is," she answers.

"Then get your Toad butts in the House," he says, motioning with his arm. The chain follows it, sliding on the ground.

It's not Sunday. And it's never breakfast time anymore. Why do they want us in the Common House?

Nobody argues or asks why. It won't change anything. Mother leads the Congregants to the entrance of the sagging building. She looks back at the Overseer for a moment, and then opens the door.

A heavenly smell rolls out into the heavy morning air. There's food inside.

The crowd hurries, and soon we are all in the room. Overseers are posted in all four corners of the room—one of them Ford, standing farthest from the exit, near Mother's altar.

But this morning I barely notice Ford, for there's something else in the room: breakfast.

Breakfast, a hot one, smelling and looking like our lives before the drought came. Three big pots of steaming oatmeal sit on the long table by the kitchen, with plenty of bowls and spoons. Baskets of apples wait at either end of the table.

My mouth waters so much, I have to swallow. I can't take my eyes off the food. I sense the other Congregants around us looking at one another and hear their whispering, but I imagine only how the oatmeal will feel in my mouth.

If Ellie had lasted only one more day, she could have feasted. I feel guilty for my hunger. But I can't help it.

"Is it for us?" Mother wonders.

Darwin emerges from the kitchen. He is wearing a dark-smeared apron and a smile that makes me nervous. But still, all I can think about is that food.

"Eat up," he calls out.

That's all the encouragement we need. The Congregants press forward, forming a ragged line—of course the Pellings are in front. Jonah catches my eye and gestures, but I look away. Mother steps aside and motions for the others to go first. I stay beside her.

"Jonah has his eye on you," she says, so quietly that only I can hear.

"He . . . He asked me to marry him."

Her eyes grow wide. "What did you say?" she asks.

"No—of course I said no."

For a moment she studies my face. Then she turns her head to stare at Jonah. "You've become a woman without me seeing it," she says, still watching him with narrow eyes.

"He only wants me because I'm the Leader," I tell her.

"A man would have many reasons to want you." Mother slides one arm around me and squeezes tight. "But Ruby, there's no room for romance—"

"I know." I tell her quickly.

She gives me another squeeze, and guilt floods me.

Jonah heaps so much oatmeal in his bowl that it threatens to overflow the sides. Will there be any left for us?

Mother is watching Darwin now. He's left the kitchen and is moving toward the doors. Then he's speaking to the Overseers who brought us inside the Common House.

Boone edges to the back of the line and stands next to Mother.

I glance over at Ford. His face lights with the briefest smile, but then it falls back into the somber watch of an Overseer.

"It's almost our turn," I tell Mother, tugging her sleeve. She moves reluctantly, still watching Darwin. Boone slides behind us.

There's a rumble outside.

"Do you hear that?" I ask Mother.

"It sounds like a truck," she answers, squinting as she peers past Darwin. "A very big truck."

Darwin slips outside and the Overseers slam the doors shut. After a moment, one tugs on the doors, as if to test them.

The doors don't open.

"They've locked us in here," Boone says.

Mother frowns. "The cisterns are nowhere near full . . ." Mother's voice trails off. But then, finally, it is our turn. Even Mother can't ignore food. She picks up a bowl and heaps oatmeal into it. Up close it smells even better.

The apples look worse up close, though. They are shriveled, with black pockmarks on many of them. Still, I take two—and for a moment, I think I'll give one to Ellie. Then I remember.

I put the extra one in my pocket. I can imagine Ellie telling me to be sure to eat every last bit of it. It's almost as if she's living in my mind now.

"Take another." Boone sets an apple on top of my oatmeal. "Before the Pellings eat a whole orchard's worth."

Jonah and his family are sitting next to the food, nearly done with their breakfast already. They're eyeing the table and I know the moment we're gone, they'll lead the charge for second helpings.

We follow Mother to empty seats and fall on our breakfast in silence. Nobody is talking: only staring at their food, spooning it into their mouths as fast as they can.

The oatmeal scorches my tongue, and it's so gummy that it threatens to stay on the roof of my mouth instead of disappearing down my throat. But I don't wait for it to cool. I eat more, and more, until my stomach feels ready to pop.

I can see the locked door from my seat. Both Overseers stand with their backs to it, arms crossed, as if a lock isn't enough to keep us inside.

All they had to do was give us the oatmeal, to keep us in here.

Nobody else seems to notice—or perhaps care—that we are trapped. But my skin crawls with the knowledge of it. The air feels thicker, pressing on me, when I know I can't run out the door. Is this how one of Mother's quarries feel when locked into one of her traps?

Mother takes a savage bite of her apple. Brown spots dot the yellow flesh, but she eats those, eats all of it except the stem.

I should eat one of my apples too—maybe all of them. But the oatmeal has stretched my stomach to near bursting. I close my eyes for a moment and pray to Otto for strength.

There's a steady loud beeping sound outside, and the grind of something that I think is a big truck. It's the same noise that the Visitor's truck makes when he starts the drive back down the hill.

"What are they doing out there?" Boone wonders.

Mother takes another bite of her apple. She wipes her mouth with the back of her hand, and then licks the juice off her skin.

Boone taps the side of my bowl with his spoon. "Go get more, Ruby, before it's gone."

Then comes a loud crash, so loud that our seats shake from the sound of it. That makes some of the other Congregants, finally, look up and stare at the door.

"That can't be the cisterns," I say. They never make a noise like that, not even when the full cistern lands on the truck.

"You got your fair share already!" someone shouts from the food table. It's Asa, and he's standing all too close to Jonah Pelling, chest to chest nearly.

Mother and Boone both scramble to their feet. I follow them to the table, but I don't hurry. Most of the other Congregants stay in their seats.

"I'll take as much as my family needs, old man!" Jonah shouts back.

A few of the Overseers are rushing to the table too. One of them is Ford. I get a little closer.

"Break it up." An Overseer pokes Asa in the back with the long part of his gun. He doesn't even seem to feel it.

"Take a seat, Pelling," Asa growls. His face is mottled red and his chest heaves with breathing.

"Step aside," Jonah answers. The other Pellings are standing now too, seven against Asa's bear bulk—and the Overseers.

It's grown silent; all I hear is Asa's breathing.

The same Overseer talks, this time his voice even louder. "I *said*, break it up."

Jonah shakes his head, a small movement, but enough for the Overseer to kick him in the back of the knees. He stumbles forward, but I reach out to steady him.

He stands but doesn't let go of my hand. I flick a fast look at Ford. He stares, lips pressed together.

Hastily, I take Asa's hand too. "We can't fight. We're all Congregants," I say. "Otto doesn't want this. Do you?"

Jonah turns so our faces are just inches apart. "I provide for my family. Always, Ruby. You can trust that." His voice is husky.

I look away, embarrassed, knowing he's asking me again.

"We're all hungry," Asa says. "Nothing special about your folk."

"Others haven't eaten as much," I tell Jonah.

He frowns, looks back at his family. But then he shrugs. His hand slides away from mine.

I let go of Asa. "Go get your food," I tell him.

Then I raise my voice. "If anyone wants more, take it now!"

Nearly half the people stand. I turn to Jonah. "Take your family to the back of the line. If there's any left, they can have it."

Jonah nods and motions to the other Pellings. "You're a pretty good Leader, Ruby," he says.

For the first time, I feel that way too.

But then Jonah has to go and spoil things, like he always does. "You'd be a pretty good wife too," he says.

I look up and meet Ford's eyes while I give Jonah my answer. "I'm not marrying you," I say.

"Not yet," Jonah answers.

Asa takes my arm and guides me in front of him. "She goes first. She needs it the most."

"I left my bowl—" I start.

"Take another." Ford stands behind the table, scooping oatmeal into the bowls. The other Overseers don't help. They take a step back and level their guns at us, as if we're liable to transform our breakfast into weapons at any second.

Ford holds out a heaping bowl; bodies press behind me, wanting more, more, and so I take it quickly.

A piece of paper crinkles beneath the bowl. Then I see

another flash of a smile from him before he turns back to filling the bowls.

I start from the surprise, but I think I hide it well. While I walk away from the line, I press the paper into a tiny ball beneath the bowl, keeping it sheltered from any glance. Then I slip it into my pocket just before I sit down.

A smart girl would throw away the paper, whatever it is. Overseers shouldn't give secret notes to Congregants. Nothing good will come of it.

But this is a better treasure than oatmeal, in truth. I gulp down my food and pray for the doors to open.

Chapter 13

Only half the Congregants are back in their seats with more food when the doors creak, and then sunshine is spilling into the room. We're freed.

Nobody stands to go to the front—all bolt more food into their mouths, but their eyes are on the door.

Darwin West steps through, the sun so bright behind him I can't see his face. But I know the silhouette of his leather hat and the swirl of his long coat.

"I'll need all the men," he announces. "And the rest of you get out to the woods."

This strange respite is over. Our normal lives begin again—except for the tiny lump of paper in my pocket.

The room is filled with the sound of spoons clattering into bowls, onto tables, onto the floor. The men rush outside and the rest of us form a line to get our cups and spoons.

I am so aware of Ford's note that it burns like a tiny hot stone in my pocket. I make sure to keep my eyes far away from him, only staring straight ahead. I take my cup and my spoon and move for the woods.

Then I see what the trucks were doing, though I don't understand it. There are piles of long, long logs sitting on the side of the road. Already the men are working on stacking them in pyramids. Are they firewood? Why, in the middle of summer? But if not that—what?

One of the men staggers away from the logs, gripping his stomach. Zeke Pelling, Jonah's older brother. He falls on his knees, and then he empties his stomach onto the dirt.

My own clenches, and I look away fast.

"Move slowly at first." Mother is next to me, her spoon clattering loosely inside the cup. "Our bodies aren't used to so much food."

An Overseer yanks Zeke to his feet and motions for him to return to the logs.

"What a waste," Mother mutters.

She stalks off into the woods and I hurry too, but not in her direction. I will find a quiet, shady spot to read my note—far from anyone's eyes.

I slip through the woods faster than a fox hunting in moonlight, barely brushing the bushes or branches as I seek a hiding place.

But Hope finds me first.

"Ruby!" She waves from a clump of goldenrod.

I sit beside her. The paper makes a small crinkling noise, but I keep my head down and try to act as if nothing is different.

"My buttons are about to burst!" Hope pats her stomach.

"Breakfast was fine." All I want to do is race away and read Ford's note.

Her smile falls away. "Are you all right? Is it Ellie?"

"I . . . Yes." I keep my eyes away from hers.

"I could just imagine her telling us to eat as much as a Pelling breakfast. Couldn't you?"

I grin. "There's no keeping up with the Pellings."

"No fooling." Hope lifts her spoon to start working, but her dreamy smile is back. "Remember how we'd tell those boys we were having a race—then we'd sneak away and play pretend without them?"

"You made us crowns from ferns," I say. I kept mine for weeks, in the cabin, until they crumbled.

"And magic wands too." Hope holds her spoon up with a rueful look. "Think we could do something with these?"

"Get water, is all."

She sighs and nods.

"I . . . I probably shouldn't harvest so close to you," I tell her. "The Overseers might not like it."

"Oh. I suppose." She looks hurt.

After Hope took up with Gabe, I could never find time alone with her. Now I'm lying, just to get away.

"I'll look for you later today. Farther away from the Overseers," I promise.

"Find lots of water, Ruby." She lifts her cup, briefly.

I tap my cup against hers. "And you."

As soon as I'm out of sight, I start to hurry again, trying to find a place to read Ford's note.

Finally I find a fallen tree, surrounded by half-browned clumps of greenery: a hiding place. I slide between them and pray nobody can see the colored bits of my dress through the screen of the tree. I'll have to be fast.

I smooth the note over the curve of my bended knee. The writing is blue, and thick, the edges blurred as if the note was written on damp paper. There are only a few lines — small, sloped handwriting that seems almost feminine.

She's in the field near the birch grove. Look for the tallest clump of grasses.

At first I don't understand. Who's there? But then I remember: Ellie is dead. And only Ford, and that other Overseer, might know where she is now.

The birch grove is far away from us. We don't usually harvest there; it's a long walk, and not nearly worth the energy. The birches have pushed away all undergrowth and don't offer drops of water from their leaves. Most places in the woods are better than the grove for meeting our quotas.

I want to go to her. I want to see her grave for myself, say good-bye at her final resting place.

But this isn't the time to visit Ellie. One cup, full, by sunset. It's nearly impossible. Mother might suffer tonight if I fail, and I can't add any more lashes to her shoulders. And yet, and yet, I can't stand to think of Ellie there alone, no prayers said over her.

I crawl out and stretch to standing. Nobody seems to be near. I start toward Ellie's grave in a trot, the fastest I dare go with water in my cup and roots reaching out to hobble me at every step.

I pass through thick underbrush and tall oaks, and then a

shorter group of pine and blueberry bushes. The birds have picked the berries clean, mostly—all that's left are the green berries and a few shriveled ones. On any other day I would stop to eat them, as Mother taught me. But Ellie's grave is more important, and I press on.

When I see a plant or tree that looks very wet, I stop to gather water. I scrape a little off a cypress tree's ragged bark, and coax more moisture from the underside of a half-dead toadstool. But more than anything, I hurry toward Ellie.

Before I reach the birch grove, I hear the wind rattling the leaves, a dry sound that feels like a rebuke. My cup is not even a quarter full, at midday, and here I am anyway.

"I should go back," I tell myself. But instead I step into the grove, looking at the field beyond it. The birch roots are thick and knobby, poking up through the ground and reaching for my toes. I have to look down and work carefully not to trip, always keeping my cup steady.

And then my toes land on the yellowed, pointy grass of the field. It's not grown very tall this year. But still, bright flowers poke above, with pink- and purple-fringed edges. They are surviving the drought, growing the same as if it rained every day.

I stop walking. I look over the field and its determined flowers, wondering where they put Ellie. And then I see it, perhaps fifteen paces away: a long fresh-turned line of dirt. Something glints from it, for a second, but then the breeze rattles the birch leaves again and it's only dirt, no shine.

Now that she is so close, I can't make my feet hurry. I take a deep breath and take one forced step, then another.

It feels wrong to come without something for her. The apple still sits in my pocket—I can smell it, even though it's tucked away—and I imagine leaving it as a gift, a tribute, for Ellie.

But I know what she would say.

Save it for yourself, she'd tell me. *Don't waste that on a dead woman.*

So instead I bend and pick a fistful of wildflowers for her. I am careful to take them sparingly, one here, one there, so it doesn't look like I was here. Ellie wouldn't like me taking a pretty thing and making it ugly.

It feels right to go to Ellie now, gripping my small bouquet in one hand, my cup in the other. The flowers spill over the top of my hand, tickling my skin with their feathered edges. I lift them to smell, but find only the scent of dirt.

I take one step, and another, and then I am at her grave.

The clumped pile of dirt seems too short, as if for a child. It is mounded higher than the rest of the ground, and another pile of dirt sits to the side of her grave; they didn't bother to put all the dirt back when they put her in the ground.

I set my cup carefully to the side, making sure it won't tip. Then I kneel to touch the edge of the dirt.

"It's me, Ellie," I tell her. I set my flowers near the top of the dirt, where I imagine Ellie's hands would be.

She's in there, our Ellie. Darwin denied her. Otto didn't save her. And I failed her too. I'm Leader. But I didn't change anything. I let Mother and the Elders convince me different. Then I didn't even bring the medicine in time.

Anger fills me so fast that it's hard to breathe.

"I'm sorry," I tell her. "I should have found a way . . . a way to get you help."

I bend low over the dirt, my palms flat against it. My eyelids sting and I know the tears are coming—until I see a glint, again, tucked in the grass near her grave. The surprise makes me sit up and forget my tears.

It's nothing natural. Perhaps it's a trap left by the Overseers. Did Ford give me his note only so he could catch me? So he could hurt me, like all the others?

I creep close, checking the grass for ropes or loops that might set off a trap. Mother's taught me enough to know how to be careful.

But then I see it's not a trap. The glint comes from a shiny, thin sheet wrapped around an enormous bunch of flowers. I pull the bundle close; a heavy scent comes from them.

I've never seen anything like these big, thick-headed things. I bury my nose in the flowers, already half limp, and breathe deep. They smell like nothing else I've ever smelled—like nothing to do with Ellie. But even so, they are beautiful.

This is nothing you can find in the woods. Someone from the outside world came here and left these.

I know who it was, even before I see the card tucked into the middle of the flowers. A chill runs down my arms as I pull the card out and read it.

Rest with God.

And then: *I'm sorry.*

There's no signature, but the handwriting matches the note that Ford gave me.

"He's sorry," I tell Ellie.

The flowers' color makes me think of blood, half dried. I squeeze one and find its petals so tightly packed that it pushes back against my touch.

"I don't want him to be sorry." A sob chokes off my voice.

I wish I'd been brave enough to tell Ellie about Ford. But I'm not sure what there was to say.

"An Overseer left flowers for you, Ellie." I turn back to her grave and set them on the dirt. "Can you believe that?"

I lift my face to the sun, at its high point, punishing me with its brightness. I have to close my eyes to keep its rays out.

"They took you away, Ellie. They wouldn't let us bury you."

When I open my eyes, I see how wrong, how sorry, my wildflowers look next to the bounty of shiny-wrapped modern flowers.

Ellie belongs to the Congregation, not to an Overseer—no matter how strange and kind he is. So I pick up his flowers and walk to the edge of the woods. I fling them so hard that the plastic splits open in the air and the flowers scatter over the birch grove floor.

Then I return to Ellie, still fresh with anger—anger at Ford, at Darwin West, at Otto, at Ellie even . . . and at myself. I stand over her grave, pick up the pewter cup that I left sitting next to her. There's even less water than before, I think. The noon sun probably boiled some right out of the cup. I should leave now and start gathering, if there's any hope of meeting my quota.

"Is this what Otto wants?" I ask Ellie. "He wants us to suffer?"

Perhaps she's with him now. Perhaps she knows the answer to that question.

The wildflowers on her grave are already limp. Soon they'll go dry, and then the wind will blow them away. In another year or two, her grave will be covered over with grass.

Nobody will even know she was ever here.

"Otto didn't save you," I say. "You believed, and he didn't come."

I tip my head back and howl out all the rage and desperation in my body.

Will Overseers hear me? I don't care. Let them come.

Let them beat me, and see how I heal. Let them spill blood on Ellie's grave. It's too late for her. But maybe it will nourish the grasses and roots that are her new family.

The birds scatter from the trees and rush away. I imagine their finding the Overseers and telling them where I am, and what I am doing—or not doing.

I think of how Ellie held me when I was smaller and then even as I grew too big, my legs dangling past her knees. She stroked her hand over my hair and whispered things to ease my life. She whispered stories, and sweet things, and reminders to believe in Otto.

"You never came!" I shout to the skies.

She tucked me in her bed when my stomach hurt or when I skinned my knee. She picked sweet clover and taught me to break its flowers with my teeth and suck the sweet honey out. She told me stories of my mother before she became a hard wall between the Overseers and the Congregation.

"Why didn't you let me help you? Why did you die?" I shout.

Nobody comes, and nobody answers. I howl until my body is limp and there's no sound left in it. I collapse on the grass next to Ellie's grave and stare up at the sky.

I came here to pray over her grave. But there aren't any prayers in me now. All I have is questions, and rage.

"You're the last one," I whisper. "Nobody else is going to die a slave. I swear it."

A bug lights on my forehead and I brush it away; my hand comes away wet. Tears.

I can't waste any sort of water. I sit up and carefully wipe the tears from my cheeks into the cup. It's disgusting, and necessary, and that makes me cry even more.

There's a loud crack in the woods. Fear dries my tears instantly, and I look around. All I see are the birches, with little place for someone to hide, and the stubby yellow grasses. Nobody is here but me.

Still, it's better if I leave. I've got to find water and get back to the clearing before dark. Ellie wouldn't want me to linger any more—indeed, she would have told me to not come at all.

"Good-bye," I say. "I'll come back some time to see you."

I wish I could tell everyone where she is. But they'd ask too many questions. This is not a place you stumble upon.

With one last look, I step back into the birch grove. My toe lands on one of the flowers from Ford. A sweet smell winds up to my nose.

My rage softens, a little. He was doing a decent thing, marking her grave with flowers—and telling me where to find it. It doesn't change the fact that he's chosen a terrible path, being an Overseer.

But the flowers are beautiful . . . a single petal couldn't hurt. I tug it away from the flower and lift it to my nose, then tuck it in the waist of my dress. It's softer than anything else that's ever touched my skin.

Chapter 14

Tonight there's only a sliver of moon. I walk to the cistern, slow, my feet a little uncertain after so long away. Every night brought a reason to stay away.

But no reason is enough, anymore . . . not since he told me where Ellie rests.

I see Ford's shadow before I hear him, a darkness that doesn't belong under the cisterns.

I walk to him, slowly, pushing away the flutters I feel every time I see him. He's given me no reason to fear him, I remind myself.

No reason except being an Overseer.

Ford doesn't stand. I get close enough that I can see he's wearing a trim white shirt with short sleeves and pants so dark that I can't see his legs in the grass.

"It's been lonely," he says.

"I knew I shouldn't see you again."

"Huh." He pats the grass near him, then slides away a bit,

as if making room. "What if you talk but you don't look at me?"

"What?" I ask, confused.

"You said you can't see me. But you didn't say anything about not *talking* to me."

I can't help smiling. But I know I shouldn't talk, see, listen, think of, touch . . . the last word makes me shiver.

"No. I should really . . ." I glance up at the cisterns.

"Just for a little. Then you can pray. Please?" he asks, patting the grass again.

I am tired from a long day of gathering, then digging. Again there was no supper. Couldn't I sit, if only for a few minutes?

And don't I owe him something for pointing me to Ellie? Isn't that what made me return, finally, to the cisterns?

So I sit, closer than I probably should . . . much closer than the last time we talked here.

"Thank you for telling me where Ellie is," I say.

"I'm real sorry she died."

"I know."

"They made us check the cabin. I didn't want to," he tells me.

"I went to her grave right after you gave me the note." I brush my fingers over the tips of the lush grass. It's damp, so different from the yellowed field that Ellie lies in.

"I thought maybe you'd want a funeral," Ford says.

"I can't tell anyone. They'd wonder . . . how. How I knew." Shame wells in me, and I stare at the ground.

"I guess that's better for both of us," Ford says.

"It would be better if we stopped . . . this." My chest feels tight, with barely any room for air.

"You can leave if you want to," he says.

But I slide closer, just a bit closer, to him. And he slides a little closer to me.

"You brought Ellie flowers," I say.

"That's what you do when people die . . . people you like."

"I never smelled anything like them." The petal didn't last forever, tucked in my dress. So I pressed it beneath a rock, by our cabin door. Maybe soon I'll bring it inside and hide it under my mattress.

"Ellie seemed like the type that'd like roses—I think." Ford clears his throat.

"Is that what they're called? Roses?"

Ford laughs. "You're kidding, right?"

"No."

"Oh. Sorry. I forget . . . I forget how things are up here, sometimes."

How can he forget? I can't forget for a second, not ever.

I glance up at the cisterns. I haven't climbed up there tonight. Before I leave, I have to add my blood. It's been far too long.

"Do you stay here all night?" I ask.

"Mostly. Sometimes I sneak back and catch some sleep if I know Darwin's gone for the night."

"He leaves? Where does he go?"

"Darwin's got a whole other house off the mountain, a real nice one with a huge backyard and an in-ground swimming pool," Ford tells me. "You didn't know?"

It would be *our* house, I suppose, if Mother ever promised to love him.

"What's a swimming pool?" I ask.

"It's . . . Really? Really, you don't know?" Ford inches closer to me, as if to get a better look at my face.

I turn my face so we're gazing at each other, straight on. "There's a lot I don't know about," I tell him. "Most things in the modern world, I don't know."

"It's like your lake, here. Only it's much, much smaller. And people build them. They're not natural."

"He made his own lake?"

"With a fountain and everything. The guys say he has a party there every summer—a picnic for all their families. He treats their families real well."

As soon as he says it, Ford ducks his head and stares at his feet.

"Real well, huh?" I look up again at the cisterns. Our Water pays for that house, and that swimming pool, and takes care of all those other families.

"It's the best job in town," Ford says softly. "Not even the jobs in Albany pay like it. Especially if you haven't gone to college."

"That doesn't make it right."

He lifts his head to look at the cisterns, then me. "I know."

"I need to . . . I have to go soon." I will myself not to look up at the cistern but he taps it with his knuckles.

"Do you have to . . . um, pray?"

"Yes." I stand up fast and hope he doesn't follow.

For a moment, it looks like he'll get up. But then he settles back on his hands and looks in the other direction. "I'll be here if you need me."

I won't need him. I can't ever let myself need him.

My feet make a soft *clank-clank-clank* on the metal steps to the top of the cistern. I roll my sleeve back and hold the knife over my arm.

What would he think if he knew what I was really doing up here?

"Praise Otto," I say, loud enough for him to hear. "Bless this Water."

I make a quick slash with the rock, and my blood flows. It hurts more than usual tonight—I don't know why—and I let out a small gasp.

"Are you all right?" Ford asks. I hear rustling. Is he getting up?

"I'm fine. I just bumped my . . . finger. I'm fine," I say quickly.

He doesn't answer. I count the drops into the cistern—twenty, today, to make up for the time I've stayed away. Near the end I have to squeeze my arm; the blood doesn't want to leave my body tonight.

As soon as I can, I wrap my cut in a handkerchief and hurry down the ladder.

There is Ford's shadow, under a cistern. I want to go sit next to him and talk more. I want to do bold things . . . touch him, even. What would it feel like, the brush of his skin against mine?

But it's wrong and dangerous. "Good night, Ford," I say softly.

"Wait!" He stands up too fast and knocks his head, hard, on the cistern.

"Are you . . . Are you all right?" I ask.

He grips his head and staggers a step sideway. "Fine," he grunts.

"You don't seem fine." I go closer, and closer, and then I am reaching up to touch the part of his head that he bumped. The short bristles of his hair are soft, not the hard spikes I imagined. I run my fingers once, twice, over them before I realize what I am doing.

I drop my hand fast. "It doesn't seem to be bleeding."

"I'm too hardheaded for that." He is smiling, I can tell, even though it's so dark in the shadows that I can't see much of his face.

We are so close that I can smell him: a clean, soapy smell. And there's something else too; a familiar tang, like woodsmoke.

"Stay awhile," he says. "I like talking to you."

"You're an Overseer. And it's late . . . and . . ."

"It's not an Overseer asking. It's just me."

And then he reaches out and takes my hand, gently, slowly. First only our fingertips touch, and then his skin slides against mine until our hands are knitted together.

Mother used to take my hand when I was smaller, tugging me here and there. Sometimes it was a sweeter touch at the end of a long day, or when we sat in front of the fire. But it never felt like this.

Heat travels from my fingertips, up my arm, until I feel like my body is made of embers.

"I'll stay," I say.

"Good." He bends his knees to sit. I follow, even though worry and shame squeeze my heart. I edge away a bit to make sure only our hands touch.

He still holds my hand—I still hold his—but his other hand strays up to his neck. I see the glint of the gold that he wears on the chain there.

"What is that?" I ask.

"What?" Ford looks over at me, then follows my eyes to his hand.

"You touch that necklace a lot," I say.

"Oh . . . I do?" He lets out an embarrassed laugh and his hand falls to the grass. "I didn't know that."

"You don't wear other jewelry," I say. Some of the other Overseers do: bracelets like small chains around their wrists, or big rings that cut cruelly, if they punch or slap a Congregant.

"It's a medal, really. I wouldn't say that it's jewelry. My mother . . ." He draws in a deep, shaky breath.

I don't push him. I close my eyes and listen to the wind in the trees. It's a little cooler at night, these days. Soon it will be darker earlier. Will Darwin lessen our quotas?

Our fingers drift apart. I feel cold without Ford's touch, but I don't reach out for him.

"It used to hang from my mother's rearview mirror, in her car." Ford slides his hands away from me and runs them over his head, tilting his head back to look at the sky. "It's a picture of Saint Jude. He helps desperate people."

I wonder if Saint Jude knows Otto. Has he told him what's happened to us?

"How does he do that?" I ask.

"Well . . . you pray. He's supposed to take your prayers to God and sort of . . ." Ford waves one hand in the air. "He convinces God to listen to them. That's what saints do."

"Maybe we need a saint to talk to Otto," I say. I mean it as a joke, but then I wonder: is that why Otto doesn't listen? Do we need someone to remind him of us, to convince him our prayers are worth granting?

What if I'm supposed to be that person? An idea starts to tick in my mind, something too small to name—yet.

Ford's hand goes to his neck again. "Otto isn't God, Ruby."

"How do you know?"

"I went to Sunday school for eight years. Nobody ever talked about Otto."

"They just don't know about him. He's real," I tell him.

Ford turns to face me. Even in the dark I feel his eyes, steady and firm, on me. "Do you really think he's God?"

"He's . . . Otto." I never went to a Sunday school. I only know what my mother has told me for my whole life.

We sit quiet for a while. Ford's fingers twine around mine again. I feel his pulse, slow, steady, where the webs of our fingers meet.

"He's all you have, out here," Ford says. "I get that."

"He's not here." I can't keep the bitterness from my voice. Suddenly Ford's fingers feel too heavy, too thick, and I slide my hand away.

"You pray to him, though," Ford says.

"Yes."

"Then doesn't that make him your god?"

"He's everyone's god," I say. "Otto heals all."

"Otto isn't my god." Ford crosses his arms. "I've got the Holy Trinity. That's what the Bible talks about."

"Trinity . . . so you have three gods. Couldn't there be one more?" I ask him.

He lets out a loud puff of air, like he's been punched in the stomach. "The Trinity is all God. There's only *one* God, Ruby. The Father, the Son, the Holy Spirit . . . all one God. Didn't your mother tell you any of this?"

I raise a hand in the air. "Don't tell me what to believe, Ford." I sound more like Mother than I mean to—hard, final.

"I'm sorry," he says. Then he shifts so he's not facing me anymore.

"Otto performs miracles. The Congregants saw it," I tell him. "Does your god do that?"

"Sure. There are all kinds of miracles in the Bible."

"You've seen them?" I ask.

Ford pulls his legs in close to his body and hugs them, lowering his chin to his knees. "No."

"Has anyone?"

"I don't know. Not for a very long time, I guess. Or . . . at least there's nothing recent in the Bible."

Then maybe it's Ford who's found the wrong god. But I don't say that. I know how it feels when he presses his god on me.

"I pray to God to save my mom, every day. *That* would be a miracle."

"Like we prayed for Ellie," I say.

"Yeah. And she's probably going to die, like Ellie."

We feel so far apart now. I edge closer, and closer, so our hips touch. Then I rest my head on his shoulder.

"They don't seem to be listening, do they?" he asks.

"Who?" I whisper.

"Otto. And God."

"Sometimes I wonder about that too," I confess.

Ford strokes his hand over my head slowly, like a mother comforting a child. It leaves a trace of shivers behind, every hair feeling his touch.

I pull my head off his shoulder and shift away a bit. "What's wrong with your mother?" I ask.

"Cancer," Ford says. "She's got it so bad, they can't even treat it."

"That sounds terrible," I say.

"And worse every day." He leans his head to the side so it's touching mine, just for a second, then sits up.

"You could give her Water," I say.

"No. Never." He says it quickly.

It stings. I feel like he's rejecting me, my blood. Would he feel the same if he knew my blood made the Water special? "You gave me medicine for Ellie. Is it any different?" I ask him.

"You ever give that to her?" he says.

"I didn't get a chance, did I?"

"I'm sorry," he says.

"Could it have saved her?" I ask.

"No. Just less pain," he says.

"The Water might save your mother," I say.

I could give him a tiny bit, couldn't I? Just enough to help? Maybe then he'd believe in Otto's miracles.

"If an Overseer steals Water, he's done. Even one drop and Darwin will kill him," Ford says.

"How do you know?" I ask.

"You think nobody's tried?" Ford points up at the cisterns. "I've heard all the stories. Last guy who tried ended up strung up . . . never mind. We'll just say it wasn't pretty."

"I never knew."

"It'd be the same thing for a Congregant." Ford's voice is soft.

"I'm not stealing," I say.

"I know."

"I wish I could help your mother," I tell him.

"I wish I could've helped Ellie."

The cicadas in the woods let out a burst of sound, shrill, like a warning. There's no breeze, suddenly: it is hot, airless, and a bead of sweat trickles behind my ear.

He leans closer to me, and I to him, until there's barely any space between our lips. I imagine the rose petal between us, soft, touching his lips and mine.

"No. No!" I scramble away, and his head jerks back for a second—in shock, I think. He reaches out as I stand up, and then he is standing too. But he doesn't make a move to come closer to me.

"I can save you," he says. "I can take you somewhere safe, away from Darwin West."

It all comes out easily, like he's planned saying it to me.

"Only Otto can save me," I tell him.

"We could be together if we were away from here." His voice cracks.

"We can't be together. Not ever." I take one step back, then another. I want to tell him to leave me alone—to never talk to me again.

But I can't get those words out. So I whirl and run and pretend I can't hear him calling me.

He doesn't follow.

And I don't stop running until I've reached our cabin, and then the safety of bed, Mother breathing deeply across the room.

I am back where I belong. I can't ever stray again.

Chapter 15

He said he could take me away.

He said he could take me somewhere safe, somewhere that Darwin West couldn't reach. But I ran, like a child. I didn't listen, all because of a kiss that didn't even happen . . . an almost-kiss I can't stop thinking about.

Mother's right. I am still a child.

"I sure hope all you Toads are paying attention!" Darwin has us gathered around one of the holes; the Overseers are carrying a long pole to it. "This is going to be *your* job, starting today!"

Already we gather and dig. Now we have something else to do for him too.

"Will there be a reward this time?" I ask Mother softly. "Or only more hitting?"

She gives me a sad smile and touches her fingers lightly to one of the cuts she garnered in last night's beating. "Otto is our only reward."

"I know." But is it wrong to hope for bread? For soup? For far, far more?

Ford isn't here today. Perhaps he stayed at the cisterns all night, hoping I'd return. But I didn't. I lay in bed, trying to sleep. When Mother woke for the morning, I hadn't slept one bit.

It's still a little dark; I have to squint to see exactly what Darwin is doing. He kneels by a pole, knotting three long, thick ropes around it.

"These will hold the poles in place until you pour the cement," he says.

He motions and one of the Overseers gives him a short metal stake with loops at the top. He drives one into the ground, a fair distance from the pole; the Overseers drive two more into the ground at equal distances.

"How 'bout give us one of those stakes, boy," I hear a man's voice say quietly behind me. I turn to look; it's all Congregants. But who? Maybe Jonah's father Earl, standing at the edge of the pack. When he's not giving Darwin West a murderous look, he spares an angry glance for Mother.

"We'll be counting stakes before you're released today." Darwin looks around our group, eyes stopping on each of us, it seems, with a hard warning. "If one of you Toads tries anything—and I mean *anything*—with one of these . . ."

He whips around and swings his rifle straight at the Congregant closest to him—Mary Evans, already near fifty when she came to the woods. She hunches and throws her hands over her head.

But Darwin stops the rifle just before it strikes her.

"You don't have to be afraid of me," he says, his voice soft, too sweet. "As long as you behave." Darwin smiles. "Tell me you understand, Toads. No games with the stakes."

The Congregants mutter.

"Make sure the rope is secure. No slips, got it?" Darwin says.

This time he does not have to tell us what to do. We nod, all of us, quickly.

He watches as the Overseers raise the pole and then tie the ropes to the stakes.

"That's when you get cement. Load up a wheelbarrow and head to the hole." Darwin points a finger into the crowd. "No spilling! Cement isn't cheap."

A beefy Overseer, nearly twice my height, struggles to get a heavy wheelbarrow up the short hill to the hole. Darwin lets out a sigh and the Overseer looks up. There's fear in his eyes.

Good. I don't feel any compassion for this man. Ford told me all the good things the Overseers get, in exchange for terrorizing us. Let him taste what is forced on us every day.

I wonder where Ford is right now. Sleeping, I warrant. Is he dreaming of the place he'd take me? Is he dreaming of him, me, together there?

Tonight I could go to him at the cisterns. He could take me away. No more pain, no more starving, no more holes or scraping water off leaves.

Joy bubbles in me, just thinking of what it might be like. I don't need much. I just need to be away from here.

But then I hear Mother murmuring prayers to Otto under her breath. How could I leave her—how could I leave the

Congregation? They would die without me, unless Otto finally comes. And I've sworn to be their Leader.

As wrong as it would be to leave the Congregants to die, it would be even worse to leave with an Overseer. For all of Ford's kindness, he chose this job . . . and he has not left it. Who's to say what he would be like away from here?

"And that's how you raise and cement a pole!" Darwin finishes. "Go to your assignments *now*."

It's almost noon, and my stomach cramps with hunger. No breakfast today—the oatmeal and apples seem so far away now, like a dream, or something from Darwin's gentler days long ago.

"Ruby? Ruby." Mother stands close to me so we're eye to eye. "We've got to go to our hole."

"Our hole?" I ask.

"The one they assigned us to just a moment ago." Mother squints at me. "What are you dreaming about, daughter?"

"Noth—nothing. No one," I stammer.

Mother stares at me for a moment longer, then gestures for me to follow her deeper into the woods. "Has Jonah Pelling swayed you?"

"No . . . No, it's not him," I say.

It doesn't seem to quiet her mind. She frowns. "This life leaves us little room for dreaming, Ruby."

She's right. But even as I follow her past a line of holes, all covered in clear sheets, I think of Ford. So long as my feet are doing as they're told, what does it matter where my mind travels?

Soon three of our men arrive carrying a pole with three ropes draped over it. One of the men is Boone. They drop the pole on the forest floor, and two of the Congregants head back down the hill. Boone lingers behind, looking first at the pole and then Mother and me.

"How will you lift this by yourself?" he asks.

I wonder the same thing. Are we really supposed to lift something as tall as a tree, just the two of us?

"We'll call for help if we need it," Mother answers. "Go back before they decide you've been gone too long."

He hesitates, looking at the other two Congregants already disappearing into the leaves. Then he follows them.

"Boone fancies himself our protector," Mother grumbles. "It only gets worse and worse."

"What's wrong with a protector?" I ask.

"What's wrong is that eventually they go away . . . or they give up. Then where are you left?" Mother kneels and pulls the first rope away from the tree. Then she hands it to me.

"Boone carries you home, Mother, after Darwin's done hurting you."

She pulls a knot tight around the pole and grimaces.

I think about Ford's eyes, steady on me—asking for something. And then I think of how Boone looks at Mother.

"He . . . He loves you," I say. "Doesn't he?"

As soon as I say it, I know I shouldn't have. Mother comes close to me and grips both my wrists tight. Her eyes are narrowed.

"That hurts," I say.

She loosens her hold a bit. "Girls your age want romance. But Ruby . . ." She gives my wrists a small shake. "There's no romance to be had here."

I drop my eyes; I feel a flush crawling over the back of my neck. I can't let her see my secrets.

"Do you understand?" she asks.

"That don't look like working." An Overseer is upon us, right behind Mother—neither of us even noticed.

We both scramble to our feet.

"Just one more rope and we'll be ready to raise it," Mother says.

"You do that. No more holding hands, Toads. I'll be back in ten minutes to make sure you're doing your fair share." The man looks at the pole, then aims a wad of spit at the ground. "Here's your stakes."

He drops three stakes on the ground, then ambles off to check on Jonah and Earl Pelling, set up not too far from us.

Just that sentence is the spark my mind needs to go racing. He'll be back—he's not gone for good. He's only stepping away for a bit.

That's what I could do too. I don't have to run away forever.

"Hurry," Mother says.

She drives one stake in the ground; I manage two, stomping on each so they're in deep, set at an angle like I watched the Overseers do.

"What're these poles for?" I ask, even though I know Mother won't want to speculate.

"They're torture enough, aren't they? We don't need to know more," she answers.

We finish tying the ropes, then stand and each take a deep breath. We roll the log until the end is over the hole, then Mother stands near the bottom and I in the middle.

"Walk it up," she says, and we do, though the log is entirely too heavy and my muscles tremble with the effort. I see Mother's shoulders and arms shaking too.

The worst part is knowing that we'll have to do this again, and again, today.

"Otto help us," Mother grunts.

I echo her prayer, but the pole is no lighter. I think of Ford's saints. We need one to make Otto listen.

But even without Otto's help, finally the log is in the hole, standing upright like a tree stripped of branches.

"You hold and I'll tie," Mother says.

I balance the log while Mother ties the ropes to the three stakes.

We stand back to admire the pole for a moment.

"It's real ugly," Mother says.

"Almost as ugly as Darwin West," I answer.

She looks at me, a smile twitching on her face. It makes my own smile want to come out. And then, she laughs—a real laugh, not a tired or angry one. I haven't heard her laugh all summer, I think. It makes me laugh too.

"Look out!" a man's voice calls behind us. "Run!"

We turn in time to see a pole falling fast, right toward us. One tree catches it, then lets go—then another. The ropes that were supposed to hold it fast are flying alongside it.

Our laughter dies in an instant.

"Move!" Mother grabs my elbow and drags me away. We stumble over one hole. And then, a *boom*. The ground shakes, and leaves scatter from the trees. We were barely clear of it.

The Overseer who was watching us comes running from another part of the woods. As he runs, he pulls out the chain from his pocket.

We creep closer to the Pellings. I pray the Overseer won't notice us.

Jonah and Earl are standing at the foot of the fallen pole. It's ripped up some of the hole it was meant for. Clods of dirt are plastered on both father and son.

The Overseer folds his arms. "You Toads drop something?"

More Congregants are sliding through the woods now, watching, but not getting too close.

"These ropes don't want to stay knotted." Jonah hunches his shoulders and looks to the side.

The Overseer bends to pick up one of the ropes scattered around the pole. He holds it close to his face, then drops it. "Looks like you're just too stupid to tie knots."

"We know how—" Jonah starts, but Earl presses his hand against his son. Jonah doesn't say anything else. He stares at the Overseer though, bold.

"I'll get the pole up real fast. I promise you that," Earl says, still not meeting the Overseer's eyes.

"You better get these poles up like Darwin said to, or else." The Overseer turns his head to look at Mother. "She don't look like she wants for another beating."

"There won't need to be any beating," Jonah says.

"What did you just say, Toad?" The Overseer whips the chain behind his head; its path knocks leaves off the branch behind him.

"He said we'd better get back to work." Earl puts one hand on Jonah's shoulder.

Jonah pauses. He looks at me.

I shake my head slowly.

"Yep," Jonah says. "That's what I said."

"Good." The Overseer lets out a huge yawn and looks back at the deep shade he was standing in. "I'll be watching."

As soon as he's out of earshot, Jonah whispers, "Or napping."

"Watch your tongue," Mother snaps.

"If you were some kind of good Leader, you'd stop this," Earl growls at me.

"I—But we have to. They'll beat us—" I start.

"Someone should stand up to him. Tell him we're not hoisting poles," Jonah says.

"Like a Leader," Earl says. "Worthless girl."

"The only reason you're mad at Ruby is because she refused Jonah," Mother says.

"She couldn't do better." Earl gives me a sour, measuring look.

"She's better off staying with me," Mother answers.

"Stop," Jonah says. He won't look at me. Pity fills me.

I put a hand on his arm. "I can show you how to tie the knots."

He jerks away, but then he nods. "That'd be fine."

I kneel by the fallen log, and Jonah joins me. The smell of him makes my nostrils flare of their own accord.

"I'll ask for our cement." Mother gives me a quick nod and hurries off toward the Common House.

Earl settles against a tree trunk with a grunt and closes his eyes.

Jonah catches me staring. "Dad feels the heat."

"We all do." Then I lift the rope and start tying. Jonah watches.

When I'm near Ford, I only want to get closer. But Jonah makes me want to get farther away.

"You tired of waiting for Otto yet?" Jonah asks.

Mother wouldn't like such talk. I look past Jonah, but there's no sign of her on the road.

"Mama won't let you say, will she?" he mocks.

"I've my own mind," I answer.

"I know you want to fight. I see it in you," Jonah says. "You don't want to wait around."

"I wonder, sometimes, if he's coming," I admit.

"Yes! If. Not when. If." Jonah gives me a smile that makes me feel like I've said the wrong thing—or just far too much.

"But—But of course Otto's coming," I stammer. "We pray for it . . ."

"And what does it get us? No food. Work every day, all day. God only knows what these poles are about," Jonah says.

"Devilry," Earl yells from his resting spot.

"Likely." Jonah nods. "Can't think of one good thing they could bring to us."

"Otto will come and then . . ." But I stop. These men don't believe it, I know. And if I let myself think, if I set aside what I've been told, I'm not sure I believe either.

"A whole world out there and here we are, stuck." Jonah shakes his head. "What's the point of living forever?"

"Because Otto wants us—" I start, but Jonah cuts me short with a stare.

I swore on Ellie's grave that I'd not let another one of us die a slave.

"What if we could find my father?" I ask. "What if we could remind him of our prayers—that we're waiting?"

Jonah picks up a nearby rock and makes a show of peering under it. "You under there, Otto? You listening to my prayers?"

"Not in the woods—not these woods, anyway," I tell him. "What if we could find him wherever he went, after he left us?"

"And bring him back?" Jonah snorts.

Earl speaks up again. "We went looking, way back when. Never found a trace of him."

"It's a different world now. Maybe it would be easier to find him . . . or someone who could help us."

"Who'd want to help us?" Jonah stands up and brushes his hands on his pants. "Not one Overseer ever lent us a hand."

I shiver, remembering Ford's touch. "I believe there are kind people in the outside world," I say softly.

"Based on what?" Jonah raises his eyebrows.

"There's Otto, at least. You believe that much, don't you?" I ask.

"You want to run away. Is that why you refused me?" Jonah crosses his arms and gives a look up and down the length of my body. It makes me want to cover myself, every inch. But I stay standing tall and stare back at him.

"I want to get help," I say. "I want to get Otto."

"Here I thought you were more of a fighter," Jonah says. "Like me."

"It's the best way to help the Congregation," I tell him. But the thought of Mother twists my stomach. I know how furious she'd be if she heard talk like this.

But she hasn't saved a single one of us, has she? Maybe I could do more.

I hear the *squikety-squik* of a wheelbarrow; Mother has nearly returned. We don't have long.

"If I go to find Otto, will you come with me, Jonah?" I ask.

Jonah might be bad company, but he's better than no company. I don't know anything about the modern world or what kind of protection I might need there.

"You gonna marry me?" Jonah asks.

"No," I say too quickly, I think, since a blush rises in his cheeks.

The Congregants with the wheelbarrow are nosing into sight now. Two of them, with Mother leading the way.

"You'll change your mind," Jonah says.

This time I stay silent.

"You tell me when and where," Jonah says. "And we're gone."

"Ruby! Come help with the cement!" Mother calls.

"Not for much longer," Jonah says quietly.

"We'll talk soon," I promise.

Then I go and help fill the hole with the gloppy wet cement. It'll dry eventually, they tell me, and then the ropes will come down. That pole will stand tall for years and years . . . maybe forever.

But we won't be around to see that.

I'm going to make sure the Congregation is free, and soon.

Chapter 16

The next day, Mother shakes me awake when the night is just starting to give way to sun.

"We've got Ellie's cabin to clean," she whispers.

"The harvest—" I start, but she shakes her head and gives my hand a small tug.

"We'll be quick. She didn't have many things left. Less maybe, now." Mother turns her head and stares in the direction of Ellie's cabin.

Waiting even a day could have been a mistake. The Overseers might have gone through their cabin, or Congregants who don't care about who the Elders think deserve Ellie's extra things.

Still, I have to drag my body from bed. I don't want to see her cabin without her in it. And I especially don't want to see it once we've taken her things out.

"Hurry." Mother tugs my dress from its hook and tosses it on the bed. I slide it on, along with my boots. Then we make the short walk to Ellie's cabin.

Ellie's cabin is cool, clammy, and dark. Mother gropes for the lantern, but it's not on its shelf by the door.

"The Overseers took it," I tell her.

"It's better we work without it anyway." Mother props the door open a bit with a stick she finds by the steps; there's barely enough light to see the outline of Ellie's bed, trunk, and stool.

The last few times someone withered, we cleaned out their cabin. Once, Hope helped. Another time, Boone was there. Of course there was nothing to do when Asa's Mabel withered. We tried to bring flowers and food to his cabin. But he wouldn't open the door for two weeks.

This time it feels right for it to be just Mother and me.

I go to Ellie's trunk. Even after hundreds of years, rich swirls of gold-painted vines and flowers cover the top and spill over the sides. I can see their glint in the dark. When I was small, I used to sit by the trunk and trace the path of the paint with my finger, trying to find the beginning and the end.

"Should we empty it here?" I ask. "Or carry the whole thing?"

"Help me lift it," Mother answers.

We each take a handle and heave, but we barely can lift it from the floor. When Mother shakes her head, I drop my part. The floor makes a loud cracking noise, and for a moment I think it will give way.

"Quiet, Ruby," Mother snaps.

"I'm sorry."

"Whatever makes it so heavy?" she asks.

I kneel by the trunk and flip up the hasp. "I think I know."

On top there's her extra blanket, with bits of dried lavender folded into it. Below that, the few scraps left from Ellie's wine-colored wedding dress, the ones too small to do anything useful with. And then there's more lavender. I slide my fingers below the crisp rustle of the dried flowers. And there I find smooth shapes, one after another. Tears rise fast in my eyes, surprising me. It's been so long since I gave her that last rock.

I didn't know it was the last one then. I thought maybe I'd bring her one the next week, or the one after that. But somehow there were other things to do—helping more with the harvesting, I suppose, or slipping away to find berries for the Congregation when the Overseers weren't watching.

"It's all the rocks," I tell Mother. "She saved them."

Mother shakes her head, looking puzzled. "Why would Ellie save rocks?"

My fingers close around one; I pull it gently through the layers of lavender and tattered red fabric. They flutter from my wrist as I stand and show Mother the rock.

"I gave them to Ellie," I tell her. "Over one summer, when Darwin was especially . . . harsh."

It was another dry time, but I was so much smaller . . . and I remember that it did rain, a little. It was just never enough for Darwin.

"We all took turns filling your quota back then," Mother says.

Yes. They'd each taken my cup and filled a bit—just as we did for Ellie in her last days.

I remember Ellie's kind smile. "Run and find me the prettiest acorn in the woods," she'd urge me, taking the pewter cup from my fingers. I let it go reluctantly, wanting to be an adult like the others—but not wanting the backbreaking work either.

So I crept through the woods and found all the dark spots and boulders that help me creep through them even today, without an Overseer seeing me. I found all kinds of treasures: acorns, yes, and rocks with streaks of shining crystals in them.

Mother smiles and shakes her head. "I'd forgotten how Ellie sent you on all kinds of treasure errands."

"She wanted me away from you, and from Darwin—didn't she?" I ask. I'd never realized it until now.

"We've always protected you from him, Ruby. All of us."

Sometimes I wish I could still run into the woods and look for treasures, instead of watching him hurt her.

"We haven't much time." Mother points at the chest. "Bundle what you can into her blanket and take it back."

I stand to spread the blanket on the floor, but Mother holds her hand up.

"Wait," she says. "I'll sweep the floor first. I can't bear—"

"I know," I say. Seeing Ellie's beautiful old quilt spread across a dirty floor.

Mother uses a small branch broom from the corner to sweep. I unfold the blanket, then, and start to put the rocks inside.

"Leave those," Mother says. "No one will want them."

My eyelids prick with tears, but I nod and set them against one wall of the cabin—all but one. I'll keep that.

Then I pull her spare dress off the hook on the wall and put it in the center of the blanket, along with her boots.

She was buried without them—without one bit of anything Darwin gave her. It makes me smile.

"Her watch," Mother says. "Isn't it in there?"

That was her greatest treasure. I pat my hands in the trunk, but there's nothing left but scraps and lavender.

"It's not in the trunk," I say.

"Those Overseers took it," Mother says in a sharp voice.

Anger flares in me, and for a moment I almost tell her that Ford wouldn't do that: Ford's kind, honorable, not a thief. Even if he is an Overseer.

"Maybe she hid it. We haven't seen it in a long time," I say.

Again Mother looks out the door; it's lighter, yes, but I haven't heard a single Overseer's truck rumble past.

"We've got a little time," I say.

"You finish there," Mother orders, pointing at the blanket. I tie the corners into a bundle while she runs her fingers along the high edges of the rough-hewn log walls, then on top of the doorframe. But she finds nothing.

"Under the bed," I say. "Try there."

Mother slides her hand under the bed, frowning. A smile lights her face and she pulls out the watch.

Without a glance to the outside, she settles on the ground and cradles the watch in her hands.

I slide next to her, feeling like a small girl again. "Can I touch it?" I ask.

"Of course." But she doesn't let go of it. Mother holds out her palm, the watch and its long delicate chain nestled inside.

Once the gold chain shone; now it seems dull, like the

clouded glass over the face of the watch. Or perhaps that's only because it's so gloomy in the cabin. It might shine in the sunlight. I brush one finger over the tiny gold vines that are worked into the piece.

"It was her husband's," Mother says. "And before then, his mother's."

"Jeremiah," I answer. He died before Mother and her father moved to Hoosick Falls: a farming accident. Ellie sold their tiny farm and opened the boardinghouse on River Street instead.

I wonder if she would have given him Water, if she had the chance. Would she have saved his life like I wanted to save hers?

"They're together now." Mother's voice is gentle. Her fingers close around the watch for a moment, then open again.

We should stand and finish our work; the horizon is bright enough for watery light to steal into the cabin. But I don't want to break the spell. Mother might be in a rare mood for stories.

"It says eleven fifteen," I say, prompting her. And it works.

"Ellie stopped the watch the day Darwin found us here." Mother holds the chain high so the watch dangles in the air. She squints at the face. "She said she'd wind it when we were free."

I tap the watch with my finger and it swings a bit. We'll be free soon, Ellie. I swear it.

"Why didn't you run farther?" I ask Mother. "You stopped so close to Darwin and the town."

"They only said we had to leave the village. Besides, I was pregnant. I couldn't go very far or very fast." A tiny smile crosses her face, and she presses her free hand to her stomach for a moment. Then she lowers the watch into her palm again.

"All of this was meant to be, Ruby," she says.

"Otto might still have found you, if you had run farther," I say. "You could have had more babies—"

"I had you. And Otto . . . he'll come." Her smile is a little too bright, I think, and she blinks back tears. "We still have time."

"Why didn't you fight?" I ask.

"Ruby." She says it like a sigh, her voice edged with tears.

"Things might have been different," I whisper.

"We . . . *did* fight, once," Mother says slowly. "You wouldn't remember. I forget that, sometimes."

"What? You never—" I turn to face her fully.

Mother doesn't look at me. Instead she presses the watch against her cheek.

"There were more of us, eight more of us, when we came to the woods. There was another child, even. He was five." Her voice chokes off.

The shock roots me to the floor like Ellie's heavy trunk. "Nobody talks about this."

"Louis. He was so bright and bold." Mother squeezes her eyes shut and takes a deep breath.

"What happened?" I ask.

When Mother answers, she speaks with her chin tilted up, a tear sliding down her cheek. Her eyes are still closed. "They ran. Louis led the way. But the Overseers were faster."

"Did you run?" I ask.

"You were a tiny baby," Mother says. "I never could have escaped."

She slips through the woods like a fox. Couldn't she have tried?

"The Overseers killed them all, Ruby. Killed them and strung them from a tree in the clearing."

"Nobody escaped?"

"Not one." Now she looks at me, eyes bright with tears. "Darwin said you'd be next if anyone tried again."

"Me?" I shouldn't be shocked. He's always known I am Mother's weakness.

"If anyone even tried to escape, he said, he'd hang you."

"Nobody talks about it."

"No. But we all know it. It helped us to accept that escape isn't what Otto wants . . . and it isn't safe for anyone, especially you."

Then all the Water I've made for the Congregants these years has been payment. Payment for saving my life and sacrificing their freedom.

I think of the nights I've skipped the cisterns, of late, all because of a boy. The Water might not be strong like it usually is, now. Is that how I repay my family?

Mother lets out a low gasp. "It's nearly time for harvest."

She hurries to her feet, sliding the watch in her skirt pocket.

I grab the blanket from the floor. Mother picks up Ellie's stool and the pillows on her bed. The fresh-stuffed new one looks wrong in this dim, sad place.

"Wait." Mother pulls the watch out of her pocket. The growing light catches one of the edges and splashes golden marks around the walls.

"The Overseers—" I start, for once the one hurrying us.

"Ellie would want you to have this." Mother presses the watch and chain into my hand. I curl my fingers around it. It feels too cold for a summer morning.

"But you love it."

"You'll let me look at it, from time to time . . . won't you?" she asks.

I'll bring it with me when I leave. I'll carry it each day until I return, with Otto or help or some kind of salvation for the Congregation.

"Of course I will," I say. She gives me a sharp look, then her eyes narrow.

"With Ellie gone, that's one less tie to us," Mother says. "Isn't it?"

She is watching me so intently. I only shake my head no. "I miss her, is all."

"We are here to endure, and you are here to sustain," she reminds me.

"I know."

"Good. Now"—she smoothes her skirt over her hips—"as you said, the Overseers are waiting."

We hurry Ellie's things back to our cabin, and then it's time to harvest. Mother leads the way out the door, but I outpace her on the way to the clearing . . . always checking, though, to make sure she follows close behind.

Chapter 17

I told Mother I'm going to the cisterns tonight—but I was lying.

"I could come," she offered—but her eyes were half shut already. Darwin spared the chain, but he didn't feed us either, and the woods were terribly hot today.

"Rest," I said. "I'll only be a little while."

By the time I'm back, she'll be asleep. She'll never know how long I was gone, really. She'll never know that I didn't go to the cisterns at all.

I'm going to see Ellie.

The path to the birch grove is long, and barely a quarter of the moon peeks from the sky. I'll have to be careful not to trip in the darkness . . . or be discovered by an Overseer.

I want to bring Ellie something, again. I could pick flowers. But then I remember how sad my little bouquet looked, lying on her grave. The flowers are starved for water like everything else here. They didn't last long away from the soil.

There is her watch. I could give her that. But I know Mother was right: Ellie would have wanted me to have it.

Perhaps I should have brought one of the rocks that she kept in the bottom of her trunk. But I've gone too far to turn back now. I'll need lots of time to go to the birch grove and back, before Mother wakes.

I cannot think of another thing. So I continue my path to visit Ellie, hoping I will see something along the way.

The wind carries dust off the ground and scatters it in my eyes. Once I have to stop and squeeze my eyes shut against a swirl of dust—too late. Tears slip from beneath my eyelids and roll down my cheeks.

Just in time, I hear the laughter before I reach a section of sparse pinewoods. I slow my pace to an agonizing tiptoe, then peek from behind a tree.

Overseers, two of them on the ground, and then another on a tall ladder propped against one of the new poles. One on the ground is holding a silver can to his mouth, drinking from it and shining a bright light on the ladder. The man next to him holds a large round disc with black rope coiled around it.

They laugh again.

"Fool . . ." One word drifts over to me.

"No training . . ." This one sounds more serious, without laughter behind it.

"Hazard pay!"

Again, more laughter.

The man on the ladder takes the end of the black rope and climbs higher, his companion unspooling the rope as he climbs. He loops the rope around the pole and pulls something from his belt. It looks like a thick, short version of the guns they point at us. I duck behind the tree, waiting for the shot.

But there's no shot. Only a loud buzzing sound.

I dare another peek and see him lowering his strange gun. The rope is attached to the pole now. The man on the ladder seems to relax so much that his body threatens to sag off the ladder.

"The juice ain't even on, idjit!" the man with the silver can shouts.

All three of them laugh.

I want to know what they're doing—terrible uses for long black rope flood my mind. Hanging, dragging, torturing . . . but I don't know what Darwin's plan is.

And there won't be any finding out tonight.

I edge back into the woods.

I hear the grove before I see it, the leaves rattling in the wind. When my eyes first fall on the tall white trunks of the birches, the hairs on my arms raise up. They stand like ghosts, the kind Asa tells me tales about when Mother isn't listening: murderous ghosts, watching, waiting for a victim to come close. I can fairly sense their angry spirits.

Then I see it, the perfect gift: an oak sapling, just knee high, standing in the middle of the grove. It is a wonder that the birches haven't choked it out already. I'll save it and bring it to Ellie's grave.

Having a task pushes away my fancies of angry ghosts. I find a stick, long and wide enough to dig with, and with a few heaves I free the sapling from the soil.

"You'll shade Ellie," I tell it. "And keep her company."

Ellie would like this, I know it. I hold the sapling close to me and cross the rest of the way through the grove. The edges of the baby leaves gently tickle the inside of my arms. I try to hold all of the dirt around the roots so they aren't left bare and exposed. I want this tree to grow tall and strong, to be with Ellie when I cannot.

The dirt on her grave is drier now, and the flowers I left are shriveled bits of straw. It is hard to tell in the dirt, but I think I see the tiny tracks of a squirrel across Ellie's resting place.

This is a sacred spot; can't they sense it? But to them, death is common. It is not like being a Congregant, being someone who pushes away death for hundreds of years.

"I brought you something," I say out loud.

The wind pushes my hair harder, and I imagine that it is Ellie giving me her hellos. I push my hair behind my ears and look for a place to put her tree. Not too close to her grave, but close enough that it will give her shade.

There—perhaps five steps away, near where I imagine her head to be. I tear away the long dry grasses by the root and use the stick again to dig a hole.

"I've been planning," I tell Ellie. "I haven't forgotten my promise to you."

It doesn't take long to make a hole big enough for a small sapling. I nestle the tree into the earth, making sure all the roots are pointing down.

Lately we've dug and filled so many holes with dead trees. It's nice to put a live tree in this one. I form my hands into a scoop and push the soil back in around the roots.

"I'm going to find him, Ellie," I say. I look back at her resting place, somehow feeling like I ought to wait for her to respond. "I'm going to bring our prayers to Otto."

The tree looks limp in its new home. I push more soil against its tiny trunk, but it only tilts more. It needs water, I think. But I haven't any of that.

I can feed it, though. Do trees flourish from my blood like people, and animals?

It will only hurt a little bit to try.

My usual stone is not in my pocket. I had left it at home, under my bed, so I wouldn't be tempted to stop at the cisterns—to make the same dangerous mistakes with Ford.

I sweep my fingers along the dirt, through the grasses, but I only find more dirt and grasses. There aren't many stones in this field. Perhaps once it belonged to a farmer trying to convince the mountain to give his family enough food to survive. He picked away all the stones—perhaps his children and his wife helped, bent over the field, like Mother told me she used to see the farmers do in Hoosick Falls.

I'm not surprised he's long gone—he and all his family. This is a hard place to live. Besides, it all belongs to Darwin now.

The stick is sharp enough, I think. I make a hard, fast swipe across my arm, and it makes a deep scratch. It's not deep enough to bleed, though. I make another swipe and a low bleat, like an animal caught in a trap, escapes my mouth. It hurts more than a stone.

But now there is just enough blood welling from my arm to give to this tree. I hold my arm close to the dirt and wipe the blood off it with my other hand, careful to drop it on the dirt I've put over the roots.

Perhaps the tree will spring from the earth faster than all its cousins. Perhaps there will be shade for Ellie in the summer's end, instead of years from now.

"I can change things," I tell Ellie. "Even if Mother thinks I am only supposed to *sustain*."

What would Ellie say if she were still alive and I told her my plan? She'd ask me to stay, like she had all those other times. She'd make me swear it, even, thinking of the Congregation.

"The best thing I can do is leave," I tell her. "But I'll come back. Soon."

A long shadow crosses over the tree; I glance up. I didn't hear anything. Surely it's only a cloud over the moon.

But there is a man standing there.

I was a fool not to turn back when I saw those three Overseers. I scramble back, and then I am on my feet, pulling both arms behind me. I push my sleeves down frantically, feel the fabric get stuck on the wet part of my arm.

He takes a step forward and a chain jingles. An Overseer, of course.

"I was only . . . I'm going back now." I step back once, twice. Still, I keep my arms behind me.

"Wait. It's me." Ford's voice, low, not wanting to be heard by anyone except me.

Relief floods me—followed fast by shame at how happy I am to see it's him. This is more than relief. It's feelings that I can't afford.

"I was visiting Ellie," I say. "But I'm finished."

"Please. Wait. I've been hoping you'd come to the cisterns after . . . but . . . you haven't." He takes another step forward and turns a bit; now I can see his face. He is staring at his hands, which are squeezing the brimmed cap that often shades his eyes.

"I have to go back there soon. But only to pray . . . nothing more."

"Why haven't you come?"

"We can't be anything to each other, Ford."

"No. That sucks." He slaps his hat on his thigh, and his other hand forms a fist.

"I'm a Congregant. A prisoner. And you . . ."

"I keep you that way. Yeah." He lets out a long sigh, then looks back at Ellie's grave. "I couldn't even help her."

"Me either," I say softly.

"What were you doing with that tree?" he asks.

A sour taste fills my mouth. What did he see? "Planting it for Ellie," I say.

"No—after. You cut yourself." He reaches for my arm.

Everything slows, and the world goes silent. *Run*, I tell myself. *Run, before he learns your secret.* Or at least one of them.

But I stand there, frozen—or perhaps just unwilling to go—and I let him take my hand. He lifts it carefully, turning my arm and gently sliding up the sleeve so he can see where I cut myself. He runs one finger softly above the cut, not touching it. The path of his skin against mine feels warm.

"I guess it's like fertilizer, adding blood to new plantings," he says, running his finger over my skin again.

I can only nod.

"Does it work?" he asks, glancing at the tree.

Relief, sweet and cold, unties my mouth. He's not discovered my blood's secret, not really.

"It works," I answer.

"I hate seeing you hurt." He bends, slightly, and drops the faintest kiss on the scratch.

"I'll heal," I tell him. Gently, I slide my arm away. I rub the spot where he kissed it—it's still tingling.

"Look. I have an idea," Ford says. I can smell him: the metallic tang of sweat, but that clean smell too, the one that makes me want to bury my face in his shirt.

"This can't happen," I tell him.

"Just give me five minutes. Two minutes, even," he begs.

"Just . . . Just one," I say. He's so hard for me to resist.

"Run away with me. Please. I can get you far away from here," Ford says.

He slides his hand down my arm, gentle, and then laces his fingers in mine.

As if it belonged to someone else, my free hand reaches up and lands on his chest, on that soft clean-smelling shirt. I spread my fingers wide. It feels as if warm rock lies beneath the fabric.

"I'd keep you safe," he whispers.

Maybe he would. But questions race through me. Who would I become, if a man took me from here? Would he own me, only in another way?

Like the other night, our faces draw closer together. But this time I don't pull back, even though I know I should. A bigger part of me wants this.

"Are you sure?" he asks.

"Yes," I say.

Then he closes the last tiny space and touches his lips to mine. His lips feel dry, and plump. A thousand tiny thrills run down my body and leave behind prickling points of sensation. My body feels like an entire starry sky.

I edge a little closer. He slides his hand behind my head. We kiss again, and this time there is no hesitation or space between our lips. Finally I have to pull back to draw in a breath.

Maybe I don't need answers. Maybe I should run first, and find them later.

But Ford has his own questions. "That Jonah kid . . . ," he says.

"Why do we have to talk about him?" I sigh.

"You with me for me . . . or because I'm not him?" he asks.

How do I answer him? I know I don't want Jonah. But do I want Ford because he's *other*? Or because he's Ford? I'm not sure.

For an answer, I put both my hands on his face, and give him the tenderest of kisses. But then he shifts, and I hear the jingle of the chain in his pocket.

It is a faint sound, one that maybe a normal person wouldn't even hear. But a Congregant must jump for the chain, away from the chain. My lips freeze against Ford's.

He pulls away and looks around. "What is it?"

I can't. I can't be with him as long as he's an Overseer and I'm a Congregant. I can't trust an Overseer to help me.

"I thought I heard something," I lie. "It was probably only a fox."

I have to remember: I am the Leader now. I've sworn to free us. That's what I have to do right now. There's no room for romance, like Mother says.

I have to trick him.

I look up at him and smile, willing my lips not to tremble. "How would we leave?"

"At first, I thought my truck." Ford pulls back a bit but keeps his eyes on me. "But then I remembered . . . Overseers have to search each other's trucks, when we leave."

"For Congregants?"

"For Water, I think. You can't take any liquid away from here." He looks away, as if embarrassed. "But we could still take my truck. I'll just park it off the property and we can walk to it."

"The woods are guarded at the edge," I say. "And there're fences."

"True. But . . ." Ford looks around and lowers his voice, so soft I can barely hear him. "I know a place where we could slip ·through."

He slides his hand up and down my back, the barest of touches leaving behind a burning trail. My heart is pounding, but I know I have to do right by the Congregation.

I have to find this place.

"Where is it?" I breathe.

"It's not far from here. If you go about a mile that way—"
he jerks his chin. "There's a tree right by the fence."

I haven't climbed trees since I was tiny—since the Overseers
thought I was risk enough to watch closely. But I was good at that,
I remember.

"Can you climb?" he asks. "In your skirts and all. I mean . . .
not that I'm asking you to . . ."

"I can do it," I say.

"Then . . . you'll . . ." His face is alive with hope.

"I don't know if I can leave," I say quickly.

"Just think about it. Promise?" He dips his lips close to mine,
and I crave him in that second more than food, more than soft
pillows, more than a morning spent resting instead of crawling
over leaves.

I crave him more than keeping my promises, even.

"I'll think about it," I say.

"I'd treat you right," Ford says. "You'd never be sorry."

"I know you mean what you say," I tell him.

He lets out a frustrated sigh. "Whenever you're ready, I'll go.
But . . . I don't know how long I can stand it here."

"What about your mother?" I ask. "Don't you have to be here
for her?"

"And one day—probably soon—she won't be . . ." His voice
trails off, and he shoves both hands in his pockets.

"I'm sorry." I look at Ellie's grave. Soon he'll feel a loss just as
great. Even greater.

"You could meet her, if we leave soon," he says.

"I'll think about," I tell him.

And just like that, I can't bear to be near him for another second. I can't bear lying to him, and I can't bear being the kind of girl who shares kisses with any sort of boy, let alone an Overseer, in the woods.

"I have to go," I tell him.

"You always say that," he answers.

He pulls me in for another kiss. I don't stop him. It is my good-bye kiss. The last one ever, if I'm brave.

I pull away before he does, and when he lets out a small sigh, I turn away fast.

"Be careful," he says. "There're Overseers in the woods tonight."

And look at what happens when you find one.

Chapter 18

Darwin has declared we must all give him a full cup today.

It is the hottest day of the summer yet, and the gathering work in the woods is brutal. I'm working near the cisterns, at the base of a hill.

It's impossible to keep my attention on the task—the heat alone is enough to make my mind wander, but it's something more today. Ford is near, standing in a pool of shade only five or six steps away.

We are alone.

Even as I bend and scrape nothing, nothing from the leaf, I feel him watching me. "You're staring," I say.

"You're the prettiest thing in the woods," he whispers.

His slow, sweet smile makes me blush. I look back at my cup, nearly empty. There's no time to talk. I've got to find water.

"Do you have a lot?" he asks in a low voice.

"No. Not hardly any."

"Damn, Ruby."

"I can't help it." Now I stop working and turn to stare at him. How can he curse me for not finding water? He's no better than Darwin.

He takes a few steps closer, eyes getting wider. "I'm not saying it's your fault."

"Careful," I warn him, looking around. Another Overseer— or a Congregant—could come at any second.

"I just can't stand to see you get hurt."

"Then . . . I'd best work." I turn back to the task.

But as I work, I feel the memory of his lips on mine. I sneak a glance—or two—and see the muscles that I ran my fingers along. They glisten with sweat, and his thin shirt clings to the ridges of his stomach.

He looks at me too, when my eyes are away from him. I know it.

Even though I told myself I'd go to that tree with Jonah, I'm not sure. I could still tell Ford yes. I could still be his, and he mine, away from here.

"Darwin's coming," he whispers.

I nearly look up at him, but stop at the last second. Instead I bend more into the plant, keep my eyes far from him like I would from any other Overseer.

Should I hurry away? Attention from Darwin is never good. But maybe he'll leave. Maybe I'll have another few minutes to be tortured by Ford's closeness.

I tilt my head, just a little, to see what Darwin's doing. He hands a big bottle of water to Ford; beads of water drip off the container and fall on the dirt. I imagine scuttling forward and opening my mouth to catch them.

"Thought you might need this. It's hot out here," Darwin says to Ford.

"Thanks." Ford doesn't even look at me; he lifts the bottle to his lips and drinks.

I can't help staring, tracking it with my eyes. It's not Ford who has my attention now. I haven't had anything to drink all day; every drop has been for the cup and Darwin's impossible quota.

"That little Toad behaving for you?" Darwin asks.

"She's working," Ford replies.

"Make sure she doesn't get lippy. Some of her mother in that one." Darwin comes close to me, and I return my gaze to the bush I've been crouched beside for a long time.

He's looking in my cup now. He's so close I can feel his breath. Goose bumps rise on the back of my neck.

"Looks like you've got a lot of work left yet, Toad," he says—sounding happy, as if my near-empty cup is the best thing he's heard all day. I know he'll be cruel tonight, if we don't all make our quotas.

Darwin retreats—but not too far. He's in the deep shade of the pine trees, perhaps ten paces away from Ford and me.

Ford backs up too, and for a moment it feels nearly normal. It's a lonely feeling.

Before long, though, Mother is walking down the hill to me. She holds her cup carefully as she steps close, watching it as she walks.

Does she known Darwin lurks? I lower my head and let out the robin's call.

The crunch of Mother's feet on leaves slows. But then she closes the space between us and stands over me.

"Have you found much yet?" she asks.

"Only a dozen drops." I look up at her. Framed in the sun, she's only a dark figure with a halo around her head.

"Me too." She sighs and squints up at the sky. "It's nearly noon."

The water is hiding today. Or perhaps it's all gone already, evaporated with the first touch of sun and heat. When we woke this morning, I was already sweating, my shift stuck to my body as if I'd been swimming instead of dreaming.

"Keep me company," I say. Having Mother close will stop me from wanting to stare at Ford every few moments.

"Yes!" Darwin calls out. "Do stay, darling!"

Mother shifts her jaw from side to side; her fingers grow so tight around her cup that her knuckles are white. But she kneels next to me and lifts her spoon.

I shift to make room next to the large bush I'm crouched beside. The water in my cup dances, mocking me. *Drink me,* I imagine it saying. *Don't give me to Darwin.*

"I thought there'd be water coming off the mountain, maybe." I point along tiny rivulets in the soil where water passed, at some point.

"And did you find any?"

"No. I thought maybe this bush would have some, deep inside the branches." I put my arm into the greenery, up to my shoulder, to demonstrate.

Mother nods and sets to work.

I dare to look up at Ford again; his eyes flick away, fast, and he scans the hills above me as if searching for enemies. His eyes narrow and his hand makes a vague shape around the lump of chain in his pocket.

Then I see what Ford does: another person comes out of the woods. It's Asa, headed straight toward Ford. His face, usually flushed red on a hot day like today, is gray. But his eyes still burn blue as he speaks to Ford.

"It's hot. I need a drink," Asa barks.

Ford caps his bottle and slides it back in his pocket.

"Work," Mother hisses at me, and I bend over the plant again. It doesn't have a bit of water to give me, but still I run my spoon over each leaf—and watch.

"Give me some water," Asa says. His voice is not as steady as it was a moment ago.

"Don't let him boss you around!" Darwin calls from the shade.

Ford's lips press together tight and he gazes away, over Asa's head.

Mother is working too, but her spoon moves slowly, and her eyes flick from Ford, to Asa, back to Ford.

Asa's hand flashes toward Ford. Did he poke him? Shove him? I'm not sure. But Ford doesn't move, not even a little. "You want me to drop dead?" Asa asks.

Ford ignores him.

I hold out my cup, a little, offering it. Let him drink the bit that I've gathered.

"Put it down, Ruby," Mother says softly.

But Asa doesn't seem to notice, anyway. Why doesn't he drink his own cup? Or perhaps he has, and it's dry. He'll suffer tonight for it. There's no way to catch up.

Asa's upper body is swaying now, like a tree in the wind. Still, his hand grips his cup. But his eyelids are flickering.

"Asa!" I move, try to go to him, but Mother puts out a hand to stop me. She gives a glance toward Darwin, still watching us from the shade.

"Asa won't thank you for getting hurt." Her voice is hard, but I see tears welling in her eyes.

I try to catch Ford's eyes. He stands less than a foot from Asa, and the near-full water bottle protrudes from his pocket. He could help. He *has* to help.

But he doesn't look at me. He only stares at Asa with a hard, unreadable face.

"Water. Please," Asa moans.

I know what that *please* must have cost Asa, a man who never begs.

Ford shakes his head. "No water."

"That's right!" Darwin calls from the shade. "Let them get their own . . . when they're done getting mine!"

Asa's body gives up. He hits the ground, hard, landing on his side. Ford does not reach out to break his fall.

"Get up," Ford tells him. His voice, low and rough, isn't the same one I heard at the cisterns or in the woods.

How can this be the same boy I kissed? There are the same swirls of ink down his arms, the same stubbly red hair on his head.

"Water," Asa says.

"Please help him," I say.

I don't think Darwin can hear me. But Ford must.

Ford turns his head back, a bit, as if he's going to look at Darwin. But instead his eyes move to me, just for a second. "Better get used to the hot weather, *Toad*," he says.

Toad. It never stung before—never meant much before, except that the Overseers hated us. We always knew that.

But I thought Ford liked us. Or at least he liked me.

Toad.

Ford nudges Asa with the toe of his boot again. "It's real hot in hell too."

Hell: Mother's told me about it. Asa likes to use it for a curse. But it's a place where bad people go—people like Darwin West and the Overseers. Otto will reward every Congregant for their suffering. He would never let us go to a place like hell.

"You'll be the one in hell," Asa says, each word an obvious effort.

"Get up, blasphemer," Ford growls.

"Can't," Asa groans.

"Please—Mother—let me . . . ," I whisper.

Mother sighs, but then she gives me a little push. I stand and go to where Asa lies. I hold my hand out. "I'll help you."

He shakes his head and looks up at Ford. "You give me my water," he says. Even half collapsed on the ground, Asa's got more vinegar than all the other Congregants put together.

"You remember who pays your mama's hospital bills," Darwin calls out.

Ford's hand slides in his other pocket—the one that hangs heavy, heavier than the one holding water. He gives his wrist a flick and the chain flies out of it. I step back just in time; one second later and I would have gotten a good lick from it.

"Go on and beat me," Asa says. Then he closes his eyes and lays his head on the ground.

Ford takes a deep breath. He does not look at Darwin, or me. He keeps his eyes on Asa.

"Get up or else," Ford warns.

Asa doesn't move.

"Do it," Darwin orders.

The chain arches up, then down, the silver glinting in the afternoon sun. It lands across Asa's chest, hard enough to make his body jerk. He grunts and his body goes limp.

"No!" I shriek. Mother is there, suddenly. She grabs me around my waist, stops me from getting any closer.

"He'll hit you too," she says in my ear, holding me so tight and strong I can barely wriggle. "You want that?"

"Is he . . . He's not . . . ," I say. Asa's body is far too still.

"No. Only stunned," Mother answers. "See? He breathes."

Ford is staring at Asa, the chain limp in his hand now. His shoulders are heaving up and down, as if he's just run a long race.

Then Asa's eyes open. He does not ask for anything this time.

"He only wanted water," I say. Ford shows no sign of hearing me.

"Quiet," Mother warns.

Darwin finally ventures from the shade to come stand next to Ford. "You know I was worried about you being soft, boy." He claps one heavy hand on Ford's shoulder. It looks small, almost fine, next to Ford's bulk.

"I'm not soft," Ford says in a low, strangled voice.

"You're getting good and mean now." Darwin's voice is proud, cheerful. "Maybe I'll have you do the whippings tonight."

"It's the job," Ford says, still staring at Asa.

I can't help the low moan that escapes me. Mother gives me one last tight squeeze. "I'll get Asa up," she whispers in my ear. "Don't you interfere."

Mother kneels by Asa and says something very quiet. She looks up at Darwin and Ford, like a dare.

"Get back to work," Ford says.

"You saw what the boy can do with a chain." Darwin gloats.

My stomach heaves. I can't stand to be here, not for another second. I take my cup and spoon and hurry into the woods— sliding behind a tall, broad pine just before I wretch.

There's nothing in my stomach, but still my body heaves, and heaves, as if it's trying to rid itself of that memory: the chain, rising, falling, the dead look on Ford's face. The proud look on Darwin's face.

Mother's right. There's no room for love in the Congregation.

Chapter 19

I have never been to any of the Pelling cabins.

It seems impossible, to have lived here two hundred years, never going to visit them. But the Pellings have always chafed and complained; Mother never sought them out. So I never did either.

It's time for me to make my own choices about who I talk to.

Even when Jonah, Zeke, Hope, and I played together, we never came here. Usually it was Ellie's cabin, where we all hid and played with silly piles of sticks and stones.

But tonight, I need Jonah. It's time to talk of leaving.

It's late, but all three Pelling cabins still have light spilling under the doors. I hear soft laughter coming from one. I wonder what could make them sound so happy. I wonder what I've missed, staying away.

My knocks on Jonah's door are harder than they should be, probably. Someone eases the door open a crack and peers out.

"It's Ruby," I whisper.

The door shuts for a second, then opens wider. Jonah flashes me a smile and runs his fingers through his long, dark hair. It's unbound, hanging to his shoulders.

"Come to marry me?" he asks.

"Let me in," I tell him.

Jonah puckers his lips and crooks an eyebrow. I shudder and shoulder past him.

Inside there're two beds, with three blankets apiece—and pillows, fluffy ones. I count five pairs of pants, and some extra shirts too, hanging on the wall.

Earl sits on a fine wood chair near the fireplace, resting his stockinged feet on the hearth. He grunts and gives me a curt nod.

"Where'd you get all this?" I ask.

"It was all honest enough—some in trade. Other in gambling," Jonah answers.

"Shut it," Earl warns. "Leaders don't need to know what goes on after harvest. 'Specially those who think they're too good for marrying."

"I'd provide for you, Ruby. I told you that," Jonah says.

"Trade with who? Gambling with who?" I ask. I never knew anything like this happened in the Congregation.

"Most Congregants aren't as uppity as your Elders," Earl says.

"Dad, let Ruby sit," Jonah orders.

"No, he doesn't have to," I say, but Earl gets up with a dramatic groan and waves me toward the seat.

Jonah settles on the floor near me. The wood planks are as clean as ours, I realize. And the mudded walls are smooth. I suppose the Pellings can spare some effort for things that matter to them.

"I'd offer you some tea, but we lost our kettle to the Bakers last week, along with my chair. Unlucky night." Jonah shrugs.

"That's fine." I stare into the fire.

"You ready to leave this place, then?" Jonah asks.

"Yes." The answer comes fast and certain. "We need to go soon."

Jonah leans back on his palms and stretches his legs toward the warm fire. "How soon?"

"Tomorrow night." I have some things I need to do first.

"Freedom." Jonah smiles, slow and easy this time, and I see what he might have been before he came here: a Jonah without bitterness or anger. I wonder how I would have been different, if Mother had been able to raise me as a free person.

"First thing I'm doing is finding some food, fried up in fresh grease," he says.

Alarm makes a dull ping in my heart. "We're going to find Otto," I warn him.

"Right. Otto, of course." His smile doesn't slip a bit.

There might be better people to take with me. But I want to go now, and Jonah is ready and willing.

"Meet me behind our cabin," I tell him. "When the moon is at its highest."

"Why not tonight?" Jonah looks around. "You feel sentimental about these woods?"

"I just . . ." I have to put my blood in the Cisterns—but Jonah doesn't know about that. And I have a few things burning in me that I have to say to Ford. "Tomorrow, is all," I say.

"All right then." He shrugs.

"What supplies do you have?" I ask.

"What do *you* have?" Earl retorts.

Jonah laughs.

I try to keep irritation out of my voice. "I'll bring what food we have—and rags, for binding wounds."

Earl reaches under one of the beds. He lifts something high in the air—a spear? No, a stick, nearly as tall as him, with a whittled point. "Won't hurt to have some defense," he says.

I imagine driving the stick straight into an Overseer's gut. "Do you have another?" I ask. "For me?"

"No," Earl growls.

"Yes," Jonah says, tipping his head back to stare at his father. "And we've got some jerky too."

"It'll be enough to get us started," I say.

"It'll be plenty," Jonah says. He looks so joyful; I can't help feeling it too.

Suddenly, strangely, I feel a surge of affection for Jonah. We are going to do something brave and bold together. For this moment, at least, I love him.

"We're going to do it. We're going to find Otto, and I'll tell him all our prayers," I say.

Does Jonah pause a second before he agrees? I think he might.

"Wish I'd gone when I was younger," Earl says.

"You should've," Jonah says.

"If even one of us was gone, Ruby here would've gotten it."

Earl draws his finger across his neck. "Otto might not like that."

"I'm grateful," I say quietly.

"That doesn't put food on the plate," Earl answers with a shrug. "You want to thank us, go fix things."

I swallow and nod. "When we go—we'll have to be quiet. Overseers are in the woods sometimes," I say. For a moment I feel Ford's arms around me—the warmth of his lips against mine—and I am grateful for the dark that hides the flush rising in my cheeks.

"You know how good I am creeping around the woods," Jonah says.

"And at scaring people," I retort.

"You shouldn't be so jumpy," he says.

I draw in a deep breath to stop the string of things I'd *like* to say to him.

"Do you know a bird call?" I purse my lips and let out the robin's trill that Mother and I use. "We could use it for a signal, if we separate."

Jonah answers me with a perfect cardinal's chatter.

"I guess I'll go, then." I stand up. Jonah doesn't.

Earl steps up to me.

"Mind you keep my boy safe and comfortable." He says it with a twisted, knowing grin that turns my stomach.

Any joy left in me ebbs away fast. "Otto will keep all of us safe," I say. I sound a little too perfect, a little too much like Mother, I know.

"You stay in one piece, boy." Earl claps a strong hand on his son's back.

I wish I'd be able to say good-bye to Mother. I wish I'd have her blessing, like Earl is giving to his son.

Once I'm back with Otto, she won't be able to stay angry.

"We'll come back soon, and everything will be different," I say.

"So we go. Tomorrow night," Jonah says. I feel a stab of guilt—making this plan, doing this thing with the wrong boy. But Ford *is* the wrong one. I have to remember what he did, and who he really is.

I'm going to go tell him that now. I have to, before I never see him again.

"Tomorrow," I say. "After midnight."

When the door shuts behind me, the lights in the other cabins are turned off. It's very late now.

But not too late to go tell Ford just how much I hate him.

Chapter 20

Tonight will be the last night I see Ford.

Tomorrow I'll be creeping through the words with Jonah. I'll climb that tree and start my search for Otto. And then, when we find him—freedom.

The moon has slipped behind clouds, and I stumble on my way to the cisterns. Once I go down, hard, and my knee lands square on a rock.

"Damn it," I say, tasting the curse that Asa loves and Mother hates. It's satisfying.

When I get to the cisterns, the wind is still. It's so quiet that I hear my every soft footstep on the road, the grit grinding and sliding under my toes.

But even with the quiet, I don't hear Ford, sitting under the cisterns. I wonder if he's holding his breath.

"You're here," he says, but he doesn't stand. His voice doesn't sound joyful either.

"Yes. I'm here."

"I guess you have to . . . pray."

"Later." I draw in a deep breath and try to steady myself for what I have to say. Even after what he did, this is hard. "I'm done with ever seeing you, Ford. I'm done. I'll have to be done . . . with ever thinking of you, even."

"Ruby, no . . . please don't." Ford stands and comes close enough for me to smell the clean soapy scent of his skin. But he's not close enough to touch. Even if he were, I wouldn't want to.

"You whipped Asa. You pulled that chain out and you laid it right across him. And you didn't even look sorry," I say. My voice shakes. I take another deep breath.

"Do you really think I wanted to?" Ford's hands are both formed into fists. "Do you think I don't hate myself?"

"How could you?" I ask, my voice too loud, but I can't control it.

Ford takes one step closer. "Quiet! You want them to find you?"

"You *whipped* him." I throw out both hands and shove him hard, on the chest. He staggers back a bit, looking surprised.

"It was only once. And I swear, it wasn't that hard—"

"You raised that chain high in the air . . ." I shove him again. "And you whipped it across his body."

"I was as soft as I could be, with *Darwin* watching."

"You were different. That's what I thought," I tell him. "But now I see you're like the rest of them."

"You said I was kinder, once." He lifts his hands, reaching out, but I step back.

"I was wrong," I say.

"Did you want Darwin to hit your friend, instead of me doing it?" he asks.

"At least I already knew he was evil. But you . . ." Tears cut off what I was going to say next. I hate them. I want to stay clean and burning-fire mad.

"I'm not evil," Ford says softly. "I'm a guy trying to keep his job."

"Why? So you can become like them?" I ask.

"So I can keep my mother alive. If I lose this job . . ." Ford turns away from me and paces to the next cistern.

"Would your mother be proud of you?" I ask, loud enough to make sure he can hear me.

I can't tell for sure, but I think Ford shakes his head. His back is turned to me and he's looking up at the cisterns.

No. I won't let him ignore me. I walk close to him. "What *won't* you do?" I ask. "Is there anything you wouldn't do to keep your mother alive?"

His shoulders tense. "Your friend will be fine. I did what I had to do."

"I hate what you did. I think I might even hate you," I say. But those words feel wrong on my tongue. I do hate what he did. But in truth, part of me still wants him.

"You think you're the only one who's mad?" Ford turns to face me.

"What do *you* have to be mad about?"

"I saw what you do here." He reaches up and knocks on the cistern. "I saw what you put in here."

Shock silences me. I look up at the cisterns, and back at Ford. Mother always warned the Overseers might find out, and now it has happened.

"When?" I ask.

"There was a night you came and I hid. I wanted to see what you were really doing." Ford jerks his head toward a thick stand of pines; in the dark I can barely see their trunks.

"You . . . You watched me?"

For a moment he looks almost sorry. But then his face hardens. "I had to know."

"I pray, is all."

"You . . . You *cut* yourself, Ruby. And then . . ." He swallows. "You put your blood in there."

So he knows. My body feels hot with shame. But why? I wasn't the one hiding behind trees.

"I didn't get it. Not until you put your blood on that plant. And even then . . ." He shakes his head. "I didn't want to understand, I think."

"You shouldn't have spied," I say.

"So it's true. You're not even trying to deny it. Ruby . . ." He shakes his head again, as if perplexed, horrified. "Why would you do that?"

Mother has taught me to lie to Overseers, always. But no lies are coming to my lips.

"It's a secret," I say. My voice sounds so small.

"Why? Well . . . I see why. It's disgusting."

Anger is flooding over my shame. Why should I feel as if what I'm doing is wrong?

I clear my throat and try again, but still my words come out quiet. "It's sacred."

"Sacred?" Ford's voice raises, loud and high, and his eyes go wide.

"Yes." I take a step forward, but he steps back. For once I am the pursuer and he is the quarry.

"Do you hate me?" I ask.

"No. I just . . ." Ford puts both hands up in the air, a clear signal: stop. Don't get near me.

"I can't explain more. I've promised my mother, and the Elders," I say. "But it's not . . . a bad thing. I promise."

"Sacred blood. Yeah, that doesn't sound like a bad thing." His voice is heavy with sarcasm.

"It's not bad," I say. It sounds weak, I know.

"You're mixed up in something evil, Ruby. Something really evil." He drops his head and stares at the ground. "I'm sorry for you."

"I'm not evil," I say. "Darwin is evil. Darwin West and the people who work for him."

"I told you. I had to do something or he'd have fired me." He sounds so tired.

"Well . . . I have to do this . . . this thing at the cisterns. Or people would die." I've said too much, I know it.

"There's only one person with sacred blood," he says.

There are two, at least. Otto, and me. Maybe more, even. "You're wrong," I tell him.

"I'm right. I was raised to know this."

"Who, then?" I ask.

"Come on, Ruby, you've got to know that." He speaks with such contempt.

"Otto, then," I tell him.

"The guy you pray to every week? No."

Ford suddenly bridges the space between us and takes both of my hands. "Only Jesus has sacred blood, Ruby. Because he's *God*. Don't you get it?"

"Otto too," I say. And me.

"What you're doing, Ruby? It's a sin," he says.

"Hitting people is a sin. Standing by and letting someone get hurt has to be a sin," I say.

Ford drops my hands. "Don't."

He's backing away again, like I'm something dangerous.

"It's a mortal sin, Ruby. I know it, right here." He forms a fist and thumps his heart.

"You're wrong," I tell him.

"I shouldn't—I can't be with you. Not so long as you're doing . . . *that*." He looks up at the cisterns again and shakes his head.

"Then . . . good-bye." Saying it hurts, hurts as bad as if he'd whipped the chain across my chest today.

"Good-bye." He comes closer, closer.

I mean to fight him. But my body does the opposite, curving near him. Then he is even closer to me, and I to him, and our bodies press together until there isn't space for even a breath of breeze between us.

When he kisses me, I kiss him harder. I slide my hands up, and around his neck, and then down his back, as if I know exactly how to do this. He lets out a low moan, nearly a growl, and his hands slide low, lower until he is pressing the most burning part of me against the hardest part of him and I press even more into him.

This time, it's Ford who pulls away. "No more."

He turns and walks down the road—fast. So fast that it's nearly a trot. I wonder if he'll run as soon as he's out of sight.

He's not asking me to run away with him anymore.

Now he's running away from me.

Chapter 21

It is time to go, nearly.

Mother sleeps in her bed, pain from the day eased with Water.

Boone and the others have all gone home. There is only one last thing to do before I go.

It will be a little while longer before Jonah comes—a little longer before I leave the only home I've ever known. It feels like the wait will be forever, and yet everything is happening too fast. Maybe I was wrong to make this choice, and to pull Jonah into it. Maybe I should keep waiting for Otto, as Mother and the Elders counsel me to.

But then I pull Ellie's pocket watch from under my pillow. I remember the promise I made her.

"Nobody else will die a slave," I say softly, and I slide the watch into my skirt pocket.

The only way I can keep that promise is to go find Otto. We have waited too long already.

drought

There is that one last thing—but I cannot bring myself to do it, not yet.

So I take our makeshift broom—one long tree branch with thin twigs tied to one end—and sweep out the cabin. The dust disappears in a puff when I push it outside the door, lighting the dark for just a second with its whiteness.

Then I straighten our few special things: the picture of Otto, hanging just so, and the soft red shawl that Mother wore the first time she met Otto. I brush away any dust that might have gathered on it.

"Do what you must do," I whisper to myself. But it still feels too soon, too final. So next I take my boots and Mother's boots outside. I clap the soles together and clods of dried dirt fall out. I brush off the toes, the sides, the tops where dirt works its way into our skin.

What new places will my boots find tonight?

Then I return to Mother's side. Her breathing is deeper already, and her cheeks have a little color in them. Darwin was brutal today, but I believe her body is getting better at healing every night.

Still, she will need me—or my blood—while I'm gone. The Congregants will need me too. Without my blood, there will be no Water. There will be nothing to heal Mother, to sustain the rest, until I return with Otto.

It's time to do the last thing, the thing I must do.

Mother keeps a small box beside her bed, filled mostly with nothings: a leaf I gave her on a particularly beautiful fall day, or a twig she found growing over a hidden spring.

But there are four important things in that box too.

I sit on the floor, cross-legged, and set the box softly on my skirts. Then I open the box, slowly, quietly. But the hinges squeak.

There, nested inside a soft clean rag, are the four vials. They are empty now, and cleaned of every bit of blood.

When Otto left the vials, there wasn't a note, or any explanation. But Mother knew what it meant: he was gone, but he wanted her to continue his work. Why else would he leave his blood? And he'd be back too—long before the vials ran out, she prayed.

Now the vials will be filled again. She can make them last for more than a hundred years, if she must.

But that won't be necessary. We'll find Otto soon, I know it. I look over at Mother; she is asleep, her chest barely rising and falling. Then I spread the shawl on the floor, ready to once again hold the vials. Beside it I set two rags, ones I normally would tuck in my pocket in preparation for the cisterns.

Next I tuck the first vial between my two bare feet, pressing my heels together to keep it steady and upright. The glass feels so slight against my skin. I must be careful not to break it.

One long slash lengthwise on my arm; it hurts, but I keep the stone steady and press down firm. The pain will last for a few minutes, but this blood will sustain the Congregation for as long as I need to find Otto.

I hold my arm at a slant, fingers pointing toward the floor. The blood runs into the vial, *drip drip drip*. I press at the top of the cut to make it go faster.

How did Otto fill the vials? Did he have a knife that cut just where it needed to, one slim easy cut without jagged edges? How did he steady the vial—for certainly he was alone, filling the vials while Mother slept and then slipping away.

"I'm coming," I whisper to him.

One vial is full. I wedge the old cork into the bottle, my blood still running down my arm. It falls on the floor now, dark drops, and I wipe frantically at it. The vial tips and some blood slides around the edge of the cork.

I steady the vial and press the rag against my arm. How did the blood escape the vial? The old cork must have shrunk. I wait for my arm to stop bleeding. I sneak a look at Mother to make sure she's not seeing any of this. But she sleeps steady, and my heart slowly, slowly returns to normal.

When the blood stops, I rip a bit of rag off the edge and wrap it around the cork, then stuff it in the vial. It will have to do.

I fill a second vial, and then make a fresh cut on the other arm for the third. This time, while I watch the blood, thoughts of Ford crowd my mind.

What you're doing is a sin, he said.

How does he know? Mother is our Reverend, not him. She knows Otto. She knows his holiness. How can Ford judge?

But what if he's right? What if we were never meant to live this long? I don't know what I was meant to do, or even whether I am the same kind of human that my mother is.

All I know is that Otto has the answers . . . and salvation for the Congregation.

Another vial full. I set it next to the first and make a third cut on my other arm. My head buzzes a little as I watch the blood roll down the side of the glass. I've bled more to heal Mother, I'm sure of it. But somehow this makes me feel weaker.

I wish I'd asked Ford more questions about the modern world; I wish he'd somehow taught me everything I need to know to survive it, to thrive in it.

Finally I can start the fourth vial, and a final cut. Both arms sting from the necessary slashes. But already the wounds are knitting together; by the time I leave, my arms will be smooth.

Then, a tap on the wall behind me.

Jonah is here.

He can't come inside—he knows nothing of my blood, and he can't ever know. I cork the half-full vial, set it down, and hurry outside.

Jonah stands in the shadows of the cabin, staring at what's left of the Lake. "You ready?" he asks, without looking at me.

"Wait a few minutes more," I tell him.

"Not backing out, are you?" Now he looks at me, and I see his eyes are puffy.

"I'll be here in a moment. I promise," I tell him.

"Hurry," is his answer.

When I'm back inside, I have to cut my arm again. Then the final vial is full.

All four finished vials sit on the shawl, nestled against one another, waiting. I wrap them up and set them on my pillow. The red fabric is like a pool of blood.

I can leave now; everything I must do here is done.

But first, I kneel beside Mother's bed and clasp my hands together, fingers knitted through each other, and look up to heaven.

"Otto," I whisper, "let this be the right decision . . . and watch over her while I'm gone." Then I stand up and drop a last kiss on Mother's head.

When I step outside, my way to Jonah is blurred with tears. But he meets me before I reach the back of the cabin. He offers me one of the tall pointed sticks.

"This place don't deserve tears."

"But the people do," I say.

Jonah reaches back and touches the wood wall of the cabin. He shakes his head, lowers it for a second. "Some of them."

I struggle to swallow the tears that want to swamp me. Feeling Jonah's stare, I duck my head, let the tears drip onto the leaves by my feet.

"You ready?" he asks.

I nod and lead the way into the woods.

As I slide my feet over the leaves and roots, I barely hear Jonah's passage. When I reach a stand of trees, I stop for a moment and look back to make sure he still follows.

Jonah is directly behind me. He gives me a grin.

"Pretty scenery," he whispers.

I turn away before he can see my face, or the blush that crawls over it. I couldn't have chosen a worse ally—except for his strength and his willingness to do this.

"No sign or sound of the Overseers," I whisper. "But keep quiet anyway."

Jonah gives a tense nod.

I lead him deeper into the woods; as we go, our path

crosses the line of poles sometimes, the black rope arching over our heads. Still, I wonder what these are for.

When we're nearly halfway to where I think the tree is, I motion for us to stop. There are blurred edges around everything I look at, and the air seems to waver. Perhaps I took too much blood for the vials.

"We'll rest here for five minutes," I tell Jonah, sitting on a stump. It's old, soft, and it sinks a little into the earth from my weight.

But Jonah stays standing. "Let's get out while we can."

"We've got all night. If we're tired, we'll be noisy," I tell him.

"You think you're the boss, don't you? A little Darwin West?" Jonah asks.

"It was my idea, wasn't it?" I ask.

"I could've run anytime I wanted, except for you." Jonah gives me a glare, then looks up the hill again.

"I owe the Congregation, I know it," I say.

"You hear that?" Jonah asks, his voice a little unsteady.

I hear leaves rustling against one another in the wind. I hear the cry of a night bird, far off. Jonah's breathing is growing shorter, more frightened.

"I don't hear anything," I say.

Jonah makes an impatient motion with his hand—*wait*.

I close my eyes so there's nothing to distract my mind. I try to push away the sound and sense of Jonah, listen to the thing that's made his eyes go wide.

And then I hear something. A faint rumbling sound, coming from below, where we started from.

"A truck?" I guess.

"Overseers are out tonight," Jonah says grimly.

"We'd best hurry." I stand up.

"Like I was saying." Jonah motions up the hill and gives me a smile to curdle milk. Now my feet seem to find every stick, every stone to send tumbling down the hill. Jonah is noisier too. But we're moving faster—and in the end, as long as we escape, does it matter if they hear us first?

All we must do, I realize now, is keep the Overseers behind us.

Chapter 22

Only a few more minutes and we'll be at the birch grove. Ford said the tree was only a bit farther, past that. How many heartbeats before we're in the tree, across the branches, into freedom?

Will it feel any different?

I pick up the pace into a run. I don't want to wait another second—and there could be Overseers behind us. I see the birch grove, off to the right, ghostly columns rising atop the hill.

"Keep going," Jonah whispers from behind me. It spurs me forward, past Ellie's grave and over the hill.

Now the land slopes down, down; I stumble once, and then again. But then I see it: the fence, long, tall, with curls of sharp wire all along the top. It's been a long time since I've seen it . . . a long time since any of us bothered to go all the way to the fence. It might've even been when I was playing with Jonah and the others.

And there, a tree. It's a sapling, still, with a slender trunk. But it's tall, and its branches reach even higher than the cruel wires that stop anyone from climbing the barrier.

Ford told me the truth. Joy courses over me. I don't know if it's because I've found the way out . . . or because there's proof, there in a tree, that Ford is truly a good person.

But before I can reach it, I stumble again. This time I cannot catch myself. I sail through the air for a moment, and then land hard. My body is betraying me again and again tonight.

I can't breathe. I try to pull in air, but my chest is impossibly tight. I close my eyes and pray.

Otto save me.

Otto protect me.

Then, hands under me, lifting me. "You can't fly, you know," Jonah says. "Not even you."

And my breath returns to me, hard, like the wind that comes before a storm.

Jonah traces the fence with his stick, looks up at the sharp wires that top it. "This tree of yours is a skinny thing."

"But look at the branch—there . . ." I point up. "It's thicker than the others. And it goes right over the fence."

"If we move fast . . ." He studies the tree.

"We'll make it. And then we'll be gone from here," I say.

Jonah lets out a soft whoop and jabs his stick in the air. Then his face sobers. "We got lazy. We should've been checking for things like this. Glad *you* found it."

Guilt, familiar now, stabs me. But I don't correct him.

Then I think of all the Congregants sleeping in their cabins, the long walk between us and them. We get to leave. They must harvest again tomorrow.

"Should we go back and get them all?" I ask.

"I'm not going back all that way. I'm going up"—Jonah points to the tree, making a long arc with his arm—"and over, and gone."

"You're right. We have to go now," I say. "We'll find Otto, and then everyone will be saved."

I don't know if I'll be strong enough to leave again. Haven't I been dreaming of it forever? And I never found the strength, never found the way, before Ford . . . and my promise to Ellie.

"And Darwin West . . ." Jonah makes a cutting motion with his finger across his throat.

He catches my revolted look. "Like you haven't dreamed of doing it yourself?" Jonah says. "Like you haven't killed him a thousand times in your mind?"

"I—I haven't," I stammer.

"After what he's done to us, Otto better kill him. As long as that man is alive, we'll never be free." Jonah spits on the ground—in the dark, it could just as easily be his father standing there.

But I can't argue with him. For the first time, doubt steals into my heart. Can Otto save us? Is this why he never did come back—he couldn't find a way to fight Darwin?

"Do you still hear it?" I ask Jonah in a low voice. "Those noises?"

"No. Not for a while. But—" He looks behind him too.

"I know," I tell him. "We need to hurry."

"Climb, then," he says.

When I hesitate, Jonah slips around me and shimmies up the tree trunk. The tree bows under his weight, but not as much as I feared. It'll hold us. I'm nearly certain.

I follow, fast. It's easier than I imagined, branches in just the right spots.

Jonah is sitting up high, not on the long branch yet.

"Go," I urge him. "Crawl over the branch and drop."

But he shakes his head, just staring at the branch, not moving.

"What if it don't hold?" he says.

"Move quickly and it'll be safe," I tell him.

"How do you know?"

"I . . . don't. But this has to work. It just . . . has to."

Jonah's lips move, but no noise comes out.

"Please go," I tell him.

"What's out there?" he asks.

Otto. Freedom. Food. "I don't know," I tell him. "But we'll find out together."

Jonah shakes his head again and wraps his legs tighter around the branch he's sitting on. "You go around me," he says.

"You're the one who just shoved around *me*," I say.

"Just go around," he says again.

"I can't. It's too narrow. The branches above—"

"They'll break, I know." Jonah looks up, then down again. "I'll move as soon as I can."

Here we are at the edge of freedom, and now he is too afraid to move?

Then I hear a strange noise. It's a low, persistent hum, as if a cloud of mosquitoes hovered near us. It doesn't change, doesn't get closer or farther away. It only *hums*.

I want to ask Jonah if he hears it. But he's frozen in fear

already. And now fear slides over me too, like ice forming on the top of the Lake—slow, but certain, freezing me. I am as stuck as Jonah.

"Go," I tell him.

"I can't. I can't. I can't." Jonah is rocking now, back and forth, his legs swinging.

"Don't you want to be free?" I ask.

"Yes," Jonah says.

"You want food? *Good* food?" I ask. "The kind without mold, as much as you want?"

"Yes." His voice shakes. He looks down. But he does not jump.

"Hurry," I say. My voice shakes.

I know we must go *now*, that this is our chance—our only chance—that somehow the hum means soon we will be caught.

"Hurry," I say again, louder. Jonah shakes his head again—if I could move myself, get a little closer, I think I would push him with the bottom of my boot.

Panic makes me forget myself. I shout it as loud as I can. "GO!"

And then, sun: sun, coming from above, everywhere, all at once. There is no sunrise, no warning, no birds singing. Only sun, blinding.

Jonah lets out a string of curses, better than anything I've ever heard from Asa. And I? I squeeze my eyes shut, like a coward. It hurts too much to keep them open.

"What did you do?" Jonah growls.

"Nothing. I only—" I only shouted. I only did something to make the world change, somehow. I brought him here and now . . .

How else can the sun rise, all at once?

But then I hear noises—shouts, men's shouts, coming from below us, and close.

"There's some of 'em out here!" someone yells.

The voice isn't familiar, at least from the top of the tree, but I know who it belongs to: an Overseer.

I open my eyes again and see that this is not the same kind of brightness that comes from the sun. Instead the woods are lit in pools of light. We sit in the middle of one.

How did the Overseers do this? It's as if they lit a hundred lanterns, all at once.

"It's the poles," Jonah says. He points, and I squint to follow the line of his finger.

He's right. Every pole that we Congregants dug a hole for— every pole that we struggled to put up straight—now has a lantern glowing from the top.

Every hiding place in the woods, every shadow I crept through, is gone. All there is now is light.

Away in the woods, there is the familiar squalling sound that came from Ford's talk box, every night we talked. Someone is close. The light in our faces makes it impossible to see them, though.

"They're coming," I tell Jonah. "You have to go, or we're caught."

"Kiss me," he says. "Kiss me or I can't do it."

How can I not? I lean close to him, our lips hovering. I expect him to take a kiss like a Pelling takes everything—greedy, fast, wanting more.

But the touch of his lips is so gentle, I almost don't know he's touched mine. "You'll marry me yet," he says. Then he edges out onto the long branch.

The tree makes a groaning sound. Jonah freezes, but only for a second. Then he slides farther on the branch. It bends low, and then lower.

No. It's not safe. It won't hold him.

"Jonah," I whisper. "Come back."

He shakes his head and inches out. There. He's far enough to let go and make it over the fence.

Then he looks back at me and grins. "Freedom!"

Crack. The branch snaps and Jonah is plummeting.

The whole tree shakes and sways; I nearly slip to the ground. But I hold on to the branches and watch the flurry of green and brown and Jonah falling.

He lands over the fence, out of Darwin's rule at last. But he doesn't say anything when he hits the ground. There's the rattle of the leaves, and the terrible heavy thump of his body.

"Jonah?" I whisper. "Jonah?"

He lies crumpled on top of the branch that betrayed him, not moving. His head is turned at an impossible angle. I can't tell if he's breathing.

Can I leap over the fence without the branch to take me close? I have to. There's still a chance. Maybe I can help Jonah if I go now.

But my body is frozen.

There's something—a breaking branch, an exhalation—something. I look back and see a hand snaking up, reaching for me.

I grasp the trunk of the tree. But the fingers find me and circle my ankle. Then they tug.

Chapter 23

Ford's fingers are tight around my ankle. His eyes are open wide, shocked—but not for long.

"Get out of this tree *now*," he growls, and he gives my leg a strong tug.

What will Jonah do if he wakes up and I'm not there? What if he needs healing? Worse—what if he doesn't? In my heart, I know the answer.

"Hurry," Ford orders. His voice is still rough. Nobody would believe we've shared kisses.

I do what he says: I scramble back down the tree, tugging at my skirt any time it catches on the rough bark or a short branch. The light shining on the tree makes coming down even easier than climbing up was.

"Where's the boy?" Ford asks.

I point at the fence, and the branch and body behind it.

"Great." Ford lets out a groan. "Get down on the ground, Ruby. Get on your stomach and cover your head. Whatever you do—"

"Why?" I ask.

"—don't move until I say," he finishes, as if I hadn't spoken at all. Then he reaches into his pocket.

Would he really do it? Would he really hit me? I don't want to know. I fall to my knees and press my cheek against the cold ground.

They won't kill me—will they? For this? I'm a good worker. But they'll whip me. They'll hurt me.

"Don't hurt me," I say. "Not you."

But Ford doesn't answer. He only paces. I watch the path of his boots, back and forth.

There are other voices, closer now, more men. More Overseers. All coming this way, and us lying like broken birds in the bright light.

"You could have been hurt," he whispers. "I would've brought ropes. I would've made sure you were safe."

"We thought we could do it." It's all I can say. I look at Jonah's crumpled body again.

"Is that all of you?" Ford asks. "Just you and . . . him?"

"Just us," I answer. "But Ford—Jonah, he doesn't mean what you . . . used to mean. He just—"

"Why should I believe you?" His voice cracks. Then it quiets. "Stay where you are. Don't get up when they get here. Just . . . Just shut up." When I look up, Ford is looking straight at me, his lips trembling.

I put my cheek back on the ground and mutter a prayer.

"Save us, Otto," I say. "Spare us from pain."

I chant it once, twice, three times.

And then more Overseers arrive. I watch their boots rush into the clearing—four, eight, at least ten pairs of boots. They jostle together, as if excited. I think of Jonah touching the cabin wall before we left tonight. It feels as if that was a week ago. How could we have been safe—or at least the same as we'd been for hundreds of years—just a few hours ago?

"What's this?" Darwin's voice comes from near my feet, but I don't turn to look. Ford's warning is enough to keep me still.

"It's, um, an experiment," Ford says.

"Whaddya mean?" Darwin answers. "An experiment?"

"Yeah, well, I had this idea." Ford sounds too nervous. Too weak. It will make Darwin far too interested in hurting him.

"An idea," Darwin says.

"The lights—the, um, Toads have never seen anything like them, right?" Ford asks.

"Duh," Darwin replies, and all the men laugh. They were so quiet up until now, I could have almost forgotten they were there, listening, watching—waiting to do whatever Darwin tells them to do to us.

"So I grabbed a few of them and brought them out here," he says.

"You grabbed the Queen Toad's little baby?" Darwin's voice is full of doubt.

"Her mother's half dead. It's not like she could fight me." Ford lets out a laugh. It sounds forced to me, but some of the other men join him.

"Where's the others, then?" Darwin asks.

"There's just one more. He tried to run when the lights came on." Ford picks up my stick, abandoned on the ground, and pokes it at the fence.

Darwin walks away. I hear him grunt. "Pity. He was a strong one."

And then he returns to me. His boot nudges my rear end. "Roll over, Toad."

I obey—but I sit up too, wrapping my arms around my knees. Now I see all the Overseers: eleven of them, in a half circle around me.

"He telling the truth?" Darwin asks me.

I nod. "He came to the cabin and yanked me out."

Another Overseer speaks. He sounds disappointed. "But nobody's allowed in the cabins."

"That's right." Darwin pauses for a second, still looking at me. Then he looks over at Ford. "You broke my rules, boy."

"I wanted to see how bad it would scare them. And it scared them good." Ford sounds so proud of himself, I almost believe he did the thing he's saying he did. "Look how that one broke his neck."

"How about that." Darwin looks up at the lights. "Never thought about that part."

"They never seen anything like it," an Overseer says.

"Probably think the moon exploded or something," another laughs.

Darwin squats beside me and grabs my chin, hard, so I'm forced to look at him.

"You scared of the lights, Toad?" he says in an overly kind voice.

"Yes," I say. I'm scared, mostly, of what it means. Will we ever have dark woods to hide us, now?

"Get used to it," Darwin says. "You'll be seeing a lot of those pretty, pretty lights."

"You're the same age as your mother, when I met her." Darwin gives me a wink. "Or close enough, eh?"

I shiver. "I'm younger," I say.

"She was the prettiest girl in town. And she wanted me." A flicker of a smile changes his face, for only a second. "Can you imagine that, Toad?"

I lower my eyes and give him a very small shrug.

"Too bad your pa came round, huh? Too bad for everyone." Darwin slides his hand in his pocket, and I can't help it, I flinch— but then he stands and walks to Ford.

His steps are slow and certain.

Save him, I pray to Otto. *Protect him.*

"These Toads belong to *me*," Darwin says. One more step and he is so close to Ford, their chins nearly touch.

Ford is taller than Darwin, by almost half a head. Darwin takes off his hat and tilts his head up to meet Ford's eyes.

"You don't touch them unless I tell you to." Darwin's slices his other hand through the air and deals a hard slap against the side of Ford's head.

Ford's head jerks sideways. He doesn't cry out.

"You don't *look* at them unless I tell you to." Another slap.

"*My* Toads. *My* operation. Got it?" Darwin asks.

"I got it."

"You like this job? You *want* this job?" Darwin asks.

Ford squeezes his eyes shut for a second. "Yes, sir. I want this job. I need this job."

"We'll see." Darwin takes a step back and puts his hat back on his head.

He looks at me. "Might as well work, since you're here," he says.

Darwin points at one of the Overseers. "You bring any cups with you?"

"There's some in the truck," the man says, sounding surprised.

"Go get one, and a spoon," Darwin orders.

Then he grins and spreads his arms wide, looking up at the lights. "Now you can harvest at night too. Woods are a lot wetter, then. I wonder how long you Toads can go without sleep?"

I try to harden my face and press back the tears that threaten, but it's no use. They spill down my face and puddle along the neck of my dress.

Darwin *tut-tuts*. "I'd cry too, Little Toad."

The Overseer is back from the truck. Two men drag me to my feet, and then I'm holding the cup and spoon.

"Half a cup, and then you can go back to bed." Darwin looks at the thick gold watch on his wrist. "Work quick and you might see your pillow."

I wait for my directions, but Darwin turns to Ford first. "We're going to have a good time together, now," he says. Then he gestures to a man behind him. "Take him to the tool shed. Tie him up real good."

Ford drops his head and stares at the ground.

The other Overseer has hesitated for too long. "You want to go in there with him?" Darwin asks.

Then two of them step forward, one for each side of Ford, and grab his arms. They treat him as roughly as if he were a Congregant.

Darwin watches them take Ford away, but he doesn't follow—not yet. First he turns to me and gives me the sort of sick smile that he usually saves for my mother.

"A half cup for you, by sunrise," he says. "And if you don't?"

He partly pulls the chain out from his pocket.

Darwin doesn't tell me where to start my harvest. He only turns and leaves, pointing at a few Overseers to stay behind and watch me.

"Remember—*my* property," he warns.

All that is left is to do the thing I do best. I obey. I kneel by the fence, and scrape leaves, and put drops of water in the cup.

And I whisper to Jonah.

"Jonah," I say. "Wake up, Jonah."

But he never stirs—not even when my cup is half full and I stand.

"I'll marry you," I tell him. "I'll marry you, Jonah Pelling." And maybe I would, if he woke—if it meant he didn't die because of my childish attempt to escape.

Still he doesn't answer, and the sky is tinged with gray at the horizon. Morning is coming.

"Good-bye," I tell him.

And then I leave Jonah alone, behind the fence—free, and gone.

Chapter 24

I do something terrible: I don't go to Earl's cabin. I slink home and hide the vials with my blood in the deepest shadows under my bed. Then I slide under my covers, willing sleep to hide my sins.

"I'm sorry," I whisper—to Ford, to Jonah, to Otto, to whoever can hear me. "I never wanted to hurt anyone. I only wanted to help."

Maybe Otto does hear, for he grants me sleep. When I wake, my pillow is wet. Mother is shaking me.

"You will sit up *now*, Ruby Prosser," she barks.

I squeeze my eyes shut and will the day to go away. Let me slide back to last night, let me change everything. Please, Otto.

But then someone coughs—a man, here in the cabin. That makes me sit up fast.

There, at the door, stand all the Elders—and Earl. They're ghostly in the gloom of the cabin, barely lit by the light filtering in around the door and through the cracks in the wall mud.

"Found my boy," Earl says. "Me and Zeke had a bad feeling."

I am pinned under his stare. I try to say something, but I am held by the hatred in his eyes.

Then Asa comes closer. He tilts his head as he looks at me, studying me. "Earl here says you tried to run."

"He's dead," Earl says.

"Is it true?" Hope asks. Her voice quavers a little.

"Jonah's dead," I whisper.

"Yes, we know, but . . ." Hope reaches for Earl, but he steps away from her, never taking his eyes off me. His fists are balled tight.

"Did you try to run?" Asa asks. "That's what we need to know."

"He was dead on the road, like an animal," Earl growls.

"Yes." The word barely comes out, and I clear my throat. "We tried to run. The tree branch broke."

"I should have known," Mother says. Then she turns her back on me.

"Mother, please . . ." But I don't know how to ask for what I need, and I don't know if I deserve it.

She walks away from me and cracks open the cabin door. "There's not much time," she says to the group, as if I weren't here at all.

"Best we could do was touch him through the fence." Earl's voice chokes off and he looks to the side, brushes his arm over his eyes.

Only Boone hasn't spoken. He stands behind the rest of them, arms folded, lips tight.

"I stayed with him, as long as I could," I tell Earl. "But . . . I think he was already gone. He fell hard."

"Must've been real broke up, being able to sleep and all," he says.

"You're nothing but a child, Ruby," Mother says.

Now I find the strength to stand. "We had a plan. We were going to find Otto."

"But Otto will come to us!" Hope exclaims.

"Hasn't yet," Earl says.

"I thought he might need a reminder—someone who could bring prayers to him," I say.

"You're lying." Mother springs forward and grabs both my arms. She gives me a good shake. "You only wanted to get away from here."

"No, Mother! We were going to come back, just as soon as we found Otto."

Then Mother drops her hands from me, letting out a low laugh snagged with tears. "If it were only that easy, Ruby."

Finally Boone speaks. "You were going to do this with *Jonah*?"

Earl swings to stare at Boone. "Girl needed protection."

"You knew about this?" Mother exclaims.

First Earl tries to meet her eyes, but then he drops his head. "I knew."

"Should've told us before they scrammed," Asa says.

"Seemed like a good plan, fighting. Gave them weapons," Earl says.

"We weren't going to fight," I say quickly, even though I know it's what Jonah truly hungered for. "We only went to find Otto."

"So you had *weapons*. And how many Overseers did you conquer, Ruby?" Mother says.

"None," I whisper, thinking of Ford, who saved me with his lies. "But the Overseers found me there, with . . . Jonah. After he fell."

"Are you hurt?" Hope asks. "Did they punish you?"

"They didn't hit me. They made me work," I say. "I was up most the night harvesting."

Mother snorts. "What good is a cup and spoon in the dark?"

"Perhaps that's why they made her do it," Boone says softly.

"No," I say. "Those poles have lanterns on the tops of them now—the brightest lanterns you've ever seen.

"Last night, they turned them on. Right before . . ." I look at Earl.

He crosses his arms and lets out a low curse.

"Darwin said we'll harvest all the time now," I say.

Hope sucks in a shuddering breath; then tears well in her eyes.

"He's the devil." Earl spits on the floor, ignoring Mother's sharp look.

"Did anyone else go with you?" Hope asks. "Is anyone else missing?"

"No," I tell her quickly. "It was only Jonah and me."

"Jonah, of all people." She shakes her head.

"Some of this falls on you," Earl snaps at Hope. "He never would've tried to leave if you'd taken him."

"Oh . . . I think he would've tried to find a way out, with or without me." Hope gives me a small smile. "This was his idea, wasn't it?"

It would be so easy to say yes. But it's my fault, and mine alone.

"It was my idea," I say.

Mother grabs my dress off the wall peg and tosses it at me. "Get dressed. It's nearly harvest time."

"She's going to pay. My boy's dead," Earl says.

"Something's got to change." Boone glances at the drawing of Otto hanging on the wall, and I follow his eyes. Even in the dim, I feel like my father's stare is on me too.

"I'll pay for it," I say. "Somehow. I'm sorry, so sorry."

I take a step closer to Earl, then another. In such a small place, it only takes one more step until I am inches away from Jonah's father.

"I know I can't fix it," I say.

He lifts his face to meet my eyes. And then his face crumples.

"Jonah wanted freedom," he says. "That's how you can pay, you worthless snip."

Then he shoves past me to the door. He flings it open, and the sudden glow of predawn light makes us all turn our heads a little.

"I'll go talk to the fool." Asa jerks his head toward the door. "And as for my vote, I say she's gone."

When he leaves, Asa slams the cabin door behind him. It's dark again.

"What does he mean . . . gone?" I ask.

"You set yourself above us, Ruby," Mother says. "You put yourself above everyone else."

"No. No! I didn't."

"We sustain. We endure. We *wait*," Hope reminds me.

"If you knew . . . ," I start. Then I swallow. "I only wanted to do the right thing for the Congregation . . . as the Leader."

Mother lets out a short, barking laugh. "Leader. That was the last thing you were last night, Ruby."

"Selfish. Childish. Cowardly," Boone says.

"Disobedient," Mother adds.

"I think she was brave," Hope says softly.

"Enough," Mother snaps.

Hope doesn't say anything more. In truth, Mother rules the Elders.

"Are you going to make me leave?" I ask.

"Leave? Isn't that what you just tried to do?" Mother asks.

"Asa said he'd vote for me to be gone."

Hope takes a few small steps and then my hand is in hers. She squeezes softly. "He means he doesn't want you to be Leader."

I wasn't sure I wanted to be Leader, when they asked me. But now I feel panic, shame. I've become used to it—proud of it, even. "And you?" I ask her.

"I want a Leader who won't abandon us," Hope says.

"I was only trying to save us," I say.

Mother lets out another snort.

"But I won't . . . I won't leave again." I look over at her, but she does not return my glance.

"Then my vote is that you stay, Leader," Hope says.

"It's up to Boone, then," Mother says. "Since Ruby can't vote."

"You said you wanted to pay for what you did," Boone says. Still he hasn't moved; he stays near the door, as solid as a wall of stone.

"I'd do anything," I say.

"It's simple." Boone draws in a deep breath and lets it out before he continues. "No more secrets, Ruby. None."

"No more secrets," I echo. But one secret will stay buried: Ford.

"And if we ever catch you lying . . ." Boone trails off and looks at Mother.

"Then you're done," Mother finishes.

"As Leader," Hope adds.

"Done," Boone says.

A chill runs down my back, but I stand up straight and lift my chin. "No more secrets, I promise it."

I'll keep them all safe until my father comes to save us.

Chapter 25

The Overseers come in the middle of the night, with loud horns and bright lights shining from the tops of their trucks. A loud, distorted voice comes from one of the trucks: Darwin, speaking as loud as if he had ten pairs of lungs.

"Sleepy time is over!" he shouts. "Come out and get to work!"

It's been three nights since Jonah died, three nights since the Overseers took Ford away to Darwin's tool shed.

"Wake up, Mother." I give her a gentle shake, but her eyelids only flutter. "It's time to work."

There's a little Water left in the bucket beneath her bed. I dip my fingers in it, then flick the drops onto her face. She does not even twitch.

"Darwin's waiting. He might hurt us." I give her a harder shake; her body is heavy and limp.

"Come when you can," I tell her.

Then I draw the sheet a little tighter under her chin and throw my dress over my underskirts. There's nothing I can do—

she will not rise; she will not walk. For once we will have to harvest without her.

All the dark and shadows are gone from nighttime. Pools of stark light fill the woods, with softer light that is more like sunshine between each bright spot. The road still has some dark spots. As I stare at the woods, I stumble in a few of them. Even my feet are shocked by the change the lights bring.

Up ahead, I spot Hope and Gabe, small and tall, striding down the road and holding hands. I hurry my pace to a trot until I reach them.

"Good morning," I say.

Both are looking at the woods; Gabe gives me a nod but doesn't tear his eyes away from the strange lights.

Hope gives me a smile. "It's good that you told us about the lights."

"Never seen the like," Gabe mutters.

Hope rests her head on his shoulder, only for a moment. "They're like candles, hundreds of them, is all," she says.

"Some will say they're the devil's work," Gabe answers.

Devil. I think of Ford, who thinks maybe I am a devil, but still helped me. "Isn't it the devil's work?" I ask. "Is anyone more devil than Darwin West?"

"Quiet," Hope warns. "And Ruby . . . where's your mother?"

"I couldn't wake her," I answer. "She breathes . . . but that is all."

"Otto save her," she says.

When we get to the clearing, the Congregants stand about, bodies hunched as if still trying to steal sleep. Some shade their eyes against the harsh lights, while others stare straight at them.

Overseers stand in a circle around us, but some are still coming up the road in their trucks. And there aren't as many as usual. I guess Darwin has to let them get some rest. I don't see Ford among them.

We stand close and wait for Darwin to speak.

His eyes fall on me, and look around me—for Mother, I'm sure. But he doesn't ask for her. His smile only grows bigger.

"Tonight is a new kind of night!" he calls out. "Now we can work without the sun!"

Darwin pauses as if he expects something—for us to cheer, perhaps? Or groan? When nobody speaks, he grins and holds up two fingers.

"Double cups today!" he calls out.

"Two cups? We'll all be beaten," Gabe says to Hope.

But we all shuffle into line to get our cups and spoons. Arguing won't make the inside of the cup any wetter.

"There's a lot more water in the night, hiding in the leaves," I say.

"Guess you'd know what's out here at night." Gabe looks back to give me a quick glance.

"Where are the cups?" Darwin asks.

The Overseers all stare at one another. Finally one answers. "Nobody brought 'em."

"*Get* them!" Darwin roars.

The man he shouted at raises his talk box to his mouth and mutters something into it.

Then we all wait. The Overseers shoulder their guns and watch us with bleary eyes.

The evening breeze moves over the back of my neck and raises goose bumps along my hairline. Until the sun comes up, it will be damp and cold. I wonder if the bright lights will bring any warmth.

If they do, they'll also drive the water away. The best place to be this night—or is it early morning?—will be in the few shadows left between the lights.

A few minutes after the Overseer speaks into his talk box, one more red truck pulls up. The man who gets out of the driver's side is like all the rest: tall, beefy, interchangeable.

He flips down the back of the truck to pull out the box that holds the cups.

Then the other front door opens and shuts; I can't see who's come out until he walks around the other side of the truck.

It is Ford—Ford, with long deep bruises on his arms, with a cut on his face that's red and festering.

I gasp.

"Ruby? Are you all right?" Hope's curious glance makes me realize I must look away from Ford.

Instead, I look at the cups. "They look bigger than usual," I say. "Filling them will be hard."

"As I said," Gabe answers.

"I . . . I changed my mind. You were right," I tell him.

He gives a satisfied grunt and turns back to his place in line. I let Hope stand next to him, and take the place behind her. Now I can look at Ford more carefully.

For a moment, he stands to the side, not holding a gun or offering cups to anyone. He looks lost.

But then Darwin comes close to him and says something in a voice so quiet that I cannot hear.

Ford lowers his head for a moment and stares at the ground. *Look at me*, I will him.

But he doesn't. When he looks up, his eyes are straight on Darwin. He nods.

Darwin claps him on the back, a move that makes Ford wince, then points at the cups.

Ford takes a step, then two steps, to the man with the cups. He is limping, favoring his right leg. His foot dangles oddly.

Our line moves twice as fast now, having two Overseers up front; I wonder if I'll get to go to him when it's my turn. Will he at least meet my eyes?

The closer I get, the more damaged he looks. There's a lump on his temple, and his lips are cracked and bleeding.

Only four people wait in front of me now. One goes to the man in front, another to Ford. Then Gabe and Hope get their cups, and it is my turn to go to Ford.

He gives me my cup. Our fingers don't brush; no part of us touches, save the air that flows between us.

He doesn't look at me.

It's time for me to move. "I'm sorry," I say. "I'm sorry you ever met me."

He doesn't even seem to hear me. He looks over my shoulder at the line and shouts, "Next!"

Chapter 26

Seven nights I've come to the cisterns, no longer hiding from Ford. But he's never here.

I check the shadows beneath each cistern and peer into the pools of dark in the woods. The lights aren't on yet; in a few hours, I'm certain, the lights will be burning and we will be harvesting. I might only have an hour, even.

Ford isn't anywhere.

"Come soon," I say out loud, quietly, and then louder.

But of course there is no answer.

I finally know what I should do; I know what I should say. But I know better than to find him during harvest to say it. He might not want to listen. And it might take some time to get it out.

The night is cooler, with a hint of the fall that's to come soon. When the weather cools, it happens fast, the leaves changing in what seems to be only a few days. Mother says things were gentler off the mountain, that spring and fall crept in slowly. But here the weather seems eager to be its most extreme, nothing in between.

Still no Ford. There's no more time to wait. I climb up the ladder to the cistern — nearly full, I think, from all the harvesting we've done at night — and make the quick cut to my arm. It barely hurts. I murmur my prayer and count.

One. Two. Three. Finished.

Finding time to get out to the cisterns has been hard. Darwin gives us a few hours to rest after the sun sets, but that is all. Far before the sun is up — when the sky is still only stars and moon — the trucks are driving around the Lake again, blasting their wake-up warnings.

On the second night, Mother was strong enough to come with us. When Darwin announced our quota — three cups, as he's seen how easily we find two — her lips pressed together so hard, they turned white.

But she said nothing. And we meet our quotas, every night. The work is crushing. But there are no beatings and we get food, sometimes. Nearly all of Mother's cuts and scars are faded.

When I climb back down the ladder, something feels different. The air is warmer, somehow. I'm not alone. I should be afraid. But instead, joy jumps in my heart — too much. I can't forget what I'm here to tell Ford.

"I'm over here," his voice says softly from below.

Ford is standing beside the other end of my cistern. When I come close, he gives it a knock. The sound is solid. "It's full," he says.

"And the others nearly. The Visitor will come to collect soon," I tell him.

"Maybe things will be easier for you then." He touches a cut on his face, lightly, like a habit.

"I'm sorry," I tell him. "It's my fault you were hurt."

He lifts his chin for a second and stares up at the sky. Then he meets my eyes. "I chose it."

"I wanted to stop him . . . but I couldn't," I say.

"Yeah. Know how that feels." He gives me a small, tight smile.

"Where were you?" I ask.

"My mother, she's . . . sicker." He swallows and looks down at his boots.

"I'm sorry."

Ford draws in a hissing breath and presses his hand to his cheek. "Crap, that hurts."

"What?" I ask. I feel so helpless.

"He . . . My teeth . . . Never mind. It'll heal."

"What did Darwin do?" I breathe.

"Forget I said that."

My own teeth and cheeks ache, imagining it.

Ford lets out a low, bitter laugh. "He's only keeping me so he can watch me."

"I . . . I have to say something. I've been waiting all these nights to say it. I came here every night but . . . you weren't here."

Ford stares over my shoulder at something, or nothing, far behind me. "You stayed away for a long time too. You didn't have anything to say then."

"I wanted to be here," I tell him.

He takes one, two, three steps forward. And we're only inches from each other. It feels as if the air between us is like a tender waterdrop; one more move and it will burst.

"Are you still afraid of me?" I ask.

He answers with his arms, and his lips. My hands are hungry, traveling down his back, tugging at his clothes like they're something good to eat. He touches me too, gentler touches, but daring enough to make my breath stop.

But then I touch something tender—a bruise or a cut— and he jerks away with a pained gasp. It's only for a second—he reaches for me again—but it's like the slap of a chain across my back. I step back from him.

"Why? Why did you do it, Ruby? Because you wanted that guy instead?" Both his hands clench, his fists hanging low against his hips.

"I never wanted Jonah."

"You tried to leave with him," Ford says.

"It was for the Congregation. Not Jonah."

"All you had to do was ask me to help," he says. "I would've gotten you out of here. Both of you, if that's what you really wanted."

"It was wrong of me to leave without—" I start.

"Without me?" he asks, not meeting my eyes.

"Without . . ." I swallow. The truth will hurt him.

"Who?" he asks through gritted teeth.

"Without everyone." I look over my shoulder.

"Don't you just want to be happy?" Ford asks. "Do you need all of them for that?" His hands aren't in fists anymore. He lifts one to trace a path down my arm, gently.

"I want to do what's right," I tell him.

He shakes his head and looks away from me. "You're a better person than me."

"No, you're wrong."

"I wouldn't love me, if I were you. I'm an Overseer, and you're . . . a prisoner," he says.

It gives me the chance to say what I've been trying to tell him since he came. "We never should have . . ." I stop.

"I'm not sorry," Ford says.

"Me either," I admit, and his soft smile makes my stomach plummet. "But we can never be together, Ford."

"Not here—but out there—"

"It doesn't do any good to dream of *out there*," I tell him. "It only makes things harder, knowing there's something else."

"So come with me and get something else."

"No. I'm here until Otto comes. My family needs me."

"I need you," he says, his voice cracking. He takes both my hands in his. I don't pull back, but I don't return the soft squeeze he gives my fingers.

"They need me more," I say.

He drops my hands. "So you're picking them," he says in a flat voice.

"It's what I'm meant—"

"*God* wants you to be happy. But not Otto, huh?" He turns away from me and slams the cistern with an open hand.

"It's Darwin who doesn't want us to be happy," I tell him.

"Then *fight* him," Ford says.

"Fight?" I ask. "I can't. And you . . . you could get hurt."

"I don't care. Fight him. Don't worry about me." Ford falls to his knees and pulls me with him.

He puts one tender hand on my cheek, and I match him with mine.

"One last kiss," I whisper.

Our lips touch gently, sweetly. Then we slide closer, closer, and our kisses are full of need. Ford slides his fingers through my hair and tugs away the pins that hold my curls in place. A flush travels over my body. The weight of my hair hanging down my back makes me feel nearly naked in front of him.

"Beautiful," he whispers. Tenderly, he wraps one strand around his finger and gives it a tug. I slide my hands behind his neck and up the back of his head, loving the soft bristle beneath the fingers. Ford shivers under my touch.

Then the sun explodes against my eyelids in a harsh second.

"The lights," Ford says, his mouth still against mine.

I scramble to my feet. Ford follows.

"I'll come back tomorrow," he says.

"No. No. You can't ever come back," I tell him.

"I'll come back every night."

"And I'll ignore you every night," I tell him.

A squawk sounds from the end of the Lake by the Overseers' cabin.

"The bullhorn," Ford says. "They'll be driving around any second."

He slides his arms around me and gives me a last hard hug. I mold my body against his, try to memorize how the print of his body feels against mine.

"Good-bye, Ford," I say into his shoulder.

"For now," he says, his voice thick.

The first loud words come from the road, not too far from us. "Wakey, wakey!"

"You'll change your mind," Ford says.

I won't. But there's no use arguing with him. I hear the rumble of truck tires on gravel. Ford must too; he looks over his shoulder again.

"Run, Ruby!" he says.

And so I run, with no shadows to hide in, hoping that my feet can outpace the slow trucks.

Chapter 27

Today is Sunday—Communion day. It's been five days since I told Ford to stop coming to the cisterns.

He listened. That hurts more than anything.

Mother is quiet as we walk to the Common House. It's still dark out, but sunrise is coming soon—the sky is already a lighter blue toward the horizon.

We both crept into our beds two, perhaps three, hours ago. Sleep is even more delicious when Darwin denies it of us. I crave sleep now, the way I used to crave food.

Our breath is on the air this morning. Cold creeps out of the ground to remind us that summer will draw to a close, and soon. But the sun will still be fierce by noon.

"When you were small, you tried to chase your breath," Mother says, breaking the silence.

She smiles and points at the puff of white coming out of my mouth.

"I don't remember," I tell her.

"I do. I remember everything about you, from the day you were born." When she looks at me, her face crumples a bit.

"Are you crying?" I ask her.

"No, certainly not." She sniffs once, deeply, then clears her throat.

Something's bothering her, but I'm not sure what. I take her hand in mine, like I did when I was smaller, and she squeezes my fingers. We walk the rest of the way to the Common House like that. It feels nice, being linked to Mother, no arguments, no trying to persuade her.

We reach the Common House, and Mother pulls away first. My hand feels cold where her fingers lay atop the skin. She hurries ahead without looking back.

I take a seat in the back, where I used to sit with Ellie. By rights I should be near the front, to take my assigned place in the Communion line when the time comes. But I don't want so many pairs of Congregant eyes fastened on my back.

They've been none too friendly, still. But I accept it. In time they'll forget, or at least forgive, our attempt to leave. They'll see I am steadfast and loyal. They'll accept me as their Leader.

"Good morning!" Hope slides into the chair next to me and pulls my hand into hers. "Did you sleep well?"

"For hours and hours, upon silk sheets and plump pillows," I tell her, and she grins.

"Remember that game we'd play? It's been forever," Hope says.

"I always loved it," I tell her, and she squeezes my hand.

We'd pretend to be women of leisure and wealth, surrounded

by luxury—just like the stories Ellie would tell us about princesses. Each tree was our servant, each rock another gemstone to pick up and treasure.

"Why did we stop?" I ask Hope.

She looks at Gabe, who's sitting next to her, then shrugs. "I suppose we both grew up, Ruby."

Yes—and she with her love, and me without mine. But Ford isn't mine, was never meant to be mine. Still, I can't help stealing looks as he stands at the front of the room.

"There's time for a sermon today," Hope says.

"Are we all here?" I ask, looking around. About the right number of chairs are full, but something feels off.

"Earl spent all night in the woods," Hope says.

"Why?" I ask.

"He filled Asa's cup," Hope says. "Truly, Ruby. I couldn't believe it."

I can't believe it either—but I should. The Pellings have good in them too.

Mother calls from the front of the room. "Congregants, rise!"

As we stand, Hope slides her arm through mine.

One short reading from the Bible, another prayer, and then Mother speaks, but briefly, before it's time to line up for Communion.

"These have been tiring days—and nights," she says. "But we are strong, and we will stay strong."

Fear makes my fingertips tingle. Why must she provoke Darwin?

But he only smiles, then nods at the Overseers as if they've all done something wonderful.

"Otto keeps us strong. Praise Otto," Mother says.

"Praise Otto," the Congregation answers in somber tones.

"We will take our Communion, and we will keep working. And we will pray that the day Otto comes is soon." Mother spreads her arms wide and looks up to the sky. For one moment I imagine Otto is about to burst through the roof of the Common House and land beside Mother.

Then she leads us in our prayer; I stumble through it, surprised to hear it come so soon.

"Ruby." Mother's voice, sharp because she can see the daydreams wandering in my eyes, I think. My mind wandered far, thinking about my father.

"Please come up front," she says.

Mother gestures for me to hurry. As I walk to the front, she calls out, "Make your line for Communion, please."

Behind me I hear chairs scraping and feet shuffling to make a line.

"She doesn't get to go first," Darwin says when I reach the front.

"Today Ruby is giving Communion." Mother says it to Darwin, but she looks at me.

At first I don't understand what she's saying—because it's too impossible. How could I give Communion? That's what Mother does, and it's always been only Mother.

"Me? Why?" I look back at the line of Congregants who are waiting for their Water. I've never given Communion. I don't think I've even ever touched the bottle, or the dropper. It feels entirely wrong.

Mother holds out the dropper and the glass bottle with a warm, certain smile. "It's your turn, daughter."

"I never give Communion."

"You're grown, Ruby," Mother says.

"You've always done it," I tell her in a low voice. I don't want anyone to hear me doubting her, not right now, not about this.

Mother sighs. "There's no time to hesitate," she says.

I take the bottle and dropper from her. They're so light.

"Squeeze it gently," Mother says, "so there's enough for everyone. Just one drop."

"I know," I say. Then I motion to her. "Mother? Open your mouth."

She shakes her head. "Everyone else first, Ruby. Always."

I suppose she's right. I can give her all the Water she needs, whenever she needs it. But it feels wrong to leave her standing here, waiting, while everyone else gets a turn.

"Hurry," Mother says.

Zeke Pelling is first in line—the strongest, by the Overseers' judgment. His eyes meet mine, and I brace myself for anger. But instead he bows his head, slightly, as if acknowledging me. Then he tips his chin up and opens his mouth.

It makes me feel powerful. I lift the dropper and hold it over his tongue. I am so slow and careful that he squints at me for a moment as I gently, gently shake the drop onto his tongue.

"In the name of Otto," I say.

"Amen," he answers, stepping to the side quickly.

Next is Thomas—taking the place of Jonah, who always used to go second. He gives me a small smile before opening his mouth.

"Hurry up," Darwin warns.

Darwin slams his gun on the floor. Thomas swallows, whirls, and hurries back to his seat.

"Don't go sneaking extra to your favorites," Darwin says. The drop that lands on Thomas's tongue must have been too big.

"I'm not, I swear it." I hate that my voice shakes.

"Look at me," Darwin orders. I drop the Water on the next waiting tongue, then swing my eyes to him.

"You going to take beatings like your Mother too? How grown up *are* you?" The intensity of his stare makes me look away fast.

There's a loud clatter behind me; I look and see that Ford has dropped his gun. As he bends to pick it up, his eyes bore an angry hole into Darwin's back.

"Leave Ruby alone," Mother says. I'd forgotten she was there, standing a bit behind me, watching my every move—and Darwin's.

"You've got five minutes," Darwin says. "Or less."

"Hurry," Mother tells me.

The faces come quicker now—all of the familiar faces that have smiled, frowned, stared at me for hundreds of years.

There's Meg Newman, one of the few brave enough to take her own lashes. She nods her head, once, before she opens her mouth.

And Joan, sweet Joan who made Ellie's pillows. She is

beaming the entire time she stands in line. I wish I could give her an extra drop.

I would I could give them all more.

Every Congregant says *Amen* to my small prayer; nobody refuses Water or even gives me a suspicious look. Nobody turns me away, not even the people who have given me the most sour looks since we tried to escape.

I wonder why Mother really did this. Did she want the Congregation to remember who I am—to stop punishing me for what I had done?

Or did she want *me* to remember who I am?

They accept me here, each one, and it makes me feel even more ashamed that I thought to leave them behind—even for a short while.

"One more minute, Little Toad," Darwin says, and there is delight in his voice.

I count six more in line, Boone's aunt Mary and her brother John among them. Mary slips her hand under John's elbow to support him as he opens his mouth.

Then the last one is Earl.

He has come straight from the woods, I think. He is breathing heavy, as if he's run a long way, and sweat stains his sides.

Just after I drop the Water on his tongue, he smiles at me, with none of the anger I've seen on his face since Jonah died.

"You are a fine Reverend," he says.

"Pack up and head out!" Darwin shouts. But he doesn't reach for what I am holding. He just picks up his gun. His hands are too busy to stop me.

drought

There's only a drop or two left in the stopper, with none in the bottle. I let the drop hover over Mother's tongue, and then let it go.

I say to her what she always said to me, every single Sunday. It feels holy. It feels bigger than us, bigger than this building, to say those words to her.

"In the name of Otto," I say.

"Amen," she answers.

Chapter 28

The line to the cisterns is moving slowly tonight. I am near the back, Hope and Gabe in front of me.

Hope lifts her hand and caresses Gabe's cheek. He smiles back at her.

Ford is here tonight, standing in the circle of guards around the edge of the woods. I can't see him from where I stand. But I am so very aware of where he is, as if there's a glowing rock just out of my sight. I feel its heat. I see the edges of its glow.

Mother slides behind me, drops a light hand on my shoulder for just a moment. "Do you have your cup?" she asks.

"Yes. Barely," I tell her. "And you?"

She whispers her answer, glancing to the side, where the Overseers stand. "I got enough for me—and helped Asa."

I helped only myself today. But I don't tell her that. I just step to the side so she'll come next to me.

My legs and arms are shuddering with exhaustion. Every Congregant has got to be as tired as I am. Just because we can live with little sleep, little food, does not mean we thrive.

"The lights aren't on. That's something," Mother says.

It grows darker earlier and earlier. But the Overseers don't switch on the lights as the sun falls into darkness. Perhaps they understand that the woods are dry—they need the night to gather water again.

Or perhaps it's more fun for them to roust us from our beds, turn on the lights then, watch us blink against their glare like mice pulled from their cozy holes.

"They'll switch them on later tonight," I tell her.

Hope takes her turn going up the ladder. Gabe steadies her as she goes. When she's done, she climbs off the ladder, letting out her breath with a *whoosh*. Then she stands next to the ladder, waiting for Gabe.

He climbs up; I don't pay attention as he pours his water in, even though Mother is next. I look for Ford. I find him, finally, not so far from the cisterns. I let myself stare for too long.

Then I hear Mother gasp. "Otto save him," she says.

Gabe is still at the top of the ladder. Water is dripping over the sides of the tank.

"He's spilled the water," I say. I look at Mother, wanting someone to tell me this awful thing is true. "Didn't he?"

"He did." She nods, then takes my hand in hers.

They will punish him badly for a spill this large.

Hope darts to the side of the tank, tries to catch the drops of water in her cup.

"Go," Mother says, but I am already moving, then at the edge of the tank with my cup ready to catch drops too. The

Congregants push behind me, beside me. We all hold our cups below the belly of the cistern, until there is a line of cups. Our elbows press against each other, but nobody pulls away. There will be no room for the water to slide to the ground.

The prayer wells up in me now too, and slips from my lips easily. *Otto save him. Otto save him.*

Darwin, who was watching from the edge of the crowd, pushes through us to reach the cisterns. The crowd jostles and my cup wobbles for a moment; I think I see a drop fall to the earth.

"That's all we'll get," someone says—Boone maybe? And everyone straightens up.

My cup looks a little more full, I think. Maybe I saved a drop or two from Gabe's spill. I pray I did.

Darwin is at the bottom of the ladder now. He reaches up to Gabe, still frozen at the top of the ladder, and gives Gabe's ankle a strong tug. I remember how Ford reached up, that night when I was in the tree. He pulled at me the same way.

"Get down, Toad," Darwin growls.

"No. Please, please don't hurt him." Hope reaches out for Darwin. She touches him—no, not just touches him. She grasps one of his sleeves in her hands and pulls at it, drops her full weight into the effort.

"Hope, stop," Mother warns, but still she hangs on.

Darwin looks at her for a moment, then flings his arm. She stumbles to the side but still holds on.

"Take care of this," Darwin yells. In an instant one of the Overseers is there. He grabs Hope around the middle, and this time she can't hold on. He pulls her away. She screams, kicks, but there's nothing she can do to help Gabe now.

Gabe's legs are shaking. Now his desperate eyes follow Hope, squinting in the gloom of dusk.

"Get down," Darwin tells him again.

This time Gabe does not resist. He scrabbles down the ladder and moves toward the stand of trees where they're holding Hope.

But Darwin holds up an arm to block his way. How does Darwin move so slowly, so surely, and still be faster than the rest of us? It looks as if he barely flicked a muscle, and yet Gabe is forced to stay where he is.

"Give me your cup," Darwin orders.

Gabe swallows and hands it over. A little water sloshes over the top. He hadn't even finished pouring.

"I was careful," he says.

Darwin barely looks at the cup; instead, he holds it out and an Overseer takes it. The guard handles the cup carefully. He won't be foolish enough to spill like Gabe did.

Then Darwin makes a fist and lifts his hand high. The Congregants suck in a breath, as one.

He knocks on the tank. It's not a hollow sound; it's solid, with barely an echo to it. Darwin takes off his hat and presses it to his heart. For a moment, he squeezes his eyes shut.

When he opens them, he gives Gabe a grin. "Your Otto might have saved you today," he says.

Darwin steps around Gabe, who has opened his eyes and is watching with care. Then Darwin climbs the ladder, quickly, as agile as ever.

"Give me the measuring stick," he orders an Overseer below.

No, not just any Overseer—Ford—comes from the edges of the Congregation. "What's that?" he asks. His tone is dead and heavy. He sounds so old.

Darwin lets out a gusty sigh. "Long thin stick, notch at the top, painted red."

Ford nods once and hurries off. I turn to watch, but when I see nobody else is following his path, I tear my eyes away and look back to Darwin. For everyone else is staring, barely breathing, waiting for what might be the best news we've had all year.

There's only one reason to use the measuring stick—Darwin must think the cistern is full.

Full! Then Gabe's water couldn't have fit. Then he won't have earned a beating.

And our work is done—at least until the Visitor comes to take our full cisterns and give us empty ones. We will have a few days.

"Let it be full," I whisper, and perhaps Otto hears this prayer. Perhaps he'll grant this prayer, and give us all a day of mercy.

While he waits, Darwin raps the top of the cistern with his knuckles, softly. With every knock, the smile on his face grows wider and wider.

"Hurry up!" he shouts.

Ford is back a minute later with the long measuring stick. He hands it to Darwin, then takes a few steps back—but not many. He seems as curious as any Congregant about whether the cisterns are full.

Darwin bends the stick into an arc and slides the tip into the top of the cistern. Down, down, until all that's left is the tip between his fingers. I try to imagine the stick covered by Water.

He pauses and looks around the crowd—then down at Gabe. "You'd better hope this comes out wet," he says. "All the way to the top."

Gabe nods.

Please Otto, I pray. *Spare Gabe. Spare all of us.*

Then Darwin pulls the stick out, slow, slow. He bends close to look at the red notch—I strain too, but it's impossible to see whether the stick gleams with wet at the top.

"It's full!" Darwin cries. He whips the stick out of the cistern and it sprays Water on everyone standing around it, tiny droplets. Gabe wipes his finger on his cheek, catching a drop, and sticks his finger in his mouth.

Never waste Water.

At first we are all silent. It's as if we have forgotten how to celebrate.

Then there is a shout: Hope, released from the Overseers, running toward Gabe. "It's full!" she cries, and then again. "It's full!"

It's full. Tonight we won't have to wake up and drag ourselves through the midnight woods. Tomorrow morning, even, we won't have to wake at sunrise. But we all will. For Darwin always does one thing when the cisterns are full.

He feeds us.

"It's full!" cries Gabe, just as Hope reaches him and flings herself into his arms.

"Praise Otto!" Mother cries. She is pushing her way through the crowd and coming close to me.

The entire Congregation answers her with the same cry.

"Praise Otto! Praise Otto! Praise Otto!"

I shout too, joy welling up in me until all I can feel is the shout and the hugs and the dancing feet of the Congregation around me. Someone links elbows with me and whirls me in a circle—Mother? Gabe? Hope, even? I'm not sure, for soon I am released and whirling around with someone else.

Darwin's brown leather hat edges around the crowd, and then I spy him standing by the truck. When I turn again, I see a flash of him laughing, clapping his hand on an Overseer's back, his face as happy as any Congregant. He sips from Gabe's half-full cup casually, and for a moment hate fills me. But then I remember it is time to celebrate. I skip back into the dancing.

I tumble among Congregants until I am at the edge of the crowd—right by Ford's side. Perhaps it is an accident, or perhaps my feet know exactly where I wish I could be.

The Overseers have stepped back into the woods a bit. Their guns are still at the ready, but a few wear smiles. Ford's face is still serious—until I stumble into him.

He grabs my elbow to steady me, and when our eyes meet, he grins, for just a moment. The giddy joy in me raises even higher, so high I feel like it will flood out of me.

"It's full," he says, the smile still lingering a little on his lips.

But his touch lasts only a second. Where he touched it, my elbow feels icy. My joy ebbs, a little.

"We won't work tonight," I tell him.

"Or tomorrow, maybe," he says.

There will be work to do after breakfast tomorrow, and Overseers to watch us. But I let myself pretend, for a moment, that Ford is right.

"We'll sit in the sun and stare up at the trees," I tell him.

"I wish . . . ," he says, his voice trailing off as his eyes shoot from left to right, then left again.

Anyone could hear us.

"No." I shake my head a little, then back away. "Don't wish."

I plunge into the crowd and find Hope.

"It's full!" I cry.

"Praise Otto!" she answers.

We join hands in a circle—Hope, Gabe, Mother, Boone, me, and Asa. All of us are grinning so big, our cheeks are like red glowing apples. They all look so young, the way I remember them when I was a child.

Then we lift our feet and dance in a circle. Our circle tumbles into the others around us, and then away again, but nobody minds. All we are doing is celebrating.

And just for now, just for this moment, I will pretend that life will always be like this.

Tomorrow morning comes soon enough.

Chapter 29

Last night the cisterns were full.

Tonight, we celebrate.

One night a year, Darwin lets us celebrate. One night, we forget we are his prisoners—or at least we do our best to try.

It starts with gathering wood in the morning. Every Congregant combs the woods for tinder and logs; some team up to cut the big logs that will feed the fire into the dawn.

Then we pile them high.

Now we're nearly finished. The Congregants stand in a circle around the firewood, watching me. Always I put the last branch on the fire. I'm holding a thin twig from a pine tree. Its rough bark snags against my toughened skin a little.

Then Mother tosses the match on top—always.

I take my time, breathing in the night air, and the smell of the food. Yes, food, brought here by Darwin West. First we'll light the fire. And soon, very soon, we'll eat.

"Hurry up!" someone shouts—Earl, I think. It's hard to tell in the dark. But I don't feel irritated. Nothing can upset me tonight.

"For Ellie and Jonah!" I shout, holding the branch high. I remember all those other nights, all those other years—the years I was too small to do this myself. My mother would grasp my wrist and pull my arm high, laughing as I shouted my thanks to Otto. And then, finally, came the first year when I was tall enough to do it by myself.

This year, I won't thank Otto. I want to remember the friends who are gone.

"For Ellie and Jonah!" the Congregants reply.

I stretch to put the branch on the top of the pile, right in the middle. But before I drop it, I look into the crowd. It shouldn't matter if Ford is here. We're nothing to each other.

But I feel empty without him, even tonight.

"Drop it!" the same voice shouts. Yes, definitely Earl Pelling.

"Hush up, Pelling!" I shout back, and the Congregants cheer.

There—there's Ford, laughing, part of the circle of Overseers around our ring. He shakes his head a little as he looks at me. But he doesn't drop his eyes. In the cover of dark, he's bolder.

My skin tingles, and without even deciding to do it, I drop the branch.

Mother pulls me back, gently, and holds out the single match that Darwin has given her. There won't be any more. Flint and steel are all we have to light our fires.

"Tonight you'll do it," she says. I don't even argue. I strike the match against a rock and drop it on the wood.

The flames start out tiny, at first. Mother hums a song, soft, one I know from nights by the fire in winter. It's a song about spring.

Behind me, Gen Baker starts singing with her. Mother looks back with a grin and raises her voice. When she takes my hand, I join their song.

The flames grow higher, higher, and then it is hotter than the brightest noon we faced this summer. The heat pushes our circle back, but the singing doesn't stop. It grows louder, and the songs melt one into the other.

"*Eat!*" Darwin's voice roars over the crowd, speaking through one of the talk boxes on top of the Overseers' trucks. Everyone rushes into a boisterous line, loose, friends shifting from one part to the other as they talk.

Mother steps aside to let the line pass before we join it at the end, as always. As the Congregants pass, they greet both of us. I'm not invisible to them anymore. They're not angry.

It feels good to be accepted again.

I remember the time Darwin gave us those steaming vats of oatmeal, then locked us inside the Common House. There was no talking, no smiling, then. Nobody trusted there would be enough.

But this is the one night he gives us enough.

Long ago, I asked Mother why.

"Darwin never gives us enough food," I told her. "Why is there so much tonight?"

She looked so beautiful in the firelight, I remember—the shadows of the flames hid her scars and the circles under her eyes. She almost seemed to glow.

Mother bent low to give me her answer. "We mustn't look starved when he comes," she whispered. "Or at least we mustn't look hungry."

"Who?" I asked.

"The Visitor, of course," she answered. "Who else ever comes here?"

It took me years longer to understand why it mattered what the Visitor thought—that he never lifted a finger to rescue us, and it probably was because we didn't seem to suffer. The sparkle of the evening's party also carried in our eyes, when he was there, and the extra food plumped out the worst of our sharp edges.

Could he truly be fooled? I think I hate the Visitor more than I hate Darwin.

The food smells so good. "I wonder what it will be tonight," I say to Mother.

She shrugs. "Any food is delicious when your stomach is empty."

I've never had anything but an empty stomach, except for the days Mother brought in a big kill from her traps. Even then, the eating left me sick, like my body wasn't sure what to do with the food.

"I remember when I wouldn't eat cornbread, or green apples." Mother laughs, a strange free laugh that I'd nearly forgotten. "I'd eat twenty green apples today if I could."

Finally the end of the line reaches us, and we step in. Mother makes sure I stand in front of her.

The table is loaded with food: long sausages and soft white buns, and vats of small red beans that swim in fragrant sauce. There's a tray full of sweet yellow corncobs too, and at the end there's a pile of round white cookies studded with chocolate. Even after all the other Congregants have gone, there's so much food.

Of course we'll all be back for seconds, and thirds. We'll get leftovers for breakfast, and they'll taste just as good—even if half of us will be sick from all that food.

Mother gives me a nudge; I grab one of the thin paper plates and load it with food. Boone waves us over to a group sitting near the fire.

Nobody is eating yet—not one single Congregant. They are watching Mother and me instead, eyes wide, begging. Hurry, please.

"Do you want to do the prayer?" she asks me.

"No," I tell her. "You're our Reverend."

She sets her plate on the ground and raises her hands in the air.

"Praise Otto in thanks for tonight," she shouts.

"Praise Otto!" they reply, even louder than when I put the stick on the fire.

Then she says the thing that makes me afraid every year—the thing that will make tomorrow night, or maybe the one after that, the worst of the year. For it will make Darwin come to our cabin.

And that never ends well.

"Next year we will be free!" she cries.

"Free!" we all shout.

And then we eat, with no signal from Mother, only years of doing the same thing behind us. I start with the soft white bun, knowing to take small bites, no matter how much my body tells me to gobble the food.

Mother is eating slowly too, but not everyone shows such restraint. Boone has nearly finished one of the ears of corn.

"You'll be sick," Mother warns him.

He nods, wipes his hand across the back of his mouth. "And then I'll eat more."

I empty my plate and lob the chewed corncobs into the fire. Then I go back for seconds.

Earl is standing at the table too. I feel him staring until I return his look. Then he steps closer, so close that I can smell the chocolate on his breath.

"It could be like this every night," he says. "If we were free."

"If Otto wills it," I reply quickly.

"Don't you dishonor my boy." He crooks an eyebrow at me, but he doesn't linger. He turns to join the other Pellings, across the other side of the bonfire.

"I won't," I whisper after him. But I don't think he hears me.

I ignore Mother's curious look when I sit next to her again. Boone distracts her by rushing into the woods, gripping his stomach.

"I warned him," Mother says, but she smiles. Then she takes another dainty bite of pillowy white bun. She is still working on her first plate.

But eventually even she goes to get more food.

When we finish eating, the songs start again. Not religious songs—old songs from Hoosick Falls, instead, from the days before Darwin West and cups and spoons. I know them all. But tonight I don't feel like singing.

I want to be near Ford, even though I shouldn't be. I won't talk to him. I want only to hear his breathing, to know his body is near mine.

When I stand to brush off my skirts, Mother frowns up at me. "You're having thirds?"

"No. I—I want to be by myself for a bit."

"Stay here," Mother warns sharply, looking at the Overseers ringing the fire. "Who knows what they might try to do—they've been drinking spirits."

Indeed, many of the Overseers are holding a bottle in loose hands, no gun in sight. Though the bulge of the chain still shows in their pockets.

"I'll stay right by the fire," I promise her.

Ford stands with his back to the deepest part of the woods. He's not holding a bottle, only a gun. I wonder if Darwin wouldn't let him have spirits.

I come close to him—perhaps three steps away, then turn my back and settle onto the ground, wrapping my arms around my knees. I balance my chin atop my knees and stare into the flames.

When I was smaller, I used to imagine that an entirely different world lived in those flames. I can still see the leaping figures that live for a moment, then shift into something else. Fire ghosts, I used to call them.

"I miss you," Ford says, so quiet I can barely hear him over the roar of the fire.

I nod once, slowly. But I won't answer.

"Give me another chance," he says.

This time I don't answer at all.

"Talk to me," he says, his voice a little stronger now. There's something in it that reminds me of the desperate way Darwin talks to Mother . . . especially how he'll talk to her tomorrow night.

No. I won't let that ruin things tonight.

"It's not safe," I say to the fire.

"Nobody's watching. Come closer," he urges.

I stand and take a few steps back, as if the heat of the fire is too much for me. But I do not look at Ford.

"Let me take you out. Just one date," he says.

"What's a date?" I dare one glance back. The flickering fire shadows fall against the curve of his lips. They look thicker, more dangerous.

He doesn't answer me, not right away. His hand lifts, as if to touch me. But he drops it before he dares, and I look away from him.

"A date is when I take you somewhere else. We do something fun," he says.

"I can't leave here."

"Only for a few hours. Please."

I hear a noise behind me, and I know he's closer to me—so close I can smell him, feel his breath on the back of my neck. It sets chills over my entire body.

"Where would we go?" I ask.

"You must be pretty sick of the woods," he says.

"Only a little." I smile, bigger than I mean to, and it's impossible to tuck the smile away once it starts.

"I'll take you somewhere different. You'll feel like you're a million miles away. We'll eat—lots, food way better than this stuff." He tilts his head toward where the table is.

Food . . . and Ford. Tomorrow I'll be empty of both. But maybe I could have one more taste.

"How?" I ask. "I'm not allowed—"

"And Darwin watches me," he sighs.

A ring of Overseers stand on the other side of the fire like short, broad stumps in the darkness—watching, but never moving. Darwin is far from here, talking to one of the Overseers, holding one of those bottles.

"I can't let you get hurt again." Cold, suddenly, I take a step closer to the fire. The warmth feels less now. Will they put more wood on the fire? It can't yet be time to let it die out.

"I'll be gone soon." Ford says it quietly, but not quietly enough. I hear him far too perfectly.

I whirl to face him. "You'll be gone for the night, only. You'll be back the next day."

"I mean I'll be gone for good," he says. "Just a couple more days and I'm done."

"Gone," I whisper. The food I gobbled down settles into a hard rock inside my stomach. Being hungry felt better than this.

"The harvest is done. Darwin says he won't need so many men."

"Maybe he'll keep you. Maybe—"

"Quiet," Ford says, his voice changed. "Move away."

Fear makes the back of my neck prick. I turn, slowly, looking up at the sky as if I'm counting the stars. Then I step closer to the fire and turn my body entirely away from him.

"They behaving over here?" Darwin's voice, just a footstep

behind mine. No fire is warm enough to cure the chill down my back.

"Yep," Ford answers. His voice is deeper, dead, when he talks to Darwin.

"Are *you* behaving?" Darwin laughs. I slide away, away, until I can't hear any more of what he says or how Ford replies.

What does he mean? Does he know about us? Does he suspect, at least?

The singing is less now; there are knots of Congregants standing and sitting around the fire. They talk in low voices, mostly, but sometimes a burst of laugher rolls out from a group. And for once, they don't quiet their voices.

Ford is leaving, for good. He said it. But I can't believe it. I try to imagine it—everything as it used to be, just like it was before he came this summer. Life was never easy, before Ford came. But now it seems impossible.

I see someone waving at me. When I get closer, I see Hope and Asa sitting near the fire, Asa closest of all to the flames.

Hope smiles at me and holds up her hand. "Come sit with us. We're telling stories about your mother."

Her light tone makes me think of stolen berries and mud pies, before I was old enough for my own pewter cup. She stretches her hand even higher and grasps my unwilling fingers.

"Come on," she coaxes.

I don't want to tell stories. I want more time with Ford. I want to sit with him here, in front of the fire, and talk about nothing. I want to feel his fingers sliding over my hair, down my back, his arms around me.

Nothing will warm me, nothing ever, once he's gone.

"Ruby?" Hope gives me a nudge. "You're in another world tonight."

"I am." I give her an apologetic smile.

"Your mother was the same, when she was around Otto," Hope says.

My breath stops. Has she guessed the truth about Ford?

She gives me a sympathetic smile. "Were you like that around Jonah?"

"No—no, not exactly," I stammer.

"I'd seen sheep with more brains, compared to your mother around Otto." Asa grins.

"She wasn't stupid. She was just . . ." Hope shrugs.

"Aye. She was clumsy," Asa says.

"It's true!" Hope claps her hands together and nods. "She'd walk into furniture, stumble down hills, drop crockery."

"I can't imagine it," I tell them. Mother, so sure-footed in the woods, her hands holding her cup steady after ten hours of being in the sun.

"People change when they're in love." Hope looks behind me, and even without looking I know that she's finding Gabe.

And then, so simple, so certain, I know: I love Ford. It's more than stolen kisses and the thrill of the modern world. I love him, and I can't let him go—at least, not without one more night together.

I stand.

"Gone already?" Hope pouts.

"Only for a little bit," I tell her.

Darwin's back by the trucks; still, I know I shouldn't stay by Ford for long. Darwin is obviously watching him.

So I walk around the fire, slow, arms out wide like a small girl playing a game. Slow, patient, ignoring the people around me, I make my path toward Ford.

When I reach him, I don't even slow or change my walk.

"I'll go on your date," I say.

"You will? Good." He sounds so happy.

"When?" I'm nearly past the point where I'll be able to hear him.

"Meet me at the cisterns tomorrow night, soon as the sun is down."

"Aye," I answer, and then I keep walking.

It's not until I reach Hope and Asa again that I remember: tomorrow night will be a terrible night.

And now I've agreed to abandon her.

I should go back and tell him no. I should tell him it will have to be another night.

But I don't. I settle beside Hope again and smile, and laugh, and tell my own stories about my strong stubborn mother.

And I dream about what my stolen night with Ford will be like.

Chapter 30

Darwin comes to our cabin the next night, just as I knew he would. It's the only time he comes here—once a year, when the cisterns are full, before the Visitor comes.

"You're not welcome here." Mother is standing at the door, chin lifted high, blocking the way inside with her body. I remember the days when I clung to her skirts and peered up at him. I couldn't make out his face under the shadow of his hat.

But I always knew who it was. Darwin West, come to beg my mother.

"It's my property. My land. My trees. My cabin. All of it." His eyes wander down her body and she lifts her chin higher.

"Leave, Darwin," she says, her voice hard and low.

"You'll want to hear what I have to say." He sweeps the hat off his head and tucks it under one arm. His thick blond hair glints in the sunset.

He looks as young as Ford.

Ford, whom I promised to meet tonight. Ford, who wants to take me away, just for a night.

Let this time be different than the others. Please, Otto. Help Mother.

She never looks back at me, or says anything to indicate I'm here in the cabin. I'm back by the stove, building a small fire, even though the leaves have barely turned. The nights are cold now. Soon we'll be sharing one bed and both of our blankets.

She warned me earlier, as she always has on this day. "Darwin will be by later," she said.

"Why does he keep trying?" I asked her.

"Why does he do anything?" Her smile was small and tired. "Stay back when he comes, Ruby. Don't interfere. If he remembers you're here, it'll make things worse."

"I can help," I protested. For years, now, I've thought of the ways I could help her when things start to go wrong. I could tell him to stop. I could fight him.

"Promise me you'll stay quiet. Promise you won't do anything," she urged.

She kept me safe all these years. She survived this night, every year. How could I not give her what she asked?

"I promise," I told her. But still, I slipped out later to find a thick stick. I shaved the end to a point, just like the one Jonah gave me, and slid it under my bed. I'd be ready to use it, I swear, if I had to.

"It doesn't have to be like this," Darwin tells Mother. "Let me come in."

"Tell me we're free," she says. "Or leave."

How I wish I were as bold as Mother.

"You can be free," Darwin says.

"Then send the Overseers home," Mother tells him.

"And me? What would you have me do?" His voice is husky, and he takes a step forward. Mother's body leans back—I can tell she doesn't want to be a bit closer to him—but she stands her ground.

"Leave us, Darwin," she says. "Forget we ever came here."

"You said that two hundred years ago, and I couldn't do it. I tried. Oh, I tried." He grips the hat close to his heart and squeezes his eyes shut for a moment, as if in the kind of pain I'd like to exact with my stick.

Mother lets out a snort. His eyes fly open.

"Otto never came," he says.

"He will," she answers.

"No. He won't." His voice is soft now, like a lover's, and he takes two more bold steps toward her.

With each step there's a soft jingling sound. He brought the chain, as I knew he would.

"Leave," Mother says again. But her voice shakes a little.

The fire is built; I strike the flint.

"I've come to ask you again," Darwin says. Then he slowly, slowly drops to one knee.

He draws a small parcel out of his pocket—something wrapped in a soft handkerchief. Then he presses it to his face and breathes in deep. "It still smells like your perfume."

"Impossible." Mother tries to turn away, but he snakes out one fast strong arm and catches her by the wrist.

"You will listen," he says.

She does not try to move more. But she does not turn to face him either.

"I'd still have you. I'd still be your husband." He sets the parcel on his knee and unwraps it with his free hand, still keeping hold of Mother with the other.

A silvery thimble, carved and softly gleaming, lies in the middle of the cloth. Its brightness is so strange, so wrong, compared to the rough and mildewed wood that surrounds us.

"You accepted this, once, as a token. It was a promise," Darwin says. "Will you remember your promise?"

Mother's eyes flick to the thimble, and then away. She shakes her head.

"If you marry me, I'll set them free. I'll give them all the help they need, to find a new place. I'd do anything, if I had you," he says.

Hearing him desperate makes me hate him even more.

"I wait for Otto, always," she says. "He is the one I'm promised to."

Darwin's hand clenches into a fist around the thimble, the cloth covering its shine.

Mother turns to look at me. "Leave, Ruby," she says, breaking her own rule for me to be hidden.

Darwin looks at me—really *looks*—for the first time tonight. He wavers on his knee, as if he'll tip over.

I step close to her and wrap my arms around her in a hug, my lips pressed to her ear.

"I won't have him hurt you," I whisper.

"He can't. Not the way he wants to," she answers, pulling me into a tight hug.

"Sula?" Darwin asks, and there is anger in his voice. "What do you say?"

Mother's arms drop away from me, and I step quickly away. Still, my skirts brush against Darwin's face. His cheeks redden.

"Go to Boone's cabin," Mother orders. She is sending me to the safest place she can think of—at least the safest place she can name in front of Darwin. I always used to go to Ellie. But no more.

I step around Darwin, and the cabin door shuts behind me. I hear his voice, and no reply from her. I wonder when the begging will stop and the hurting will begin.

I can't leave her. So I find a bush to huddle behind, a safe enough distance from the cabin. I listen. And then I realize—I have left my stick and all my grand plans to protect her under the bed.

She screams, and fear ripples through me.

Otto, make him stop, I plead. *Make him go away.*

She doesn't scream again. Perhaps Otto heard my prayer. Or perhaps this year will be different.

I let myself make a terrible wish, for a moment. I imagine Mother nodding, taking the thimble in her hand. She'd slide it over the tip of her finger, perhaps. Darwin would stand up, then. Maybe he'd even kiss her.

The thought gives me the chills. Darwin's cruel mouth wasn't made for kissing anybody.

But if she agreed, he'd free us. I wouldn't just see Ford

tonight. I could see him any night. I could leave this place and be a modern girl. None of us would have to scrape for water in the woods. Never would I have to heal Mother.

Or perhaps she'd need healing all the more. Being married to Darwin would be a rough business.

Shame washes over me, hot, like water in a shallow puddle that's been in the sun all day. How could I wish for such a thing, even for a moment? Does love make you so selfish that you could sacrifice your own mother?

"No!" Mother shouts. "Never!"

Then she screams again, a long sharp scream, and I jump at the sound of it. I want to help her, but she made me promise.

"I'll heal her," I tell myself. "She'll heal."

But there's another scream, and another, and then I can't even count how many there have been, anymore.

Healing isn't enough. I have to stop him, even if she told me not to.

I rush down the hill and lunge for the door. But it opens just before my fingers close around the handle.

Darwin comes out of the cabin. I stumble back.

"Hello, little Toad." He gives me a slow, lazy smile. "Your mother refused me again."

I don't answer. I'm not sure I could speak even if I wanted to.

Then he whips his arm up high and takes a fast step toward me. I cringe away. He holds his trembling fist high above my head. In a blink he could smash me to the ground.

"I'm sick of this," he says.

"Me too," I whisper.

He lowers his arm, slowly. "You'll want a mop," he says.

Then he walks up the hill to his truck.

I yank open the cabin door.

"Mother? Mother!" I slip on something—something wet that sends me skidding. I drop to my knees and crawl in farther—and find the wetness, again, a puddle wider than me. I lift one hand close to my eyes and see the liquid is dark. A hint of metal drifts into my nose: blood, all over the floor.

"Mother. Mother. Mother." I don't mean to chant it, but it comes out, over and over, while I make my way to her. For now I see the lump by the bed.

When I put my arms around her, her body moves in wrong ways—hinging where it shouldn't, limp where it should resist me. This is worse than any other year. I know it, even without seeing.

I won't light the lantern. I won't need it. I'm going to heal her completely, no careful checks of healing scars and broken bones.

I grab the bucket and slop in all the water I can. Then I cut myself, not bothering to count the drops of blood. I pour the entire bucket over her.

Again, to the Lake. Again, blood and pouring.

The Water rolls off her body and over the floor. I slip with every trip for more of it. Once I land hard, slamming my chin against the wood.

"I hate him," I say out loud. And while I have always hated Darwin, it's a different feeling now—deeper. I know what love is now, and I know how he has twisted it.

The Water is starting to work. Her chest rises and falls, though slow. And the terrible angles in Mother's legs are easing; I lay them straight and run my hands down them, coaxing them into right lines again.

Will we do this again next year? And the next, and the next?

Will Otto ever end this?

I work, and work, and finally I believe I've done all I can. She's too heavy and limp for me to lift into bed, so instead I cover her with my blanket. She'll have to rest where she fell.

My bed feels too large without its blanket. I want to curl up next to Mother—drape her arm over my side and sleep like it's winter. But I don't want to slow her healing, or cause any more pain.

Just as my eyes start to flutter shut, there's a knock.

I do not call out an answer. Instead I slide off my bed, doing my best to be silent, and grope under my bed. There's nothing but dust, and dust, and then another knock on the door. Finally I find hold of my sharp stick and grip it tight.

A third knock. I creep closer to the door and hold the stick up high.

"Who's there?" I ask, louder than a whisper, but not loud enough to wake Mother—though nothing could wake her at this moment, I think.

The only answer I get is another knock.

Wouldn't Darwin have kicked open the door by now?

I fling open the door and keep the stick high.

It's Ford.

Chapter 31

Cold waves of shock flow over me, ice water from high on the hills. My fingers quiver so badly that the stick falls from my hands.

"Did you forget?" Ford asks.

"No, never," I answer.

Ford motions to the road. His truck is there, lights off, but I hear the engine running.

"My mother—" I look behind me. She's breathing lightly. She hasn't moved.

"Come. Just for tonight," he urges. The small smile on his lips makes my own curve up in response. My body tingles, just being near him.

"If they catch us—"

"They won't. I'll have you back before dawn. Please?" Now he takes my hand. He doesn't even seem to notice my bloody clothes, or my hair falling ragged out of its tie. He smiles at me as if I'm beautiful.

"If Mother wakes . . ." I catch my breath when he runs the pad of his thumb across the soft inside part of my wrist.

"Day after tomorrow is my last day. The truck guy comes and then—*adiós*." He shrugs, gives me a sad smile. "So this is our last chance, for real, Ruby."

"For real." I repeat the strange modern words.

"I'll take you to the movies. Nobody will even see us. I have a plan."

"What are the movies?" I ask.

"Magic. Come on. You'll see." He bounces on his toes, a bit, like a child.

It's only one night. Mother won't be awake, truly. With his truck, I'll be back safe and sound.

This one night could sustain me for years and years—until Otto comes.

"Let me change. Wait right here," I tell him.

I put on my spare dress, and use a soft green ribbon from Ellie to tie my hair back. She wore it when she was courting, she told me once. Then I slide her watch into my pocket, for luck.

It's cold outside, but Ford's truck is toasty warm. He opens the door for me and waits to get inside. "Watch the door," he warns, and then he slams it shut.

Ford snaps a strap around me—"It's a seat belt, for safety," he says—and then one around himself too. The truck moves faster than any person could run, and then faster still, the trees moving past us in the dark like one big blur. We bump along the road, and I hear the gravel scattering from our tires. For once I am inside the machine making all that noise.

"I'll drive you to near the exit," he says. "Then you'll have to hide in the woods—just until they've searched the truck for Water."

Soon the truck stops. Ford leans over me to open the door.

"Watch," he tells me. "Once they've checked the truck, I'll get them to walk away. That's when you hop in."

I creep into the woods and follow the road as Darwin drives up to two men, both holding guns.

The Overseers glance in the front of Ford's truck. Then they lift the cover in the very front of the truck and peer inside with flashlights. Finally they check the open back of the truck.

I think I see Ford's head turn toward my hiding place.

Then I hear low voices, the men talking to Ford. One laughs. And then—both turn from the truck and walk down the road.

I do not hesitate. I pull my skirts from the grasping branches and I sprint to the truck. The door is already open, a little. I climb inside.

"Don't slam it," Ford warns.

I ease the door shut, but quick. The truck starts moving. I crouch low, hidden, afraid the men will see me.

"We're almost past," Ford says. The truck picks up speed, and then we are flying, nearly.

"Can I come up?" I ask from my hiding place.

"We're safe," Ford answers. He looks down for a moment to give me a big grin.

Ford stops the truck while I settle back in my seat.

"Ready to leave the compound?" he asks.

Am I ready? Truly ready? No. My heart pounds. Part of me wants to fling open this door, tear off this trap, and run back to my cabin.

"Go. Go fast." I grip the handle that's by my wrist, and Ford makes the truck go very, very fast.

"At first I wanted to take you to a restaurant. Give you some decent food for once, you know?" Ford glances at me while he talks, but I barely notice. I am too busy staring at all the parts of the world I've never seen—it feels important to memorize every tree trunk, every field, to remember the broad world of Everywhere Else. Although, so far, it doesn't look different from my world.

"I like food," I say.

"Oh, there'll be food. I'm taking care of that too. Popcorn, to start. But more than that."

I think he says more after that—I'm not certain. For the trees start to fall away, and in between them are houses. Houses grander than any cabin, grander than even the beautiful big place where the Overseers and Darwin West live.

They are set far back from the road, with glowing windows winking between trees. Even though we fly by, there's time enough to see that they're big. I count six, eight glowing windows in the front of many. There are two levels on a lot of them.

I wish I could see how a family fills so much space. And how many people live in one house? We've already passed more than the entire Congregation put together, I think.

"They all have their own bedrooms, I know it," I say.

Ford makes a surprised sound, then lets out a short laugh.

"And a kitchen, and a bathroom, and a sink, and a shower . . . for starters," he says in a teasing tone.

I hope he doesn't see my face in the dark, amazed, shocked . . . and wondering what a bathroom is. Truly a room, just for a bath?

"Just a few more minutes and we'll be there." Ford rests his hand on my knee, lightly, for a moment. It feels impossibly warm. I reach for him, but already his hand is gone and back to the wheel he's been gripping.

The truck is going down a very steep hill now; I feel the pull of the bottom, telling us to go even faster. There's a blinking light ahead, suspended above the road.

"What is that?" I ask.

Ford laughs, again, but stops quickly when he senses, I think, that I am not joking. "It's a traffic light," he says. "It tells us to slow down—or stop—so we don't drive into another car."

"I wish Darwin West had one," I say.

"Yeah. No kidding. Only for him, it should always be red." Ford does something to make the car slow, and then stop. We have reached the light, stopped at the edge of an even bigger road. This one has many painted yellow lines on it. Cars and cars and bigger cars pass in a stream, never stopping.

There is a building too, across the stream of cars. It's small and low, like our cabin, with festive lights burning as if they have all the fuel they could ever want—why else would they waste it when the sun is up?

The sign in front says FRANK'S QUIK-EE-GRAB.

"Is that someone's house?" I ask. I can't tear my eyes away

from its lights. It's different from the other places we've passed. This one wants to be noticed.

Ford doesn't laugh this time, even though he does give me a surprised look. "It's a gas station—where I fuel up the truck. Really good breakfast burritos too."

"What's that?" I ask.

"Eggs, bacon, cheese, all rolled up in a tortilla. You have to have one."

"Now?"

"In the . . . morning . . ." Ford's voice trails off.

"I'll be back in the woods, come morning," I say.

We sit, silent, both staring straight ahead at the light. It's so quiet in the truck that I can hear it blink . . . blink . . . blink. Then Ford twists the wheel and we're on the road, going even faster.

Chapter 32

There aren't any houses, now. Instead we pass bigger buildings, most of them dark. But they keep their signs lit.

NAIL SALON, reads one.

QUICK CASH LOANS, says another.

These words mean nothing to me. A wave of embarrassment hits me, and I work hard to push it back. Just because this isn't my world doesn't mean I am less than the people who live in it.

It's hard to remember that.

Soon the lit signs give way to fields. We pass rows and rows of tall stalks. Ford slows the truck and makes another turn.

"So . . . movies," Ford says. "I guess I should prepare you."

A little fear stirs in me, but I slouch and look out the window as if I'm not afraid. I want Ford to think I'm as brave as the modern girls he knows.

"They're like pictures—only moving. That's what they used to call them, moving pictures," Ford says. "And they're big, taller than your cabin."

My bravery has nearly vanished. I swallow and stay quiet, will away the fear rising in me. He wouldn't take me to something that would hurt me, or scare me.

"Don't worry." He sets his hand on top of mine, for a moment. "It's fun. I promise."

"I trust you," I tell him.

"Movies can take you a million miles away—so far away, even Darwin West can't touch you," he says.

"Where will we go?" I ask.

"Oh, nowhere." He lets out a short laugh. "I just mean figuratively. We'll sit in the truck the whole time."

Soon a sign looms up, so brightly lit that I shade my eyes. "Hudson Drive-in," I read out loud. "Flicks, food, and fun."

"It's not exactly a movie theater. We'd have to drive to Albany or Bennington for that," Ford says, apologetic.

"It's nice," I tell him—because it is, far nicer than anything I've ever seen.

"And it's just for us." He drives the truck up to a small hut and presses a button that makes his window slide down. "I thought maybe—maybe a lot of people might be too much, tonight, anyway," he says.

I look past the hut and see only rows of sticks. There's one small building with a sign over it. A picture shows a girl opening her mouth wide to take a bit of a curly white food.

Inside the booth, a boy in a red-and-white-striped shirt waves. He's got a small sparkling bit in one ear, and hair long enough to half cover his eyes. He needs a tie to hold it back—but maybe modern boys don't do that.

"Who's that?" I ask.

"That would be Chuck," Ford says. "We used to . . . He's my friend, I guess."

"Ford, is that really you?" the boy's voice is muffled behind the glass.

"Thanks for setting this up," Ford tells him.

"I pulled out the reel for *Summer Gone*. There's kissing and stuff." The boy slides open the glass door and leans out. I think he's trying to get a good look at me.

His staring eyes are too much. I pull back into the seat and look in the other direction.

"Glad to see you're still alive," the boy tells Ford. "Now pay up."

Ford pulls something out of his pocket; I look and see a wad of green paper. He holds it out the window, close to Chuck, but pulls it back a little when Chuck goes to take it.

"Where's my food?" he asks.

"Oh that? You still want that?" Chuck looks down toward his feet and shakes his head. "It's probably stone cold, man."

Ford peels away some of the paper in his hand and cocks his head at Chuck. "I ordered it hot, right?"

There's a thread of threat in his voice, something that makes me think of Darwin.

I shiver and look around. Suddenly the wide lonely space in front of us looks dangerous. I wonder how Mother is doing, if she sleeps easily. What will she do if she wakes before I'm back?

No. I know that won't happen. And this is just one night,

one slight thing to remember when I'm crouched with spoon and cup. That's all. He won't hurt me. Mother won't find out.

"Ruby? Ruby." Ford is trying to hand me something. I become aware of the heavenly smell coming out of a tall white paper bag.

I take it and hold it up, breathe in deep. Ford is watching me.

"I never smelled anything like it," I tell him.

First he smiles, but it doesn't last long. Something like anger flickers on his face. "You miss a lot up there on the mountain, Ruby."

My only answer is to open the bag more and smell deeper. My stomach lets out a tremendous growl.

Ford hands all the money to Chuck.

"That'll do fine," the boy says. "Enjoy the show, et cetera, et cetera." He waves for the truck to move forward.

Ford drives past rows and rows of the short sticks, not even half the height of all the poles we installed for Darwin. "What are those?" I ask.

"Speakers, so you can hear the movie," he says.

Ford pulls close to a tall white screen. I know the pictures will show there. But how do they get there? Who does it? How do they start and stop them?

The window next to me is going down—Ford's pressed a button somewhere, I think. Then the truck rumbles off, and it's silent. Silent save for the crickets all around us, and peepers too. They're not as loud as you'd think they'd be, though. Maybe it's been just as dry down here.

We sit quiet for a second. I breathe it in. I close my eyes. It's almost like I'm back on the mountain, away from the constant press of the modern world.

"Last summer, we used to come out here after the midnight show, almost every night," Ford says.

I open my eyes to look at him. He's got a small smile on his face, staring straight ahead as if he can see something—but it's still just the blank screen.

"Why come after the show was done?" I ask.

"Chuck gave us free popcorn. It was better than hanging at the Quik-ee-Grab." Ford shrugs.

"What's popcorn?"

"Dinner first." He says it like I'm his child. It bothers me, a little. He doesn't own me. He's not better than me.

But then he unrolls the bag with the food inside, and all I can think of is eating.

He hands me a white fork, the same flimsy kind that Darwin gives us. Then a big white container that squeaks a little when he moves his fingers on it. I squeeze it, a little too hard; the side cracks.

"Careful, there. You're supposed to eat what's inside," Ford teases.

Inside there's long white thin strands curled in a red sauce. There's something yellow melted on top.

Ford has one just like it. He sticks his fork in the middle of the strands and turns it in the circle.

"Can't beat Leo's spaghetti," he says.

Spaghetti. I wonder if that's the white part, the red part, or the yellow part—or all of it. But I'm too hungry to ask any more questions. I do like he does, twirling and pushing the food into my mouth.

But it falls off my fork before it touches my lips.

Ford laughs, but gently. "Takes practice."

He uses a paper napkin to grab the pile of food from my lap, tosses it back into the bag. A waste. I could put it in my pocket, save it, eat tomorrow night when Ford is gone.

But I want to be like a modern girl, so I load my fork with fresh spaghetti and try again.

The flavor explodes in my mouth. I close my eyes and pay attention only to the food, the flavor, the fact that there's a pile more of it waiting for me.

"You like it?" Ford asks.

I swallow and nod while I put more on my fork. "But it's not food, Ford," I tell him.

"I promise you it is . . ."

"No. It has to have another name. Food's not this good." I put another forkful in my mouth, and another, and as I fill my belly I realize that pictures are flickering on the screen in front of us now.

"Movie's starting," Ford says. He reaches out his window and does something to the pole next to the truck.

Sound rolls into the car, so loud that I drop my fork and the little bit of food that's left skitters out of my container.

"Is it kind of loud? I should have warned you." Ford slides his hands over my ears and smiles. I rest my hands on top of his, for a moment, and smile back. The music is muffled, not like modern people hear it, I warrant. I want to be a modern girl at the movies, so I pull his hands away, even though the sound seems loud enough to make my teeth rattle.

"I'll turn it down," Ford says.

Now I can barely hear the music and the talking, but I like it that way. Just looking is more than enough. The people are so big on the screen, and nearly transparent, somehow. I never pictured them flat either.

It's beautiful, so beautiful, in colors brighter than real life. The girl on the screen wears a trim green dress with a skirt so tight and short, I don't know how she sits down. She strides confidently on shoes made of only a few strips of leather. I want to be her, so joyful and carefree.

"I've seen this movie, like, four times," Ford says. "You'll like it. You can see all the fancy stuff you've been missing. The people in it are über, über rich."

"Like Darwin West," I say.

Ford laughs. "If Darwin has money like these people, he's not spending it like them."

I think of his cabin with blazing lights and water that runs inside it, and how his shoes are always fine and new. I think of the thick gold watch on his wrist that glints when he pulls the chain back over his head.

Could there be any richer?

"You'll see." He shifts in his seat and suddenly, somehow, he is much closer to me. I feel the heat coming off his body, and the movie feels less consuming now.

The girl on the screen is driving a tiny, sleek thing that is nothing like the bulky trucks the Overseers drive.

"That's a sports car," Ford says. "I bet it goes from zero to eighty in, like, two seconds."

"Sports car," I say, testing it in my mouth. If I lived in the modern world, could I drive one?

Would I want to? She's missing so much flashing past her while she hurries to the next empty thing.

The girl eats, and flirts with boys, and breaks their hearts. But she doesn't do anything that matters. She's not kind. And she doesn't help a single person.

Is this modern life? I don't know if I like it. But I like watching it. I try to remember every little thing. I'll remember them again, and again, when Ford is gone.

I watch the movie, but I feel Ford's eyes on me, not the screen. I shift a little closer to him too—but I use the softer end of my fork to poke his side gently.

"You don't have to buy tickets to look at me," I tease.

"I just like to watch you," Ford says. "It reminds me of how to be happy."

He slides one arm around my shoulder, and I know what to do. I leave my fork in the empty container and rest my head on his shoulder. It's hard, but not bony—a strong place that will barely even feel the weight of me on it.

"You just watch the movie," I tell him.

The boy from the ticket booth sticks his head in Ford's window and grins at us. "Ah, romance."

I sit up straight; my cheeks flame.

"Table for two, Chuck," Ford growls.

"Popcorn delivery, Mr. Touchy." The boy puts an enormous

white paper bucket in Ford's lap; it's spilling white fluffy bits on the floor.

"Thank you," I tell him.

"Nice girl you got there," Chuck says.

"Chuck," Ford says, none too quiet.

But Chuck doesn't seem to notice or care that Ford's annoyed. He snakes his arm in the window and grabs a giant handful of popcorn. "That guy is such a sucker," he tells the screen. "Chasing after her. She'll never end up with the nice guy."

"Don't you have to clean up or something?" Ford asks him.

"Maybe." The boy tilts his head sideways and looks in at me. "Unless you want company."

I know Ford wants to be alone—I suspect he wants to do more than watch the movie. I feel it in his fast breathing, in how he's pressing the side of his body into mine.

Maybe that's too much for me. But I don't mind finding out for myself.

"We're fine," I tell Chuck. My voice shakes a little, but neither boy seems to notice.

"Maybe next time," Ford says.

"Yeah, right. This girl's way too smart for there to be a next time." Chuck gives me a wink. Then he tosses one of the popcorn pieces at Ford and strolls away. I don't watch him for too long. The movie is taking us inside a gorgeous, tall house with white pillars like trees. I gasp at the beauty, and Ford gives my hand a squeeze.

The people in the movie seem more real than us, their lives

more important, the colors of the world brighter than what I see every day.

"Try some popcorn," Ford says.

I put one piece on my tongue and close my mouth over it; the salt and fat melt slowly. It is heavenly. More flavor than I've ever had, except for the spaghetti.

"Told you it was good." Ford puts the bucket in my lap and pulls me close with his arm again. I wriggle my hips until I'm right next to him. Again I rest my head on his shoulder, still putting popcorn in my mouth, piece by piece.

His hand gently squeezes my shoulder, his fingers draped down over my arm. I wonder what it would feel like to wear the smallest of clothes like the girl on screen. I would feel Ford's skin all over me, right now.

It might be too much to bear.

My stomach feels too full. I set the popcorn bucket on the floor of the truck and lean back against Ford.

He puts his hand against my cheek, pressing—not hard, but not easy to ignore either.

I turn my head, like he wants me to. Then I kiss him, like I want to.

It feels different than when we are under the cisterns. There's no limit out here in this wide space, far from the eyes of Darwin West. Ford's hands travel over my shoulders, across my bodice, find the ties and buttons that he never dared to touch before.

I'm greedy too—I tug at his shirt, up, up, until he realizes what I want and he pulls it off. I pull back from his kisses for a moment, look at the inked designs crisscrossing his chest. They outline the muscles and hardness. I trace my fingers over them, and Ford pulls me tight for another kiss.

More of our skin is touching now. And still all I want is more, more, more.

But his hands slide there—and there—and suddenly it's too much. There's not enough air to breathe. I pull back, gasping. Ford eases back too.

"I've never . . . ," I say. "I don't know. . . ."

Ford smiles, his face half shadowed, half bright in the light of the movie playing. "That's okay."

He tugs his shirt back on, then he rests his arm on the back of his seat. I straighten, tighten my clothes. Then I rest my head on his shoulder. We stare at the people on the screen, in their jewel-bright clothes, doing things I only half understand. Ford's fingers gently trace a circle on my shoulder.

"You don't have to go back," he says.

All the heat still stirring in my body freezes. "I do," I tell him. "I have to go back."

Ford's hand on my shoulder stops. I feel his arm go tense. He swallows hard and looks out the window.

"They need me," I tell him.

"Darwin can live with one less pair of hands," he says, still looking away from me.

I reach up to touch his cheek—but still, that feels wrong, to be close to any part of him. Instead I lean forward and cross my arms tight. "They need the Water."

"You mean your blood." His voice is flat.

"Yes."

"It's heresy, Ruby. And it's . . . crazy. Your blood isn't magic."
His voice is low, but hard.

"You don't have to believe me." I edge away from him until
I'm as far away as I can get, pressed up against the window on my
side.

"Look, Ruby . . ." His voice is gentle now, and he reaches out
to take my hand. I let him hold it but keep it limp. I think about
the strong girl in the movie. She would have snatched her hand
away and stalked off to another boy.

But there is no other boy in my heart. I only want to be here.
I can't, though.

"Take me home," I tell him.

"I'd take care of you. I'd do anything for you," Ford pleads.

I look down at the empty box of spaghetti, the empty rows
meant for modern people's cars—it all seems wrong. I've tried
something I'm not meant to have.

"Take me home," I whisper. "Please."

"Unbelievable." Ford picks up the popcorn bucket and flings
it out the window. The white scatters everywhere like snow.

Did he ever think I would go back? Had he planned to put
me in his truck and never see the Congregation again?

"You think you can control me," I say. "Like Darwin West."

"Don't ever compare me to that man," he says.

"You want to tell me what to do. You want me to obey," I say.

Ford twists the key, and the truck's engine roars to life.
"One more day, Ruby. One more day and I'm gone. No more
chances."

"I know," I say. Tears blur my eyes. Does he think I don't realize this is all coming to an end? That the rest of my life is before me, the same as all the other years before I met him?

"I thought you wanted me," he says.

"I do," I tell him.

But the Congregation needs me. That is where my promises lie.

"Doesn't seem like you want me much," Ford mutters.

We don't wave at Chuck when we leave the movie behind, even though he leans out of the window and waves wildly, with a big grin on his face.

We don't talk all the way home.

Chapter 33

Ford stops the truck when we reach the edge of Darwin West's property.

"One last chance," he says.

Then he takes my hand, softly, and traces a circle on my skin. He doesn't look at me. He looks only at our hands, joined.

I can't speak. I lean my head back against the seat and close my eyes. I listen to the rumble of the truck, inhale the stale spaghetti smell. None of this is my world. None of it feels right.

"They'd die without me," I say.

Ford lets out a long breath. His hand falls away, and the truck moves forward again. The road feels so bumpy after being on the faster, smooth ones.

"You don't have to go all the way to my cabin," I tell him.

"It was a date. That's how you do it," he says.

I don't want to remember him angry. "I'm sorry," I tell him.

"I know."

Now that we are close to the cabin, he switches off his lights.

The truck slows and then we are there. The cabin looks so much smaller now. I notice the roof, half its shingles sideways or missing, and the crooked door with mold growing on the parts that never see sun.

"When will you be gone?" I ask.

"Two days," he says. "At most."

"So . . . good-bye," I tell him.

He turns to face me, and I face him, even though every part of me screams: get out, hurry away, make sure nobody sees you.

When we kiss, my tears slide between our lips. Ford wipes them away when we part.

"I could've saved you," he says.

"Otto saves," I tell him.

"Right." His hand goes to his necklace, for a moment, and then he comes around to open my door.

As soon as I step outside, I sense it: someone is out here, someone besides us. I don't know if I saw a shadow move, or heard breathing, but I'm certain.

"Careful," I whisper.

"What?" Ford says, far too loudly, looking around.

I stand still, as still as a hunted animal. But I don't see anything, hear anything. My skin crawls with being watched, though.

"Go," I tell Ford.

"Not until you're inside," he answers.

Yes. Yes, inside I'll be safe, safer than out here. I want to kiss him again. I want to say good-bye. But I only raise my hand and half run, half tumble down the hill to the cabin.

It's dark inside; the sun hasn't started to come up yet, and I extinguished the lamp before I crept out to be with Ford. I stand still to let my eyes adjust; in the silence I hear the truck's engine grow to a rumble, then gravel spitting from under its tires. Ford is leaving.

A sob pushes out of me. I take careful steps to Mother's bed, barely visible in the near black.

"I did this for you. I did this for the Congregation," I say. More tears spill over my cheeks.

When I kneel to touch her on the floor, my hand passes through where her body should be. I feel only damp blankets. Has she moved? I stand and check her bed — but no.

Someone took her. I left for the first and last night in my life, and someone took her. Darwin West, I warrant, breaking the very few rules he ever followed.

I burst out the cabin door. I'll get Boone. I'll get ten men. We'll go to Darwin's house and we'll save her; we will, I don't care if we're not supposed to fight back.

Then, a voice.

"I'm over here, Ruby." Mother's voice? Impossible. I scramble away from the sound, coming around the corner of the cabin.

I'm halfway up the hill when the person speaks again.

"Stop running, Ruby."

It is Mother.

I spin around, looking for her. Everything is dark, and she says nothing more. But then I spy a sliver of white fluttering near the road. She's in the bushes, only feet away from where the truck was parked.

Part of me wants to run. I'm afraid of what she saw, what she heard. But where would I go? I made my choice when I let Ford's truck drive away.

"Mother?" I ask. My voice quavers. "Please come out."

"Come here," she says. The white fluttering grows, and I see now that she's waving her arm at me.

What did she see, so close to the truck? What did she hear?

Slowly, I come close to her. She's got one arm wrapped around a slim pine tree trunk, her face as pale as the bloodstained gown she wears. But she stands, and breathes.

"Do you still hurt?" I ask her.

"Not enough. You healed me well," Mother says. "Too well."

"I'm not sorry you're better." I can't think of what else to say. So I offer her my hand. "Let me take you back to bed."

"Your blood grows stronger every day, Ruby. That's what I think. How else could I have healed so fast tonight?" She sighs and lays her head against the trunk, the brown of her hair blending until all I can see is the unnatural white of her face.

"I made a lot of Water," I tell her.

"Still, you didn't think I'd wake so soon, did you?"

No. I thought I could go away, and come back. I was more worried about Darwin West catching us.

Mother shakes her head. "There's no room for romance here, Ruby."

So she saw something—so she knows enough. My stomach feels like a rock. My arm drops slowly, slowly, as if passing through mud.

"And with an Overseer." Her body slumps a little, and she grabs at the trunk with her other arm.

"Mother!" I wrap my arms around her chest and pull her upright. She twists against me, not wanting my touch, I think.

"You'll let go of me now," she says.

I obey, but I do not step back. "Let me bring you inside. You're still healing."

"They beat us. They starve us. And you . . . you *kiss* one?"

"Yes," I whisper, familiar shame filling me. She's telling me the same thing I've told myself.

"Never did I think, Ruby. Never did I think you would betray your family."

"I didn't betray us. I only . . . I only wanted . . . love."

"To think I worried about what'd you do with Jonah Pelling," she says.

"Ford's a good person," I tell her.

"No. No, he's not." Mother fixes a grim stare on me. "What did you tell him, Ruby? What does he know?"

I told him I craved escape. I told him I loved the short bristle of his hair. I told him I knew what it felt like to lose someone you loved, inch by inch.

"I didn't tell him anything," I say.

"Your blood? Our age? Does he know these things?"

"Only my blood," I whisper. "But he doesn't even believe it's sacred."

"Ruby! Your greatest secret, gone," she says.

"He's leaving," I tell her. "He's leaving for good. None of this matters."

"And you?" she asks, her voice rasping, dryer than bark peeling off birch.

First I don't understand. "And me? What do you mean?"

"Don't mock me." Mother grips the tree and turns so her back is to it, both hands behind her for support. Then she inches up, up, until she is standing very straight.

We are exactly the same height now.

The force of her stare pushes me back a step, then another.

"You'll go with him, won't you?" Mother says.

"No. No!" I look down the road, imagining the taillights I didn't even see—because I was already in the cabin looking for Mother, worrying about her. "I'm a Congregant."

"And a fine, fine young lady in love." Mother's laugh is terrible: low, bitter. She doesn't think I'm fine. She thinks I'm soiled.

"I don't—" But no. I can't tell her I don't love him, even though it's the only thing I can say that might help.

So I swallow and give the best truth I can. "It doesn't matter if I love him."

"Does he give you pretty things? Trinkets, or food?"

I think of the spaghetti, and the popcorn, and his kisses. He gave me far better than trinkets.

"He's kind to me," I tell her.

"It's far more than that, isn't it, Ruby?" She moves as if to fold her arms, her usual powerful stance when she questions me—but when she lets go of her support, her knees betray her and she sinks to the ground.

I plunge to the forest floor next to her. "You're not well enough to be outside," I urge.

"No. But I woke and my daughter was gone." Mother bows her head for a moment, and when she looks at me again, her eyes are bright with tears. "I thought Darwin took you. I was . . . I was walking to his cabin."

"I thought he took *you*," I tell her.

"He could have, couldn't he?" She gives her eyes a vicious wipe and looks away from me.

As long as my mother has been conscious, I do not think I have ever seen her so vulnerable before. It kills every bit of fight in me.

"I'm sorry. I never should have left you, not even for a few hours. Not for a moment." I grasp both her hands and fold them together over my heart. "Please forgive me."

She lets me hold her for a moment, then finds the strength to yank her hands away. "I can't forgive a betrayal."

"It was for one night. It was a good-bye."

"You sold yourself for trinkets," Mother says.

That lights anger in me. "I would never—"

"I saw your kiss. I saw how he watched when you walked down the hill. That boy desires you, Ruby. You made that happen."

If she's trying to make me feel worse, it doesn't work. A small, proud flame lights in me. After we fought, after I put him aside, he still desires me.

That will carry me through many a long, hard day.

"He's left," I say simply.

"And what did he leave you with?" She looks down at my waist, then back up.

This time I do not miss her meaning. "We didn't do that. Not like—" I stop before I say it. But she finishes the sentence for me.

"Not like me? Not like Otto and me?"

I nod.

Her slap hits me so hard, my head snaps sideways. Overhead, something flutters away. A bird, I suppose.

She hasn't hit me since I was very small and I crept away from her. It was a game to me. She thought I had fallen into the Lake.

"Don't ever leave without telling me," she said then.

I've sinned the same way again.

"Sneaking about with an Overseer is *nothing* like what I had with your father," Mother says.

"He's not like the others," I tell her.

"I've seen him lift his chain. I've seen him level a gun against us," she answers.

"He hated every bit of it. And now he's leaving, and I'll never see him again." I can't help the tears that start down my face, even if it makes Mother snort with disgust. "He won't tell anyone about me, Mother, I know it."

"I wish it were true, Ruby. I wish it were true." Mother puts both hands behind her and tries to stand, but her legs won't hold her.

"Let me help you," I tell her.

"Seems I'll need to get by on my own, soon," she says.

"Never. Never!" I cry.

Mother lets out a sigh and stops her attempts to stand. She tips her head back and looks up at the trees. "I hate the woods. I've hated them from the day I walked into them, and I'll hate them until the day I walk out of them."

"We all hate it here," I say.

"I've dreamed of leaving. I've dreamed of fighting. But I

know what we're meant to do, Ruby," she says. "You know it too."

"Yes," I whisper.

"We are meant to wait, and pray, and endure. That is all," she says.

There's no way to make her understand. All I can do is show her it's done. All I can do is stay by her side and remember my promises.

So I don't argue anymore. I offer her my hand. "Let me take you inside. Please, Mother."

She considers me for a moment, then nods once, short. When I pull her up, she groans. My hand slides against something wet along her back.

"You're bleeding again," I tell her. "Come."

"Wait." Mother shakes me off. She is barely standing, tilted to one side, her gown shaking from her body's trembling.

"Promise me first," Mother says.

I bow my head.

"Promise me you'll never leave," she says.

Anger stirs in me. Didn't I already tell her that? Haven't I already shown it? I made my choice.

But I say it. "I promise. Now . . . please." I look up and hold out a hand.

"Promise me you'll never look at him again," she says.

He's in my memory forever and gone in two days. I keep my eyes level, meeting hers, not looking away. "I promise."

"Promise me you'll forget all about him, Ruby."

I look away from her.

"If you can't do that . . . how can I trust you again?" she asks.

"You can trust me," I tell her.

"How can I love you?" she whispers.

My breath stops.

"Promise," Mother says.

I want to say it. I open my mouth to say it. But the wind shifts, and the smell of Ford is around me for a moment, caught in my hair and my clothes.

Never will I forget him.

"I can't," I tell her.

Her body slumps, but she does not fall.

"Come inside," I say.

She shakes her head.

I want to leave her here, go to my bed, close my eyes, and forget every bit of this for the last few hours. But there's no way I can leave her here, even after what she's said.

"Then we'll lie here," I tell her.

I kneel at her feet and brush away the sticks and pinecones that surround her. Then I stand and press against her shoulders, gently. All the strength is gone from her. She sinks to her knees, then slumps onto the ground.

Mother curls into a tight ball, and I round my body around hers. Her breathing is ragged at first, and then it erodes into gasps, and then sobs. Her body shakes with them.

"Promise me you'll be here in the morning," she whispers.

"I promise," I tell her.

Her body goes limp.

I wrap my arms around her tighter and stare into the woods, waiting for dawn.

Chapter 34

I wake with pine needles in my mouth. Mother is gone; a damp reddish patch remains where she lay. The sun is already full over the horizon, but it hasn't burned the night chill off yet. Autumn is upon us.

She cried last night until sleep took her; then I closed my eyes. I dreamed of Ford, and kisses, and popcorn.

Tomorrow is his last day here. Today is the second to last. Will I see him? Do I want to?

I wipe the salty taste from my lips. I've woken into a different life now, the one I'm meant to live. I should be glad if I don't see Ford again.

When I get close to the cabin, I hear a sound coming from it—a strange, light sound I haven't heard in a long time, in the morning. It's Mother, singing. I push open the cabin door and find her sweeping.

"Good morning," I say. It's hard to say anything to her after last night. I cringe, waiting for anger, or worse—silence.

Maybe she already has stopped loving me.

But she smiles at me with no anger, no threat. "Good morning, Ruby. I thought I'd clean before we went to the cisterns."

She's got her dress and boots on. Her body is straight and strong enough to sweep the floors. Even her hair looks lustrous.

My clothes are stained from embracing her bleeding body last night; my eyes feel near swollen shut from shedding so many tears. Next to her, I look like the one recovering from Darwin's blows.

"You're better," I say.

She shrugs but doesn't stop cleaning. "I feel completely healed."

She doesn't thank me—she never does. What I give is what's expected of me, what I was born for. I try to push the irritation away. It never bothered me before. Why should it bother me now?

"Do you think the Visitor will come tomorrow?" I slide around her to pull the soiled sheets from her bed. I'll put them in the Lake, weigh them down with a stone so they soak without floating away. They'll come out muddy, at least, but most of the blood will be gone.

"We'll be readying the cisterns today," Mother says. "And I smell breakfast cooking."

I hadn't noticed the smell before, but now that I breathe in, there's grease in the air, a promise of food.

"Then the Visitor's coming very soon," I say. Darwin is working to put plump on our angles, hide the evidence of his abuse on every other day of the year.

drought

"Aye. Maybe even today." Mother stops to inspect her work, hands on hips, but whirls into motion again.

If he comes today, Ford won't be back tomorrow.

"Why are you tidying? The Visitor won't be coming *here*." It comes out as a grumble, even though I meant it as a tease.

It doesn't seem to bother Mother; nothing could bother her today, I think. "Today is a fresh start, Ruby. I want everything as clean as I can make it."

I notice her boots now; she's brushed and scrubbed at every stain, I think. I don't understand. Does she think housecleaning will make her forget—will make me forget?

When Mother sees me looking at her feet, she waves her hand at mine. "Let me clean your boots."

But then the bell rings—the dinner bell, something we rarely hear anymore. Mother claps her hands together, boots forgotten. "Breakfast, Ruby."

"I know." Does she think I'm still a child?

Mother chatters about something as we walk to breakfast—stuffing the cabin's chinks with mud, perhaps, to ready it for winter. Or maybe she's telling me about the latest dispute with the Pellings. I don't know. None of it matters. It's all the same thing we've talked about for two hundred years.

We sit with Beaulah Pelling, her face as sour and pinched as the apples set out for breakfast. She doesn't have a smile to spare.

Mother usually doesn't seek her out. Once I heard her tell Hope that the woman was harder to bear than sitting on a tack. But today she smiles and gives Beaulah a squeeze around the shoulders.

"Is your arthritis better?" Mother asks.

"For now. Trust it to flare up when the snow flies." Beulah gives a single nod, then takes a vicious bite of her apple. At least all the Congregants have kept their teeth. Our tiny bit of Water has been enough for that.

"I'll get your food," Mother tells me. "Sit and relax."

"I can—"

"I'll get it." Her tone leaves no room for argument. I watch her go up to the table and pile two plates with eggs and biscuits, plus plenty of apples and leftover sausage from our celebration. As she goes, she stares at each Overseer and looks at the corners of the room.

Ford isn't here. I knew it even as I walked in the room. When Ford's around, everything feels calmer, steadier. But today the room felt jittery and wrong.

"Soon we'll be harvesting snowflakes," Beulah sighs.

"And freezing our fingers half off," I say.

She gives me a surprised look; normally I ignore her complaints or give her a sunny reply. But I've no strength to fight her gloom today. Besides, my gloom is far darker than hers.

Mother sets the plate in front of me. The eggs nearly slide off the plate, leaving a wet trail behind them. The biscuit has black burned edges.

I try a bite of eggs. They're ice cold, and somehow I know now that they shouldn't be. I gag.

"Delicious," Mother says.

"Best food I've tasted in weeks," Beulah sighs.

All around the room, the Congregants are grinning and

jamming food into their mouths. They don't stop to look at the food or wonder whether it's better suited to be fireplace coals.

A week ago, I would have been just like them. But now I've tasted better. I know just how terrible this food is. I remember spaghetti. I remember popcorn.

I push the plate away and Mother gives me a sharp look. She's been watching me since we came into the Common House. "What's wrong?" she asks.

"My stomach hurts," I tell her. It's true enough.

"There won't be more later for you. Eat," she orders.

"I'm not hungry," I tell her.

She frowns, but only for a second, and then smiles wider. "Then take apples for later," she says, rolling her eyes a little at Beulah. What a silly little girl she has.

"You gonna eat that?" Beulah asks. Her arm snakes toward my plate.

"Take it," I tell her.

Mother's eyes narrow.

"I'm not hungry," I tell her again.

"You must stay strong," she says softly.

Is she worried for me, or worried for the girl with Otto's blood? I try to push away the thought. Why am I thinking these terrible things? I'll be here with her for a long time, until Otto comes.

The door to the Common House opens; I twist to see who's there, hoping for Ford. But it's Darwin. His face is flat, lifeless, the most frightening look of all for him.

"Come on, Toads," he says. "Time to work."

They all stand, eager almost. But I stay seated. What we will grant for just a bit of kindness, a bit of food. What if we used our energy for something different?

I look across the room and see one other not standing: Earl Pelling. He catches my eye and then looks at Darwin, and back at me. Nods once. Then he jams an entire biscuit in his mouth.

I look away. I can't give him what he wants.

The Congregants grasp for a last biscuit, a last apple, and the big dented metal bowls are empty before the crowd has left for outside. I don't reach for anything extra. Already Mother has pressed two apples on me. I'll keep them, at least for now. Eventually hunger may make them delicious.

Darwin leads us across the dirt road to the cisterns. He catches a look at Mother, standing next to me, and his eyes widen. He glances back at the closest cistern and gives it a good thump. The full sound seems to satisfy him, and he looks at a clipboard that one of the Overseers has handed him.

"I need five toads to fix the cabins up roadside. Five to cut the grass, here. And three to tidy up the outside of the Overseer cabin." Darwin looks up, expectation on his face, and Congregants step forward quickly to volunteer. It's better to speak up while you know what the job is.

It's what we do every year to prepare for the Visitor. We make this look like a different kind of place—a place where people have time to do things besides harvest water, a place that's home, not a prison.

Last year, I painted the boards on the walls of the cabins that faced the road—but only so far as the cisterns. The Visitor never goes past here. The year before, I scrubbed brown dots of dried blood off the cisterns.

Another truck with Overseers pulls up; they've got buckets and long brushes in the back of their truck. The passenger door opens, the same place I'd sat just last night. And out comes Ford.

Do I let out a gasp? Or does it just echo inside me? Mother grabs my elbow, looks at the truck, then looks at Darwin.

"Do you need another painter?" she calls.

Darwin shakes his head. "Dock scrubbers!" he shouts. "My house!"

Ford and the other Overseers he came with step up. They are holding buckets and long brushes. Ford's eyes brush past me, and I lose my breath.

"Don't even dream it," Mother says, and her grip becomes painful. I try to shake free but she only grips harder.

Ford hands out brushes to five Congregants. Mother keeps me right next to her.

"Weeds!" Darwin calls out, and Mother gives me a shove so I stumble forward.

"We'll weed," Mother says loudly.

I get a big paint-stained bucket and a small shovel with a dulled nose to dig with. Mother takes one too. I walk to the edge of the clearing and kneel. At least it's easy to find weeds, unlike drops of water.

Mother pops a weed out and tosses it in her bucket. Another, and another. Breakfast has energized her—or maybe it's anger at me.

"The Elders will come to our cabin tonight," she says in a low voice.

"Tonight? But it's not our meeting night," I say.

"You'll tell them what you did. And they'll decide what to do," she answers.

I hadn't thought about anyone else knowing. Somehow I thought only Mother would have my secrets about Ford. But of course she's told them. She loves the Congregation over me—she said as much last night.

"He's leaving," I tell Mother. "For good."

"It doesn't change what you did." She glances over her shoulder, and I look too.

The Congregants who volunteer to work with Ford are piled in the back of the truck. He's inside, staring straight ahead. The truck moves forward, and that's when he looks, for just a second, at me.

I see anguish, and love, and all the things that are in my heart too.

"Turn around," Mother orders, and she gives my ear a hard tug.

Still I can hear the gravel popping under the wheels, and the engine rumbling as the truck moves away. Ford is driving away again.

And this time, Mother is right beside me to ensure I make the right choice.

Chapter 35

It's not dark yet when the Elders come. Tonight we don't have to hide. We did Darwin's work. And then he even gave us a sort of dinner — slimy, cold, thin slices of white meat, with sticky yellow slices of cheese and crackers edged with more mold.

This time I made myself eat every bit. I'm a Congregant, nothing more. Any bit of food is a miracle.

Hope comes to the door first. When I open it, a rush of cool air comes in, laced with woodsmoke.

"Ruby," Hope says. That is all. No hug, no more greeting, no small joke about the day's work. Her face doesn't hold a hint of a smile.

"Come in." I smile wide as I step back to let her in the cabin. She looks away.

Boone and Asa come together. Boone is a step behind the older man, his hands out and up slightly, as if to catch Asa if he stumbled. But Asa is sure-footed tonight. A little food and Water has brought back his strength.

"You made a good mess, girl," Asa snaps at me.

"I only—" I start, but Asa holds up his fist.

"Your reasons don't matter," he says.

Boone only shakes his head, flicking me a glance, then goes inside.

Mother and Hope have been talking in low voices, too low for me to hear much. I've heard bits: *love, foolish, danger.* Perhaps I don't want to hear more.

Each Elder sets down the chair they've brought. There's none for me.

"Shall we start?" Mother takes her seat and looks at the other three. They follow her lead, arranging their chairs in a rough circle.

Where do I go? Uncertain, I settle on the floor, behind Asa, and ready myself for what they have to say.

"Leave us," Boone says. It's the first word he's said to me all night.

Nobody disagrees. Asa leans back in his small chair, folding his arms. The wood creaks under his weight.

I stand up and look at each of them. "Leave?" I ask.

"Yes, that's right. You'll have to find another place for the night." Mother stares straight at me with a strange, too merry smile on her face. Hope won't look at me. And Boone—Boone, who healed Mother countless times with me—gives my arm a shove. It's none too gentle.

"I'm your Leader," I say. "You can't make me go."

"You'll do as we say," Asa growls. "We made you Leader, and we can take it away too."

I feel like a small girl again.

"Go, Ruby," Boone says. "You can return at sunrise."

"It might not take that long—" Hope starts, looking up at Boone.

"It's best that way," Boone says.

Hope draws in a deep breath, then nods, dropping her eyes to the ground.

"I wanted to explain," I say. I'd been ready to answer their questions, had been thinking about it all day as I worked. I was going to tell them about Ford's kindness, his horror at how we lived, how we were treated. I wasn't ready for this.

"There's nothing you need to tell us," Mother says. "I've told them everything."

She's told them everything *she* wants them to know. But what of my side? Words tumble over my lips. I sound frantic, but I don't care. They have to listen. "I want to explain. I want to tell you why I didn't leave. I want to tell you about Ford—"

"Don't say his name," Hope says, her voice gravelly. Still she doesn't look at me.

"Doesn't matter, does it?" Asa says to her. Then he turns in his chair. "Get out, kid. Don't come back until the morning."

They are pushing me from my own cabin. They don't care what I have to say. They hate me, it's clear. It's not just Mother who can stop loving me. It's all of them.

I chose them, and they don't even love me.

"Take some jerky," Mother says, pointing at the chest.

That tiny bit of kindness stings more, somehow, than the rest of this.

"I'm not hungry," I choke out, and then I turn and hurry out before they can see any more tears on my face.

Softly, I settle on the ground beside the door, my back to the cabin. I turn my head and press my ear to the wall.

Never have I had to eavesdrop on the Elders before. Always they let me stay in the room. I heard them talk about all manner of things.

It's not easy to hear them. We've mudded the walls well, and the logs are thick. I hear the rumble of Asa's voice, and Mother's laugh—strange, high-pitched. But mostly it's quiet.

The fall chill settles over the bare parts of my skin like a wet spiderweb. I shiver, rubbing my arms for warmth. It will be a long night without fire. I wonder if I could follow the smell of the woodsmoke to find shelter, maybe even some friendship.

But I stay where I am. I might catch a little of what they're saying. And the cabin—and the people inside it—are my home. They are the people I'm meant to be with. I'll stay out here, if I must.

But then the door opens. Hope peers out, catches sight of me almost right away. Her eyes widen and she puts her finger to her mouth. A signal: be quiet.

"I'll be but a minute," Hope calls inside. Then she shuts the door.

"What are they saying?" I scramble to my feet and take an eager step toward Hope.

She holds up both hands, warding me off. "Why do you ask when you were listening?"

Finally our eyes meet. But her look does not hold any warmth. What happened to the girl-woman I played with in the woods? What happened to the person I whispered my secrets to?

"No . . . I . . ." I look down at my feet. There's no use in lying. I was lurking only a few footfalls from the door. "Yes. I was listening. I've never been sent away from an Elders meeting before."

"You never did . . . *this* before either." Hope looks over her shoulder. "I'll have to tell the others I found you."

"No. Wait. I'll go." Things won't go any better for me if all of them know I was here.

"Go to Ellie's cabin. I'll get you there when it's done." Hope jerks her head in the direction of the road, her mouth a grim thin line.

"At sunrise?" I ask her.

"Sooner, I hope. But . . . I don't know." Hope draws in a deep, shuddering breath, and for a moment I think she's going to cry.

"I'll go. I'm sorry, Hope." I want to touch her, hug her, but I can tell I shouldn't, not right now.

"Promise me you'll wait there," she says. Now a tear slips down her cheek.

If she's upset, it's because of me. "I'm terribly sorry," I say again.

"Just go," Hope says.

So I do. I hurry up the road; when I look back, she's still watching me. Then she looks back into the cabin, as if someone has called her. I don't wait longer to see what she'll do, or if Boone chases me even farther away.

There's still a streak of sun on the Lake when I reach Ellie's cabin, but already gloom has settled over it for the night. It never seemed so dreary when Ellie was alive, not even when she was sick.

When I push open the door, the hinges creak. A damp smell rolls out. I open the door wider, and fan at the air with my hands. It's wrong for Ellie's cabin to smell like this.

All her dried flowers are growing mold, and her mattress is streaked with it too. It's as if the walls have been weeping since she died.

Nothing is left of Ellie here. We took her things, yes. But now I can't even close my eyes and breathe in. The woods and the mold have already started to reclaim the cabin.

The cabin lets out a creak; the sound sends chills down my arms. I feel like I've invaded a place where I'm not wanted— worse, a place where I don't belong. I can't stay another moment.

Ellie. I'll go to her, just for a little. I'll be back before Hope comes to find me.

And if she finds me missing? Well, maybe they deserve it, a little, for the things they said. Let them worry they've lost me.

Even though the sky is blue with sunset, the woods are nearly as dark as the middle of the night. The lights aren't on tonight, of course. We're not harvesting. I wonder if Darwin will push us to work day and night after the Visitor brings fresh, empty cisterns. Or will he wait until the heat of next summer to do that?

Tomorrow the Visitor will come. He'll have the Overseers put the full cisterns on his long truck, after taking the empty ones off. Everything will start over again.

But tonight they're full.

Would Darwin let them sit unguarded? He hasn't trusted us all summer. Why now?

And would he still send Ford to do it?

I feel the tug of Ford's presence. He might be in the woods now. If I turn left instead of right—if I swing around that tree instead of ducking through those bushes—I could be with him.

But no. I made my choice. I have to live with it.

As I walk to Ellie's grave, nothing feels right in the woods. I hear noises that push my feet forward, send my heart racing—noises that any other night I might have not even noticed. Skittering. Crunching leaves. Scrambling. It's only animals, and small ones, I know. But none of it feels friendly.

The Elders are against me, Mother is against me, and that makes it feel as if all the world has decided I deserve to be punished.

But not Ellie. Ellie would never do that. I ignore the noises and press forward, even when a sapling branch whips me straight across the face. I know every tree in the forest, but this one seems to have picked up its roots and set itself in my path. After one branch surprises me, they all feel out of place. Three more lash me before I finally slow my pace.

What are they talking about, back in the cabin? Are they thinking of a punishment for me? Or maybe even deciding I'm not a worthy Leader, like Asa said they could?

A root plucks at my toe; I stumble, my ankle twisting, and barely manage to stop from falling. But then another step, another root, and I go sprawling across the forest floor.

My chest lands on the hard knob of the root. It pushes all

the air from me in a *whoosh*. I gasp, desperate for air, and at first nothing comes.

The air seems to shimmer around me. I imagine I see someone standing ahead—Ellie.

Finally I can breathe. I suck air into my lungs, lying on the dirt, and the figure I imagined is gone as suddenly as I first saw it.

Every part of the forest has fought me tonight. Why do I keep fighting back? Ellie is gone. I know I can't really talk to her there—if she is listening, she'd be listening everywhere, not just by the patch of dirt where they discarded her.

I should go back to her cabin. I should wait. If Hope goes there before I do, she'll think I ran, maybe. Or at least she'll know I didn't obey her.

But that's not the way my feet turn. And now the forest is familiar again—the branches are where they are supposed to be, easy to push away or to duck. Stones and roots are vaults for my toes instead of blocks.

I'll be at the cisterns in moments.

Maybe Ford will be there. Maybe he won't. I'm not sure what I'll do if I see him.

But I do know there's nowhere else I want to be right now. And before I go back to living the same dreary Congregant life, I want one last chance for something more, just for one more night.

Chapter 36

I am nearly at the cisterns when I hear the scream.

It bounces off the birches, so loud I imagine it sets their leaves rattling. Is it a bobcat? A bear? Whatever it is must be wounded, or battling . . . or both.

When I can nearly see the tops of the cisterns, another scream echoes around me. I duck into the bushes and peer through the branches. There, ahead, is the dark bulk of the cisterns. I creep closer, and closer, until I am at the ridge of the hill that looks down on them.

There are shadows at the cisterns, ones that don't belong. I crouch farther into the leaves before risking another look.

People, six or seven or them, are standing in the shadows of the cisterns. They are in a wide circle. I cannot see their faces, or what they wear. But I do see the glint of something silver cascading from a hand.

I force my breath to slow. Now I hear other noises: the sickening rattle of an Overseer's chain. And then a hard thump.

A silver line arcs high above the people's heads and lashes in the middle of their circle. When the chain finishes its arc, there is another scream. This one sends shivers down my spine, clenching my toes in my boots.

The chain passes from one dark figure to the next. Each arcs high and strikes hard. But the person they are beating does not always cry out. Perhaps it is because their victim is brave—or perhaps it is because he, or she, is losing strength.

I know I cannot stop them; I know they would only turn their chain on me. So I will wait until they are finished. I will creep out of the woods and get help for the Congregant who lies in the grass under the cisterns.

Another scream; another lash. I sink onto the ground and push my hands tight against my ears. This beating is lasting longer than any I've ever seen.

Congregants are strong, I remind myself. Our bodies can endure. This pain is temporary, and this Congregant will heal. I'll make Water to help, if I need to. I don't care what the Elders think.

The screaming has stopped. The chain falls once, twice, three times again. Then I hear a voice—a familiar, silvery, and impossible voice—come from one of them.

"Is it finished?"

It's Hope, I know it. A gasp escapes from me, and I shrink back into the woods.

"He's good and beat," another voice says. Earl?

I dare to peer out again. In a flash, I recognize other figures too: Asa's slight list to one side, Boone's broad shoulders, Mother's proud straight bearing. There's Earl, next to her, holding the chain. There's one more figure besides them: Zeke Pelling, maybe, or perhaps it's another Congregant. Six of them, in all.

"But is he dead?" Boone asks.

Mother kneels, looking at the person or thing in the middle of them. "He's got to be dead. He's not one of us."

Hope lets out a loud moan. "What have we done?" she cries.

"The right thing," Boone answers.

"Go get Ruby, Hope," Mother says. "Bring her home."

Then she steps aside, and I see into the middle of the circle. A body, crumpled. White scraps of a shirt, darkened and shredded. Dark swirls of designs on skin torn and bloodied.

"No! No!" I burst out of the bushes and race down the hill to them. As one, the group turns and stares at me. Earl drops the chain. It makes a heavy terrible thud on the forest floor.

I shove my way between Mother and Boone. There is Ford, in the middle, though I can barely recognize him. He lies in a pool of blood. His limbs are bent in wrong ways; a dark river runs from the top of his head, down his cheek, to pool at his throat.

"You killed him!" I reach for him, but Boone grabs me roughly around my elbow, stopping me.

"We had to do it," Hope says.

"You didn't have to do this." I fix Hope with a fierce stare.

She looks away.

I struggle against Boone's grip; he grimaces, trying to hold me. "Let me. Let me touch him." I don't beg. I snarl, wild.

"Might as well," Mother says.

Boone lets go of me suddenly; I stumble back and land hard

against Mother. But I scramble away from her, fast as I can, and kneel beside Ford.

His body is entirely, shockingly, still. I take one of his hands in mine, trace my fingers over his palm. A shudder rocks my body.

"He's dead," I tell them. "Dead!" I scream it, loud enough to echo off the hills.

"Good," Mother says.

Boone looks at me, his face blank. "Now you'll stay," he says.

"And he won't tell anyone about you." Mother's eyes flick to Earl and Zeke. I wager they're good enough for helping dole out a beating, but not good enough to hold all my secrets.

"He wanted to steal you," Hope says. "He wanted to take you from us."

"He only wanted to love me," I whisper.

"You were both very selfish," Mother says. "You left us no choice."

"When did Otto ever say that killing was a choice?" I ask her. "You always said violence wasn't our way."

"Otto needs you here. We all agreed." Mother looks at the others, one by one. Slowly, each nods.

"I told him good-bye. I *told* you it was over." I look up at Mother.

"And what if you changed your mind, Ruby?" she asks.

"Love makes you do dangerous things." Hope steps through the circle to come close to me; at first she moves to kneel next to Ford, I think, but then she takes a step back and looks up, quickly.

"Look at him, Hope," I urge. "Look at what *you* did."

She claps a hand over her mouth and dashes into the woods.

I try to smooth the scraps of fabric back over Ford's broken chest; it seems even more indecent, his blood and guts exposed. A sob escapes from me; my tears drip over him, in him, but I only cry harder.

Asa speaks, finally. "Wasn't us who made this happen."

"It was you," Earl adds. "Could've had my boy. None of this had to happen."

"Instead you ran round with trash." Zeke spits a wad on Ford's battered cheek. I wipe it away, tenderly.

"They're wrong," I whisper to Ford. "It wasn't me who did this."

I lay on the ground next to him, body in blood, hair nested in the leaves. But I don't care. I only want to be close to him.

"We're leaving, Ruby," Mother says. Then she holds out her hand.

"Good," I tell her. "Go."

She pulls back as if she's touched something hot. "You'll thank me one day, Ruby. You'll see."

"Never," I say.

Mother whirls on her heel and starts to the road. The others follow—all but Boone, who lingers for a moment.

"Visitor's coming in the morning," he says. "I'd clear out by then."

"I'll never forgive you," I tell Boone. "Not any of you."

"Maybe not." He draws in a deep breath and looks up at the sky. "But you'll stay."

Boone walks away, feet crunching over leaves as dry as bones.

I pick up Ford's hand—every finger at wrong angles—and trace my finger over his skin, the way he touched me once.

"Wake up," I tell him.

And then I say it again, louder.

"Wake up."

Then I feel it. There is the faintest of pulses, in the web of skin between his thumb and his pointer finger.

He is alive, but barely.

Chapter 37

He's alive.

I sit up and look over Ford's body again, this time to see what I need to fix first. There are wounds everywhere, his body sunken in the wrong places. Bones pierce the skin over his ribs and his thighs.

But there's hope. And if anyone can save him, it's me.

"You're alive." I chant it softly, over and over, as I gently press and examine. The words run together faster and faster until they're one word. Alive. Alive. Alive.

He needs Water—but from where?

There's no way to get water all the way up here from the Lake. I haven't any buckets.

The leaves. I can get it from the leaves. I scramble to my feet and grab at the nearest bush. Dry. Ferns—they'll be wet. A single tiny drop of water slides over my finger for a tantalizing moment . . . and then it drops onto the ground.

I run my finger over the soft lumps of veins in my arm. I

could find a rock and cut my arm open. I could drip my blood
into his wounds.

Would it work? I don't know. It might. Or it could kill him.
Nobody has ever drunk my blood unless it's diluted in water. I
can't experiment, not now.

There's only one place left that has Water: the cisterns.

Five full cisterns stand behind us. Surely there is enough to
save anyone's life.

The Water belongs to Darwin West. Nobody has ever broken
that rule. Perhaps that is because the Overseers stand ready to
punish any theft. Or maybe it seems wrong to meddle with consecrated Water.

I look up at the cistern looming above us like the only cloud
in the sky. The large lock looped over the spigot is rusty, and old.
It moves slightly in the breeze that's sweeping over us.

"I'm going to help you," I tell Ford. "Just . . . Just keep breathing."

Then I push to my feet. My clothes are stuck to my body in
strange places, plastered with blood and clods of dirt. When I
take a step, I notice for the first time that my legs and hands are
shaking.

I find the biggest rock I can and hold it high over the
lock.

The Visitor comes tomorrow. There will be no hiding the
theft—unless I use only a little.

I smash at the lock. The rock leaves bright scratches behind
on the rusty metal. But the lock does not break. Again I swing
the rock. The lock swings wildly on the hasp, mocking me, still
unbroken.

The chain still lies by Ford's feet in a bloody heap. It is the strongest thing in the clearing. I lift the chain and swing it, slowly at first, and then faster. Then I smash it against the lock.

The lock swings, but it doesn't break.

It's only one small lock. One small, rusty lock sits between Ford's death and life. I have to find a way to break it.

I finger the links and remember the hands that held this chain before me. Mother, Boone, Hope, Asa, Earl, Zeke . . . they all held this chain with hate. They all would want me to fail, tonight, if they knew what I was doing.

I won't fail. I can't.

The lock has stopped swinging. I take a deep breath and study it. There's a big gap between the bottom of the lock and the hasp—big enough to push something through. I could use a stick as a lever, or maybe . . .

Maybe I could use the chain.

I slide the chain's end through the lock, then grasp one end in each hand. Then I pull against the chain with all my might. For once, let these terrible chains do some good.

But the lock stays closed.

Please, Otto, I pray. *Please break the lock.*

I wrap the chain around my arms, my wrists, and then I push my entire body against it. I heave. Nothing. Then I jump back and land against the chain. My feet slip and I tumble on the ground, but I hear the lock groan.

It's working. I stand. Jump. Land. Fall. Scramble up and do it again. My back screams. I feel the fabric of my dress split, more with each leap.

"Otto!" I moan. "Help me!"

And finally I am thrown into the grass. The lock is broken.

The chain has landed across Ford's body. I push it away, shuddering, then hook my hands under his arms and pull. His body reluctantly comes my way, with a sickening slide over the rocks that lie under him.

Now I have him positioned under the spigot. I twist it open.

At first, no Water comes out. But then there is a trickle, a beautiful terrifying trickle. For a moment, I am frozen, staring at the Water leaving the cistern. We worked all year to gather this Water. Tomorrow the Visitor will come for it.

But then I look down and see Ford, broken, waiting to be healed. I take a deep breath and cup my hands around the spigot to make sure that every drop lands on him. The Water drips on his neck and rolls down his chest, disappearing into the holes made by his broken ribs.

Please work, I pray. *Save him, Otto.*

Ford said the Water, my blood, was blasphemy. He said it was the devil's work. But I don't care. I only want him to live.

He doesn't look any better, and the edge of the sky has a blue tinge. There's not enough time. I give the spigot a savage twist and the Water gushes onto Ford's body.

But it does not land on his broken face. I rip at his soft, now shredded shirt, and hold the fabric under the running Water.

The blood wipes off his face easily. I keep wetting the cloth, keep running it over the wrong-shaped planes of his face, hoping it will restore him to the Ford I know.

Ford's breathing has changed. It is deeper, longer. Still, a wet rattle comes from his chest. And all his limbs stay bent at wrong angles. I pull on his arm, trying to straighten it into the right shape, like I do with Mother after a bad beating. It feels a little less limp.

The Water is working, though slowly.

I stand, stretching the kinks from my body. When I take a step, my foot slides in the mud. I didn't realize how much Water had pooled around us. The dirt is small lakes of mud, and a steady stream is running down the road now.

When I kneel beside Ford again and run the cloth over his face, it feels different. I lean close, my breath mixing with his. His nose looks straight now, and his lips are no longer crisscrossed with bloody splits.

I drop a tender kiss on his lips.

"You won't die. Not tonight, you won't," I tell him.

I check the sky. It's dark, still, but the stars aren't as bright. How long do I have?

"Wake up, now," I tell him. "We'll go get more popcorn."

Ford doesn't hear me, or if he does, he can't reply. But I imagine his lips move in a tiny smile.

"We'll take a ride in your truck too," I say. "We'll drive fast, and far."

I am soaked to the waist from kneeling to mop Ford's face. But I keep wetting my cloth and mopping—and now I move my attention to his broken hands. Even as I run the cloth over his bones, straightening them as I go, they seem to lie flatter and knit together.

His skin has smoothed together too. There's no more blood, save the stains in his shredded clothes.

I shake his shoulders and dare to speak loudly. "Wake, Ford."

But he does not wake, and the Water seems to be coming more slowly now.

I catch some Water in my hand and dribble it into Ford's mouth. At first it slides out, running down his cheek. I try again. And then he swallows.

"Good," I tell him. "Good!"

A gurgle comes from his throat.

"Ford?" I ask.

He doesn't answer. But he moves his head from side to side, and his eyelids flutter.

With all my might, I pull him up to a sitting position, still letting him rest against me. He coughs wildly. I whack him on the back, once, twice, thrice. Then he leans forward and vomits Water onto the grass.

I come around to his front and put my hands on his shoulders, to keep him from tipping back. "Ford. It's me—Ruby. You're going to heal. You're going to live."

The sky is light between the tree branches now. At any time we might hear the rumble of the truck.

"Ruby," he groans. Then he reaches out one hand and gives my arm a strong squeeze.

"I'm sorry. I never knew they were coming here. I would have stopped them. Somehow. I never . . ." There's so much I want to say to him. But there's no time.

"The Water. Gone?" Ford looks up, then moans and tips his chin back down. He holds his head in both hands.

I realize the flow of Water has stopped. It took us months—two, maybe three—to fill it. And I have emptied it in one evening, for one person.

"You're alive. I don't care." But my voice wobbles.

"You healed me," he says.

"Yes, I did. I mean—the Water did. But come." I stand and hold out both hands. "You can't stay here."

His hand gropes for his necklace, but soon falls limp to his lap. "Can't move." Ford falls back to the ground and rolls onto his side, spewing more Water from his body.

"I'll help you to the trees," I say. "But you have to walk, at least partly."

He's heavy, but his legs are half working. We stagger to a thick stand of pines. I roll him onto the soft bed of pine needles; the low-hanging branches hide him. His eyes are fluttering shut. He'll need sleep, lots of it.

"Hide until sunset," I tell him. "You'll be strong enough to go, then."

Maybe, with luck, the Congregants will walk right by him.

Ford swallows, and clutches his stomach—but nothing comes out. "Where will you go?"

"To the cisterns, and to harvest after." Perhaps if I pretend all is normal, others will too. I don't know what else to do.

"Ruby, be careful." Ford tries to reach for me, but his arms are too heavy. He can barely lift them.

"I love you," I whisper.

Ford grins, then shuts his eyes. "I knew it."

Then he's asleep, that quickly. I pray he doesn't snore.

I think about running—or hiding somewhere too. I could go someplace and think, try to understand everything that's happened this night.

But then I hear the roll of truck wheels behind us—not driving past, but slowing.

I dive under the trees, just in time.

A white tanker truck pulls up next to the cisterns. It looks anonymous, like it could carry anything, for anyone. But I know it is special.

It is here to collect the Water that I stole.

Chapter 38

The truck door opens and a knife-thin man dressed all in white gets out. His clothes fit him like they've known him for a very long time.

The Visitor has come for the Water for as long as I can remember. That he's never changed tells me he drinks the Water too.

I've never been this close to him before—something about him always made me stand at the back of the crowd. Perhaps it's the way he licks his lips, as if tasting the Water, his tongue darting out like a snake's.

Or maybe I'm afraid of him because he's the only person that I've ever seen Darwin West show fear of.

The Visitor lifts his head and sniffs the air, then looks around, a smile creeping on his face. He can't possibly know we're here— can he? He mutters something, but I can't hear it.

Ford lets out a small groan in his sleep. I press my hand over his mouth.

"I smell something delicious," the Visitor sings out.

A new sort of fear washes over me, freezes every muscle. I watch as he stalks around the clearing, nose high in the air. I am grateful for my dark hair and browned skin, blending into the woods around me. I cast my eyes down, lest he see their bright whites.

The Visitor can't know my secret—can he? But if not, why is he looking for me?

"I'd treat you better," he calls out. "You'd have a new life."

I draw in breath as quietly as I can, careful not to shift a single muscle. I'm not sure what he's talking about, but my instincts tell me that I shouldn't answer—that this man is dangerous.

There's a cloud of dust on the road. People are coming. Relief warms me. Soon I won't be alone with the Visitor.

He walks to his truck and opens the door—not the one where he sits, but the other, just the same place where I sat when Ford took me to the movies. Then he looks all around the clearing. His eyes stop, I think, where I am.

I squeeze my eyes shut, like a child who's playing peekaboo.

"Come out! I'll take you away from here!" he calls.

Slowly, slowly, I open my eyes to see if he's coming closer. But still he stands by the truck. He gives a grand wave toward the open door.

When I don't answer, he shrugs and closes the door. He doesn't slam it like Darwin or the Overseers. He pushes with just enough force. It shuts with barely a sound.

Then the Visitor walks to the closest cistern—the one I emptied for Ford—and pats it with his hand. But then the look on his face sours, and he glances down at his feet. He is standing in a mud puddle.

Does he suspect what it means? I can't tell. He has stepped back, now, to dry grass. He pulls a white handkerchief from his pocket and wipes at his shoe.

The first Congregants have arrived. I've never been happier to see Congregants, especially since none of Ford's attackers have come yet.

The Visitor glances up at them and gives the air a slight sniff. His face twists, just a little, as if he's smelled something bad. Then he returns to cleaning his shoes.

Ford would be safest if I wasn't next to him. If I make a noise, or someone catches sight of my dress, then we'd both be found.

I lean down to drop a last kiss on his lips.

"Sleep well," I whisper.

I trace my finger down his cheek. He's beautiful again. He's breathing. I did that.

More Congregants have come now. They join in small knots, chattering. Darwin might give us one more meal before the day is out. He's always in a good mood after the Visitor leaves.

He won't be today.

I study them, the people who have been my family for so long. I look at the wrinkles across their faces, the white hair that has slowly, slowly, crept over their heads. They have protected me for hundreds of years.

Some betrayed me last night. But not all lifted that chain.

I hurt every single one with my theft.

If Darwin demands a price, shouldn't it be me who pays it? I chose to use the Water; nobody else did. Why should they suffer?

But fear stills my feet. I don't want to feel the lash of Darwin's chain—or worse. Perhaps he'd save some special torture, some new kind of pain, for the person who steals the Water.

Then I see Mother coming down the road. She walks with Asa, her head bent, nodding, agreeing with something he is saying. Anger surges in me. How can she act as if this is any other day? How does her body not show remorse for what she's done?

She doesn't even seem to miss me. Not once does she glance up, or look about, as if she wonders where I am. Is she so secure in thinking that I won't run away now?

I won't lurk in the woods. I won't hide away. I want her to know that she didn't just kill Ford—nearly.

She killed things between us too.

I step away from the tree, staying close to the tall bushes at the side of the road until I edge into the middle of the Congregants. The crowd is massing around the truck.

I don't come close to Mother. Not yet.

The truck is long, with a bright red cab up front. The back is flat and open, and it holds five empty cisterns. They are to be swapped for the full ones.

"Good morning, Ruby." Mother stands beside me, Asa not far behind. A slight smile hovers on her face. It reminds me of the same look that Darwin gives her, in the mornings, when she walks with a limp from one of his beatings.

Asa doesn't look ashamed either. He's got the same stolid, watchful face. And right now, he is watching me.

"It's the worst morning I've ever lived," I tell them.

Mother moves to stand next to me, so our shoulders are pressed against each other. Our eyes do not meet, and our voices stay low.

"I will never forgive you," I say. "And neither will Otto."

"We did what we had to." She wraps one arm around my shoulder and squeezes.

"You're soaking wet," Mother says. "Why are you wet?"

"I held him," I tell her. "It's his blood you feel."

Her arm drops away.

By the cisterns, Darwin West is greeting the Visitor, shaking his hand and smiling broadly—but there's a tremble on his lips. The Visitor's smile gets bigger and bigger until it's broader than Darwin's. He is relishing Darwin's discomfort, I can tell. Perhaps this should make me like the strange man. But it makes the dread in me grow.

Darwin issues orders to his Overseers. "Lee. Mathis. Schuyler," he barks. "Let's get to work. The rest of you keep an eye on the Toads."

Schuyler. That's Ford. So Darwin doesn't know he's missing, not yet. He will in a moment.

The Visitor steps back from Darwin, and the truck—and toward the Congregants. His eyes rove over us. I shrink farther behind Asa.

Darwin folds his arms and watches as the other two Overseers amble to the truck.

"Where's Schuyler?" he asks.

"Schuyler's not here," shouts an Overseer holding a clipboard.

"Useless townie!" Darwin roars, and the other Overseers laugh.

Darwin orders someone to take Ford's place, and the work begins. They move the empty cisterns off the truck bed and then hook a chain up to the cistern farthest from us—one that I did not touch last night.

"Where is he?" Mother asks, her whisper low and harsh.

"I . . . I buried him," I tell her. I gesture down at my dress, dark-stained from blood and mud. "It took hours."

"That was . . . wise . . . ," she says warily.

Asa clears his throat and glances over his shoulder before he speaks in a low tone. "He was awful big. How'd you move him yourself?"

"It wasn't easy," I tell him.

"With what shovel?" Asa asks.

"I used a stick. And my hands." I hold up my hands, equally stained from fighting the locks on the cisterns. There are still scars from the cuts the chain gave me too.

"You protected us. Good." Mother moves as if to pat me on the back, but my stare must make her think twice. Her hand flutters back down to her side.

Asa shoots me a squint-eyed look. Then he takes a step in front of Mother and me, shielding us.

Darwin is watching his men work, his arms crossed and legs wide. A pleased smile plays on his lips, though he flicks occasional nervous looks at the Visitor.

The Visitor is not paying attention to the transfer of Water. Instead, he edges into the crowd of Congregants. I take another small step, deeper into the shelter of Asa's shadow.

They've moved two of the cisterns onto the truck now, cranking the chain so it drags them across the grass and then up the ramp of the truck. They leave long lines of flattened grass behind them.

Mother lets out a gasp. "Mud. Mud, up there, by the cisterns. There's been no rain."

Fear freezes me. I stare straight ahead.

"This is more than blood." Mother grasps my sleeve, squeezes it. A trickle of Water comes from it and lands on the ground. "This is Water."

"You did what you had to," I say. "And so did I."

Mother lets out a low moan.

Now the Overseers have reached the empty cistern. They clasp the enormous hook over the top. I close my eyes and send a silent prayer to Otto.

Have mercy, I beg him. *Save us. Save me.*

"Where did you get it, Ruby?" Mother asks.

I do not answer.

The Overseer operating the crank pushes a button. The cistern jerks—and then it flies high through the air. Without the weight of Water, the tug of the truck is too strong.

The chain is slack at first, and the cistern flies toward the crowd. Darwin dives to the ground, but the Visitor, nearly in the middle of the crowd, only turns and watches while we Congregants scatter.

The cistern reaches the end of its tether, landing just inches from Mother.

She swings her head to stare at me.

"Is he alive?" she asks me.

"No." I meet her eyes. "You killed him."

Darwin strides up to the cistern; the Visitor follows, just a foot away from me now. The hair on the back of my arms pricks like it's tipped with needles.

"I'll fix it. I'll fix it all," Mother mutters.

The Visitor raps the cistern with his knuckles. It sounds hollow, not the satisfying thud of a cistern ready to be capped and delivered.

"It's empty," he announces.

Then he looks at me and smiles—his tongue slipping over his lips again. A roil of nausea sweeps over me.

The Congregation explodes into noise: hot sizzles of worry and speculation, suspicious eyes flicking over everyone's face.

"Who did this?" Darwin roars.

Chapter 39

"It wasn't us." Mother is edging in front of me, shielding me from Darwin. "We didn't take any Water."

Darwin's eyes dart from Congregant to Congregant, never settling on one more than a second. His look barely lands on me. Even if he did, he might not notice my dress is wet. It is so thoroughly soaked, it simply looks darker.

Still, I take another step behind Mother.

"Those cisterns were full." Darwin takes two steps, and then he is but inches from Mother. "You greedy Toads always want more, don't you?"

Behind him, the Visitor lifts a hand, nearly touches him — but lets it drop. He pulls a watch from his pocket, the chain gleaming in the sun. "I should have been gone by now."

"A minute. Just . . . give me a minute," Darwin says. His voice is an unfamiliar whine.

"The Water—" I start.

The Visitor's eyes flick up from his watch, landing on me.

"Ruby." Mother snaps out the command without turning to look at me.

"What does she know?" Darwin asks Mother.

"That girl? All she knows is sleep. I had to wake her this morning. Lazy thing." Mother turns around and aims a slap so hard on my face, it sounds like a branch snapped off a tree. I press my hand against my cheek, sure it must be bleeding.

The Visitor draws in his breath so sharply, he hisses like a snake.

"Stop wasting our time," Mother orders me.

She doesn't want me to confess, I think. Mother wants to control everything in this world.

"You know where my Water is?" Darwin asks me.

"My Water, actually," the Visitor corrects. He gives me a smile. But I do not return it.

"Where is it?" Darwin roars at me.

My mouth is as heavy and unmovable as if stuffed with gravel.

"None of us Congregants took the Water," Asa says.

"Nobody else would," Darwin says.

"Did you say one of your men was missing?" Mother asks.

Darwin looks around at the Overseers, then nods slowly. "Schuyler didn't show today."

"Missing Water, missing man . . ." Mother waves one hand in the air, slowly. "Doesn't that make sense?"

"It wasn't him," I blurt out.

Mother's head drops heavy, chin against her chest.

"The girl does know something," Darwin says.

"Ruby doesn't know anything," Mother says.

"Leave them alone." The Visitor lays his hand on Darwin's shoulder, lightly.

Darwin flinches. "They're thieves."

"No. They're not thieves," the Visitor says. "You are."

"It wasn't me. I swear it. I would never take anything from you." Darwin sweeps his hat off his head and holds it against his chest. His head looks wrong, too vulnerable, the blond hair matted in a ring where his hat sat.

The Visitor folds his arms, a simple movement, no energy wasted. The rest of him is very still. "We have a contract, Darwin West. You owe me this Water, on this date. Not a day later."

"I know. And I had it. I *had* it!" Darwin whirls to face Mother, then stares at me. "She knows where it is."

The Visitor looks over Darwin's turned back, straight at me. "Tell me something, girl."

I push back the urge to turn and run. "Yes?"

His eyes travel over me. I school my eyes to stay steady, not to move for one moment toward Ford's hiding place.

"A promise is a promise, isn't it?" the Visitor asks me.

"You'll get your Water," Darwin says.

"Isn't it?" the Visitor asks me.

"Yes," I answer, my voice cracking over that one word.

"How will that promise be met now?" the Visitor asks.

"We'll harvest," I say, my voice so small, tiny, I sound like a little girl.

Now the Visitor smiles, broader, broader, and gives the air a delicate sniff. I look down at the ground and will his eyes away.

He comes closer to me, leans near.

"Blueberries," he whispers. "And mint."

I step back quickly. Mother frowns, but she says nothing.

"The girl's right. We'll work double hard. We'll work all night. Won't we?" Darwin gives Mother a threatening look.

She does not answer.

The Visitor raises his voice, only a little, but even that tiny bit of extra power is more dangerous sounding than Darwin's bellowing. "I want it today."

"They're not all empty." Darwin points at the two remaining cisterns.

"How do you know?" The Visitor arches an eyebrow at Darwin.

"I'll show you," Darwin says.

The Visitor circles behind me first.

"That was a little excessive," he whispers. "A few gallons heal even the worst wounds, don't they?"

He steps back around me, faces me. Our eyes meet and a chill travels down my back.

"I'll show you," Darwin says loudly.

I watch as they slowly, slowly make their way to the other cisterns. Darwin wants to rush the other man, but he will not be hurried. He stops by nearly every Congregant and breathes in deeply. Always his face looks disappointed afterward—and always he looks back, again, at me.

The Visitor's walk is so light, it's almost as if he doesn't touch the ground. And yet, it's clear that he is the most fearsome person here. One need only watch Darwin's face to know that.

"What did he say to you?" Mother asks me.

But Hope rushes up to us before I'm forced to answer, Boone directly behind her. He has eyes only for Mother.

"You killed him," I say.

Hope closes her eyes tight and nods.

"We had to," she says.

"You don't have to explain," Boone tells her.

The Visitor raps his knuckles on the first cistern and makes a satisfied face. Then he slowly moves to the next—but not before he glances at me.

"The Visitor is staring at Ruby," Mother says. "Like she's not ours."

Boone gives the wrist of my dress a brief squeeze. "You're soaking."

"We know what you did," Hope whispers.

"There's no way you can punish me more," I say.

Her eyes go to Mother. But Mother looks away, toward the cisterns.

"Then . . . the Water didn't work?" Hope asks.

"Nothing worked," I answer.

The Visitor is saying something to Darwin that we cannot hear. Darwin holds up his hands, as if to defend himself.

And then Darwin begins to cry.

"Who took the Water?" Darwin screams to the crowd, tears running down his face. He reaches into his pocket to pull out his chain.

But the Visitor grabs it first. He whips the chain from Darwin's pocket and drops it on the ground behind him.

"No," he says.

"Tell me!" Darwin rages at us all.

The Elders move as a group to the front, and I follow.

The Congregants are whispering, staring at one another as we move through the crowd. Now a few eyes are skimming down my dress.

But nobody speaks a word against me. Not even Asa, who is behind us now, muttering something.

"You must pay," the Visitor tells Darwin.

"We'll get it to you, twice as fast as before," he says.

The Visitor shakes his head. "That's not enough."

Darwin nods at the Overseers around us. A few lift their guns to their shoulders, aim them at the Visitor.

"If I'm not home in an hour, the police come," he says.

Some drop their guns. Others swallow, but keep their weapons firm.

Police . . . Darwin told me about them. They're supposed to protect people, save them, even. They've never come here before. Why should anyone believe they'd come now?

But the Congregants are excited. A current of whispers grows, again, even as we all strain to hear what the Visitor will say next.

He points at two of the closest Overseers. They are among the shorter ones of the bunch, but thick, with ugly blue tattoos on their necks. They are nothing like Ford.

"Bobby Saunders. Gary Markham. You think you want to go back to jail?"

They look at each other, startled.

"You know our names," one says, slowly.

"I know all about you, each of you—and if I'm hurt here

today, then the worst you've ever imagined *will* come true. For each and every one of you." The Visitor looks from Overseer to Overseer.

And one by one, they drop their guns.

Darwin's breathing becomes fast and shallow, like an animal panting, like he's run a very long way to be here.

"Will anyone help?" the Visitor asks.

He looks directly at me—but not at my face. His gaze travels down my sleeves, to my wrists, and lingers there.

I could answer him. I could offer my blood, now, and refill the cisterns.

Somehow, I think, he knows this. I don't know where he comes from, or what kind of person or beast he is. But he knows my secret, even if Darwin West doesn't.

The Overseers are looking at one another, muttering, shaking their heads.

The Congregants stand still, silent.

Once I asked Mother why we all grew quiet just before Darwin West pulled out the chain—how we all seemed to know, before he told us, that pain was coming.

"Congregants know the smell of violence," she told me. "We smell it before we see it."

All are still now. Something terrible is coming; something has wafted over us already.

The Visitor bends at the waist—hinges, almost, a spare and elegant movement.

Darwin whirls and takes three frantic, stumbling steps away from him. But running away from the Visitor means running into the Congregants. Asa stops him, grips his upper arms—then turns him to face the Visitor.

The Visitor stands and holds a shining knife high in the air.

"Put that away," Mother orders. "We don't want anyone to be hurt."

I let out a harsh laugh, one I didn't know was waiting until it burst out of me.

"I'm a good supplier. I give you all that you want, year after year—even when there's a drought," Darwin says. "You can't hurt me."

The Visitor smiles slowly. "Oh, but I can do almost anything I want."

He swings his arm wide. The Overseer closest to him leaps back.

The knife arcs down and across Darwin's stomach. He makes an animal sound before the knife's arc has finished.

Everything happens so fast after that. First he's standing and then he's crumpled, both hands pressed over his belly. The Visitor looks down at him, his face blank.

Darwin sinks farther. Blood pools around him.

"Give me my Water and he will be healed!" the Visitor tells us.

It would be so easy. We'd fill the cisterns from the Lake, or with any sort of water. Then I could give the cistern enough blood in one day, or two.

But if I did that, all would know my secret. And Darwin would live. He would still own us—or worse, the Visitor would.

Finally I can be the Leader the Congregation needs. I can

pay back the debt I made when I took the Water. I can do what Jonah said I could: I can free all of us.

I will stay silent. Let Darwin West lie and suffer. I will end him by doing nothing.

Boone releases Mother. She kneels beside Darwin, puts his head in her lap.

A wave of shock hits me like a slap. How can she give him tenderness?

When Mother looks up at me, there are tears in her eyes. "What will I do now?" she asks. "Help him, Ruby."

The Visitor hears her. He sniffs the air, again, and smiles at me.

I've let Mother and the Elders command my blood for so many years. But my body is my own. My blood is a gift that I choose to give.

It's a gift I can choose to withhold.

The blood has soaked Darwin's shirt. Already his eyes have slid shut. I can't tell him all the things I've dreamed of saying. He won't hear them.

I won't endure any more.

"Darwin West doesn't deserve your comfort," I tell Mother. "He doesn't even deserve to live."

She bows her head. I wonder if she will speak. Will she give up my secret to save him?

But she stays silent.

"Then he dies," the Visitor says.

Chapter 40

Mother starts the singing. It's a hymn, one we sing in the woods sometimes.

Let us die in gentle grace
Let us die in his embrace

We might have sung it for Ellie or Jonah, if we had buried them. But instead, they sing it here. He doesn't deserve this. Not a single note.

At first some stay quiet. Boone keeps his lips sealed shut, even though he crouches next to Mother. And I catch sight of Earl, arms crossed, silent.

But then Mother gestures and the sound swells, every Congregant soon picking up the tune—except me. I stay quiet.

Mother still sits with Darwin's head in her lap. She leans close, ear by his mouth. When she pulls her head back up, her face is streaming in tears.

Then she lifts her head and rejoins the song.

I've never seen a person die so fast before. It takes weeks to wither—months, sometimes, for the body to disintegrate, a little each day. That is all the dying I've seen.

But Darwin was alive just minutes ago, screaming at us, so sure that he controlled his future.

Now he lies in his own blood, pale, motionless.

The sun is full up now, without any clouds in the sky. A trickle of sweat runs down my back, where the most of the rays shine. My dress doesn't feel wet anymore.

Mother lays Darwin's head on the ground, gently. As she rises to her feet, she still sings.

But when she faces me, her song stops. Her lips quiver. "Otto save your soul, Ruby."

She beat an innocent man. I let a devil die.

"Otto would be proud of what I did," I tell her.

"You did nothing." She looks down at Darwin.

I did nothing, and I did everything.

The Visitor glides up to us, close, and lays his finger on his lips. "What should I do with you now?"

"He's dead." Mother lifts her chin and gives the man the same defiant stare she used to save for Darwin.

"Yes. He repaid his debt." The Visitor looks around. "But now I'm left with this mess."

"Just take your Water and go," I tell him.

"Ruby," Mother says in her warning voice. "You let us talk."

"I hate this place." The Visitor looks around.

The song is fading, quieter, fewer people singing, and even those lowering their voices, I think.

The Overseers are picking up their guns, one by one. But instead of looking at Darwin, they are looking at the Visitor.

Soon we will have a new master, and everything will be the same.

This time I won't let her ignore me. I grab Mother's sleeve and lean close to whisper in her ear. "We're free. Don't let him have us."

She shakes her head and turns away.

"It would be easiest to kill you all—well, most of you," the Visitor says. He draws his words out, as if tasting them.

The Overseers look at one another. One lowers his gun. But most only shoulder them higher.

"Spare our lives and we can give you more Water," Mother says.

"That's an interesting proposal." The Visitor tilts his head and looks at me. "How much Water could you give me?"

"Two cisterns," Mother answers.

"Darwin West gave me five." He waves his hand toward the cisterns.

"He worked us nearly to death," she says. "This summer, especially."

"It's not difficult," the Visitor says. "I never understood why I only got five. Unless . . . it's just the one."

He points at me.

Mother looks at me, then back at him, a confused look on her face. "Ruby is only one of many."

"She's special," he says.

"She's a lazy, disobedient girl. She's near worthless." Mother gives him a firm shake of her head. "I've got nearly sixty others who work harder. We'll harvest every day."

"Harvest? What a distasteful word for something so beautiful." The Visitor gives me a sympathetic look that turns my skin to ice.

"We scrape the Water from the leaves," Boone says loudly. "With pewter cups and spoons."

The Visitor's eyebrows jerk up. "How oddly unnecessary."

"It's what Otto taught us. We're blessed," Mother says quickly.

"Ah, Otto." The Visitor wipes his hand over his mouth. I can't tell for certain, but it looks like he might be hiding a smile. "This Otto. Is he coming soon?"

"You'll get your Water," Mother tells the Visitor in a steely tone.

"You'd still need guards." The Visitor looks over at me. "Besides, someone has to feed you, don't they?"

"Three meals a day," Mother says quickly, stepping a little to the left so his line of sight to me is broken.

"Of course," the Visitor murmurs.

This would have been a miracle to me, a few months ago. But now I've tasted what freedom can mean. And I made a promise on Ellie's grave.

I turn to face the crowd.

"Do you really want things to stay the same?" I call out.

They look at one another. They look back at me.

"I want breakfast!" someone calls from the back of the crowd—and nearly the entire Congregation nods.

"Lunch too, maybe," someone near me says.

"We've been slaves for two hundred years and all you can think about is food?" I ask.

"Ruby, silence!" Mother orders.

"What about freedom?" I ask. "What about going where you please, when you please?"

"What about staying alive?" Meg Newman asks.

"We can do that without . . . *him*. And them." I motion behind me to the Visitor and the Overseers.

"Otto would come if it was time for us," Zeke Pelling says, staring at the ground.

"Your brother believed in something better," I tell him, my voice trembling.

He shrugs.

"We should show Otto that we can save ourselves," I tell them all.

"No, Ruby. Otto saves. We only wait, and endure." Mother tries to take my hand, but I pull away and face her.

"You've said that for two hundred years. And he's never come. How much longer are we supposed to wait?" I ask.

Mother raises both hands in the air, palms out, as if pressing me away. "We'll wait as long as Otto wants us to."

"He's not coming," I tell her.

I never admitted it to myself. But I've known it for a long time now. If Otto were going to save us, it would have already happened.

"Don't let him do this. Don't let *her* do this," I plead to the Congregation.

But nobody looks at me. They only glance at one another, and whisper—and then they look at Mother.

It's no use. I am alone.

"It's time for me to go," the Visitor says.

The Overseers look uneasy, shifting their weight from foot to foot, looking at their guns and then back at us.

"Two cisterns, each year," Mother says. "That's our offer."

"Or else?" A smile plays around the Visitor's lips, but it fades fast.

Mother doesn't give him an answer. She crosses her arms and raises her chin, meeting his eyes steadily. "Then Otto's judgment is on you."

"Otto." The Visitor closes his eyes for a moment. He breathes in deep. Then he looks at me. "She stays?"

"We all stay," Mother tells him. "Until Otto comes."

The Visitor makes a face like he's unimpressed, or maybe as if the bargain doesn't even matter. "Two cisterns, then."

The Congregation sets up a cheer.

But I'm different. I want to be free. I can't live another day like this, when there's any chance at something better.

"A deal, then?" The Visitor holds his hand out to me—an invitation, I think. I shake my head and he drops it.

"Soon enough," he says.

I do not answer.

"Next September, then," he tells Mother.

A smile spreads on Mother's face. "Next September."

The man turns to the closest Overseer. "I have ten minutes. Come discuss arrangements with me."

They wander a bit from the crowd. All around us, cheers and prayers to Otto are erupting. If the Congregation were free, I don't think they could be happier.

Boone picks up Mother and swings her in a circle.

"Put me down!" she cries, but she's smiling.

"You saved us," Boone tells Mother.

"I did, didn't I?" she says. "Meals three times a day, Ruby! And new clothes, I'll warrant. With blankets, pillows perhaps."

Her cheeks are flushed red, her eyes a bright sparkle.

"What about me?" I ask.

Now she frowns, a little. "What of you?"

"You promised *my* blood to him."

"Quiet," Boone warns.

"I promised him Water." Mother looks around the Congregants, checking, I think, to see if anyone heard me.

The back of my neck pricks. I turn to see the Visitor staring at me. The Overseer is talking to him, earnestly, I think, hands moving, nodding his head. But I don't think the Visitor hears a word.

He's paying attention only to me.

"He wants me, not Water," I tell them.

"He won't have you." Mother crosses her arms. "You belong to us."

She's said that before, I know it. But it never quite struck me like this before. I've been a slave to Darwin West for hundreds of years. But I am a slave to my own Congregation too.

"I don't belong to anyone, not anymore," I tell Mother.

She looks at the Visitor too, then back at me. "He's in charge now."

"Not of me, he's not." I take a step back from her, bump into someone behind me who's singing a song of praise to Otto.

I've got to get away from the Visitor now. He's promised to spare our lives in exchange for Water. But he wants me, I can feel it. He might not wait another year before he comes back. He might not even leave today without trying to take me.

I won't let him have me.

"I'm leaving," I tell Mother.

She nods. "Lunch should be in only a few hours. We'll see you then."

For a moment, I want to tell her that's not what I meant. But she doesn't deserve a good-bye, and I don't want one.

So I raise my hand, briefly, and push my way through the crowd, away from the Visitor. Once I get past them, I'll slip into the woods.

"You're running away, aren't you?" It's Hope, whispering. She walks at my side, so close our shoulders touch.

"I won't be a slave anymore," I tell her.

"But how will you live? You'll be all alone."

"Otto will guide me—and if he doesn't, I'll find a way." I tell her. "Are you going to try and stop me?"

"No. Maybe—maybe I'd leave too."

We're at the edge of the crowd now. The Visitor is barely visible on the other side of it. But he could reach me in a heartbeat.

"I've got to go," I tell Hope. "That man keeps looking for me."

"I know. He wants you—for what, I'm not sure. Nothing holy," Hope says.

Then she grabs both my hands in hers. I look down. Her hands are scrubbed clean, mine still filthy with Ford's caked blood. Clean killing hands laced with dirty healing hands.

"You tried to kill him," I say.

"Tried. Tried! Ruby . . . is he alive?" Her voice sounds hopeful.

"Do you want him to be?" I ask.

"Yes," she says in a low voice. "I only wanted you to stay. I hit him but once. And then—then I nearly fainted."

My heart cracks open, a little. I wonder what sort of fear made her lift the chain.

"There's blood," I tell her. "I filled the four vials. They're under my bed."

"Thank you," she breathes.

"It's more than any of you deserve," I say.

"I'll pray every day for your forgiveness," she says. "And your safety."

"Pray for me to find Otto," I say.

"Otto will find us here," she says. "Not out there."

"Or maybe I'll find him," I tell her. "Good-bye."

Hope releases my hands and takes a step back. "I'll make sure he doesn't notice you're gone—for as long as I can, at least."

She smiles, and I remember mornings spent playing chase

in the woods, nights painting rocks with crushed berries, secrets whispered while we harvested.

"Thank you," I tell her.

Then I slide into the woods that have held me all my life. I pray they shelter me one last time—long enough for Ford to heal. I'll go back to him, as soon as the crowd is gone.

Then we will start the long walk down the mountain. And by nightfall, I will be free.

Chapter 41

As soon as Hope turns from me, I slide into the place in the woods where Ford lies.

He's still sleeping, but his breathing seems deeper, more even. I drop a kiss on his cheek; it's soft, softer than I've ever felt it.

"I'll wait for you," I tell him.

The Congregation is barely visible through the thick screen of leaves around him; I hid him well.

But I can hear them.

"Praise Otto," they sing. They are laughing too, and some are dancing.

It is a very strange funeral for Darwin. I can't see his body, from where I crouch. I imagine him lying in the pool of blood, a silent, motionless witness to the joy of a Congregation without him. Do they celebrate because he is gone? Or do they celebrate because they'll only have to fill two cisterns this year?

"I'll never forgive them," I whisper.

I run my hands down his limbs; they feel straight and true.

His skin is clammy, perhaps from lying on the forest floor. But he lives.

Then I notice the swirling designs on his skin. They are faded, some gone almost completely. It's as if the Water erased them.

He's swallowed a lifetime's worth of Communion in one night. How else did it change him? What's he become?

Do we have far longer than just his lifetime together, now?

The gold medal still sits on his neck. I lift it gently with my fingertip and study the small man engraved on the disc.

"I had no choice," I tell him.

The noise is quieting, through the leaves. I peek out. The Visitor is talking to Mother, but his eyes are casting about, seeking. And he is sniffing the air yet again.

My skin prickles; I am being hunted, I know. What will he do if he finds me?

The man points at three of the Overseers and says something. They nod and shoulder their guns. For a moment I think he's sending them after me. But instead, they move to the place where Darwin's body still lies. They stand in a group. One looks down, then back up quickly. It's too far for me to make out his face. But I think I see him move as if to be sick.

They never showed such remorse when one of us bled on the grass.

Disgust washes over me. How could Mother not want to fight these men? How could she take a new yoke from a new master?

Now the Visitor is moving back toward the truck. Even when he is nearly obscured by the Congregants, pushing through them,

I can spot the white blaze of his suit. It moves farther and farther from me. Every step away eases the band of fear around my chest.

But the new fear floods in: once he's left, they'll be crawling through the woods.

I can't let them find either of us. I know the Elders will kill Ford if they discover him—and as for me, I don't want to fight them anymore, or say good-bye, or even look at them. I only want to be gone.

Ford can't go anywhere until he's awake. I glance at the crowd, just in time to see the truck door slam shut. I've got to hurry.

I grab sticks, leaves, anything light I can find from around me. Then I pile them on his feet, then his legs, then his chest. The sticks slip from my hands; fear has made my fingers slick with sweat. But I keep working until only Ford's face shows. I even put leaves on his hair.

"Be safe," I whisper to him.

The safest place for me will be far in the woods; I can come back for Ford later.

But I can't make my feet go. I can't leave him here, not knowing if he's found, or if he wakes from his sleep. And what if he does? What if he leaves, not knowing I've decided to follow him to his world?

A tall, firm tree spreads its arms above us. With a last glance at the crowd—merrily waving good-bye to the truck as if their own family waved back from it—I step around to the side they can't see and shimmy up. Then I curl into a croft that's shaded with plenty of leaves.

As long as nobody looks up, they won't see me.

From here, I can see the top of the truck as it slowly rolls away. The sun glints off the dirtless shine; I squeeze my eyes shut, for a moment. When I open them, all I can see is the corner of the truck. Then it's gone.

I think of another tree, of Jonah edging his way across it. "I'm going to be free," I whisper—hoping that, somehow, he'll hear me.

I pray that he's free too, wherever his soul has gone.

The Congregants stay in loose groups, for a bit; the Overseers don't order them about or wave their guns. One does go to his truck and pull out the crate that holds the pewter cups. So it will be a workday, like any other day.

Slowly, each Congregant moseys to the Overseer. They accept their cup and spoon. There's no sign of struggle or argument. They move into the woods as if it's any other morning.

I watch for Mother; she is hanging back, talking to all, before going to get her cup. But I see Asa take his cup—standing tall, almost as if he's proud, and then he moves straight toward me.

Please Otto, shelter me, I pray. I duck deeper into the cover of the leaves.

Asa kneels only a few feet from the tree and scrapes his spoon over the leaves. There's no water, though. He lets out a familiar curse and pushes past us.

He doesn't discover Ford. He doesn't even come close.

I let out the breath I've been holding. We'll be safe. We need only wait. I have to believe it.

Three more Congregants pass by us. And then they all have their cups, all fanned out, all away from us.

All except Mother. She has her cup, now, and she's following the same path that Asa did. She moves more slowly, though. Her eyes seem to catch and sort every branch. Mother knows where all the water hides.

She didn't go to get me at the cabin, to help harvest. This is her way of saying she's sorry, I think. It's the most she would do or say to show it.

Her hair is still so brown and glossy, with none of the gray that's appeared on other Congregants' heads. I hang over her, watching, keeping my breath as quiet as I can. I can hear her breath—slow, even, as she takes her time across the roots and rocks. Her feet slide easily over each obstacle.

I won't see my mother again. I won't see the woman who carried me, birthed me, protected me from Darwin West for two hundred years. She knows me better than any, I think—though now I see just how much distance there is between us too.

I pray she uses the blood I've left to sustain the Congregation until Otto comes . . . if he comes.

A tear slides down my nose and drops on the leaves below. Mother's eyes fall on it.

She doesn't look above to see why there's water. She simply lifts her spoon and carefully, carefully, scrapes my tear into her cup.

Her back is to Ford. When she stands, she walks away from him, and my tree. I turn my head to watch her path until she is gone.

Then it is just Ford and me in this part of the woods—the same woods where we started. But we will not end here.

I watch the sun climb high in the sky, from my perch, and then sink with agonizing slowness. So many times I nearly leave my shelter, to check on Ford—and just to be close to him. But I know I must be careful. So I try to be satisfied by watching him. His chest rises, and falls, and now his eyelids are fluttering, as if he's dreaming.

Soon he'll wake.

The sun is sinking over the trees; soon the Congregants will be back with their water. But still Ford doesn't wake.

I hear singing behind me, not so far away; someone has finished harvesting, and they're coming back. I grip the tree trunk harder and watch the file of Congregants return to the clearing.

Never before have they taken so long to deposit their water.

But nobody beats Mother.

Nobody even says something about a quota.

Then they begin to file home. I watch Mother, alone, walking away from the cisterns. It's too dark to see her face. But I can tell that she is not hurrying.

Does she know I am already gone? Or does she not want to see me any more than I want to see her?

Then, darkness. A cool breeze wraps around the tree, rattling its leaves and raising goose bumps on my skin. In a few more weeks, that breeze will whip browned leaves from the tree. We were lucky, so lucky, this happened now.

Or perhaps we were even blessed.

"Thank you," I murmur—whether to Otto or to Ford's God, it doesn't matter. It seems like something that must be said.

It's safe, or as safe as it will be. Now is the time to go.

When I start to climb out of the tree, I nearly fall; my legs and arms have knots from sitting for so long. I didn't even feel them until now.

Ford's eyelids are not fluttering anymore. His skin is rosy, and softer still. I run the edge of my thumb down one cheek.

His eyes open.

"You wake!" I exclaim, but softly.

He does not answer, only blinks fast, three times, then stares at me. Then his eyes move from side to side, slowly. "Where? How?"

"You were hurt. I helped you . . . You've been resting for a while," I whisper.

He struggles to sit up. I want to stop him—I want to tell him to rest. But I know we've got to move on soon. Mother will find the empty cabin soon. She might come back. She might send fifty Congregants to search the woods.

"Your . . . mother . . . ," he says. "She came to the cisterns. She said you were hurt—that you were asking for me."

The news of her lie stuns me as much as seeing her hold the chain above Ford's body. "I wasn't hurt. I didn't . . . I didn't ask for you."

"Then they all came out." Ford looks around wildly now, then at me. "Where are they?"

"At dinner, if there is any," I tell him.

He puts his hand behind my head and presses me close to him. Our lips touch, softly at first, then hard. I want to taste him, believe that he's alive.

But now isn't the time. I pull away. "We've got to go. Can you stand?"

Ford pushes to his feet; he wobbles, but stays up. "I'm fine," he answers. "We'll take the truck."

"Yes—" I start, but then I realize that's not what I need. I've ridden down the mountain in that truck. The world goes by too fast. Houses, trees, other trucks flashing by, no time to understand or truly see any of it.

I hold out my hand. "If you're able, let's walk," I say. "I have to take this slow."

I'll take every bit of it slow. But for now, all we have to do is leave. After that I'll decide what comes next for me.

"It's miles down the mountain," Ford says. "Can you make it that far?"

He's the one who will weaken first, I think. But I only smile. "I've harvested water day in and day out in these woods. I've spent most of my days walking and stooping."

"You're strong," Ford says.

"Yes." I tug at his hand. "This part will be easy."

We walk down the dirt road, keeping to the shadows, and in my mind I tell every tree and branch and bush good-bye.

I won't see you again, I tell them. You'll have to get by without me.

They're strong too, they answer. I needn't worry about them.

There are no guards tonight. The whole Congregation could slip away. But it will only be me, and Ford.

When we reach the end of the dirt road—the start of the hard black road with a yellow line and cars zooming past—I pause. I hold one foot over the road.

"Are you ready?" Ford asks. He gives my hand a squeeze.

There's so much for me to learn—and so much for me to tell him, still.

I close my eyes.

Otto, give me strength.

I'm done waiting for someone, even my father, to save me. Today I'll be the one doing the saving. I already saved Ford.

Now I save myself.

I open my eyes. "I'm not ready," I tell Ford. "But I'll learn to be."

Then I set my boot on that beautiful terrifying hard black road.

ACKNOWLEDGMENTS

My greatest thanks must always go to my family: cheerleaders, salespeople, therapists, all of them, without fail. I offer special gratitude to Patty, who is my one-woman street team, and to my sci-fi consultant, Nick.

Jason, you carry me when I cannot walk further, and you fly alongside me too. Thank you for always clearing the path to my writing desk.

Noah, thank you for pulling me away from that writing desk. Let's go play some baseball.

My community of writer friends is a true treasure. Thank you for your friendship, good advice, and perspective. In particular, I am grateful to Vivian Fernandez, for guiding me away from the revision ledge and always believing in this story, told my way.

I owe much to the talented editorial, marketing, and sales teams at Egmont USA, especially my editor, Regina Griffin. Thank you for always believing in my books, and for working so hard to bring them to the world.

Thank you to my agent, Emily van Beek, for being such a wonderful partner and co-dreamer. Thanks, too, to Elana Roth for helping to bring *Drought* to the printed page.

My colleagues in my "other" work life are so supportive and always excited about my writing. Thank you.

Just as I was finishing work on *Drought*, our family suffered a terrible loss. My father, just sixty-eight years old, died suddenly. I want to thank all of the friends, colleagues, and family who offered their love and support. I could not have stood again, let alone found joy, without all of you.

Dad, I will always miss you.